The
VIOLIN
CONSPIRACY

The
VIOLIN
CONSPIRACY

BRENDAN SLOCUMB

RANDOM HOUSE
LARGE PRINT

Copyright © 2022 by Brendan Slocumb

All rights reserved.
Published in the United States of America by Random House Large Print in association with Anchor Books, a division of Penguin Random House LLC, New York, and distributed in Canada by Penguin Random House Canada Limited, Toronto.

Cover design by Ervin Serrano
Cover photographs: man © G-Stock Studio/Shutterstock; violin © Gerald Kelsall/Shutterstock; textures: LUMIKK555/ Shutterstock and Miloje/Shutterstock

The Library of Congress has established a Cataloging-in-Publication record for this title.

ISBN: 978-0-593-58412-5

www.penguinrandomhouse.com/large-print-format-books

FIRST LARGE PRINT EDITION

Printed in the United States of America

1st Printing

This Large Print edition published in accord with the standards of the N.A.V.H.

To my youngest brother, Kevin B. Slocumb
My hero for more reasons than I could ever count

PART 1
The Disappearance

Chapter 1

Day 1: White Chucks, Size 10¹/₂

On the morning of the worst, most earth-shattering day of Ray McMillian's life, he ordered room service: scrambled eggs for two, one side of regular bacon (for Nicole), one side of vegan sausage (for him), one coffee (for Nicole), one orange juice (for him).

Later, he would try to second-guess those choices and a thousand others that, in hindsight, vibrated in his memory: What if he'd ordered French toast instead of eggs? What if grapefruit juice instead of orange? What if no juice at all?

Breakfast had materialized before he'd gotten out of the shower. He'd lost track of time, caught up in the fingering of the Tchaikovsky Concerto's triple-stops, and water sluiced down for ten minutes while he gaped at the tiny bar of hotel soap.

When he'd walked naked out of the bathroom,

the aroma of bacon wreathed the suite. The break-fast tray was waiting on the tiny dining table, the dishes' lids still in place. "I didn't even hear them come in," he said. If only every morning room service could magically deliver eggs and sausage.

Nicole was curled up in one of the armchairs, watching CNN. She twisted and untwisted a lock of auburn hair, the eighth-note tattoo above her wrist rhythmically flickering and disappearing. "You never hear anything." Another bombing in Jerusalem, and a hurricane bearing down on Indonesia. "I have a confession," she said, not looking away from the TV.

"What did you do this time?" She wasn't looking at him, so he took a giant step forward and blocked her view of Indonesia. Gave her something else to look at.

"I stole five bucks from your wallet to tip her. Hope that was okay." She eyed his nakedness. "You gonna eat like that?"

"Do I need clothes to eat?" He leered at her.

"This definitely works for me," she said. "I was just trying to figure out if you were going to get dressed now or if you want to eat, or—"

"We need to be out of here within an hour. You need to finish packing."

"I'm already packed," she said. "You're the snail in this race."

Ray slid on underwear and a T-shirt, grabbed a

plate of food, lay back on the messed-up bed. He propped the plate on his stomach.

Afterward, he relived all the other choices of the morning: cluelessly packing his suitcase, scouring the suite one more time, pulling up his roller bag's handle. He slung the violin case over his right shoulder (should he have put it on the left?), gestured for Nicole to go first with her two roller bags. The door clicked shut behind them, sealing the suite—and what remained—inside.

Down the elevator, through the Saint Jacques lobby, checking out, tipping the doorman, who flagged down a cab for each of them: Nicole's, first, to Penn Station. He hefted her suitcases into the trunk, leaving his own roller bag on the sidewalk, the violin case slung securely on his shoulder.

She turned to him, pressed her hand against his chest. Her warmth spread through his shirt, her touch like pizzicato—plucking violin strings with fingers he could feel shudder down his spine. "I meant to tell you," she said, "when you're playing the Mozart, I think you're playing the second movement too fast. Just try taking it maybe two clicks slower? Really milk it."

"You think? Because Ben Amundsen said to keep the tempo bright."

"I know, but you play so much more passionately when it's a little slower. Just a little. Try it, all right? For me?"

New York battered against them, cars zooming past, splashing last night's rain onto the curb.

"Just come to Charlotte. Find a sub," he said.

"You come to Erie," she said.

"You know I have to practice—"

"You can practice just as easily in Erie."

"I can't. There's Janice, there's my space, you know I—"

She grabbed his head with both her hands, pulled him toward her, and leaned forward, so their foreheads touched.

He closed his eyes, breathed her in. "I'll see you next week," he said.

"You've got this. Rayquan McMillian, future Tchaikovsky Competition gold medalist. Just focus. Visualize it. You can totally do this, you know that? It's going to happen."

Another breath he could feel deep in his abdomen. He tilted forward to kiss her.

A voice from the cab: "Hey, buddy, you almost done there?"

Another moment ruined by New York City's transportation system. Before he could kiss her, before he could even say "Call me when you get in," she'd jumped into the back seat and the taxi door slammed and he stood there like an idiot as the car moved off into traffic.

But already the day was hammering at him, his taxi had rolled up, trunk popping open, and he was spilling into the back seat with the violin, his anxiety level rising again. He wanted to be through LaGuardia, back in Charlotte. This morning he hadn't even practiced his music, so now he was itching to pick up his violin, assure himself that he could really make Tchaikovsky's voice his own.

Only one month left until the competition began: the world's most prestigious, most difficult classical music competition—judged by the top musicians in the world, as well as an online audience of millions of listeners. Even if he practiced every day, fourteen hours a day, he didn't think he'd be ready. He resented wasting the time to fly home.

At the airport, he filed into the TSA PreCheck line. Had he only gone through regular security. Why had he been in such a hurry? He should have waited in the long queue. If he'd waited, the screener might have randomly pulled his suitcase aside or asked him to open the violin case. Someone would have noticed or asked; it was security, after all.

Instead he placed the roller bag on the conveyor belt, violin case behind it, and they sailed through the X-ray and he sailed through the body scan, oblivious.

Later, over and over, he replayed in his mind the next two hours: boarding Delta Flight 457, stowing his luggage (the violin case could manspread alone in the overhead bin), returning to Charlotte, home to his little house, the air musty and stale. He lay down on his bed for half an hour, grateful to be back, violin case on the floor next to him, where he always set it. He let the travel wash itself from his skin, into the air, felt himself getting centered. Getting focused, ready to play.

It was just after 2:00 p.m. on May 16 when he kicked himself off the bed. He stood up, took three strides across the room, picked up the violin case, and set it on his bureau.

He flicked open the left clasp, then the right, and the lid lifted back.

His violin was gone.

Inside sat a white tennis shoe: a Converse Chuck Taylor All-Star high-top canvas shoe, men's, size 10½.

Ray wore a size 12.

Poking out of the shoe's mouth like an obscene tongue: a sheet of white office paper, folded in thirds.

He unfolded it.

SEND $5M IN BITCOIN FROM BISQ TO WALLET 34U69AAV89872

TRANSFER ON JULY 15 BETWEEN 12:00 PM EST–1:00 PM EST

YOU WILL RECEIVE NO FURTHER COMMUNICATION

Chapter 2

Day 1: Darkness

The next few hours were a blur, and all that he could remember afterward was how he'd repeatedly opened and closed the violin case. Every time he was absolutely certain—absolutely convinced—that if he opened the case one more time, this time—**this time**—the violin would be there, glowing, its tiger stripes shimmering like flames: because **how could it not be there?** Instead the obscenity of its empty mouth yawned back at him. Its barrenness was impossible, as if water were no longer wet.

He'd called the Charlotte police and none of it made sense: he was calling to say that the violin was stolen (but of course it wasn't stolen, it was right in its case where it belonged). The house was filled with uniforms and pale faces turning toward him and then they were taking the violin

case away from him—how could they take it away
from him?—and for moments at a time he forgot
how to breathe, as if the air had suddenly become
something difficult and foreign. He was talking to
New York police and the FBI and then he was on
another Delta plane back to New York and it was
impossible: because the violin was not on his shoulder and was not within arm's reach and he couldn't
touch it. Its absence gaped on his back, where the
case should have been slung.

The violin's absence was like nothing he'd ever
felt before. He could tell you the exact pressure
that he should feel—that he should be feeling—of
it against his jaw, knew the flare of its ribs the way
he knew the flare of his own. His thumb should
rest against its neck right where the wood darkened
at the seam. The smooth roundness of its back was
lit with orange and gold and brown, but those
were words and couldn't touch the reality of how
the pattern rippled and called out to him in a voice
that only he could hear. How could anyone say it
was just a violin?

When he arrived back at the Saint Jacques, the
hotel clerk—the skinny blonde who'd been so rude
to him last year, so long ago, that first day—put
him up in another suite on the same floor as his
and Nicole's previous suite. The police were in
his old room, but they wouldn't let him in. He
wanted to show them exactly where he'd stood,

where the violin case had rested, but the crime scene crew was dusting and measuring and keeping him out. It didn't matter. The room had already been sanitized for the next guest: all the irreplaceable, priceless forensic evidence vacuumed, Windex'ed, bleached away.

He stood for a while outside the room, looking in, and then found himself back in this new alien suite. He had no violin case, which was just insane, because of course always near him was a violin case and a violin, inside. People—detectives, the hotel manager, the concierge, even Mike the doorman—would appear in the doorway to take Ray's fingerprints or to ask an apparently random question: Did he have it in the elevator? Was he sure the housekeeper left with the breakfast cart? Over and over he repeated his story, every detail: practicing the afternoon before; dinner, drinks; back to the hotel, sleep, shower; breakfast, orange juice; flight.

There were Delta Airlines representatives. There were agents from the FBI Art Crime Team—Ray hadn't known that an art crime team even existed. He couldn't keep anyone straight and didn't bother trying.

He tried not to snap at them: they were here to help. He tried to breathe but his ribs had been wrapped in piano wire. He tried to remain calm. He tried, very hard, not to cry.

"I'm telling you," he kept telling them. "It was either my family or the Marks family. It had to be one of them. Go check them out."

His words seemed to disappear into the air, to vanish unheard.

"We hear you, sir," said a NYPD detective, a fit, muscled guy with cheekbones that looked sharp enough to puncture the skin. "I assure you we're looking into it. We just want to get more information about your own movements. Yours and your girlfriend's. When did you say she was coming back?"

When was Nicole coming back? Ray couldn't remember. His hands were trying to hold on to something that wasn't there. It was gone, of course it was gone. How could he have imagined that he could have kept it, that he was worthy?

Everything that everyone had ever thought about Ray—about people who looked like Ray—was now turning into reality with an inevitability that he almost welcomed, it was so expected. He was bringing their words to life. He was exactly what they said he was. Incompetent. Irresponsible. It was all true, true, true. He not only wasn't good enough, but he'd never been good enough. He would always, now and forever, be the dumb nigger who lost the most important thing in his whole worthless life.

For hours he paced, roaming the bedroom and adjoining living room/kitchen/dining room, turning the television on and off, opening the door to ask the police officer outside if there'd been any news, if he could help. They'd taken his suitcase, taken the clothes he'd been wearing, and the T-shirt and jeans he now wore felt wrong, strange, not his.

Nicole called him again. Her flight was boarding in forty minutes; she'd been calling for an hour but he hadn't picked up to talk. But suddenly the silence of the room hurt his ears and he was desperate to hear the sound of someone else's voice—a voice saying something other than his own internal accusations. When her name flashed across the phone, he answered.

"Stop pacing," she said to him.

"What are you—"

But she was talking over him. "Stop pacing. Sit down. Close your eyes. I'm here. Take a deep breath."

He stood in the middle of the room, phone pressed tight to his ear. Tears burned as they slid down his cheeks, and he closed his eyes.

"Seriously. Sit down," she said. "Listen to me. Take a deep breath."

He sat, the mattress giving beneath him. He tried to breathe but his lungs no longer breathed air.

"You know, I really would have just come to Charlotte," she said. "You didn't have to do all this just to see me again. When you want something you really go for it, you know that?"

Despite himself he released a breath, a strangled guffaw, and suddenly the air was flowing into his lungs again. "Nicole, I—"

"It's not your fault. You hear me? It's not your fault."

"It is, I—"

"It's not. Nobody—nobody—could have taken better care of that fiddle. And you know what else? They'll find it. You're going to get it back. You will. I absolutely believe it."

The tears were coming soundlessly, his breathing ragged, and he closed his eyes against the world, now reduced to the exact size and shape of her voice.

"Who's there with you?" she asked.

"What do you mean? A bunch of cops."

"Did you call Janice? Your aunt? Is anyone else coming?"

"I called Janice. I didn't call the others. I couldn't talk to them."

"Not even your aunt Rochelle?"

"Especially not Aunt Rochelle."

"Why? You should give her a call."

The one person in his fucked-up family—besides his grandmother, but he couldn't even think of her—who had faith in him. "I can't," he said. **I can't tell her that I lost it. I can't tell her that I failed her, and everyone, and most of all, Grandma Nora.**

"Well, what does Janice say?"

"I don't remember. No, she said she's coming. I think she said she's coming."

"I talked to her, too. She'll be there tomorrow morning."

"Oh. Yeah."

"She told me that she was sure they'd find it," Nicole said. "She said that people almost always get it back in a couple days. A week at most, she said. Remember Yo-Yo Ma got his cello back in a couple hours? He'd left it in a cab in New York City."

"Oh," he said. "Right."

"I'll be there in two hours, okay?"

"Okay," he said.

"Look, we're boarding, I'll be there soon. Just stay calm. It's not your fault. Ask the police if there's anything else you can do in the meantime. Get some food. Maybe one of the cops brought vegan doughnuts."

"Haha," he said without humor. They hung up.

The evening folded into night, and a blustery, beer-gutted guy in a suitcoat that didn't begin to cover his paunch knocked and entered, introduced himself: Bill Soames, head of the FBI's art crime unit. He led Ray through the same questions that the other cops had asked.

When was the last time Ray locked the case? He locked it only when the violin was out of his sight, and it hadn't been out of his sight for days.

When was the last time Ray had actually seen

the violin? A little after 6:00 p.m., between 6:05 and 6:15, when he'd finished practicing for the day. He'd slid the violin in its case before jumping into the shower and heading out for dinner.

Who else had access to the violin? Just Ray. And his girlfriend. Yeah, she was on her way back, she'd be here in an hour. And maybe some of the housekeeping staff, but he was always there when housekeepers came in.

Who had a motive to take it? Ray couldn't help thinking, **Is this guy fucking high?** Everyone had a motive. Everyone. Did any of these cops even talk to each other? He'd already told this to at least four different detectives. And, meanwhile, the people who should be investigated—the Marks family, for starters—were probably laughing their fat asses off, thinking they got away with it. "Black people are so dumb," they were probably saying. For once, he agreed with them.

"Calm down," the FBI guy said. Ray had already forgotten his name. "We're looking into them. I know you're upset. Just know we're doing everything that we can do."

Ray knew that whatever they were doing was not enough. If he couldn't protect it, they sure couldn't. For these cops, retrieving a missing violin was just part of the job—like finding a lost dog or a misplaced umbrella.

After the guy had left, Ray was too exhausted to even pace. He lay on the bed, hating himself.

Just before midnight Nicole returned and the police pulled her aside before she could do more than give him a hug. An hour later she returned to the room: her skin sticky, dark hair tousled and greasy. Neither showered: it was as if by showering they'd somehow be washing off some last trace of the violin. They lay together on top of the yellow satin hotel bedspread. Nicole held his hand as he stared up at the ceiling. It shone silver and gold in the midtown night.

At 3:07 a.m. he told her, "You know what? I'm rich."

"What are you talking about?"

"When the insurance company pays out. But I guess I'm not that rich. Because of my family."

"You still won't be poor." She squeezed his hand. "It's not your fault. You need to know that. You did everything right."

His own hand was suddenly sweaty and he pulled free, rubbed his eyes. "The Marks family is probably partying tonight. I bet they're playing it right now. That fucking niece. What's her name? Heather? Heidi?"

"It's Holly, and, uh, the Marks family probably has about eighty FBI agents ransacking their house and bank accounts," she said. "I doubt they're partying. They're definitely not getting any sleep tonight, either."

"I hope they never sleep again." He laughed, a harsh guffaw in the dark.

He imagined the violin dropped, damaged. He'd been entrusted with this instrument, this glowing talisman that possessed a sound unlike any other. His audiences drew in a collective breath when he played. Now he imagined it smashed under the wheels of a car, the shards of wood poking out like the feathers of a run-over bird.

He went over to the window, pulled the drapes fully closed. Now it was too dark, too stuffy, and he opened them again. The window looked out onto an air shaft.

"Have you even practiced today?" she told him.

"Are you fucking out of your mind? What am I going to practice with? The fucking bed?"

"Don't be so shortsighted. They're going to find it. In the meantime you still have a lot of work to do. That Mozart's not going to play itself."

"Nicole—"

"Ray. We've just got to find you another violin, just until yours is recovered. Unless you want to call and drop out of the competition? Nobody would blame you."

He looked over at her, a shadow lost in shadow. "You think I should?"

"Should what? Get another violin? Fuck yeah,

you should. We're already in New York. Janice is coming. What's the name of the guy that did the appraisal? Mike?"

"Mischa Rowland."

"Yeah. He could help you find something. Just temporarily. They're going to find your violin."

He said nothing and she went on, "Ray, you're about to make history. But you can't do it if you don't do it, dumbass. Just get the violin so you have something to practice on while they're getting it back from Holly Marks. Let's call Mischa Rowland first thing tomorrow. We can do this."

"Can we talk about this in the morning?"

"Okay, but promise me that if your violin isn't back by ten a.m., we're standing on Mischa Rowland's doorstep when he opens up."

"I think he opens at nine."

"Ten's fine. Let me sleep in a little, okay? It's almost four now," she said. "If I were you, I'd be saying, 'You need to do this. This is a temporary setback. You're one of the best young violinists in the country. Maybe the world. This won't stop you. This is your best opportunity to show everybody who always said you couldn't.'"

"But I—"

"Ray, there are no buts. This is it. This is your moment. You grab it. That violin is amazing but you're even more amazing. And now you're going to show everybody."

"I'm going to win," he said. "Even without the violin. How long will it take the insurance company to pay? Maybe I can get a message to the thieves, tell them I have the money and they can get it back to me early?"

"I have no idea," she said, putting out her hand in the dark.

He took three steps toward her, reached out, grabbed the note, held on.

TRANSFER ON JULY 15 BETWEEN 12:00 PM EST–1:00 PM EST

"I want you to come with me," he said.

"Of course," she said. Her face was a smooth oval in the half-light. "I have a good ear for tone, and I think I know what will suit you."

"No," he said. The empty windows across from the air shaft gleamed at him, and he felt almost as if he were falling into them. "Not to get a violin. But I want you to do that, too. I mean to Moscow. I want you to come with me."

"What?" She sat up. "Are you serious?"

"I'm very serious. I need you there with me. Especially after this. Will you come? Help a brother out?"

"But I have to play," she said. He could tell from her voice that she was just going through the motions. Her grip tightened on his. "I can't just take off three weeks from work—we're doing that Sibelius retrospective, remember?"

"Nicole. You're coming. We can do this together. I might not have a violin, but I have you."

"I think the violin is worth more."

"True. Maybe I can sell you in Russia and use the money to pay the ransom."

She slid off the bed and slipped over to him, wrapped her arms around his back. Her face was cool against his cheek. "I'm sure I can probably get time off work." He could feel her mind working, so close to his. "You'd probably have a lot of money left over, after you sell me."

"Yeah, I'm planning on it. So you'll come?"

"I've got to figure out flights." Letting him go and sitting down on the bed, she pulled out her phone, compared various offerings.

With his eyes he traced the nape of her neck, the elegance of her finger as she scrolled across the screen. Her eighth-note tattoo flickered almost as if it were a melody. Even after the longest day in creation, she was still beautiful. How could she love someone as damaged as he was?

"There's actually a flight from Erie that's $493, with a three-hour layover in Frankfurt," she said.

He'd lost his violin and she was still with him. She still believed in him. How was this possible?

Ten minutes later, he lay on the bed and stared

up at the ceiling. She kept thumbing her phone, whispering travel options that he only half heard. "This one goes through Rome. Oh, but that one has a twenty-four-hour layover. Want to spend a day in Rome?" One thing about Nicole: she loved to travel, but was stupidly cheap about it. She always looked for the cheapest routes.

Twenty minutes later she tucked the phone away. By 5:00 a.m. her breathing had grown deep and even. He lay there, holding her through the broken remainder of the night, until the ceiling's silver warmed into dawn.

Chapter 3

Day 2: Temporary Solution

News of the theft broke sometime around dawn, and by 7:00 a.m.—when Ray next turned on the TV—his face peered out from CNN, FOX, and every other news channel. Underneath talking journalists' heads, and shots of the Saint Jacques's gold-and-white awning, the theft slid into the chyron: "$10M Stradivarius Stolen from NYC Hotel."

Bill Soames had told him the night before not to do media interviews: the FBI would release a statement. They told him that doing an interview could compromise the investigation, and, anyway, Ray had no intention of sitting across from Anderson Cooper to explain how he had managed to lose the violin.

"So let me get this straight. Two days ago you carried your violin in an unlocked case, up and down New York's Upper West Side? Do I have that right?"

Yes, you have that right.

"Did you take it on the subway?"

No. Only taxicabs, and to a couple bars. That's it. Swear to god.

By 8:15 a.m., his voice mail was full and he had a hundred and twelve unread texts.

He would have turned off his phone entirely, but Soames had said that there could be further communication from the kidnappers, so he needed it on and charged.

There will be no further communication.

He flipped channels.

"Turn that off," Nicole said from the bed, eyes still closed. "Please."

He turned off the TV.

Nicole was groggily checking her phone. "Hey, Janice texted. She's here. She said you haven't texted her back."

Janice Stevens, his violin teacher—mentor, friend, and surrogate mother—had taken the first flight out of Charlotte that morning to be with them. She, more than anyone else in the world, understood what the violin meant to him. He was terrified to see her, afraid that he would read disappointment in her eyes. He'd failed her, too, like he'd failed everyone else. After all the time she'd spent with him, the extra hours she'd wasted, touring over the summer, teaching him how to talk to music directors—

"I didn't want to talk to her."

"I'll tell her to meet us at Mischa's, okay? It looks like she can be there by nine fifteen." Nicole groaned. "Let's have her meet us there at ten. We both need a shower, and I need to get some breakfast. I bet there's media outside."

"They're definitely out front," Ray said. "We should go out the back."

"So I'll tell her ten a.m. at Mischa's? She can call the shop and tell him we're coming."

He felt unable to make decisions, incapable of even nodding assent, so he just shrugged.

The news spread. Texts swirled in from his family.

Aunt Rochelle: **Are you ok call me**

Uncle Thurston: **Why you let somebody steal it**

And then his mother: **When u think we get paid???**

His lawyer, Kim Wach, called and texted—probably to say **I told you so**. No way was he talking to her.

Meanwhile Nicole ordered breakfast. "You've got to eat," she said, ordering the same food as yesterday—how could it have been only yesterday? "Hope you're not hungry," she told him when she hung up. "They said it'll be an hour. Let's jump in the shower so we can be ready to go right after we eat."

"I'm not hungry," he said.

They'd both showered when someone knocked on the door. "Here's breakfast," Nicole said. "I'll get it. I'll get the tip, too. Just don't get used to it."

Ray managed to smile.

But it wasn't housekeeping with their eggs: instead Bill Soames and another FBI guy whose name Ray couldn't remember came in. "You find it?" Ray asked, standing.

"Not yet, but we do have some promising leads," Soames said. "Several people from the housekeeping staff didn't show up for work today."

"What's promising about a bunch of people skipping work?" Ray said. "Maybe the hotel down the street pays better."

"Or maybe one of the housekeeping staff knows something about the violin and skipped town," Soames said evenly.

"You think so?" Nicole said. "What makes you think that? I don't know if I'd want to show up for work if the place was crawling with cops."

Soames shrugged. "Maybe they got something to hide. We're checking their home addresses. We'll keep you posted."

Another knock, and breakfast arrived. Soames and the other agent left. Nicole sat down to eat and she forced Ray to have a few forkfuls of egg. He felt better.

Janice met them just inside the door to Rowland's Fine Instruments on Fifty-Sixth Street. She embraced him and would not let him go. Worn from the flight, her black hair grayer than he remembered, she was nonetheless sturdy and solid. He wept in her arms.

In the showroom, Mischa Rowland clasped both of Ray's hands in his enormous ones. The pinned-up violins and violas glared down from the walls: what a traitor Ray was. His bones ached to think of playing some other instrument.

"I have treasure for you," Mischa said. "It will not be what you had, of course not, but it will be special, and it will be worthy of the Tchaikovsky Competition." How did Mischa even know Ray had entered the competition?

"You know, thanks, guys, but I don't think I can do this," Ray said. A wave of nausea had swelled up in him. The scrambled eggs burned at the back of his throat. "Let's just go."

Nicole reached for him but he ducked away, heading back the way he'd come. Every other violin in the entire world was in that showroom— every one but his. How could he think—even for an instant—that he could replace his violin with something else? These were only glued pieces of wood, horsehair stretched over pernambuco, varnished and shining.

His violin thrummed in his blood.

His violin was not there.

He was almost out of the shop when Janice said his name—so quietly—but something made him pause, hand on the front door's worn brass handle. "Ray. This is not your fault," she said. She didn't raise her voice—but all the days and years of practicing with her made it impossible for him not to hear her. "They're going to find your violin. You have to believe that. We all believe it. Finding a loaner instrument isn't a betrayal. It's just a tool to get you to the next step."

"It's just too soon," he said. He could barely get the words out.

"It's just temporary," Janice said. "Once they find your fiddle, you'll return this one. You can make Tchaikovsky sound good playing on a cardboard box with rubber bands."

"That's what I was playing when I met you," he said, forcing a laugh. Outside, three gray-suited men with black briefcases filed down Fifty-Sixth Street. He wished he were one of them.

"My point is that of all the obstacles you've had to face, you've never backed down. You're not a quitter. You've worked too hard to let some selfish asshole destroy your dreams. It's about the music, remember? It's about what you bring to the music. I didn't want to work with you because of your violin. I wanted to work with you because I'd never seen someone love music so much. You can't lose that. Let's just choose an instrument to practice on so you don't lose everything you've worked for. Okay?"

The Tchaikovsky Competition was less than a month away. He'd given up the last six months of his life to prepare for it.

He turned back to the room.

Mischa, expressionless, was holding out a 1959 Lehman, and almost despite himself, Ray took it, smooth and cool. It lay in his hands like a wet fish, glinting. And yet there was a part of him that was relieved, as if some bow hair inside his skull tightened, or loosened. This was familiar; this was his world; this was music. He would continue to play. He would continue to connect with his listeners. All this would not be in vain.

Ray tuned the Lehman, lifted into a G scale, then fumbled into Ralph Vaughan Williams's "Rhosymedre," the opening notes coming almost unwillingly, haltingly. He hadn't played the simple melody for so long but somehow it always lay there, just beyond the furthest reaches of his hearing, the song he played so often for Grandma Nora, and he played it for her now, the unpretentious tune pouring down and echoing and repeating. **Lovely** was the word "Rhosymedre" translated, and he closed his eyes and for a moment just let its sweetness wash him clean.

And then, somehow, the song was over. The

Lehman's full ripe sound hung in the air. It had resonance and depth, and a familiarity that Ray immediately liked. But you never go with the first car you drive, so he handed it back to Mischa.

Next was a 1986 Vitacek, gorgeous and showy, with a sharpness that cut through the air, commanded attention. Holding it felt wrong, though—it was beautifully balanced, but not balanced like his violin had been; it didn't sit quite right under his jaw and looked slightly awkward as he stared down the fingerboard. The 2003 Henner was too tight. No way it would open up enough before the competition. The 1907 Gorman was not bright enough.

Finally, with most of the morning gone, Ray turned to Mischa. "You knew right off the bat which one I'd like," he said.

The big man smiled, slid the Lehman across the counter. Ray picked it up.

"Great choice," Nicole said. "You rocked that thing."

Twenty minutes later, Ray, Janice, and Nicole headed back to the hotel, the Lehman slung securely over Ray's shoulder in a black Tonareli case. He wasn't ready to play it—not quite yet—but he felt centered again, having the weight at his back.

Bill Soames and the NYPD were tracking down "dozens" of leads, he told Ray back in the hotel.

It sounded promising, but Ray didn't want to let himself hope.

That afternoon, as they waited for further news, Tommy Reed, the Benson Insurance Company representative, phoned. Benson was offering a $25,000 reward for information leading to the Strad's recovery. In the meantime, they were sending their own investigator. Although it was too early for them to pay out—it would be at least six months, if not longer, before they closed the file and paid the $10 million—they'd already hired a private art detective, Alicia Childress, to investigate the theft. One of the top art recovery experts in the world, she'd cleared her schedule to get started immediately, given the ransom note's tight deadline.

"That's great," Ray said. "She's coming to New York?"

"Tomorrow. I'm warning you, she can be a little brusque," Tommy Reed told him. "But she's a total bulldog and smart as hell."

The FBI. NYPD. Benson's reward. Alicia Childress.

Ray was not alone.

All the world was marshaling.

Chapter 4

Days 3–4: Alicia

Around nine the next morning, Nicole went shopping. "I'll be back in an hour," she said. "I'm just going to get stuff to eat so we don't keep spending this insane money on room service. In the meantime, Mozart's waiting on you."

"What?" he said, looking up from the game he was playing on his cell phone. He'd slept a couple hours last night, but as soon as he awoke and the Strad's loss drenched him, he lay under the covers unable to move, wishing that breathing was not automatic and that he could just stop. An hour later, when Nicole awoke, she immediately bounded into action—opening the curtains, ordering breakfast, forcing him to take a shower.

Now she was dressed, standing near the door, slipping into sneakers. "Time to practice."

"I don't really feel like it," he said, but he knew she was right. The Lehman lay where he'd dropped it last night, propped in the corner of the bedroom. He could feel it pulsating there in the dark, the weight of it unfamiliar and a little uncomfortable, like an extra sack of potatoes in his shopping bag.

She gave him a long hug. After she'd gone, he trudged over to the Lehman and stared at the case, as if he expected it to apologize: **Sorry, dude, but I'm all you've got.**

So here's what you do if you're a Black guy trying to make it work in an unfamiliar world: You just put your head down and do the work. You do twice as much work as the white guy sitting next to you, and you do it twice as often, and you get half as far. But you do it. You just sit down and practice, over and over, and eventually someone turns to you and says, "Wow, you're way better than I expected you'd be." And all those extra hours of practice, they build themselves into the marrow of your bones, they electrify the nerve endings on the tips of your fingers, until they become habit. Now his bones were pricking and his fingertips were tingling, and even though picking up this unfamiliar instrument was the very last thing he ever wanted to do, he did it. He'd built that into himself—that discipline, that strength.

The Lehman felt light in his hands—too light. It was someone else's violin. He'd have to relearn the

Mozart, the Tchaikovsky, the Ravel, the Bach, and the other pieces, all with someone else's violin.

But unexpectedly, the Lehman felt familiar to him. Like the violin he'd had back in high school: he'd made that one sound good, too. Playing that violin hadn't been a betrayal—playing the Lehman wouldn't be, either. Both were just tools. They were the means of making music.

He started with the Mozart, the Violin Sonata no. 21 in E Minor, trying Nicole's suggestion of slowing down the second movement. Mozart had written it around the time that his mother had died, and the dark minor key reflected his mourning—and Ray's, too. The piece felt like an appropriate way for Ray to begin. He tucked the Lehman under his jaw and imagined fat little cherubs tiptoeing across clouds, borne up by the music lingering below, jumping from cumulonimbus to cirrus, sunlight slanting through the blue. Nicole was right: slowing down the tempo meant that the cherubs didn't have to zip around frenetically—they could glide from cloud to cloud, rolling in an upward current of warm air.

He didn't even hear her return, but eventually became aware that she was standing in the doorway. Almost two hours had disappeared inside the Mozart.

"Wow," she said. "You're doing Mozart proud."

"You're right about the second movement," he said. "Ben Amundsen could take a tip from you."

"I'm really feeling it. Sounds like you are, too. Don't get too cocky, son." She disappeared into the living room, and he lifted the bow again to the Lehman's strings.

An hour later Bill Soames brought them news. "We checked out one of the people who didn't show up to work yesterday. The woman who brought you breakfast the morning you left."

Hope leaped blindly, like a fish jumping out of a lake. "Where is she?" Ray asked.

"We're checking her residence now. Her name is—allegedly—Pilar Jiménez." A bloom of razor burn coated Soames's neck, and he scratched at it.

"What do you mean, 'allegedly'?" Nicole said. "Don't you know her name?"

"There is a possibility that she didn't provide her real name."

"That doesn't make sense. Doesn't the hotel have to get passports, visas, something?" Ray said.

"Yes, we're reviewing her documents now," Bill said. "But there are red flags. It looks like a fake passport. False social security number."

"Fake? You're fucking kidding me," Ray said. He wasn't sure if he was furious or elated.

"How long has she been with them?" Nicole asked.

"Almost two months."

Ray said, "And you went to her house?"

"We went to the apartment she listed as her residence, yes. She wasn't there. Nobody would say where she was, only that she left yesterday."

"So what are you doing?"

"We're talking to everyone. Checking everywhere she might have gone," Soames said. "Buses, cars, planes, trains. Door to door to the neighbors. Her church. We'll find her."

They hashed out various possibilities: that someone had bribed Pilar Jiménez to swap the violin for the Chuck Taylor shoe. That Pilar was maybe a violin aficionado and had targeted the violin herself. That she'd infiltrated the hotel for the express purpose of stealing the violin, since Ray regularly stayed there. "Ten million dollars is a very good motive," Bill said.

Bill Soames drilled Nicole again for her version of the breakfast delivery that morning. Ray had heard the story several times by now—each time she seemed slightly more broken, her voice even shakier, as if she were reliving the part she may have played in the violin's loss: the fatal mistake of letting the housekeeper out of her sight, if only for a moment.

Nicole was sitting in the armchair next to the window when the knock came: "Room service." She let the small, dark-haired woman in. Nicole didn't really get a good look at her behind the breakfast cart. The woman kept her head down. Her hair was smooth, with straight bangs, caught in a bun at the nape of her neck. She pushed the breakfast cart past the bathroom on the left where Ray was showering; past the kitchenette, also on the left; into the living room. She'd stopped the cart in front of the small dining-room table and started transferring the plates.

"I should have stayed right there," Nicole said. "I never should have tipped her."

"Why didn't you have the tip ready?" Bill asked. "You knew she was coming. Don't you normally give a tip?"

"Ray usually does it," Nicole said, looking at him.

"Yeah," Ray said, "I do."

But Nicole's purse was in the bedroom, so she went in to retrieve it. "I could still see the cart," she said.

"Could you see the woman?"

A long pause. She stared at the FBI agent, then down at her hands. "No," she said finally. "I guess I couldn't."

"Could you hear anything?"

"I heard her moving plates and glasses." Her voice cracked. "But I wasn't really paying attention. I only had a twenty so I had to find Ray's wallet."

"How many plates did you hear her move? Did you hear the violin case open?"

"No!" she said. "I was looking for Ray's wallet. I

just heard him taking a shower." Tears gleamed in her eyes, and she looked at her hands in her lap. Ray wanted to reach out, grab hers. Hug her tight.

"So what happened next?" Bill said. "Did you get his wallet?"

"Yeah. I found it and got five bucks."

"Where was the wallet? Could you see the cart when you found it?"

"No," she said, and now Ray could hear the panic in her voice. "His wallet—it was on the floor. It fell on the floor. Between the nightstand and the bed. I had to look for it. It was maybe thirty seconds, but I found it and gave it to her. Gave her the money."

"Five dollars, you said before?"

"Yeah," Nicole said. "It was only thirty seconds."

"How did you know where his wallet was?"

"He always has it on the nightstand. Don't you?" she appealed to Ray.

"Yeah," he said, "I always put it on the nightstand at night."

"But it wasn't there," Bill said to Ray, and then to Nicole, "so how did you know to look on the floor? Did you look through his coat first? Anywhere else it maybe could have been?"

"No," Nicole said. "Why would I not look on the floor? Wouldn't you? That's normal. This whole thing is normal." Now her voice was breaking. "I went into the bedroom, I came back out, I gave her the money, and she left. That's it."

"That's not it," Bill said. "Somewhere during that time, the violin disappeared."

Nicole had been inching toward him, as if she could convince him by her proximity, but now she fell back in her chair as if her spine could no longer hold her up. "It was thirty seconds," she repeated. "It was a minute."

"Was it?"

"It couldn't have been more than a few minutes. Three. Five, tops."

"She probably swapped out the violin in less than a minute. Stashed it underneath the cart. It would have taken her seconds."

Because the violin, all this time, lay casually in its unlocked case across the chair closest to the wall. The cart would have blocked Nicole's view of it.

Ray remembered seeing the violin case there when he went to grab breakfast. He'd been slightly surprised, because he usually left it in the bedroom, but the night before they'd all had a bit too much to drink. He'd probably come in, laid the violin on the chair, and collapsed into bed without thinking.

"So she had the opportunity to swap the violin for the shoe," Bill Soames confirmed.

For a moment no one said anything. Nicole sniffed—a tiny sound, but it seemed very loud in the silence.

"I'm not saying this is what happened," Bill said, "but it seems very possible."

"You mean it's my fault," Nicole said flatly.

"I didn't say that."

"You're damn right you didn't say that," Ray said. "It's not her fault."

"It's not a question of fault," Bill said. "It's just a question of opportunity. This was an opportunity, and it's possible that the woman took advantage of it."

"All the stars must have had to be aligned perfectly in order for her to pull this off," Ray said.

Bill Soames shrugged. "You'd be surprised. A lot of crimes really boil down to moments of opportunity. This woman may have been coming by, delivering your breakfast, a bunch of times, with the shoe and the ransom note in her cart. She finally got lucky."

Ray squeezed Nicole's hand. Maybe now his luck would change.

He spent the evening practicing, even though it still felt traitorous to be playing the Lehman. Stradivarius violins were unique. They commanded a mystique unlike any other instrument, with what many believed to be the purest, most extraordinary sound a violin could make. But the power and pull of the violin went well beyond its sound and its beauty: his own violin was in his blood, in the pulse that beat in his wrists and temples.

He skipped dinner. The Tchaikovsky Concerto blossomed.

Just after 8:00 p.m., the phone buzzed. A woman's voice, firm and no nonsense. "Rayquan McMillian? Alicia Childress here. I'm downstairs and I'm coming up." Minutes later a stout woman in her late fifties or early sixties was shaking his hand. Her curly gray hair was trimmed very close to her skull, and she wore khakis and a loose sweater. Without asking, she moved past him into the suite, pulled out her laptop, cleared a space on the dining-room table, talking the whole time.

She was done with pleasantries. "So let me make this clear," she said without preamble. "I'm focusing on three factors, and I'm going to drill into all of them: access, forensics, and motive."

He and Nicole sat down across from her. Ray removed Nicole's cup of cold half-drunk coffee from the table, laid it on the sideboard behind him. Where it had rested on the glass top, a half-moon glared up like a giant ghostly fingernail.

"So my first job, Rayquan," Alicia said, "is to determine who had access to the violin—I'm going to start by going over your story, every inch."

"Ray," Ray said.

"What?"

"Ray," he said. "Please call me Ray. Nobody calls me Rayquan."

"Ray it is, then," she said. "I'm still going to go over your story," she told him, "and then I'm going to go over yours," she said to Nicole. "You both had the most access, obviously."

"Pilar Jiménez," Nicole said.

"I keep telling everybody, it was either my family or the Marks family," Ray said. "It had to be one of them."

"I've heard this, and I'll get to them in a minute."

Ray twined his fingers with Nicole's. He felt more confident: this woman really was a bulldog. No time to chat and be friendly; Alicia was on a mission and he was not about to stand in her way. "Anything you need."

"Second, forensics. The FBI and the art squad have already shared everything with me, and I'm in the process of reviewing it. It's unfortunate that you didn't discover the theft until after the crime scene was tainted."

"You're assuming the crime scene is the hotel room?" Ray said.

"I am, but you're right. Since you didn't lock the case, it could have been stolen elsewhere—the airport, the airplane, plus the evening before, when you were wandering around the city. Pilar Jiménez is our primary person of interest, of course. But keep in mind that no matter where the violin was stolen, we still have a tainted crime scene."

"What about the ransom note?" Ray put in. "Are you tracking down the Bitcoin account?"

Alicia's brown eyes were carefully blank. "Yes, we're all working on tracking down the account."

"What about the letter itself?" Ray asked.

"Waiting to hear back from the lab for fingerprints or any other DNA. But, honestly, I wouldn't hold out much hope for that. Whoever planned this did it very carefully, and I doubt he left his fingerprints or a saliva sample on the paper."

"What about tracking down the ink and the paper?" Nicole said.

Alicia didn't look away. "Already did. It's from an HP OfficeJet 5258, using standard HP black ink. HP has sold fourteen thousand of the printers over the last year. The lab is still analyzing the paper, but I'll tell you right now that it's from a cheap ream that you can pick up in any office supply store in the country. The physical note itself is a dead end."

"The shoe," Ray said. "The shoe is the key. It's got to be a clue. Did you find out Dante Marks's shoe size? I'll bet you it's a ten and a half."

"He wears a size nine," Alicia told him. "And in the meantime there were three hundred purchases of men's size ten and a half Chucks in the tristate area over the past month. And another two hundred online across the US. We're tracking down every one we can, but it's a monumental job."

"Oh," Ray said.

"The third factor I'm focusing on is motive," she went on, holding his gaze. "Who would want it? Is it for some black market collector? Is it for the insurance money?" She eyed Ray, sizing him up.

He stared right back. "The people with the biggest motive are my family," he said. "They have the most to gain." He didn't want to explain again about the deal he'd made with them—how his lawyer had begged him not to. How he'd thought it was his only option. "And if it isn't them, it's those crazy Markses. It has to be."

She nodded, not asking for details yet—she clearly already knew. "Yes, when it comes to motive, they all have a strong one." She paused, her eyes drifting beyond him, staring at the blank cream wall of the hotel suite. "And you need to know that we're looking into you closely. The insurance money makes you a pretty obvious suspect."

"If he wanted to sell it, he would've sold it already," Nicole said.

"I've certainly had offers," Ray said. "For more than ten million bucks. Someone offered me fourteen a couple weeks ago."

"That's good to know," Alicia said. "I'll want a list. In the meantime I'll start with you," she said to Ray.

It was now after 9:00 p.m. Despite the lateness of the hour, Alicia asked Nicole to go into the bedroom, close the door. Then she spent the next two hours grilling Ray about every movement he'd made the day of the theft. The FBI guys and the police detectives had been polite and thorough, but this woman took it to a whole new level, drilling into every step of the evening and night.

"When you went to the bathroom, you took the violin with you?"

"Yes."

"Number one or number two?"

"The night before it was stolen, only number one."

"Where was the violin?"

"Slung over my right shoulder, in its case."

"You never took it off?"

"Never, especially not in the bathroom. Humidity. It stays on my shoulder."

"How about if you have to go number two?"

"I always find a stall that has a hook on the inside of the door so I can hang it. Always within arm's reach."

"Always?"

"Always," he said firmly. "Okay, let's get this out of the way. I'm just some Black dude who got lucky. I know what you're thinking, but I'd never do anything to put my violin at risk."

"I can see that." She nodded. "But the case wasn't locked when you were having dinner, right? Or drinks? Or in the cab?"

"No."

"Why not?"

"Because I don't lock it when I have it on me. And I always have it on me."

"So you never lock it, you're saying."

"I've locked it," Ray said defensively.

"Mm-hmm." Alicia looked down at her notes. "But it wasn't locked when you were in the shower, right? When the housekeeper was in the room?"

He just looked at her. She was right.

"I don't think you get it," Ray said. "I don't take any risks with it. Ever. I never leave it alone. I don't walk around with the case unlocked and leave it lying on a park bench. That violin is my life. It changed everything for me."

"From what I've heard, you're a very talented musician in your own right."

He shrugged, still feeling a little defensive. "It took my playing to a whole different level. It was an enormous shortcut to having people pay serious attention to me."

"Nothing good is ever easy," she said.

"I guess not. But I don't come from a family that really nurtures music."

"Not even now, with all the attention you've gotten? You certainly are a media darling these days."

"No, not even now. I haven't talked to my mom in months."

"Really," Alicia said. "Why is that?"

"She did everything she could to stop me from

playing. She just wanted another paycheck coming in."

"Was she hurting for money?"

He shrugged. "I didn't think so, but she was a single mom, and I have a younger brother and sister, and they always need something. It's worse because they're twins, and she has to buy for both of them. She's always wanting more money." He thought about it. "But, honestly, I have no idea. You think my mom would steal my violin?"

"Do you?"

"I don't know. My family has the best motive, but I really don't think they'd be able to get away with it, not with all the conditions we put around the deal. My lawyer made sure of that. They're definitely greedy but they wouldn't have the slightest idea of how to pull something like this off. Getting fifty dollars' worth of groceries for fifteen? Yeah, sure. But this? Not even."

"There's a lot of money at stake," Alicia said. "You'd be surprised what a motivating force money can be."

Where Ray's mother was concerned, Ray thought, Alicia Childress didn't know the half of it.

Alicia pulled her laptop over, donned a pair of reading glasses. "Some of those relatives of yours have racked up some serious debts," she was saying. "Thurston and Joyce in particular."

"They always wanted money from me," he said. "I never made very much but I still sent them what I could. It was probably twenty thousand dollars, all told. But it was never enough."

"Which is why you made that deal with them back in February," she said.

"Yeah," he said. "That's why. It got them off my back."

She'd been studying her laptop as if she could read some hidden map in its screen, but now she looked up at him, shook her head. "Your family is at the top of my list of suspects. A stolen violin plus insurance money equals a big fat life-changing motive."

Chapter 5

Day 17: Mom

He returned to Charlotte, and Nicole went back to Erie. Within a few days he was already considering a return to New York, as if being there would make it more likely that he'd stumble over the violin on a Midtown street. Late one morning, as he was working through the Bach Chaconne for the third time, his phone rang. Alicia. He snatched it up. "Any news? Did they find her yet?" He laid down his bow on the music stand. The house echoed.

"Not yet." No one had tracked down the housekeeper. The community wasn't talking.

"What about the reward?" Ray said. "Did you tell them about the reward?"

"Oh, good idea," she said. "Wish I'd thought of that sooner. Darn. Missed opportunity."

"She couldn't just disappear," Ray said, pacing

around the house. "What about airports? Bus stations? It's New York."

"Exactly. It's New York. She absolutely could."

He asked if there were any leads about the Bitcoin account (nothing), the printer (nothing), or the Chuck Taylor purchases (no news).

"So Pilar is still the best shot," he said.

"She is. There is a serious manhunt out for her. Bill Soames promised to alert me immediately when they track her down."

"I guess you haven't turned up anything with my family, then?"

"We're monitoring all their accounts. They've all been interviewed multiple times." Alicia's voice turned deceptively casual. "I also had a chat with the Marks family."

Ray sat up. "What did you think? They're trippin', right?"

"They're certainly a piece of work. Denied everything."

"Well," Ray said, "if the violin is gone, so much for their lawsuit against me."

"They definitely don't seem to have a motive to steal it."

He parsed her words. "But you don't trust them, either."

"I don't. But we haven't found any proof yet of their involvement. I'll keep you posted."

They hung up soon after, and Ray went back

to practicing the Bach. He couldn't concentrate, though, and finally took a shower and lay on his bed, staring up at the ceiling.

Midmorning next day, Alicia texted.

Alicia: **I've found her. Honduras. The house-keeper.**

Ray: **I'm going down there, send me the address**

Alicia: **Leave this to the pros, grasshopper. I'm at the airport now.**

Ray: **Are you sure it's her**

Alicia: **Pretty sure. We want to talk to her in person, not risk spooking her again. I'll report back asap.**

Alicia called the next day, just after 11:00 a.m. He'd barely slept, staring at the phone, willing it to ring or text.

"I just left her," Alicia said. "She says she doesn't know anything about the violin."

"Why did she leave, then?"

"She refused to say. Absolutely refused."

"That's bullshit," Ray said. "She must have said something. What made her disappear?"

"There's clearly something going on," Alicia said. "But all she would say was that she was homesick. I kept asking her other questions, and that's all she'd tell me."

"You speak Spanish?"

"Enough. And I hired a translator that I use when I travel to Central America."

After they hung up, Ray sat for a moment, thinking. Then he put the violin back in its case, went out to his car, drove the forty minutes back, down familiar streets.

The house seemed exactly the same: left gutter pulled away from the siding, rust stains oozing like acne down the white vinyl, new weeds elbowing their way through the old ones along the walkway. It felt so routine—like he was just returning from a trip to the grocery store—and so alien, like perhaps the grocery store had been on Mars.

He knocked. For a few minutes nobody answered, and he felt sick. He was stupid for not having called first. Ever since the twins finished elementary school, his mother's schedule had become erratic. It was the middle of the day, though: she should be home. He knocked again, hopeless now.

Then he felt the slight rattle of footsteps, and a moment later his mother stood in the doorway. "Well, look who comes crawling back," she said. "Not so high and mighty now, are you?"

"Hi, Mom," he said.

"Now that you lost your fiddle, guess you're wanting me to help you out, huh?" She eyed him. "Well you might as well come in." She sauntered back in, leaving the door ajar.

The living room looked just the same—faded couch, beaded lampshade, scuffed carpet, glass-topped coffee table—but what hit him hardest was the familiar smell, the slightly musty mix of old upholstery, unwashed sneakers, and nail polish remover. His mother sat grandly in her chair in front of the TV, gestured for him to sit across from her. He sat.

"You stopped sending money," she observed. "You could have at least told me."

"Nice to see you, too. You got all the money in the settlement. I'm going to be paying you off for the rest of my life. Plus I haven't been performing lately, I've been practicing."

"Seems by now you should have gotten good enough to stop practicing."

He held his breath a moment, let it out. "I have a big competition coming up. In Moscow. It's one of the biggest competitions in the world. It's a pretty big deal."

"Well, whoop-dee-freakin'-do," she said, studying her nails, which were very white and glowed. "Shouldn't you be 'practicing' then? Everybody else has been coming by, asking me where I was, did I know what happened to your fiddle. They got some kind of court order to look at my bank account, you know that? And not one word of apology from my son. Not one."

"Why would I apologize?" he said. "The fiddle

was stolen. The police were just doing their jobs, trying to get it back."

"You should have known it would have inconvenienced me." She said the word like it was something she'd heard someone else say, then practiced in front of a mirror. "I was very inconvenienced. All these people coming by, asking can they talk to me, scaring the twins? You know your sister didn't even want to let them in? You know that?"

"You and the family are the prime suspects," he reminded her. "Because of the money."

"You think nobody else mentioned that, genius?"

She was looking down at her chair, fumbling for her phone, which had chimed, so he was staring at the top of her head. "Do you know who took it, Mom? Did Uncle Thurston? Uncle Larry? Because if it's about the money I'll figure out how to get it to you. I just want the fiddle back. I don't care about the money."

"You don't care about five million dollars?" she said. "Sure you don't." She was still groping in the chair for her phone, which she found, lifted to her face.

"Mom," he said again, trying to be patient, "just listen to me. If you know anybody who could have taken it, can you tell them to be in touch with me? I'll start crowdfunding. I'll get you the money."

"How would I know where it is?" she said. "You got a lot of nerve, barging in here and accusing your mother of stealing that fiddle! You got some nerve, that's all I can say."

"So you don't know where it is? And nobody else in the family knows anything?"

"You are getting on my nerves with this. Will you stop pestering me? I told you I didn't know nothing. Seems to me that those fancy white folks that're suing you would be the people you'd be thinking about right now, not the mother who fed you and clothed you."

"The Marks family, you mean? Yeah, the detectives are looking into them, too. But I wanted to talk to you myself."

She picked up her phone. "You know something, you gotta leave." She stared into the depths of the phone screen, which looked blank from Ray's angle. "You need to go. Accusing your own mother. After all I did for you."

"Mom, I—" There was so much he wanted to say. He just looked at the top of her head, smooth and gleaming, as if she'd spent twenty minutes in front of the bathroom mirror, brushing her hair and pursing her lips. "Got it," he said. "Sorry to bother you."

As soon as he got home, he logged onto the crowdfunding website he'd been clicking on for days, called Nicole.

"Hey," he said when she picked up. "I think we should do the crowdfunding."

She'd been after him to set up RaysFiddle.com, a crowdfunding site to raise the ransom money himself—just in case the police or Alicia Childress didn't recover the violin on their own.

"Okay," she said without hesitation. "What do you need me to do?"

Together they spent the afternoon and evening preparing the files and uploading photos under the heading "Please Help Me Rescue My Stolen Violin," with a donation goal of $5 million, due by July 13, two days before the ransom date.

"This is gonna work," she told him. "You're gonna have the money in no time."

"I sure hope so," he said. But he already felt lighter and more confident.

That evening he struggled to get back into the mindset of practicing. The competition loomed. He was flying out in two weeks. He did his best to clear his head and focus on the Mozart fingering, on putting his whole soul and personality into telling Mozart's story, but he could feel that he wasn't emotionally connecting with the music the way he needed to.

When the phone rang, he was grateful for the distraction, hoping it was Alicia with news about the former housekeeper, but it was Uncle Thurston. Wow—perhaps the talk with his mom was already working. He should have known his family had been involved. "Hello?" he said.

"What the hell you thinking, boy, going over and threatening your mama? That's just bullshit, you hear me?" He continued to swear so much that Ray couldn't even get a word in. "I thought she raised you better than that, but what you need is to have someone take you outside and show you what happens when you threaten your mom."

"What are you talking about? I never threatened—"

"Sure you didn't," Thurston cut him off. "I don't want to hear your excuses. No excuse for that kind of behavior. How you turned out to be such a piece of shit is beyond me. It was always about you, wasn't it? You selfish son of a bitch. Always about you. Well, now the shoe's on the other foot, ain't it?"

"I didn't—"

"I just called to tell you one thing—just one thing. If you think for even a second we'll help you—any of us will help you get that fucking violin back, you can think again. You ain't never going to see that thing again. And you know what? I'm glad. You deserve what's coming to you. You earned it."

Thurston hung up, and Ray, trembling, set down the phone.

How had it ever gotten so awful?

PART 2
The Joy of Family

6 YEARS AGO

Chapter 6

The Wedding
October

One early October day in Ray's senior year in high school, he was sitting at the kitchen table watching Hilary Hahn's performance of Vivaldi's **L'Inverno** on his phone when his mother said from the doorway, "Cheryl's son Ricky is graduating next month with his GED."

He looked up, the violins soaring in his left ear; he had only one earbud in so he could hear his mom if she wanted something. He hated hearing her yell.

"She got him a job working at the hospital," his mother was saying. A slender woman, she liked looking good—even now, with her hair tied up in a scarf and wearing her favorite faded red T-shirt with **Property of North Carolina State University Athletic Department** on it. She leaned back against the doorjamb, looked at her fake yellow nails with studied casualness.

"At the hospital?" Ray repeated, not really listening. Hilary Hahn's fingering was delicate and impressive. He slowed down the replay, lifted the violin to his chin, practiced the fingering without letting the bow touch the strings. His mom didn't like him playing the violin in the house, even though he'd bought a cheap practice mute so she wouldn't hear it.

Ray was the only kid in orchestra with a rental instrument—a beat-up ancient wreck, dirty and rough sounding. He'd strapped a sponge with a rubber band to the violin's base to create a makeshift shoulder-rest.

The YouTube video swelled around him. His left arm was rigid; his right sawed the air. There were so many flats in the piece that he had to make sure his hand slid back into half position.

"Yeah," his mom was saying, "he's working in the cafeteria. He gets free food and benefits. Can't you graduate early?"

He stopped, looked up at her. "What? Why?"

"So you can get a job."

"I have a job," he said. He rewound the video twenty seconds to examine how Hahn moved up and down the fingerboard. He hit PAUSE and marked the music on the table in front of him. Of course—why was he trying to play that phrase in third position?

"Will you listen to me and stop with that noise?" his mother said. "That little part-time job ain't going to make you no money. Plus it's over in a month. You gotta help out with these bills around here. You gotta make plans."

"I think I missed the cutoff for the winter GED," he lied. "I can check, though."

"After Christmas you're going to have to start helping with the rent and the rest of the bills." She opened a cabinet door, stared at a row of cereal and pasta boxes, closed it.

He set down his phone, actually looked at her. She was serious. Terror started out as a small nugget in his chest, quickly grew fingers, tightened like a hand around his heart. "You said before that I'd pay rent when I graduated."

"I changed my mind," she said. "Ricky's already paying rent and they just got a new sixty-inch."

"So you want me to get a GED so you can get a bigger TV? Is that what this is about?" Regional orchestra auditions were in January, and Ray really wanted to try out. If he graduated in December, he wouldn't have the chance. It was a long shot to get in, but he'd spent the summer practicing and he desperately wanted to try out. Only the top players in the state were chosen, and if he got in he would be able to perform high-level music he'd probably never have another opportunity to play once he graduated and got a real job.

"This is about you doing what I say and getting a damn job," she said. She crossed back, opened the refrigerator, stared into it like she was reading his fortune in the packed shelves. "You could have been making good money at Popeyes by now."

"I don't want to work at Popeyes. Or in the hospital cafeteria."

"I didn't ask you what you wanted." She pulled out a liter of soda. "I told you to get a real paying job, you hear? You had plenty of time to find another one by now. You better have a job by Thanksgiving." His part-time job at the construction site ended next month. She poured herself a glass of soda.

"I'll find something," he said. "Maybe the grocery store?"

"You need to go ahead and apply," she said. "And go check about getting your GED." She took her soda back to the living room, where she and the twins were watching TV. The twins, who had just celebrated their eighth birthdays, were—like his mom—addicted to **Family Feud**.

Ray put in both earbuds, turned Vivaldi's **L'Inverno** up as loud as it would go, pressed PLAY. He would ignore everything except the music. Hopefully his mom would forget about the GED by the end of the weekend, but that wasn't likely— once his mom got an idea in her head, there was no shaking her. She wanted that sixty-inch.

He'd apply to the grocery store on Monday, after school. The hours were pretty much the same as the construction site, plus it was indoors. Satisfied that he had a workable plan, he spent the rest of the weekend focusing on playing **L'Inverno** on his school violin and playing a new video game on the PlayStation 5 his grandma Nora had given him last Christmas.

But that Monday in orchestra class, Ray's buddy Aiden changed everything. Before class started, Aiden sat down two seats over from him, leaned in, and asked, "What're you doing this weekend?" They'd become casual friends the year before, eating lunch together and playing duets sometimes at Aiden's house. If Ray ever needed to borrow rosin or an extra string, Aiden was the only one who would offer. Aiden was tall and slim, with long black hair that he was constantly brushing out of his eyes. He was one of a handful of Asian kids in orchestra.

"Not much. Studying. Chillin'. Can I borrow your rosin?" Ray asked.

Aiden handed it over. Ray unscrewed the lid, applied the rosin to the bow hair with long slow strokes.

"I got asked to play a wedding on Saturday," Aiden said. "The other violinist just backed out. You want to take his place? It's two-hundred bucks."

For a moment Ray couldn't breathe. "Are you serious? Quit fucking with me, dude."

Aiden laughed. "I'm dead serious. We need another violin. It's an outdoor wedding. We get to stay for the reception. Free food. Want to do it?"

"Fuck yeah, I do!" Ray calculated. Two hundred dollars was like twenty-five hours of minimum wage at the construction site or bagging groceries. Two and a half weeks of work.

"Good," Aiden said. "I'll get you the music after class."

Wait till his mother heard! She called his music "noise," but once she heard how much money he could make, she'd change her tune. No need to bag groceries. If he could get a regular gig playing music, he'd be golden.

At the end of class, when Aiden handed him the music, Ray said as casually as he could, "You have any more gigs lined up you might need me for?"

"Yeah, we do a few a month. Don't you have a job, though?"

"It's ending in November," Ray said. "I would love to play with you guys. Who was the other violinist?"

"It's Chad Horner, you know him? Graduated last year. He's a flake. This is the third gig he's bailed on. I should have asked you earlier, it's just you're always working."

Ray didn't want to sound desperate. "I'm usually free most weekends."

"Awesome," Aiden said. "Let's see how this weekend goes. If it's good, you're in."

When Ray got home that evening, he immediately hunted down his mother, who was in her bedroom, lying back against the pillows, flipping through **Essence** magazine, phone tucked almost invisibly beneath her jaw. "Hold on," she said into the phone. "What is it?" she said to Ray.

"I'm making two hundred dollars this weekend." He had never made that kind of money. Even if his mom took most of it, what would he buy? If he had two gigs he could buy his own violin—no more school instruments. He could get a shoulder rest instead of a sponge. He'd seen one for twenty-five dollars at the music store on Providence Road.

"Where?"

"I'm playing at a wedding! It pays two hundred dollars." He rolled the numbers around his tongue, savoring them.

"Oh good." Then into the phone, "What I want to know is, does she really think he don't notice? Because he sure as hell noticed."

"That's like two and a half weeks of work bagging groceries," Ray said. Maybe she didn't understand.

"That's just like her," his mom said. "I told you she was gonna do something like that."

"If I do a good job," Ray said, "they said they can use me every week. That's two hundred dollars a weekend. That's more than Ricky makes at the hospital in one week."

"Hold on, girl," she said to the phone. She stared

up at the ceiling. "He makes about three hundred dollars a week."

"Yeah, but that's working five days a week. This is one afternoon. If I can get a couple gigs a week—and my friend thinks I can—I can start bringing in serious money."

"When you get paid?"

"After each gig," he said. "One thing, though. I'm going to need a ride."

She looked at him blankly. "Well, you're gonna have to find one. I'm not your taxi. Ride your bike." She gestured for him to be quiet, waved him out.

He turned, muttering, "You are unbelievable," and hit the doorframe with his shoulder.

"Hold on, girl. What did you say?" she shouted behind him.

"Nothing. I didn't say anything." He went down the hall, flopped down on his bed. For a few moments the old familiar resentment seethed through him.

He needed to save up for a car, that was clear. Then he could book even more gigs. Then she'd see how much money he could make with his playing. And he could stay in school, try out for regionals. He'd get paid for making music—this was incredible.

He texted Aiden, asked him for a ride to the wedding, then rummaged through his book bag to retrieve the wedding music. Canon in D. No problem. "Arrival of the Queen of Sheba." No problem.

Water Music Suite. They sure were playing a lot of Handel.

He was reaching for his violin when his mom opened the door without knocking. "Let me tell you something," she told him. "When I'm on the phone, don't come in asking me anything crazy. Do you understand?"

Ray held his breath for a moment. "Okay," he said at last.

"And don't even start playing that thing. Making all that noise."

He needed a better practice mute, he told himself again. He'd pick one up once he made his first $200. He shuffled the pages around until she left. Then he just read and reread the music until he fell asleep, imagining how amazing it would be, playing in a wedding—a real wedding.

By Saturday morning, the twelve pieces of music were creased and parts were almost illegible with handling. His fingertips thrummed with anticipation. He took out the polish that Aiden loaned him, rubbed it vigorously on the violin's body to try to clear off decades of rosin buildup. By the time he'd finished, his right hand was sticky and white with the rosin. He was so determined to make a good impression that he even polished the back of the violin, though no one would actually see it.

He wiped his hands on the edge of his bed, leaving a smear of rosin behind.

Now for the suit: black slacks, stiff white shirt, black tie. He looked at himself in the mirror. Damn, he looked good. People might think he was the one getting married.

As he took his cereal bowl back to the kitchen, his mom came out of her room. "Why you so dressed up?"

"I'm playing that wedding today, remember?"

"I told you. I'm not giving you a ride."

"I know. I took care of it." He put the bowl in the sink and retreated to his room to grab his jacket and his violin case, dashing outside as Aiden showed up. Right on time.

At 11:15—fifteen minutes early—they pulled up to the wedding venue. Ray had passed this place dozens of times, but never thought that the wrought-iron gates would stand open and welcoming for him; that the tall brick pillars, weathered a soft pink, would allow him to enter.

At the top of the drive, people were getting out and heading up the walkway to the front door. Aiden pulled up behind them. "You go on in, I'll park and meet you around back."

"Okay, cool." Ray grabbed his violin case and headed up the sidewalk, lined with huge gray ceramic vases, from which ivy and roses poured. The house was even more daunting up close—it seemed to go on forever. He was really doing this.

Slightly ahead of him, a young couple and a

young woman were dressed in their Sunday best—
the young man in a navy-blue suit, the women
both in minidresses. Their wedding gifts, wrapped
in silver, sparkled.

"Hi," he said.

The people smiled with their lips, their eyes not
meeting his. The man—blond and blue-eyed—
rang the doorbell.

This was it, his first paying gig. He was on his
way to the big time. He'd hand his mother the crisp
twenty-dollar bills and she'd look up at him and
smile and hug him. Maybe they'd even give him
two $100 bills.

The door knocker was enormous, ornate, fash-
ioned in the shape of an open-mouthed lion. Was
it brass? Gold? He couldn't wait to tell his mom
about this place. She wouldn't believe it.

He was about to take a photo, to prove it to her,
when a tall man with a foamy white beard and a
speckled bald head opened the door. He looked at
all of them, looked twice at Ray.

"Hey, Uncle Roger!" said the young woman next
to him, a redhead with heels so high Ray didn't
know how she could even walk. "You look fantastic!" She offered him her cheek.

Uncle Roger was wearing a tuxedo. Ray had
never seen a tuxedo up close. Could Ray take a
picture of the tuxedo, too? He was a big dude.
Probably a football player thirty years ago.

"Melanie," Uncle Roger was saying, "We didn't think you were going to make it. Sara will be thrilled that you're here."

Ray waited for the man to turn to him. Instead he said to the couple, "Mike. Ellie. So glad you could come today. Come on in, everyone is in the living room for drinks and hors d'oeuvres." Uncle Roger leaned to one side and the three entered, Melanie teetering in on her heels.

Ray was next.

"May I help you?" Uncle Roger stepped out of the doorway.

"Hi, I'm here for the wedding."

Uncle Roger looked Ray up and down. "Whose wedding?"

"I'm playing for your wedding," Ray explained.

"I'm sorry, you are . . . ?"

Ray kept his smile fixed in place. "I'm Ray McMillian. Playing for the service."

"Hold on a minute." Uncle Roger stepped back through the door, partially closing it. Ray could still hear him. "Anne, could you come here?"

Aiden was nowhere in sight. A few more cars had pulled up: new guests with new presents. The conversation on the other side of the door was still unspooling.

"Well, who is he?" Uncle Roger was saying.

"I don't know." A woman's voice. "Did you ask him for an ID?"

"No. He was carrying something. I guess it could be an instrument."

"We don't have time for this. I have to finish getting ready. It's almost time to move everyone to the garden."

"Well, what do you want me to do?" Uncle Roger said. "I don't know who this kid is."

"Ask him for an ID. Maybe he's with the catering company."

"They all arrived at ten. It's eleven thirty."

"You're going to have to handle this. For once in your life, can you make an effort?"

The door opened partway, the man's face barely visible. "I think you have the wrong address. This is a private ceremony."

Ray couldn't even open his mouth to speak as Uncle Roger closed the door.

What just happened? Did that guy just close the door on him?

Ray stood there, in his black suit, with his black tie, in his polished black shoes, looking dope with his fresh new fade, with his violin polished and his bow rosined and the whole world waiting to hear him play—and he just stood there. This had to be a mistake. He was carrying a violin case, for goodness sake. Who shows up to a wedding with a violin case and has the door slammed in his face? He rang the bell again. It was 11:26 a.m.

The other wedding guests were tapping up the

walkway. A blond girl dressed like a thirty-year-old, with a dress that barely covered her hips, looked directly at him and then looked away. She was probably fifteen, if that. She was the only one who even looked at him.

Uncle Roger was opening the door and waving the other guests inside, his body somehow blocking Ray from entering. Ray could hear the sounds of forks on plates, and low laughter. "Come on in, everyone. We're about to go into the garden."

"I'm supposed to be playing," Ray said, holding up the violin case as if there was a sign emblazoned on it: HERE TO PLAY FOR WEDDING.

Should he call Aiden? He would, but he was so embarrassed—as if he'd done something wrong. Maybe he had and just didn't know?

Uncle Roger gently but firmly closed the door again. What the hell?

The door opened, and Uncle Roger looked directly at him. Ray sighed, relieved. 11:31. He moved as if to enter.

"Look, you're going to need to leave before I call the cops. This is a private event."

"What? I'm supposed—"

Uncle Roger lunged toward him. "This is a wedding. Not a rap concert."

"What are you talking about? I'm here to play at your wedding."

"I booked a string quartet. It's classy. No offense, but it's not your people's kind of music."

"I'm here to play—"

"I'm not going to tell you again," Uncle Roger said. "Get the hell off my property. Now!" Again the door slammed, louder this time, cutting off the din inside. From across the lawn, a bird sang, loud in the stillness.

What the actual fuck?

He called Aiden, who answered almost before the phone rang. "Dude, where are you? We were supposed to start five minutes ago. You haven't even gotten set up yet. Did you get lost?"

"You won't believe this, but I can't get in."

"What? What are you talking about?"

"Some guy told me I was at the wrong place and slammed the door in my face."

"Are you serious? Where are you now?"

"I'm at the front door."

"Hold on, I'll come get you."

11:36. 11:39.

The door opened again.

"Dude! Hurry up." Aiden led Ray through the empty foyer. Uncle Roger had thankfully disappeared. Ray caught a blurred glimpse of oriental rugs, heavy wooden and gilded furniture, and pictures in heavy gold frames suspended from wires on the walls. They sprinted through a pair of

French doors and into the garden, slowed to a walk. Garlands of roses and white lilies looped like snakes along the walkways. Twin fountains sprayed a light mist; the sunlight fell golden and in rainbows. Ray and Aiden tried to tiptoe inconspicuously around the two rows of padded white folding chairs now holding wedding guests. Most people ignored them, but Ray could feel some eyes like flies on him, clinging. The other musicians were sitting on one side under a tent. Four chairs, two empty. Ray sat down. What had just happened?

Aiden grabbed Ray's folder. "Go quick as you can. I'll get your music ready. We're starting with **Water Music**." Beth Lamb was playing viola and Christine Long was on cello.

"I'm sorry, man. It wasn't my fault. I tried to—"

"Don't worry about it. We'll figure it out later. You guys ready?"

They gave a nod and waited for Aiden's cue.

It felt as if every eye in the garden was on Ray. He wondered where Uncle Roger was, if he'd march over and drag Ray out. He told himself to calm down. It was no big deal. This was the first of many gigs. He needed to do it right. Two hundred dollars.

The music started. Suddenly his bow arm was gliding across the strings and his fingers were making the notes somersault off the fingerboard. He was doing it. He was actually playing music—and getting paid for it. People were listening to him—to him!—and paying him for the privilege. This was more fun than he'd had, ever: he loved the immediateness. The melodies sluiced off the violin and out into space, where he was setting the mood and filling his audience's senses.

The quartet played through the five prelude pieces flawlessly—these were all songs they'd played many times in class, and all four of them knew the music from memory.

At the end of the fifth piece, the groom, minister, and four groomsmen took their positions beneath the canopy, in front of a wall of white roses.

The wedding director waved at Aiden to begin music for the next processional—" 'Rhosymedre,' Prelude on a Welsh Hymn Tune"—for the family's entrance. This was one of Ray's favorites. He liked it so much that he'd researched the piece and the composer, Ralph Vaughan Williams. The title meant "lovely." It was totally, absolutely true.

The sun was high in the sky. The air was cool but not chilly. Every flower in the garden was in bloom. The guests were no longer looking at him, they'd all turned to watch the mother of the bride, in a sky-blue dress, glide down the white runner that ran between the rows of seats. She walked in perfect sync with the music. The bridesmaids, in darker blue satin gowns with their hair elaborately piled on their heads, followed.

Then Christine played the eight most familiar

notes in all of classical music: Pachelbel's Canon in D. As she played, the house's elaborately carved French doors opened and the bride appeared.

Standing next to her was Uncle Roger.

Ray's hands froze. He doubted he'd be able to move the bow, to lift the violin. He would stick there, become part of the chair itself.

Aiden began to play. Ray had only eight beats of rests before he had to enter. Those eight beats stretched on and on. He stared at the music, convinced that Uncle Roger was glaring at him.

No matter what just happened, his first gig was going to be a good one. This was the start of something great. Right on cue, as if his hands belonged to someone else, he began to play. His phrasing was even and sure. His notes were rich and beautiful. Aiden looked over at Ray, nodded in approval. Roger and the bride drew closer, and Ray drew more into himself, focusing on the music. He was sure Uncle Roger was marching down the aisle glowering at him, but when Ray dared to glance up, Roger was focused on the minister and the groom and the bridesmaids.

When the bride took her place, Aiden signaled them to stop playing. They wouldn't play again until the minister announced the couple was officially married, and then they'd start in on "Arrival of the Queen of Sheba." Ray kept his eyes on the music, on the few feet of grass that separated them from the guests, listened to the vows.

Finally Aiden brought his instrument to playing position.

"And now," suggested the minister, "may I present Mr. and Mrs. James Sinclair."

Ray was poised, ready. But just before the first note, his eyes locked with Uncle Roger's, lower lip clamped in his teeth, scowling at him from the front row.

Ray was a professional. He wouldn't let the old man psych him out. He kept his eyes on Uncle Roger and began playing "Arrival of the Queen of Sheba." The fast notes didn't deter him from the staring contest: he'd gone over the piece so many times that he no longer needed the music. Then Beth's hand slipped from the viola's fingerboard and she played a series of wrong notes. Uncle Roger stood up to applaud the new husband and wife.

They were almost done with the ceremony and soon he'd never have to see Uncle Roger again. And most important: he'd played beautifully, the beat-up old violin singing like a Stradivarius. The $200 was his.

The guests—and Uncle Roger—followed the couple from the garden back to the house.

The quartet had been invited to eat at the reception, but Ray was still on such a high from playing that he didn't much care if he ever ate again. They packed up their instruments and music while the cleanup crew took down the canopy.

"Man, you sounded awesome," Aiden told him. "I didn't know you were such a rock star!"

Beth overheard them as she packed up her viola. "You really are a great player. Where'd you get that violin?"

Ray laughed. "This is one of the school rentals."

"Are you serious? It sounded really sweet—you did a good job."

"My man." Aiden wrapped an arm around Ray's shoulders. Ray's chest expanded with pride. Of course Aiden would ask him for more gigs. No bagging groceries or getting a GED.

Just then came a voice from behind them. "Thank you so much! You sounded wonderful!" They turned. The mother of the bride was bearing down on them. Behind her, eyes fixed on Ray, was Uncle Roger.

"Thank you for having us, ma'am." Aiden slung his violin case over his shoulder. "We really appreciate it."

"Sara was so happy with the music. We look forward to seeing you inside. Roger will take care of you."

"Okay, so what do I owe you?" Uncle Roger said. As if he didn't know.

Ray leaned over to watch. This was it. The moment he got paid for his first gig.

"Eight hundred dollars," Aiden said. Ray could barely keep a goofy grin off his face as Uncle Roger reached into his jacket pocket and pulled out a thick wad of folded bills.

"Thank you all," the mother of the bride was saying. "Please follow me to the dining room and join us for the reception. Sara and James will want to thank you personally. Roger?"

A flurry of thank-yous followed. Uncle Roger extended one hand, stepped aside. Aiden led the quartet down the white runner toward the French doors. Ray was about to follow them when Uncle Roger grabbed his arm. The mother of the bride, leading the rest of the quartet, was now several steps ahead. Uncle Roger scowled at him, rage barely contained.

In that moment Ray saw something both familiar and foreign: he'd seen that same expression dozens of times, from dozens of people. The men on the corner on his way to work. The cashier at the 7-Eleven. The police officer riding by on patrol. Mark Jennings in orchestra class. He knew that expression.

Uncle Roger pulled him in closer, never breaking his gaze. "You almost destroyed my daughter's wedding. The only reason I didn't throw you out is because I didn't want to cause a scene," he growled. "I want you to get the fuck outta my garden and get the fuck outta my home. I don't ever want to see your face around here again. Fuckin' darkies need to stay on your own side of town. You are going to walk your Black ass through those doors and off my property. If you so much as cough, I'm calling the cops. Do you understand me, boy?"

Ray's mind was blank. How had Ray almost ruined the wedding? Maybe he'd missed a couple notes, but nobody cared. Beth had played worse than him. He couldn't breathe.

Uncle Roger jerked Ray's arm, waited for Ray to pass, and fell into step behind him. Ray felt daggers in the back of his skull. There was no possibility of going into the dining room, grabbing a plate of food, sitting with the others, basking in a job well done. He'd wait for Aiden in the car, if he could find it.

A few yards away from the house doors, an older man with an unkempt moustache smoked a cigarette. As Ray passed, the man said to Uncle Roger, "Niggers are getting bold, ain't they."

Ray froze for an instant, his stomach in his throat. Behind him, the man and Uncle Roger laughed.

Ray reached the house. From his left he could hear the sound of conversation, the clink of forks, laughter.

"Straight ahead, boy."

The house enveloped him. His eyes burned. Again a blur of lush furnishings, even more blurred now. At last he was in the foyer, he recognized the big carved door, open, the ornate golden lion staring at him emptily.

Wordless, he walked outside and down the

walkway. He'd wait for Aiden past the gates, on the road. Or maybe he'd get an Uber. He couldn't stand to be on this property a moment longer.

There are moments in life when the clouds lift and the curtain of rain blows back and suddenly the world stands before you, stark and vast, and you teeter on the edge of an enormous precipice of knowing, of understanding with every fiber in your soul, every hair on your head; and this was one such moment. A little breeze came from nowhere and set the early autumn leaves spinning, green-gold and yellow, and the air felt like it was being breathed by different lungs, the leaves on the ground crunching under different feet.

It's not that he didn't know he was Black—of course he did. A glance at the back of his hand was a constant reminder. And it's not that he didn't realize that there was racial prejudice in the world—it was baked into every TV show, discussed ad nauseum in the news, marched against and preached against. So how was it possible, how was it even conceivable, that he would somehow believe that racism didn't apply to him, that white people would just ignore his skin? He was dressed in a suit, with a nice tie, and he spoke with the same accent they did; his handshake was firm and his gaze direct. He knew he had a great smile on the rare occasions when he smiled. He wasn't the smartest kid, but he was smarter than most.

And none of that mattered. No matter how nice the suit, no matter how educated his speech or how strong the handshake, no matter how much muscle he packed on, no matter how friendly or how smart he was, **none of it mattered at all**. He was just a Black person. That's all they saw and that's all he was.

He would always—**always**—be seen as only half as good as everyone else.

All this time he'd lied to himself, or had he just been naive? Mr. Stinson, that jerk of a music teacher, didn't ignore him because Ray was poor, couldn't afford an instrument, couldn't afford private lessons like all the white kids did: no, Mr. Stinson ignored him because he was Black. Mark Jennings—the only other really good player in the orchestra—called him "ghetto" and taunted him not because Mark Jennings thought of Ray as a rival, but because Ray was Black.

Being Black was why Aiden had never asked him to play before—because why would you want a reliable Black guy when you could sit around waiting for an unreliable white one? Black people just couldn't play this kind of music. Ray was ridiculous to think that he could.

Everything written by James Baldwin and Langston Hughes and Toni Morrison and Alice Walker and all the other writers that he'd read in school was true: racism was real, and it was about **him**.

Today he had learned two things, and these two things were intertwined in his head and in his life. First, he learned that he could make money playing in front of an audience, and that he loved playing in front of an audience: his listeners spurred him to play better, to dig deeper inside himself, to trust his fingers and their innate sense of where the music wanted to go. Second, he learned that doing what you loved may not be enough, that all the passion and perseverance that roared like blood within you could be trumped by factors that you could never control—factors like the color of your skin, or the shape of your eyes, or the sound of your voice.

The world had been telling him these things over and over, and he'd just been too dumb to hear it.

Finally, after walking for months, for decades, he reached those elaborate wrought-iron gates that he had passed a billion years before. Only then, when he'd returned to the world with cars thundering past and a 7-Eleven on the corner advertising $1.50 Slurpees and an open-late Wendy's just beyond that, did he sit down on the curb and text Aiden: **Outside gate pick me up on your way out.**

He'd get that $200 to show his mother.

Chapter 7

Grandma Nora

November

Ray couldn't wait to see Grandma Nora. Holidays with his family could be particularly brutal, but Grandma Nora, his only surviving grandparent, was the one saving grace. Even though she lived an excruciating eight-hour drive away, the trip was always worth it. This year especially, after the wedding incident, he was desperate to see her.

He had no one to talk to about what had happened. He hadn't said anything to Aiden—he was too embarrassed. Part of him thought that by telling Aiden, Aiden would somehow agree with Uncle Roger and not invite him to other gigs, would see Ray as a liability instead of a great musical partner. He had no close friends to confide in. Telling his mother, or his siblings, seemed equally impossible.

When he'd come home from the wedding, he'd handed his mother the ten twenty-dollar bills, and stitched together for the twins the brief glimpses he'd had of the house and grounds—its high ceilings, cut flowers on every conceivable surface, oriental rugs like something out of **Aladdin**. He hadn't told any of them about Uncle Roger: he didn't want to hear "You ain't got no business being there anyways" from his mother, and the twins were too young.

Grandma Nora, though, would listen. She wouldn't think less of him.

He'd played several gigs with Aiden since the wedding—he'd made close to a thousand dollars during the past month, and given $850 to his mom. He'd bought a better practice mute and a shoulder rest, and was saving for a car. He hadn't talked to his mom yet about not going to work at the grocery store or getting his GED—she seemed to have forgotten, which wasn't too surprising. If she did remember, he was hoping that she would relent if he showed her how much money he was making by playing his "noise."

He'd talked Aiden into playing at some clubs when they didn't have gigs. The money could be really inconsistent, but he loved having another excuse for performing. Tucked into the corner of the Alibi Club with Aiden and the rest of the quartet, serenading the white-haired old ladies from the Charlotte Flower Club as they forked up their Chicken Cordon Bleu or their Eggs Benedict, he felt weightless, almost as if he were about to levitate off the floor. No Uncle Roger: just the music— a mix of lite classical and arrangements that Aiden had found online of the Beatles, Fleetwood Mac, and Barbra Streisand. Ray could play and no one would tell him to stop—and they'd actually pay him for having fun.

When his mom's Toyota pulled into Grandma Nora's driveway a little after 3:00 p.m., there Grandma Nora was, standing on the porch, waving to them in her floor-length pink house dress, holding on to the walker that never seemed to slow her down. How she knew they would arrive right when they did was always magical, and she'd just laugh when Ray would ask her how she'd known: Ray's mom never called her ahead of time. Ray struggled out of the car, jittery from the drive, ears ringing from his brother's video game and his mother's complaints, and before he even hit the porch the scents of the freshly baked pies hit him: sweet potato, pecan, and blueberry. Grandma Nora would tell Ray that she baked the blueberry just for him. The blue tint of her thinning silver hair caught the November sunshine.

He picked her up off the porch in a bear hug. She was barely five feet tall, probably didn't even weigh a hundred pounds.

"Hey, baby! Look at you," she said in her Southern drawl. "You've gotten so big!" Once he'd overheard one of his uncles say that Grandma Nora was so sweet that just hearing her talk could give you diabetes. Ray could listen to her all day.

"I'm good," he said. "You look great! I smell pie! You make me one?"

"I sure did. I put it where nobody can get at it. Your aunt Joyce tried to cut a piece but I told her to put that pie down before I grab a switch. That's when I had to hide it. I told her that pie is for my favorite grandson."

The twins were thundering up the porch steps, but she kept her gaze on him, as if intuiting something amiss. "How is school going? You still playing your fiddle?"

"Well—"

"Ray, get over here and get these bags," Ray's mother shouted, popping the Corolla's trunk.

"Be right back." Ray returned to the car and began unpacking.

His mother, carrying her purse, went ahead. "How are you feeling?" she asked her mother.

"Oh, I'm fine. My hips have been bothering me a little bit, but I'm good."

"Y'all leave your grandma alone," Ray's mother said to his siblings. They stopped climbing on her walker and trying to pull out her hair rollers— Grandma Nora was only inches taller than they were—and ran inside, the door banging behind them. He knew they were bee-lining for the TV.

A book bag over his shoulder and duffel bags under his arms, he unearthed the violin case. Should he bring it into the house now while his grandmother was standing there, or sneak it in later so his mom didn't know? Better to do it now so there would be less of a chance of sparking an argument about practicing.

His mother had gone in already, but Grandma Nora had waited. "I am so glad you brought your fiddle. I want you to play me a song after supper." She scooted toward the edge of the porch to meet Ray as he maneuvered up the steps.

"Okay. I have a concert coming up. And guess what? I've been playing a lot of weddings. Making real money."

"I'm so proud of you," she said, holding the door for him. She and her walker slid in after him.

Thanksgiving Day was always a mixed bag. Sometimes his family barely ate because his aunts and uncles would drink and laugh for hours. Other times—rarely, admittedly—Uncle Larry and Uncle Thurston would get into an argument (usually about politics) and would jab at each other, index fingers extended. Once Uncle Larry actually swept the countertop clear of the casserole dishes, furious with Uncle Thurston's needling him about his beloved Philadelphia Eagles' defensive line.

Luckily this year would have less drama than usual: only Aunt Joyce and her husband had made the drive. His mom's other siblings—Thurston, Larry, and Rochelle—had to cancel. Ray was grateful: now he had more time to talk to Grandma Nora alone.

On Thursday morning, the turkey was already in the oven when Ray volunteered to help Grandma Nora peel potatoes and slice squash. His mother and Aunt Joyce had gone to the store—ostensibly because they needed more collard greens, but in reality because one of the biggest family traditions was to keep Aunt Joyce out of the kitchen.

So Ray and Grandma Nora stood side by side next to the sink when she said quietly, "Ray, baby. What's wrong?"

Ray stopped mid-peel. He opened his mouth to answer but the words would not come.

"You know you don't have to pretend. You know you can talk to your grandma."

He took a deep breath. No one was nearby. "I was so happy. Then—then everything changed." Suddenly he was close to tears. He cleared his throat and dropped his head toward the potatoes.

"What happened?"

He tried for another deep breath, but his chest felt too full, as though he couldn't draw enough air into his lungs. "I played at a wedding last month. It was my first one. I actually got paid. Two hundred dollars."

"That's wonderful!"

"Yeah, I thought so, too. It was wonderful. Then . . ."

She waited, hands busy with the potatoes, not looking at him.

"Then something happened." He wasn't sure how to continue. "Grandma, have you ever had to deal with people that don't like you because—well, because—you know . . ."

"Because I'm Black?" she said.

Ray stared down at his hands, at the potato peelings stuck to them.

"I know it must have really hurt," she said. "Especially for a sweet boy like you. What did they say?"

The words poured out of him almost as if he weren't speaking them. "He talked to me like I was an animal. Like I was less than an animal. He hated me. I was so scared. I've had to deal with people that don't like me because they think I'm a jerk or because I get better grades than them—but it's never been about skin before.

"I didn't know what to do. He made me feel like I was nothing. Told me I wasn't supposed to be there. I played really well and he told me I ruined his daughter's wedding. Grandma . . . What did I do?"

She laid her hand on Ray's cheek. Her palm was warm, slightly damp from the potatoes, and so soft. "I want you to listen to me very carefully. That thing that happened to you was terrible. That man was sick. Nothing you do or say will ever change that. You can't think from one encounter that everyone thinks the same way he does. Don't get me wrong. There are plenty of people, men and women, young and old, that are just like him. He wasn't the first and he won't be the last one to treat you that way. You are a fine young man who has so much to offer. You can't let them take that away from you. They will try and keep trying."

"So what do I do?"

"You can beat them. You can win. You know how?"

He shook his head.

"You work twice as hard. Even three times. For the rest of your life. It's not fair, but that's how it is. Some people will always see you as less than they are. So you have to be twice as good as them."

"I don't think I can do that."

"You're already doing it," she said, her voice so low he could barely hear it. "You promise me one thing, you hear me? You stay the same sweet Ray that Grandma loves so much. You work harder than they do and you stay sweet. When you begin to hate them just because they hate you, you turn into them. And then they win. Grandma can't have that. You just have to be true to your own sweet self and not let them change you."

"But what do I do?" He felt so defeated. He couldn't win against this. No matter how nicely he was dressed or how politely he spoke, his very existence would ruin the wedding.

"Just what I said. You work twice as hard. You hold your head up high, and you keep doing what you do. You get good grades. You play your music. You find your goal, and you go after it. You be proud of who you are. You never, ever forget that your grandma is proud of you, so proud her heart could just about burst from it. Don't you ever apologize for being who you are or let someone make you feel bad for being Black."

He could feel something inside him thaw, something he hadn't even known was frozen. "Has it happened to you?"

"Oh, my lord, yes. Grandma's dealt with them people all her life. It don't stop because you get old. I seen some terrible things. And I heard of some even worse things. I prayed all my life that my children would never have to go through what I did. I could tell you stories that you wouldn't believe. One day, baby, maybe I'll tell you."

"I am so sorry."

"Don't be sorry. It's an ugly part of life but that's how things are. Probably how they always will be. You just work hard and be your own sweet self, you hear me? You stand up for yourself, but always respectfully. I want you to remember that. You stand up, you respect yourself, and you be respectful. That's how you win."

She gave him a hug. He closed his eyes and drew her near, breathed in her smell of lavender and potato peels.

"Now when you going to play something for your grandma?"

Ray drew in a shaky breath and could feel the air at the bottom of his lungs reaching a place that was suddenly open again. He said, "I'll play for you right after dinner."

"You know my PopPop used to play fiddle, don't you? I loved hearing him when I was a little girl. That's where you get your talent from. I keep telling your mama that."

Dinner went well without his uncles around to egg each other on. Everyone complimented Ray's mom on the turkey—a complicated recipe involving apple cider, orange juice, and cloves—so she was glowing with pride. The table almost disappeared beneath the plates of fluffy mashed potatoes, seasoned with butter and garlic; the omnipresent collard greens and cranberry sauce; the homemade butter for the cornbread. There was ham and black-eyed pea stuffing. Everyone ate everything except the sliced squash. It was always a mystery why Grandma Nora insisted on slicing squash, baking it, and serving it up on everyone's plate every year, only to have no one touch it. This year was no different.

As they were finishing, Grandma Nora said in her unmistakable slow southern drawl, "Ray, baby, when you gonna play a song for your grandma?"

"Of course," he said, pushing himself back from the table. "I can play you a few songs from my concert and maybe I can play my audition piece for you, too." He gathered up everyone's plates, picked clean—except for the squash.

"Lord, don't nobody want to hear that noise." Ray's mom said, taking another swallow of her wine as Ray went out into the kitchen.

"You still play the violin?" Aunt Joyce said with genuine interest. Aunt Joyce took after her mother— a shade over five feet tall and very petite. Her hair was pulled back into a ponytail. Aunt Joyce loved a good laugh, and her single dimple was always noticeable when she smiled, which was all the time.

He had two pies in hand: the pecan and his favorite blueberry. "Yup, I'm still playing."

"When I was a little girl, my PopPop would always sit us down and play that fiddle. I used to love hearing him play. You know he was a freed slave and—"

"Mama, please," Aunt Joyce said. "We heard you tell this story a million times."

"You hush," Grandma Nora said, waving her hand to silence Aunt Joyce.

Ray's mother chuckled. "I could see that one coming a mile away."

"Baby, your great-great PopPop tried to teach my daddy to play. He gave his fiddle to my daddy and told him to teach his babies music. But nobody ever learned to play. I've always been sad about that. My PopPop loved that fiddle."

Aunt Joyce reached for the wine bottle. "You still have it?"

"Yes, girl. Don't you remember when you were kids how I tried to get y'all to play?"

For the past eighteen years, Ray had been coming to Grandma Nora's house at least once a year. He'd heard that story of PopPop and the fiddle even before he'd started playing. Maybe—now he couldn't remember—he'd first gotten interested in the violin because Grandma Nora talked about it all the time. And yet, unaccountably, nobody had ever asked Grandma Nora if she still owned it. How had that never, not once, come up?

Ray's hands seemed suddenly clumsy, unable to pass the pie plates around. He dropped a fork and scrambled under the table to find it.

"Yes, Mama, we remember," Ray's mom said. She and Aunt Joyce burst out laughing.

"Your mama and your aunt Joyce never tried to play," Grandma Nora said to him as he emerged with the fork. "They just didn't want to. They thought they was too cute to play an instrument."

"Where is it now?" he said.

"It's up there somewhere in the attic," she said. "Told you I never got rid of it."

As Ray went up to his room to retrieve his school violin, he heard his mom say, "Well, I ain't tryin' to hear all that noise. Come on, Joyce. Let's go sit in the living room. And bring that bottle." The rest of the family followed them out.

So he and his grandmother were alone when he played for her—starting with "Rhosymedre" from the wedding, and then on to "Jesu, Joy of Man's Desiring," Corelli's **Christmas Concerto**, "Jingle Bells," and even the first half of **L'Inverno.** When at last he drew his bow across the strings in a final tremulous finish, she did her best to leap out of her seat as she applauded him. "Come here and let me give you a hug! That was beautiful! You sounded just like PopPop."

"I hit a bunch of wrong notes."

"Oh, you hush. It was beautiful. Just beautiful."

As he slid the violin back into his case, he said as casually as he could, "Grandma, you really still have your PopPop's fiddle?"

"I sure do. It's up in that attic somewhere. We never threw nothin' away, and I know your granddaddy didn't get rid of it. I wouldn't have let him."

"Would you mind if—if I saw it? I've never seen a fiddle that old."

She laughed. "You been in that attic? There's probably fifty years of I-don't-know-what-all piled on top of it."

"Could I look, though?"

"Well, sure, you can look."

PopPop's fiddle haunted Ray for the rest of the evening. As his mother, Aunt Joyce, and Grandma Nora drank wine, told stories, and laughed so loud that they kept Ray awake, he could think of little else. What did it look like? PopPop died sometime in the 1930s—what happens to violins when they've sat for seventy or eighty or ninety years in an attic? Probably it was warped and ruined from the heat. But he could look, hold a part of his heritage. He imagined playing to his grandmother on PopPop's fiddle, and couldn't imagine a sweeter gift for her.

Later, Ray walked with her to her bedroom, helped her into bed. She was so tiny, so frail. He could pick her up almost with one arm. His heart ached with love for her, for the way her hand reached up and touched his cheek, so gentle, so warm. He put her walker off to the side, went back to kiss her.

"Thank you again for tonight, baby. You made Grandma so happy."

"I'm glad I could do it. You sleep well."

"I love you, you know that?"

"I love you, too," he said to her, and realized in a flash that although he said those words fairly frequently—to his mom, sometimes to the twins—this time he understood how much they could mean. His heart ached with love. "Good night," he told her, and turned off the light.

Next morning, before breakfast, on the upstairs hall landing, Ray grabbed the pull string and a cloud of dust poured down with the folded attic stairs. When had someone last been up here? He climbed. At the top he felt along the wall for a light switch, then, waving his hands in front of him, he ventured forward. Almost immediately a pull chain hit him in the face. He yanked. Bright light shone forth.

He groaned aloud. The attic ran the entire length of the house, branched into alcoves front and back. In the nearest corner, a bed sagged under a faded quilt. Ray seemed to remember that one of his uncles used to tell him stories of how he would bring his dates up here.

Except for the small space around the bed, the attic was filled with all kinds of everything. Lamps stacked on dishes, chairs crawled over more chairs, spindles poked out like needles. Chests and TVs crouched in front of what looked like an old Victrola, on top of which a stereo with one corner bashed in sat deteriorating. And among and between and below all of them: boxes—an endless sea—piled from floor to ceiling.

How would he even find something like a violin? It could be anywhere, in anything. It could be propped behind that cradle or tucked inside the carpet padding.

He lifted the flap of a nearby box. Nesting china teacups peered back at him.

He'd never find PopPop's fiddle. He'd need a system. Given that the fiddle had been in the attic for as long as it had, in all likelihood it would be in one of the back corners, far from the door, with newer junk piled on top. He clambered over boxes and under hanging garden hoses to the far end of the attic.

And then he systematically opened box after box, sifting through piles of clothes, groping under a dressmaker's dummy, pulling open each cabinet drawer, even if he had to shift the whole cabinet to get to it.

"Ray!" A voice wafted up. "Rayquan, what are you doing up there?"

"Looking for PopPop's fiddle!"

"What?"

He had to repeat himself two or three times to be heard.

"No you ain't. You're coming down here. Right now," his mother bellowed.

As Ray wedged his way back across the attic's battlefield, he could hear his mother and grandmother below. "Mama, why you get him started on that?"

"You let that boy alone. He's fine. Are you and Joyce taking the kids shopping?"

"No, they're staying here, and Ray's going to mind them. We're gonna get you a new dress. We're sick of seeing you in that one."

"Ain't nothing wrong with my dress. You better get you some new shoes. Those you're wearing look like they been run over by a truck."

"Mama!"

"Get you a pretty pair. You got nice feet."

By then Ray was standing in front of them.

"Hey, baby," his grandmother said, "ain't you something."

"You are filthy," his mother observed.

"What?" he said. "What did you want?"

His grandmother said, "You got to get you some breakfast before you try chasing down that fiddle."

His mother rolled her eyes and sighed, but did not contradict her mother.

All that morning, and well into the afternoon, Ray searched. At one point he found a few boxes of piano music, so he figured he was getting close. Beneath a pile of moth-eaten coats, four huge boxes lurked. Inside he found more coats. He lifted out each one, shook it. How many coats do people need in Georgia?

His search did turn up one artifact, though. Under one of the far eaves, in the top drawer of a shiny yellow dresser with green knobs, an old tan envelope sat on a pile of 1981 tax returns. Ray was about to close the drawer and move on to the next when he deciphered **Leon Marks** in rough pencil scrawled across the back of the envelope. Leon Marks, he knew, was his grandmother's grandfather—PopPop. He searched carefully through the dresser and the surrounding area but did not find the violin.

After 2:30 he had to take a bathroom break. His grandmother was in the living room watching a soap opera.

"I found a lot of stuff but no fiddle," he told her. "Are you sure it's up there?"

She held out her hand to him, not seeming to mind that his right arm was covered in some kind of thick gluey dust, with blackened cobwebs across his knuckles. "It's up there. Your granddaddy put it up there years ago. You hungry? I can fix you some lunch."

"I did find something, though." He handed her the envelope with PopPop's name on it.

"Oh, baby, you found this?" She turned it around and around in her hands, looking up at him, but making no effort to open the envelope.

"I thought you might want it. Looks like PopPop's papers."

"It sure is," she said. "That's exactly what this is."

"I'm going to go back and look some more," he said. "I'll be back down in a little while."

"You be careful, you hear me? It's in an alligator-skin case. The handle is a little loose so be careful how you pick it up."

He lost track of time, lost himself in the rhythm of unearthing a pile, going through each section one piece at a time, putting the pile back.

"Get down here!" His mother was yelling up at him again. "You get down here right this minute."

"In a sec," he called.

"I said, right now. It's after nine and we got pizza. You wasted enough time on this foolishness."

He looked back at the stack he'd half finished processing, clambered downstairs covered in dust and cobwebs.

His mother was tapping her fake nails—now silver and red—on the wall. "No," she said.

"What do you mean, no?"

"I mean no. You ain't coming down here like that. You go take you a shower and get changed. Right this second."

After he showered and changed, he gulped down two mushroom slices, folded a third, and, chewing, started back up the stairs to the attic.

"Uh-uh, no you don't," his mother said. "You been up there enough."

"I think Mama got rid of that thing years ago and forgot about it," Aunt Joyce said, taking another sip of her wine. "You remember when she threw away your sweater with the clouds on it?"

"Girl, I was so mad. You remember that?"

"What time are we getting on the road?" Ray asked.

"Eight thirty. You go up and pack."

"Eight thirty? Can't we leave a little later?"

"No. You know I don't want to hit traffic." He knew that tone, and knew not to argue. After kissing his grandmother good night, he set his alarm for 6:00 a.m. There was that one area under the eaves, not too far from the piano music, where he was now convinced the fiddle had to be hiding. He could take one more look before they left.

He was up before the alarm clock. The fiddle was not under the eaves. It felt like only moments before his mother was calling for him. Eight a.m. already.

Downstairs his grandmother was waiting. "You find it?"

"No, ma'am."

"Well, you sure did look for it. I'm proud of you, baby."

"I just wanted to see it," he said softly.

"It ain't going anywhere, don't you worry about that."

"I told you," his mother said. "It's probably not there."

"I don't think I ever saw it," Aunt Joyce said. "Not ever."

"Hush, both of you," Grandma Nora said.

Ray gave his grandmother a tight hug. She hugged him right back. "I'll see you soon, baby." And then, in a low voice right in his ear, "It's gonna be okay. You just remember what we talked about, you hear me?"

"I know, Grandma," Ray said. "Respect and be sweet."

"That's right," she said. "You're already working twice as hard."

"I'll remember," Ray said.

Later, in the car, his mother asked, "What did Mama say to you as we were leaving?"

"Oh," he said, "she just told me she loved me," and went back to staring out the window.

Chapter 8

Holiday Excavations
December

December, with its final exams, winter concert, and practicing for regional auditions, left Ray barely time to sleep. He showed up at school early to practice his violin, and then again at lunchtime and at study hall. His construction job had ended, but he hadn't applied to bag groceries. He didn't tell his mother.

The day after the winter concert, his orchestra teacher, Mr. Stinson, announced to the class, "If you're auditioning for regionals, I'll hear you today."

Twelve students—including Aiden, Ray, and Mark Jennings—were trying out. One by one they played **L'Inverno**.

After the other students played, Mr. Stinson rose to return to his office. Ray called after him, "Mr. Stinson! Are you going to hear me?"

Mr. Stinson looked at him blankly. "Why?" he said. Just the one word, but it boomed in Ray's ears. He vowed that he'd show Mr. Stinson what he could do: Ray would play twice as well as the others at regionals.

Ray stood motionless as the other students packed up to leave, as Mark bumped his shoulder, laughing, as Mr. Stinson disappeared into his office. Only when all the other students—even Aiden—had left did Ray bend down to place, so gently, his school violin in its battered case.

A Black kid with a school violin, no private teacher, no vast wellspring of talent. Why would Mr. Stinson waste his time on such a kid?

Why? Because the Black kid could play his ass off, that's why.

Two days later, Aiden texted him the details of four gigs lined up over Christmas.

Rather than text, Ray called him. His lips had trouble forming the words. He sucked in a breath. "I can't do it."

"What? Why not?"

"I had to turn my instrument in, remember? It's the school's. I don't have a violin. I'm gonna buy an instrument over break. A nice one. I've been saving up," Ray said. "I should be getting some Christmas money." He'd been saving up for Christmas break to go shopping—with what his mother hadn't taken, and maybe some money from Grandma Nora and his relatives, he'd been planning on getting a step-up instrument. There was a good music store at the mall near Grandma Nora's.

They returned to Georgia on December 23, and Grandma Nora was again waiting for them on the porch. He sprang from the car and into her arms. "It's great to see you," he said.

"You're a sight for sore eyes, baby. I'm so proud of your concert." He'd called her after the winter concert, told her how well the evening had gone, how much he loved playing in front of an audience. She was the only one in his family who'd even asked. He'd also called her last week, when someone at the Crocodile Club had tipped him twenty dollars. Now she shuffled into the house where the adults were gathered in the living room, discussing plans for the next few days.

"The Eagles are playing the Cowboys tomorrow," Uncle Larry was saying. "That's gonna be a good game. Don't come in there messing with me. The living room is a no-talking zone."

Ray hovered behind Grandma Nora, who'd seated herself with a sigh in her huge paisley corduroy La-Z-Boy. It almost swallowed her up. He'd put one hand on her shoulder and now her hand fluttered up, patting his.

After a few minutes of listening to his uncles

berating the Cowboys and Aunt Joyce and his mom
arguing about a television show they both followed,
Ray murmured to his grandmother, "Can I go up
and look?"

She smiled up at him. She knew what he was
looking for. "You sure can."

"Thank you!" He kissed her cheek and slid out of
the living room, up to the second floor hallway. He
yanked the cord and the attic stairs tumbled down.

He started right where he'd left off a month ago.

If he was looking for old Stevie Wonder albums, he would have hit the jackpot. And how
many clothes did one family need to keep?
How many bags of stuffed animals?

That fiddle meant connection: if only he could
find the instrument, he'd connect with his grandmother and her grandfather. This was his gift
to her.

He never thought of owning the fiddle. It was
his grandmother's, and he would never take it from
her. But finding it, holding it, having Grandma
Nora tell him that he looked just like her PopPop,
standing there playing his fiddle? That would be
worth all the dust.

He was on the far side of the attic, sorting through
a stack of boxes higher than his head, when he
heard Aunt Joyce shouting his name. "Ray? Come
on down! It's dinnertime and you need to watch
the kids."

He stood still, as if she wouldn't know he was up here, as if she'd just give up and go away.

"You hear me? Ray! Get down here right now."

Reluctantly he left the box stack and threaded through the attic, back down into the main house.

"Boy, you are a hot mess," she observed. "Go wash up and change your shirt."

He lifted the attic stairs back into position.

"It's not there, sweetie," she said gently. "Nobody's ever seen that thing. Your grandpa probably sold it years ago and never told her."

"She said it's up there."

"She wants to believe it's up there. She's an old lady. She gets confused."

He didn't know what to say.

"You know if you did find it, you can't have it, right?" Aunt Joyce went on. He realized, only then, that his family must think that he wanted it for himself. He tried to tell her but she was saying, "We don't know what all is in this house. When Mama passes, we'll have to sort it all out. Including that fiddle, if it's even still here."

"I just wanted to see it," he said, meeting her eyes. "I just wanted to play it like she wants me to. Like her PopPop. I just want to play it for her."

He finished searching the attic on Christmas Eve, before they left for the annual Christmas picture at the mall. He refolded the flaps on the last box in the last corner. PopPop's fiddle wasn't up there.

Grandma Nora had assured him it was: an alligator-skin case with a loose handle. There was no way she was just a confused old lady like Aunt Joyce had said. She remembered the loose handle, hadn't she? She knew she'd never gotten rid of it, didn't she? Had she been lying to him, laughing at him all this time, snickering as she listened to him thumping around for all those hours?

His misery and confusion made it impossible for him to speak on the car ride to the mall. When they arrived, as soon as the picture was taken, he went off on his own to the music store. Violins, guitars, and other stringed instruments hung like pinned butterflies against an entire wall. There were only three brands of violins to choose from—the cheapest was $500, a shiny version of his school violin, which was unacceptable. The step-up violin was a Roth that hung behind the counter with a Christmas-sale price tag of $1,049.

The clerk, a scrawny guy in his midthirties, kept scowling at Ray.

Ray had $930 in his bank account. Could he ask Grandma Nora to loan him a little extra? She'd probably give him fifty dollars as a Christmas present—she'd done that in the past, so he only needed a little more. He could pay her back out of money from the next gig with Aiden.

Back at home, after the family finished eating,

they trickled into the living room, where the Christmas tree twinkled. Dozens of gifts poured from the tree skirt. As usual, Grandma Nora sat in her La-Z-Boy. Also as usual, each of Grandma Nora's children chose two gifts: one to give to a sibling and one to give to each of their children.

After opening his presents—a pale blue dress shirt, three pairs of pants, several pairs of socks, and a fine haul of Amazon gift cards—he watched the littler kids open Nintendo games and remote-control cars, screaming in excitement and searching for batteries. When the living room was a sea of discarded wrapping paper, ribbon, and Christmas cards, the adults all stood to give Grandma Nora her annual family gift. This year it was a new set of cookware. Grandma Nora, still in her chair, beamed. "Oh, thank y'all. I needed a new skillet."

"All right! Time for the game!" Uncle Thurston reached for the remote. The younger kids, rejuvenated, were chasing one another. Aunt Joyce and Aunt Rochelle headed toward the dining room to clean up. Ray, loaded with his presents, headed upstairs. Maybe he'd watch a YouTube video of the New York Philharmonic playing Rimsky-Korsakov's **Capriccio Espagnol**. Ray wanted to play the violin solos in that piece.

The volume level had increased in the house, so Ray was almost out the door before he heard

Grandma Nora, who'd apparently been shouting in her tiny voice. "Hang on a minute! I have one more present to give out. Hang on!"

"One more? Wait, everyone," Aunt Joyce bellowed. Ray looked back from the hallway.

With some difficulty, Grandma Nora was reaching under her chair. One of his cousins tried to help, and she gently swatted his hand away. She pulled out a long slender box wrapped in green-and-red-striped paper.

"What's that?" Aunt Rochelle said.

"Don't you worry about it. It's for Ray."

Everyone turned to stare at Ray, who stared back cluelessly.

"Mama has a gift for you, son." Uncle Larry, standing behind him, elbowed Ray in the side. "Go get it. Game's starting in two minutes."

'You didn't have to get me anything."

"I know, baby. But you earned this. Here."

The paper peeled away. Beneath was an alligator-skin fiddle case, a dull blackish brown, gray with mildew. The handle was loose.

Aunt Joyce said from somewhere behind him, "Oh my god."

Was this possible? Was this a joke? Grandma would never play a joke this cruel. Gently, impossibly, he laid the case on the floor and stared at it for a moment before looking up at her. She was smiling.

"How—?"

"Go ahead. Open it." Her eyes were shining.

His aunts and uncles jockeyed for position.

He reached out with hands that did not seem to belong to him, popped the two clasps, folded the top back.

A fiddle lay there. PopPop's fiddle. There, in front of him.

An excited babble of voices rang out. He heard only his mother: "Rayquan, that ain't yours to keep." Gently he leaned down again, picked up the fiddle, lifted it into the air. He was actually holding PopPop's fiddle.

"How do you like your new fiddle, baby?"

"Grandma, this isn't—"

"Hush, baby. It's yours now."

"Mama, you can't give him that! Nope. That thing is not leaving this house." The voices swirled around them, but right then there was only Ray and his grandmother. "I can't take this. I just wanted to find it for you. I just wanted to play it for you."

"I know you did. And now you will."

"It's yours," he said. "It's PopPop's."

"It's yours now," she told him. "He'd want you to have it. I want you to have it."

"Mama," Ray's mother said, scowling, "what are you thinking?"

"Ray, baby," Grandma Nora said, "take your fiddle and go into the kitchen, okay? I want you to play me that pretty song in a little while."

No one spoke as he reverently closed the case, carried it out of the room. Out of sight he put his back to the wall, listened.

"Every one of you hush," Grandma Nora was saying. "If anybody says a word I'm taking off my shoe and going upside your head with it. Your daddy and I tried to get every one of you to learn to play. All of you! Not a one of you would do it. It's mine, and I will give it to anybody I please. None of you has anything to say about it."

"He needs to get this music out of his head and start thinking about a real job," his mother said. "He's graduating from high school soon and he don't know what he wants to do. He can't make a living as a musician and he don't need no encouragement from you."

"It's his life. He needs to start making his own decisions."

"His own mistakes, more like."

He couldn't listen anymore. He left them arguing, set the case on the kitchen table. It didn't matter what they decided: for this moment, the violin lay in front of him, connecting him to his grandmother and to his past and to a musical heritage he barely understood.

Grandma Nora had told him that she wanted him to play tonight for her, but he saw immediately that was impossible. The tailpiece was cracked. Two of the pegs had broken off. The bridge was badly warped and the sound post rattled around inside. Decades of mildew and built-up rosin coated the instrument in a whitish film. He rubbed at it, and his fingers came away black, but underneath was more caked-on rosin. There were more hairs lying inside the case than attached to the bow.

But the violin's body was sound, not cracked or warped or eaten by insects. It could be fixed. He could take it to the music shop in the mall. Even if he couldn't keep it, he could play for her when he visited. Her gift to him would be his gift to her.

"Ray, get in here." His mother, voice sharp.

He placed the fiddle back in the faded green cushion of the alligator-skin case, returned to the living room.

"Baby," said his grandmother, "PopPop's fiddle and his fiddle case both belong to you now. No, I will not be taking them back and I better not find out that anybody tried to take them from you."

His mother had taken a step toward him when she saw him, but now she turned and rolled her eyes at Grandma Nora. She sighed. "But, Mama—"

"You hush. You heard what I said. Now you play something beautiful for us," she told him.

"It needs to be fixed," he said. "I can't play it till it's fixed. But I can take it tomorrow to that music store in the mall."

"Tomorrow's Christmas," someone said. "It'll be closed."

"The day after, then," Ray said. He never looked away from his grandmother. It was starting to sink in. He had a violin of his own.

"Thank you," he said, leaning down and squeezing her so tightly she gasped.

"You're welcome, sweet Ray," she said when he released her. "That's how much I love you, baby."

Later that night, after they'd all gone up to their rooms, Ray dialed Aiden's number.

"Merry Christmas, bro! Good to hear from you, but your timing sucks. We're—"

"So is that New Year's gig still on?

"Yeah, but when you said you couldn't do it, I asked around. Chad's doing it."

"Are you serious?"

"It's a three-hundred-dollar gig. I had to find someone."

"I have a violin now. I can do it."

"I already asked Chad. Don't get me wrong. I'd much rather play with you, but—"

"But nothing. Tell him he's fired, tell him it's canceled. Tell him something. Let me do it!"

"That is so messed up. Chad's a flake, but I can't yank the gig from him."

"Chad doesn't give two shits about you. We're homies. You give me this gig, I'll owe you for life."

Aiden paused for a long while before saying, "You know what, fuck Chad. I'll come up with something."

The day after Christmas, Ray was downstairs waiting when the first adults staggered in for breakfast. He asked Aunt Rochelle if she would give him a ride to the mall as soon as it opened. Ray didn't want to open a can of worms by asking his mother or his other relatives. Aunt Rochelle seemed indifferent about him receiving the fiddle, so she would be the least likely to give him any grief.

When they got to the mall just after ten, the parking lot was mostly empty. Aunt Rochelle stopped off at a department store that had a huge SALE sign in the front window, and Ray went on alone, violin case tight under his arm, straight to the music store. Behind the counter was the same scrawny young man with thin blond hair and an even thinner mustache shadowing his lip who had been growling at him last time. His name tag—HI! MY NAME IS ERIC! ASK ME ABOUT OUR HOLIDAY LAYAWAY PLAN!—glittered red and silver.

Ray laid the alligator-skin case on the counter. "I need to get some repairs done."

The clerk glanced up, then back down at his computer screen, kept typing.

Ray waited a few moments. "Hi, excuse me. I need—"

"This ain't a pawnshop. Get out."

Ray stood there, confused.

"This is a music store," the clerk said, as if to a five-year-old. "We sell instruments, we don't buy them." He never looked up.

"I need to have some repairs done on my violin." Ray opened the case, showed him the violin as proof.

My-name-is-Eric-ask-me-about-our-holiday-layaway-plan stared at it like he'd never seen one before. "Why you want to get it fixed? That thing is disgusting."

"It's been in storage and nobody's played it. I think the white is from all the rosin."

"Looks like mold." Leaning over to peer more closely, the clerk snickered. "Smells like mold, too. What did you do to this thing? Can't be fixed. Anything else I can help you with?"

"It's going to need—"

"You deaf, too? I said it can't be fixed. We're done here." He turned away from the counter, as if to head to the back room.

A familiar feeling washed over Ray. He remembered what Grandma Nora said about respect. Maybe this guy didn't know much about violins. "I need a new tailpiece, a set of strings, new pegs, the sound post set, the bow re-haired, and a new bridge."

Eric gave an exaggerated sigh, then spoke with

exaggerated slowness—everything overemphasized, as if to a child, or to someone deaf, or to someone profoundly stupid. "I told you, it can't be fixed."

Ray stood very tall. "It can't be fixed, or you won't fix it?"

"What did you say? What did you just say to me?"

Ray took a deep breath. "I need to have this violin repaired. This is a repair shop. I need you to fix it."

"Is that piece of shit even yours?"

Ray straightened. "Sir, I would like to have my violin repaired. I need a new bridge and tailpiece, a bow re-hairing, and the strings and the sound post adjusted. Can you do the work?"

Eric went back to his computer, typed in some keys, but in a way that made Ray think he was tallying up numbers for the repair. "Three hundred thirty-seven dollars."

"Okay. How long will it take?"

"A week. Maybe two."

Ray recoiled. "A week? This isn't a long job. Do you have a lot of repairs ahead of it?"

"Do you want this piece of shit repaired, or don't you?"

"Could you do it today? While I wait?"

Eric thought about it. "It'll cost you an extra hundred bucks."

If only there were other music stores close by. If only Ray had a car. If only he were someone else. "Okay," he said. "You'll do it while I wait?"

"You have $437?"

"Yes I do."

"I want to see the money."

"Here's my debit card," Ray said. "You can take two hundred dollars out now. The rest when the repairs are done."

"Two hours." Eric slammed shut the case and took it to the back. When he returned, Ray was still waiting. "You need something else?"

"A receipt."

Eric wrote out a yellow check-in slip, smacked it on the counter, disappeared into the back room. Hopefully to work on the violin's repairs. It was 10:18 a.m. Two hours to go.

Ray retreated outside, took a seat on a bench twenty feet from the music shop, between a Sbarro and a Gymboree. He pulled out his phone and played video games, his eye on the shop, as if he expected Eric to slip out with the violin and disappear forever.

Aunt Rochelle found him there, still waiting. "Did you get it fixed?" she settled herself with a sigh next to him on the bench, with two bulky department-store bags at her feet. She was younger than his mother, with short-cropped hair and heavier features. She tended to keep to herself and didn't engage with the family as much as the others, so he hadn't spent a great deal of time with her.

"I had to drop it off, but he said he'd have it ready by twelve thirty."

"You want to get some lunch?"

"It's only eleven thirty."

"Why don't we get some lunch while he's fixing it," she repeated. "There's a Bob Evans across the parking lot and they serve a mean sausage biscuit."

"I'm not real hungry," he said, eyes on the music store.

"You can leave it for a minute," she said. "It ain't going anywhere."

He shrugged. She patted his leg, sat with him for a few more minutes, watching him as he watched the music store. Finally, she stood. "Okay, I'll be back." She went to buy a dress she'd tried on earlier.

At exactly 12:20, Ray went back inside. An older woman with gray hair and a faded, tired face was examining the electric keyboards against one wall but turned to stare at him. He smiled at her, but she didn't smile back.

Eric was at his post at the counter. "Yeah?"

"I'm here to pick up my violin."

"Right. Your violin. That thing is hardly a violin." Eric disappeared and soon returned with the violin case. While he processed Ray's debit card, Ray opened the case. The new pegs didn't match. The tailpiece was plastic. The strings had cheap red labels and cost twenty-six dollars—Ray knew the price since that's what he'd bought for the school instrument. He was no expert on repairs, but he knew he wasn't getting what he'd paid for. "Excuse me. Do you carry Dominant-brand strings?"

"Why?"

"I was expecting a set of Dominant strings for $437."

Ray could feel the woman watching both of them. Eric just stared for a moment and said, "Get the hell out of my store."

"Why?" Ray said.

"Because I don't like you. I don't like any of you. You come in here, never buy anything, and steal half my shit. You're always walking around like you own the world with your pants around your ass, but do you buy anything? No fucking way. You probably stole that piece of shit anyway. Get the fuck out before I call the cops."

Out of the corner of his eye Ray saw Aunt Rochelle hesitating, one foot inside the shop. He thought she would come up, say something, but she didn't—she just waited as the clerk's words poured over him.

But her presence was enough for him to lift his chin high, square his shoulders, and pack up the violin. As he left the store, he said, "Merry Christmas." Neither Eric nor the older lady replied.

Outside in the mall, Aunt Rochelle put her arm around his shoulders. "Asshole," she said.

"Yeah," he said, his heart still beating hard. "But I got it fixed. I can play it for Grandma today."

"You really love that old thing, don't you?"

"Which old thing, the violin or Grandma?"

They both laughed. Ray's was forced, but he tried to pretend he didn't care about what had just happened.

"The violin," she said. "Everybody loves Mama."

"I really do love it," he confessed. Perhaps it was the incident at the music store, but he found himself talking to her more than he ever had in the past. "I didn't want it for me, before. I just wanted to find it and play it for Grandma. But if she's given it to me—well, that just means so much. It means I won't have to play with the crappy school instruments anymore. I'm the only kid of all the juniors and seniors who doesn't have his own instrument."

"You are?"

"Yeah. And all the other kids get private lessons, too. But that's okay, I know my mom doesn't get it."

"Your mom's a good person," she said.

"Yeah," he said without enthusiasm. "She doesn't like my playing, though."

"Well, if you love doing it, don't let nobody stop you, you hear me?"

"You sound like Grandma," he said.

She stopped in the parking lot and gave him a two-armed hug, shopping bags swinging against his back. "I want to hear you play, too." She didn't let him go. "You're a good boy, you know that?"

He didn't know what to say, so he just hugged her. Why had he never noticed Aunt Rochelle before? He'd always just lumped her in with the rest of his aunts and uncles—but now he realized that she was a pretty cool lady. She saw him as something more than a babysitter for his younger cousins. He wanted to spend more time with her.

When Ray and Aunt Rochelle got back to the house, Grandma Nora was sitting in her recliner in the living room. "Hey, baby. You get it fixed?"

He took it from its case, showed her the repaired instrument.

"Looks just like I remember," she said. "All that white stuff. My PopPop used to say it was good luck, all that white stuff. He called it 'Good Luck Dust.' " She chuckled quietly to herself, marveling. "I'd forgotten that."

Ray tucked the violin beneath his jaw and looked across the tailpiece, over the bridge, and past the fingerboard to the scroll. His own violin. His. Heavily coated with an extra thick coat of Good Luck Dust—which was his, too.

With his right hand he touched the bow to the string, rose into an A, and tuned the instrument, keenly making sure the A was a perfect 440. He pulled the bow from frog to tip and the note sang out clean, surprisingly piercing. Somehow the act of playing that one note had cemented his ownership of the violin; and he could feel the muscles in his arm vibrate almost as if they were adjusting themselves to its sound.

"You know what, baby? You look just like my PopPop, standing up there. I have chills. Look." She showed him her arm, where a prickle of gooseflesh rose on her thin skin. "I could swear he was standing up there. Sure brings back some sweet memories." She smiled up at him.

He played an F-major scale to warm up, and his grandma applauded. "That was just a scale," he told her. "Nothing to clap for."

"I just love hearing you play. Wait a minute. Larry, Rochelle, Joyce, Thurston, y'all come in here. Ray is going to play for us on PopPop's fiddle," she shouted. His aunts and uncles came in from other parts of the house.

"Oh lord. Mama, please," Ray's mom said, edging back down the hall.

"Girl, you stand right there. This won't take long. Ray is gonna play."

Ray closed his eyes as he lifted the violin more tightly to his jaw. He'd have to get a shoulder rest sometime soon. A nice one. No sponge for PopPop's violin. But that would wait. He touched the bow to the E string and began **L'Inverno**. No written music—he should have gotten his music!—but he knew the notes, the correct fingerings were effortless, and he switched smoothly from third to fifth, then back to first position.

The melody started slow, in the night, a plucking of strings, snowflakes falling dreamily, one flake at a time; and then a burst of cold air poured down on them, and flakes eddied, biting in the chill, the north wind coursing through the living room. Dawn came, light glistening off a frozen pond. A bird flew down, hopped on new snow, looking for seed. Bare trees reached to the sky, achingly blue in the cold.

Skaters swirled on ice. Skiers coasted down long cold runs. Then back to the house, to the warmth, to chocolate thawing on the stove and mittens steaming in front of a fire.

He painted all this for them in the air, this first time, with the music from PopPop's fiddle—of his own violin!—washing over them. How glorious this was: to touch them, to make them hear, to give them this gift.

PopPop's violin was different, easier to play. Maybe because it was his? Maybe he was channeling PopPop? Maybe he was just so deeply touched, playing for his grandmother, who was swaying there in her chair, eyes closed, a huge smile wreathing her lips? The last eight measures that had given him such trouble now seemed easy, smooth, and then before he was ready he'd played the last note. He held it as long as he could, the bow trembling in his hand.

Grandma Nora pulled herself from her recliner, clapping so hard that two of her pink curlers came loose and bounced to the floor. Moments later the rest of his family joined in.

It was assuredly Ray's imagination, but holding the violin in his trembling left hand and his right hand sweaty on the bow, as he looked out at the sea of faces, another figure grinned back at him: a small man, shorter than his mother, just behind Aunt Joyce, very thin, with hunched shoulders and deep-set almond-shaped eyes. The shadow of the brim of a hat shaded his forehead. It was almost as if Ray could feel his blessing, his pride, and his exhilaration beaming at him. A moment later, when Ray blinked, the figure was gone.

"Whoa, that boy is good!" Larry patted Ray's shoulder. The others sang out his praises, too. But he had eyes only for her, tears rolling down her face, hitting her hands together so hard he was afraid that they would shatter. "Baby, I am so proud of you. Your PopPop would be proud of you, too. I just can't believe how good you play!"

And then, almost by accident, effortless, the thought crept into his head, and he listened to it for the first time: **I can do this.**

Chapter 9

Opportunity
January

Like many turning points in a life—especially in the life of a lonely kid who stuck mostly to himself, playing a beat-up violin his grandmother had given him—Ray's life changed because someone else reached out across the gulf and touched him.

Later, much later, Ray stumbled across a quote that reputedly came from Whoopi Goldberg: "We're here for a reason. I believe a bit of the reason is to throw little torches out to lead people through the dark." Ray would type it up and stick it on his refrigerator with a local realtor's giveaway magnet, and the paper would curl up at the ends and brown; and every morning, when he'd pull out his orange juice, he would see it hanging there and for an instant he'd pause and be grateful.

He found the torch that would lead him through the darkness at the auditions for the North Carolina Regional Orchestra, Eastern Division. Regional orchestra was a very big deal—he'd never auditioned before, and never thought he had much of a chance. Two hundred violinists vying for forty spots. He was one of three Black musicians out of the 392 trying out, and the only Black violinist. But none of that would stop him from trying out.

After the auditions, as he waited in the cafeteria with Aiden and a couple other kids, someone tapped Ray's shoulder. A short, thin woman with an electric smile beamed back at him. She was in her early forties, with a few gray strands curling in her black hair. She wore jeans and a blazer. He couldn't figure out where he knew her from—she looked very familiar—and then he realized that she was one of the judges at the audition: the only Black one. "Hello, young man."

"Hello, ma'am," Ray said, instinctively standing up straighter and adjusting his shirt.

"I'd like to say that I enjoyed your audition."

"You did? Thank you." Ray could feel Aiden looking at him, but he kept his gaze on the judge. "I'm sorry about that F-sharp in the D-minor scale."

"No need to apologize. I used to miss that F all the time when I was starting out."

"You play violin?"

"I do. I'm Dr. Janice Stevens. I'm an associate professor of violin at Markham University."

Ray stood frozen with his mouth slightly open. Aiden nudged his ribs.

"I just wanted to introduce myself and wish you the best of luck. You're both wonderful musicians," she said to them.

After she left, Aiden said to Ray, "Dude. That's got to be a good sign."

"Yeah, maybe." But Ray's heart beat a little harder. She'd come up and talked to him! That must mean something, right?

Close to an hour and a half later, a scrawny man with bushy eyebrows came out with a piece of light blue paper: the violin selection list. He thumbtacked it to the bulletin board.

Then he heard Mark Jennings's voice from the crowd. "No fuckin' way." An instant later, Aiden called out, "Ray! You made it! Bro, you made it!"

Ray's name was among the chosen.

Both Aiden and Mark Jennings emerged from the kids still straining to see the list. Mark's eyes were narrow. "How the hell did you make it?" he said to Ray. "Is this an affirmative action audition?"

"Shut the fuck up," Aiden told him. "You mad because you left your white supremacist starter kit on the bus?"

"Fuck you, Asia." He shot Aiden the bird. "See this? Open your eyes. Oh wait, they are open."

"Asshole," Aiden said. But he was used to Mark slamming his Asian looks the way Mark would slam Ray's: Mark was an equal opportunity racist.

Aiden was beaming, pounding Ray on the back. "You made it. Dude, you totally made it."

Dr. Stevens appeared again. There was that smile, so bright. "Congratulations, Rayquan. Quite an accomplishment. This is a very difficult orchestra to get into. What year are you?"

"I'm a senior."

"Who are you currently taking lessons with?"

"Like, a private teacher?" he said. "Nobody. Just Mr. Stinson, our orchestra teacher. I've never done private lessons."

"You mean Gary Stinson?"

"Yeah, I think that's him," Ray said.

She looked at him even more intently.

"He practices, like, all the time," Aiden interjected. "The guy is glued to his violin."

"Yeah," he said. "I like playing." He shot Aiden a grateful look, but Aiden was watching Dr. Stevens.

"Well, you've been doing a great job," she told him. "What are your plans for next fall?"

"You mean after I graduate?"

"Yes."

"Going to find a job," he said, inventing on the spot. "Maybe the military."

"Have you considered college?"

"I've thought about it," he said, although he

never really had. "But I wouldn't know what to do. Plus all the student loans." Popeyes still loomed.

"I'm asking because you're a very good player and you obviously work hard. Your vibrato was beautiful and your musicianship was exquisite. When you played, it definitely woke us up." She reached into her purse. "Here's my card. I'd really love for you to consider applying to Markham University. You'd be one of my students."

Her card sat in his fingers like a butterfly wing, about to disintegrate if he squeezed too tightly.

"I know this may be overwhelming but it could be a real opportunity. If someone had gotten a hold of you when you were younger, you could be playing solos with major symphonies by now."

He had to clear his throat before he could speak. "Thanks. Thank you, Dr. Stevens."

"You're very welcome, Rayquan. I can feel how much potential you have. I hope to hear from you soon. Congratulations again."

Both Ray and Aiden stared after her. Then Aiden punched Ray's shoulder. "Whoa! Bro, this is amazing! Major symphony, you hear that? There might be a scholarship for you! This is your lucky day."

The bus ride home was a blur. When they pulled over to a fast-food restaurant for dinner, and Ray was away from the noise of the bus, he called his grandmother.

"That's wonderful, baby!" she told him. He didn't

think she quite understood what regional orchestra was, but she was happy for him nonetheless.

He was beyond exhausted, and still dizzy with excitement, when he unlocked the front door to his house. His mom had left a lamp on next to the couch, its glow glittering on the glass coffee table, pouring over the red, blue, and green swirls of the faded upholstery. The room felt unfamiliar, as if he'd been gone for a very long time.

A light was on in his mother's room. She was lying in bed, on the phone.

"Mom! Guess what! I made it. I made regionals!"

She stared at him blankly for a moment. "Stop screaming like you ain't got no sense! You lock the front door?"

On Friday, February 8, all the students for the regionals concert assembled in the auditorium to begin the first rehearsal, before blind auditions that would decide their seatings the next morning. Ray sat in the back of the violin section, trying to keep calm, trying to keep his lips in a straight line, trying to pretend he'd done this a hundred times before.

Two other Black students sat together on the other side of the room. As the organizers, the teachers, and the conductor introduced themselves, the Black kids caught his eye.

He gave them a **what's up** nod. During their

first break, Ray headed toward them. Shawn, from Fayetteville, played trumpet; and Janelle, from Chapel Hill, was a bassoonist. Janelle had played in regionals last year, but this was Shawn's first time. They decided to have dinner together that night.

It was really great to sit with other Black musicians at dinner. In Charlotte, he was the only Black kid in orchestra—and there were only three other Black kids in his grade. Ray had never befriended any of them—they were more interested in hip-hop. His love of classical music made him an outcast to the group: his violin case alone assured this. Plus it seemed that his classes didn't align with any of the other Black kids at school, so somehow he'd never gotten close to any of them. It felt awesome to sit with other Black teenagers who, like him, loved classical music.

None of the other students—all of whom were either white or Asian, with a couple Hispanic kids peppering the crowd—spoke to or sat next to the three of them. When Ray got a second glass of lemonade, he overheard a couple boys loudly saying something about "affirmative action" and "meet a quota." Shawn and Janelle didn't seem bothered by any of this, though.

Janelle, like Ray, was a senior, and deciding between UNC and NC State. Shawn was only a junior, and was in the middle of college tours with his parents.

"How do you decide where to go?" Ray asked Janelle.

"I think I'm leaning toward State. They have a better biology department."

"You aren't doing music?"

"I'll probably keep playing but I'm not going to major in it."

"Oh," he said. He was a little amazed that someone so talented wouldn't be majoring in music.

"Howzabout you?" Shawn asked.

"Still thinking about college," Ray said. "Haven't applied anywhere yet. Might have one option."

"What do you want to do? Music?"

Ray couldn't in all honesty imagine majoring in anything except music. He shrugged. "Why do you want to do biology? You sound amazing."

"Ha! Thanks. It's just not realistic for me. How many Black bassoonists you see in orchestras? It's already cutthroat. I'm not gonna fight it. A few years ago, when I auditioned for this group, my teacher was actually one of the judges. One of her other students was auditioning, too. Ashley Hawkins. Blue eyes. Blond. I beat her at band auditions for years. The other kids that auditioned hadn't been playing that long so I knew I could beat them. When it came down to it, the judges chose Ashley."

"I don't get it," Ray said.

Janelle and Shawn looked at each other, laughed, pointed at the tops of their hands. Then—only then—did Ray remember Uncle Roger, all over again.

"You seriously thinking of doing music?" Shawn asked him, pushing aside the last fries on his plate.

"A career in music would be awesome," Ray said.

"Good luck with that one," Janelle said. "Look around. There are only three of us in this entire orchestra. You'd be better off majoring in something that's going to make you some money. You have to think about your future. This music thing is for the white kids who can afford the instruments and the big-name teachers. We don't have much of a chance. My parents are really pushing me toward medicine."

"Mine want me to be a lawyer," Shawn said.

"Wow. I never thought about it that way. I just like playing. But if I could actually make a career out of it? I don't know."

His mother's voice echoed in his head: **When you gonna stop all that shit.** When would he? A world without playing his violin seemed to loom raw, gray, and empty.

His expression must have betrayed how he felt, because Janelle said, as if comforting him, "Well, maybe a scout will recruit you."

"Scout?"

"Yeah, of course. Haven't you seen them? Some of them have been here all weekend. They're mostly looking at the seniors. They find out where you're planning on going, then try to convince you to go to their schools. Funny thing is that a lot of these kids aren't even planning on studying music."

In the next morning's auditions, the judges wouldn't see the competitors, only hear them. When it was Ray's turn, he entered the green room adjoining the stage that had been converted to an audition room.

Down the center of the room, blocking the other side from view, an enormous white plastic sheet hung from the ceiling. Three sets of legs were visible below: two sets in trousers, and one set wearing pantyhose and high heels.

In the center of the open space before him, a lone music stand beckoned. On it lay a single sheet of music: the Offenbach solo. Ray swallowed. He knew he could play the notes, but making this solo sound good was a real challenge. Although the Berlin Philharmonic performance was the best one he'd found online, it was still a rougher recording than he wished it had been. Why hadn't he spent more time studying a better recording?

No time to think about it. No time to second-guess. He lifted PopPop's fiddle to his jaw, closed his eyes, and dove in.

The solo came from **Orpheus in the Underworld**—a spikey, brittle moment in the lushness of the rest of the piece, high-soaring phrases leaping like frogs from one high note to the next.

He pressed his jaw against the chin rest, tried to make the solo lilting and effervescent, imagining beetles scaling trees, birds lifting off one branch and alighting on another, higher branch, looking out at the view, and then leaping even higher.

One minute later it was over.

After dinner, the conductor, in a quick mono-tone, read out the results of the auditions, starting with the second violins. This was Ray's first blind audition—for the first time he'd be placed accord-ing to how well he played the music. No one had an unfair advantage. The conductor didn't call Ray's name. Had he made first violin?

"First violins. Your seating is as follows. Jenny Carlson. Congratulations. You're the concert-mistress." A tiny red-headed girl two seats over from Ray would be playing the Offenbach solo. She screamed and hugged her stand partner.

In the commotion, Ray didn't hear the next names ring out. The judge hadn't called him. Had he not even placed at all? Was he last chair? His anxiety rose. The students were shifting to their assigned seats. Ray raised his hand. "Sir, I think I missed my name being called. Ray McMillian."

"Rayquan McMillian. Yep, there you are. Third chair."

He was third chair, first violin. His legs moved on their own. The associate concertmaster posi-tion. If the concertmistress and her stand partner, the number two violinist, left for any reason—if either got sick or broke a string, or just decided to go home—Ray would be playing the solo. The responsibility of leading the orchestra would fall to him. He didn't think there was any chance of this happening, but still.

Ray had to pass Mark Jennings, three chairs back, to get to his new seat, so he heard Mark mumble to one of his buddies, "What the fuck is going on? How the hell did that nigger beat me?"

"You need to open your mouth when you speak," Ray told him. "Someone could mistake what you say for something, oh I don't know, racist?"

"Fuck you, Ray Ray."

Ray grinned and took his seat as the associate concertmaster.

By Sunday morning, they were ready. He understood now the joy of playing with a full orchestra, how the other players lifted him up, how his own notes blended and soared and twisted with the rest. Every time the conductor raised his baton, new joy blossomed in his chest. Each note felt special, a gift.

At the end of the performance, they went into the dressing rooms to pack up their instruments. His stand partner whispered, eyes wide, "You were incredible. I've never seen somebody so into the music before. It was really cool to watch. I think I learned a lot just sitting next to you."

"Um, thanks," he said. "You too." But he couldn't remember even noticing her during the performance.

Back down the narrow hallway, from dressing room to main auditorium, he and the other students headed out. The audience had come onstage. Most kids now held huge bouquets that their parents, glowing with pride, must have given them.

Mixed in with the adults were men and women wearing blazers with university insignia on their left lapels: Duke Blue Devils, Appalachian State Mountaineers, and others he didn't recognize. Scouts, here to recruit students for their colleges.

Ray paused, waiting to be acknowledged. Would they all come running to him, the associate concertmaster? Appalachian State passed him by. So did Duke. UNC looked at him vacantly and then headed toward a blond girl who'd sat a few seats behind him. It was as if he were a human-shaped block of wood or a potted plant: something to be bypassed on their way to someone else. Unaccosted, he made it to the front of the stage and was about to head down to the audience level, and then on to the waiting buses outside, when he heard his name.

He turned, almost knocking over a cello case. It was Shawn. "Oh, hey, man," Ray said. "I was looking for you. You sounded great today."

"Likewise," Shawn said, "although I couldn't really hear you over all twelve million violins. We should keep in touch. Let me know what school you end up going to." They exchanged emails.

"Great meeting you. Maybe we can catch up once school is out. If you see Janelle, tell her I said bye and that it was nice meeting her."

"Yeah, absolutely." Shawn said, looking behind Ray at someone. "Take care, man."

"Ray?"

He turned. Dr. Stevens, wearing a Markham University blazer, smiled from ear to ear.

"Dr. Stevens, hi!"

"Hello. I hope I'm not being too out of line when I first say congratulations on a terrific performance, and an even bigger congratulations on your associate concertmaster seat. That's quite an accomplishment in itself—let alone for a first-time orchestra member."

"Thank you. I just did my best."

"I know you did. That's why I am hoping you'll accept the university's offer. I'm authorized to offer you a full music scholarship to study with me."

The world seemed to slow for a moment, the auditorium lights contracting around her.

"The scholarship would cover full tuition, and room and board, but you'd have to pay for your own books and miscellaneous materials. February is a little late to apply, so we'd have to get you in the system right away. I'm authorized to waive your application fees if you apply before Thursday. Housing assignments don't begin until the summer, so you're okay on that front. How does that sound? What do you think?"

He tried to speak but just kept opening and closing his mouth.

Dr. Stevens's grin only widened, if that was possible. "I know this may seem like a lot all at once. I understand that you might need to talk it over with your family."

"Yeah." Hope and exhilaration fizzed in his veins—but his mom would never let him go. Dr. Stevens handed him two business cards: the university card she'd already given him and the other for the admissions director.

"Is your family here? I'd love to meet them."

"Uh—they couldn't make it."

"Sorry to hear that," she said. "Go home, think about what I've said. Talk to your family. Email or call me when you make a decision, but don't wait too long. If we don't hear from you by the end of next week, I'll have to offer the scholarship to another prospective student." She looked at him hard. "This could be the start of a meteoric career for you, if that's what you want."

"Uh—yeah. Yeah. It's what I want. I need to talk to my mom, though. Thank you. I'll be in touch."

"I hope so. Congratulations again." She shook his hand and disappeared into the crowd.

Outside, in the weak late-afternoon light, kids and their families were moving on, shouting good-bye, the mournful **thunk**s of car doors closing. He was one of only three students to ride the charter bus home. He stared out the window the entire way, thinking and trying not to think.

His mother and the twins were in the living room: the twins, as usual, glued to their spots in front of the TV, his mom on her phone on the sofa. "Your food is on the stove." Their dinner plates, stacked with chicken bones, glistened greasily on the glass coffee table. He dropped the violin and his duffel in his room, went into the kitchen and made up his plate. Mashed potatoes, string beans, chicken breast. He put it in the microwave.

Voices bounced around in his head:

You need to find a real job.

This could be the start of a meteoric career.

Down the hall to the bedroom. Something made him notice the pictures framed on the walls: pictures of each twin over the past three years—his brother mugging for the camera in his baseball and basketball uniforms; his sister and a half dozen other little girls squashed into white tutus at the local community center's ballet recital. There was only one of Ray, with his mom and dad, from when Ray was a baby. His mom wasn't smiling.

Ray had always been the one his mother couldn't quite understand—instead of playing basketball with the other uncoordinated prepubescent kids, he was up in his room, alone, practicing air violin with his IKEA headboard as a fingerboard. His mom never got to sit at the half-court line and gossip with her friends, whose kids were also on the team—she didn't want to go alone to an alien concert hall with a bunch of soccer moms wondering if she was lost.

He lay on his bed. There was a crack in the left corner of the ceiling he'd never noticed before. The muted TV laughter itched his skin, as if it would leave scars. Talking to her might not be so bad. Maybe she'd be excited. Happy for him. She didn't have to pay for anything.

Water rattled in the pipes. The twins were in the bathroom, getting ready for bed. A poster of Optimus Prime—Transformer, leader of the Autobots—clenching his metal fists. His corded muscles bulged reassuringly. If Optimus Prime could beat the crap out of Megatron, Ray could talk to his mother.

Ray came out of his room. "Mom. I need to talk to you. It's important."

"What, boy?" She was typing.

"The concert was really good. I was one of the top violinists and I got offered a scholarship."

"Uh-huh." Her phone chimed. She smirked at it, typed.

"Mom!"

"Who you yellin' at?"

"I'm not yelling, I didn't know if you heard what I said. I got offered a scholarship today."

"To where?"

"To Markham University."

"Well that's too bad. You're gettin' a job. I ain't paying for college."

"This is a scholarship. A full scholarship. It would pay room and—"

"No."

"What do you mean, no?"

"I said no. I ain't paying for nothing."

"You don't have to pay for anything. It's a music scholarship. I just said that. It covers everything."

"What did I just say?"

"You said no. But I think I'm going to take it."

"You ain't taking shit. You goin' to get a job and help with these kids." She mumbled something incoherent. Her phone chimed and she looked at it.

"Mom? Hello? What is the big deal? I'll have a college degree."

"In what," she said, actually looking at him, eyes narrowed. Only then did he realize how furious she was. "In music? What's that goin' to do for anybody? Let me tell you something. You're just a kid. You don't need no college and no music. You need a job."

"One of the professors thinks I can play in a major symphony."

"Ha! You can't play in no symphony. I hate to tell you, but you didn't play all that good at your grandma's. You ain't good enough."

For a moment, neither of them spoke.

"I'm doing it," he said.

She stood up suddenly, swift and sure, took two steps, leaned over him. "No, you ain't. You're gettin' a job."

He stood, too, taller than her. "So you're telling me that you'd rather me stay here and work for the next ten years at Popeyes instead of going and getting a college degree? That doesn't make any sense."

"Talk back one more time and I'll slap the shit outta you."

"This is unbelievable. I give you almost every cent I make. And why? So you can get a bigger TV? What's after the TV? I've begged you for years for a violin, but you say you can't afford it and then you get your hair done. All I've done is contribute."

"You got a better chance of makin' it in the NBA than you do makin' a living playing music. It's tough out there. You need to find somethin' steady."

"Like what? Popeyes? The hospital cafeteria?"

"Exactly. Something nice and steady that's gonna pay the bills."

"Pay your bills, you mean."

She smacked him, palm wide open, and he staggered as the backs of his legs hit the armchair and he reached out to steady himself. His left cheekbone flamed.

"Let me tell you something," she said. "You gon' do what I say. I'm smarter than you, and you will never be able to get one over on me. Do you understand?"

He held the left side of his face. The burn crept into his left eye.

"You know that you can't make a living playing a violin. That old fiddle Mama gave you is about to fall apart as it is. You think them white people are gonna let you play in a orchestra? No. You ever seen a Black man playin' in a orchestra? No. There's a reason for that. Now I'm tired of hearin' about this shit."

She sat down, stared at her phone again, snickered at it.

"You won't have to hear about it anymore." He stumbled around her, down the hall to his room. His face burned.

Moments later his mom went into her bedroom, talking on her phone loud enough for him to hear.

"Then he said he was going to go to some college for violin. Yeah. Then he got smart. I slapped the shit outta him, that's what I did."

She went into her room, closed the door. He could hear her muttering, then a cackle, long and drawn out.

He pulled out his own phone, dialed.

After the third ring came a voice—shaky, frail: "Hello?" The sound of a throat clearing, and then, stronger, "Hello? Ray? That you?"

"Hey, Grandma," he said.

"Ray? What's wrong? You okay?"

"I'm fine—nothing's wrong." He cleared his own throat, blinked hard. His left eye still stung, as if sleet were stinging the side of his face. He sat up straighter. "I'm sorry to call so late, but I had to tell you the good news."

"Oh, I'm so glad you called me. What is it, baby?"

PART 3

Treasure

Chapter 10

Janice

14 Months Ago

He'd missed two calls from her already.

"Ray?" Dr. Stevens said. "We need to talk."

"What's going on?"

Her voice sounded thin, strained. "Where are you?"

"In my room. What's going on?"

He stood up, the phone suddenly slick with his sweat. The textbook he was supposed to be reading slid to the floor. Outside the March sky lowered cold and gray, with darker clouds shadowing the trees on the horizon, but the sun shone in a distant patch of blue. He leaned his forehead against the window, concentrating on the cold circle above his eyebrows. She rarely called him, and she never sounded like this.

"Rayquan. I'm going to ask you a question, and I need you to be honest with me."

He swallowed. How would the accusation run? Someone's instrument stolen (when it was left in a storage room), a too-high music history test score (so he must have cheated), a practice room vandalized (had to be the Black guy). He was so close to graduating. "Did I do something?"

"Can you meet me outside the music building?"

"Sure, but it'll take me fifteen minutes to get there."

"I'll be waiting for you outside."

"I'll meet you in your office."

"No. Just meet me outside." She hung up without saying goodbye.

His pulse pounded in his temples, and the sweat was cold in his armpits and between his shoulder blades. He threw on his coat and pulled his Yellow Jackets ski cap down across his brow. He was almost out the door before he remembered his ID card on the desk. The cool plastic felt somehow alien—too cold, shaped wrong—as he stuffed it into his pocket. He headed out into the weak afternoon sunshine.

As promised, she was waiting for him, pacing back and forth on the steps of the music building, hands in her pockets. Above her loomed ancient brick, limestone lintels arching into a medallion with **1907** in its center. These walls had always been a refuge for him—he knew every office, every practice room, every hallway. The floors vibrated from far-off arpeggios and the faint buzz of distant pianos. For four years he had breathed in the aroma of cleaning solvent, the mustiness of old books, and the distant perfume from the vocal majors. That smell had become home to him.

When she saw him, she stopped moving. He waved, but she didn't wave back.

She was always—always—smiling. It was one of the traits he found most endearing—it was as if there were some private joke that only the two of them shared, and they were a team, the two of them against whatever came their way—from a nasty assistant in the dean's office to a sluggish bartender who didn't seem eager to serve them. He'd never known an adult to treat him like this.

Now her smile had vanished, and her hands were deep in her dark blue puffy jacket.

"Will you please tell me what's going on?" he asked her. He'd been waiting for this moment for the past four years, ever since she'd approached him with that out-of-the-blue scholarship. The entire time he'd been here, he'd felt like a fraud, and that they were waiting to kick him out. Was Popeyes hiring?

When he left Charlotte to go to college, he'd taken a series of buses to get to campus, carrying a ten-dollar suitcase, his red duffel bag, and the still-new cheap violin case. He'd paid his mother her long-awaited rent, and most of the bills, but still had saved $2,200 from playing gigs at night and working afternoons at the grocery store.

His freshman roommate, a poli-sci major with blond hair, blue eyes, and absolutely no interest in being friends, would smile and somehow quickly drift out of the room whenever Ray came in. Ray barely noticed. The music department consumed him.

The first time he sat down in Music Theory 101, which Dr. Stevens was teaching, he realized how far behind he was. He didn't know how to name intervals or relative minors. All the other kids rattled them off without thinking. Never having taken private lessons, he'd missed basic techniques—double-stops, playing in seventh position, and reading different clefs.

As that first class ended, he wondered if he could get a full refund on his textbooks—they'd set him back $250.

"Ray, can you wait a minute?" Dr. Stevens had called from the lectern that day.

The rest of the class had filed out, the door closed behind them. He stood before her, the seats spreading behind him like abandoned cars in a parking lot. Now it would come: now she'd tell him that she'd made a mistake, that he had to leave.

And then she'd smiled—warm, friendly, welcoming. "I know you're feeling way behind," she told him, smiling that smile. How did she know? "It will take a while to get adjusted. But I'm here to help. You can do this."

He could feel his misery unknot in his throat.

"Don't get caught up in all the technical stuff," she said, looking up at him. "You'll learn it. I have every faith that you will. This is what you're not seeing— there's something special about your playing, and that's why you're here. It's called **musicality**."

"What do you mean?" Hope soared in him.

"Precision and technique can be learned," she told him. "That's just practice. A lot of practice, but it's still just practice. What we can't teach is how to make a musician actually connect—emotionally connect—with the pieces he's playing. To really care about the music, and let the music tell its story."

"And I do?"

"You do," she said. "You can't fake it. It's like always looking at a reflection of the sun in a puddle, and then all of a sudden seeing the sun itself. You're that sun, Ray."

He laughed. "Uh, yeah," he said, "sure."

Her smile vanished. "I'm very serious," she said, holding his gaze. "You have a lot of hard work ahead of you, but if you want this, you can absolutely do it. Do you want it bad enough?"

You're eighteen years old. You're trying to be callous, trying to be cool, trying to show that you don't care because, after all, that's the point, isn't it—to be detached, to be above it all? You can't let your guard down because then someone might mock you, might call you a moron. And it's even worse when you're Black, right? The only Black music major, already only half as good as everyone else. So above all else: Be cool, be nonchalant. Don't care.

"Yes," he whispered. "I want this." He meant it, body and soul.

She nodded slowly. "I know. So own it. Do it. You can make it happen. You have it in you."

"Okay," he breathed.

"Good. Now go practice your double-stops in the Bach. Tomorrow I want them sounding perfect."

He went to the practice room and practiced double-stops for the next four hours.

That first year of school, he stuck out uncomfortably. "He sucks," he once overheard two other music majors say. "He only got in because he's Black." The first time Ray had to play in front of his studio, he was so nervous that he missed every high F, flubbed every run of the Kabalevsky Violin Concerto.

One Thursday afternoon in mid-February, life felt particularly tough. In his lesson he'd played Monti's **Czardas** especially poorly. The sweeping minor chords, the pining lift into hope, into desperation, into joy, catapulting into that quick, fast, danceable celebration of light and the wind across the water—it was all there. But its false harmonics just wouldn't come out. His left hand stopped working. He'd played the double-stops terribly out of tune, and he'd played the rhythm in the adagio section incorrectly every time. Finally, the spiccato and sautillé bowing wouldn't bounce at all.

He threw his violin back into its case, stomped out of the studio.

Dr. Stevens caught him on the stairs going down to the exit. "Hold on," she said, laying her hand on his arm. She wasn't angry. She wasn't even disappointed. She just smiled as if this were a private joke between them. "Give me your violin for a sec. I'll show you how I used to practice this."

"I'm never going to get it," he snarled.

"Believe it or not, I had the same issues you're having now." There on the stairwell she tugged the violin case from his grip, pulled out his violin, and played the four troublesome measures over and over, starting very slowly, and then increasing the tempo.

That's how to do it. He couldn't believe how such a simple gesture—just slowing down the phrase, lifting his bow slightly—could fix such a complex problem. He nodded, but she was already going on to the harmonics section, eyes on him. She didn't say a word, pointed at her left hand with the bow, and slowly placed each finger into position. She arched each finger higher than normal, and he understood how to do it. Yes. He could do that.

Czardas reverberated off the concrete walls and into his chest. Her playing was flawless. She handed him his instrument and bow. "Drop the bow on the string."

He dropped the bow from above his head. Nothing happened.

"Again."

Again, nothing.

Finally, six or seven attempts later, a magnificent sautillé rang out.

It would be nice to say that that was the last time discouragement overwhelmed him, but it wasn't. He often felt like giving up—but the feelings came less frequently. The moment in the stairwell cemented his belief that Dr. Stevens was watching out for him, always there to give him a little added support.

They met frequently on Saturdays and some Sundays to give Ray extra lessons so he'd keep up with his classmates. Over many months he learned her history, which seemed as rarified and impossible as the ruby-throated hummingbirds that sometimes whizzed around the trumpeter vines on the south side of the music building.

She'd studied privately as a child with Dorothy DeLay from Juilliard and was one of a handful of Black kids to go to summer music camps. Eventually she was performing across the country with several prestigious degrees in tow. But it wasn't easy: she constantly fought the stigma of being a Black woman, of not being the typical violin soloist. She

auditioned for the Boston Symphony, was a finalist, but eventually they went with someone whiter,
more conventional. She took a job teaching at
Indiana University until Markham lured her away.

Her résumé was impressive, but her connections
were even more so. She had friends in most major
symphonies, had performed with many concertmasters, festival organizers, and others in the industry.
But more important than all the name-dropping: she
loved teaching and loved music. Ray couldn't believe
how lucky he was to have found her.

**We're here for a reason. . . . To throw little
torches out to lead people through the dark.**

At the end of every one-on-one lesson, she'd compliment him. It always made him uncomfortable,
but eventually he didn't wince when she praised
him. "You're my diamond in the rough. You may
not have bionic fingers, but you're a born musician.
Never forget that." Except for Grandma Nora—
who was hours away and often only a disembodied
voice on the phone—he'd never had anyone regularly support him, watch out for him daily. It was
an odd, slightly uncomfortable feeling—as if he'd
eaten too much, his belly secure and tight. He desperately wanted to please her, and that was an odd
feeling, too—he'd always performed for himself,
and now he was performing for her, too. It made
all the difference, knowing he was seen.

At the end of his freshman year, the students

played a convocation for the entire school of music. Ten students played each week, and when it was his turn, Ray went fifth. He would play **Czardas**. He took a deep breath, told himself to put the Kabalevsky debacle behind him, and strode onto the stage. Dr. Stevens's lessons—the harmonics, the double-stops, the sautillé—felt ground into his fingers. He hurled himself in, giving the piece all of his soul. His body was on autopilot, and he could tell even as he played that this was vastly better than anything he'd ever performed before. The mournful opening notes gave way to sunlight on a park bench, to the glitter of water pouring endlessly from a waterfall on a very hot summer day. When the last note rang out, his listeners leapt to their feet.

They called him back for three curtain calls.

This is what he needed to do with his life.

Over the summer, back home with his mother, his routine continued: up at 6:00 a.m. to practice with his heavy practice mute in his room. All day working at the grocery store. Evenings practicing more, or playing in a couple jazz clubs. Weekend weddings or parties or anywhere else that was looking for a musician. Every couple weeks he caught a bus to have summer lessons with Dr. Stevens. His mother did her best to ignore him, and he did his best to ignore her.

By the middle of his sophomore year, he'd caught

up with the top students in the studio—juniors and seniors—and surpassed them all. Soon the rumblings he heard were not about him being the quota student, but that he received preferential treatment because he was Black. In his junior year, when he beat Julie Asher, a curly-haired bubbly girl from Texas, in a seating audition, Julie started a petition to have Dr. Stevens removed as the violin teacher because she was helping Ray more than everyone else. Ray defended Dr. Stevens fiercely, and the petition went nowhere.

In his junior year, Ray and a few students went out for pizza with Professor Harris, who taught music history and piano and who'd listened to them practice that afternoon.

After they ordered, Professor Harris leaned in toward Ray. "Have you ever thought about applying to the Tchaikovsky Competition?"

The restaurant was noisy. Ray thought he hadn't heard correctly. "Excuse me?"

The man leaned in, repeated what he'd said. The Tchaikovsky Competition. It was one of the most—if not **the** most—prestigious competitions for young musicians, held every four years in Moscow. The winner and finalists usually walked away with recording deals and invitations to play worldwide with the best orchestras. Hundreds applied, and only a few dozen made it to the First Round.

Ray swallowed a chunk of breadstick, which was suddenly rough in his throat. "When is it again?"

"It took place two years ago," Professor Harris said. "You should really think about it. I honestly think you have a real shot. You have two years to get ready. You should look over the application materials, see what you need to enter. Talk it over with Professor Stevens."

"Isn't that the competition where, like, no Americans have ever won?" Ray said.

"Well, Van Cliburn won the first one on piano, back in the fifties, but you're right, it's rare that Americans make it that far. I think you should consider it, though. That sautillé of yours is pretty incredible."

"Thanks," Ray said, taking another breadstick and snapping it in half. "I guess I'll think about it."

"You have some time," Professor Harris said.

The conversation moved on, but Harris had lit a flame in Ray: he burned not only to apply to the competition but to be good enough to actually qualify.

The next day in his lesson, after he'd finished the Mendelssohn Concerto, he broached the topic with Dr. Stevens. "Do you know anything about the Tchaikovsky Competition?"

"I'm glad you asked," she said, nodding slightly. "You're definitely on a soloist's track, and that means competitions. That's the top of the food chain. You're not quite ready, but you could be."

"You really think so?"

"I do. One hundred percent. But there's a lot you have to do before you get there. You'll have to really increase your repertoire, and you need to dig into basic techniques. Like double- and triple-stops. And you'd need to have a soloist's violin. But we have time for all that. You just stay focused."

She kept smiling, looking at him, as if she were delighted he'd brought it up.

From then on, he'd check out the competition's website, study past winners, follow the controversies over the judging, the various missteps that the classical music world brooded on. Americans were rarely chosen; a Black American probably didn't even have a shot.

But if he didn't apply, he wouldn't give them a reason to say yes.

So, quietly, just to himself, he set a goal: the Tchaikovsky Competition in three years. It would mean he'd have to work even harder, and he loved the challenge.

Senior year had turned into the best year of his life. He'd moved out of the dorms and into an apartment he shared with two other music students, he was concertmaster of the college symphony orchestra, he played in the community orchestra, he played jazz gigs every other weekend with a combo that played close to campus, and he worked part time behind the counter at a local bagel shop.

In the spring he would prepare for major orchestra auditions. Dr. Stevens had pulled strings to find the most promising auditions on the East Coast, and some in the Midwest. So when she said that it was time he had a concert-level instrument, he immediately agreed. Grandma Nora's beat-up old fiddle wasn't going to cut it. Luckily, hidden away in Charlotte was Fischer Luthiers, a musical instrument store and repair shop that was one of the best in North Carolina. Ray had been in a couple times with his string-repair class.

Dr. Stevens drove them out one Friday afternoon. They'd made an appointment ahead of time. Jacob Fischer—"Call me Jacob, son, don't call me Mr. Fischer"—was waiting behind the counter and came out to meet them in the middle of the showroom floor. A grizzled man with a tonsure surrounded by wild, wiry black-and-gray hair, a hooked nose, thin lips, a back hunched from years of bending over a worktable, he'd seemed daunting each time Ray had met him, and today was no exception. He shook both their hands, called Professor Stevens "young lady," and was deferential to them both. This was a far cry from the music shop in the Georgia mall years before.

Fischer had heard Ray play several times. "Your

Brahms A major sonata reminded me of Nigel Kennedy at your age."

"Wow. Thanks, Mr. Fischer. That's so nice." Ray was getting better at accepting compliments.

"Jacob. And I mean it."

Dr. Stevens explained that Ray would soon be making the audition rounds and needed a violin that was up to the task.

Fischer led them over to the violins that hung like hourglass-shaped jewels on the wall. "Try this one on for size," he said to Ray, reaching for a tiger-striped, honey-colored beauty with mother-of-pearl inlaid pegs. He lifted it from its rack, extended it to Ray, who grasped it cautiously. Ray slid his bow across the strings, tuned the D string—it was slightly flat—and played an A-major scale all on the G string to get the feel of it. Then he launched into the third movement of the Mendelssohn Concerto, the vast sound reaching up from the ground and growing leaves and blossoms. The tone on the E string seemed to float from his chest, not from the instrument at all. He closed his eyes and let the violin serenade him.

"That's what a high-level violin can do," Dr. Stevens told him. "And that's why you need one."

Mr. Fischer—Jacob—nodded. "That sounded most impressive, young man. That's the kind of instrument you should have."

"How much is it?" He was afraid to ask. He wanted it desperately.

"This little beauty is thirty-six thousand dollars," he said. "It's a Eugene Lehman from 1959. It's actually a steal at this price—in New York, you'd probably pay one hundred thousand for it."

Ray swallowed. "That's what I was afraid of." Gently, he handed the Lehman back to Fischer. "It may be a bit much for me."

"He needs something top tier, though," Dr. Stevens said. "You can see how much talent he has. Audition season starts in May, and he has a shot at some very interesting possibilities. We need to find him something that's more affordable but will showcase his skills."

They spent the next two hours trying various instruments. Ray kept circling back to a 1997 Rinaldi. It was definitely a soloist's instrument, with only two previous owners. The sound was as pure as light and easily filled the shop. At $5,200, it was a steal but still vastly more than he wanted to pay. He had just over $8,000 in his savings account. So it was possible. But that was money he planned to live off—to pay rent and to travel to auditions. He'd have very little left.

"Are we sure that mine can't be fixed?" he said. PopPop's fiddle still rested on the counter, where he'd deposited it when they'd come into the store. He'd long ago replaced the alligator-skin case with a lighter hard case that had much more padding as well as four bow compartments. The alligator-skin case he'd wrapped carefully in a garbage bag and stowed beneath his bed.

"Let's take a look." Fischer opened the case, pulled out PopPop's fiddle, glanced at it. "This looks like early factory made, right off the assembly line. You'd be investing in a new fingerboard, new bridge, fitting the pegs. At the end of the day I don't think it would be worth my time or your money."

"It's not factory made," Ray said. "It's been in my family for more than a hundred years. When I first got it, I had one repair job done. Maybe that's what you're looking at?"

"It's a filthy mess," Jacob said. Despite Ray's best polishing efforts, the violin was still whitish from decades of unremoved Good Luck Dust. Jacob pulled out a bottle of solvent, dabbed a little on a cotton swab, rubbed it on the violin's back, and the rosin magically disappeared. He dabbed the cotton swab in a few more places, front and back. He slipped behind the counter, into a back room, and returned with several tools—calipers, screwdrivers, magnifying glasses, a jeweler's loupe. He examined the violin front and back, looking into the F holes with a portable light.

"You're right, the craftsmanship is good. Very good. You see how the sides flare, and the feminine winding on the scroll? See the shape of the back, how it bows, and how it's solid, not two pieces? Even underneath all the grime, it's definitely Italian."

Carefully he removed more built-up rosin. "Nice underlying varnish, actually. Maybe if it were cleaned up I could better assess it." He pulled out a slender tape measure, took several measurements. "The dimensions . . ." He looked at Ray. "They're very interesting. You might have something here."

"Can it be brought up to a soloist level?" Dr. Stevens asked.

"I don't know." Fischer paused. "Maybe." He turned it over and over. "Yes, maybe. I think it could be. You're right and I'm wrong. It's actually a nice instrument. There's a bit of warping, but I think I can correct it. Whoever did this repair work"—he gestured—"did a terrible job, but that's easily fixed. The question is whether it can really be restored to the way it should play."

"How much do you think it will cost? To try fixing?" Ray asked.

"Once the top comes off I'll have a better idea. I can tell you right now that the inside is really dirty, and the grime on the varnish alone is a job in itself. The sound post might need to be replaced."

"And the bridge, and the pegs . . ." Ray said.

Fischer waved that away. "That's just cosmetic. This old beauty needs someone to really pay attention to her, really clean her up and bring her back. That takes time. Let's say fifteen hundred dollars."

"Goodness," Dr. Stevens said. "But we're not

even sure if it will be at the level of at least the Rinaldi when you're done?"

"Correct."

Ray took one longing look at the Rinaldi tempting him from the wall. There really was no question. A tiny figure in a pink housecoat, her hair in curlers and her hands on a walker, stood behind him, just out of sight. If he turned quickly enough, perhaps he'd catch a glimpse of her—perhaps he'd hear her "Ooooh, baby" again.

"Okay, let's do it," he said. "Do you need a down payment for fixing mine?"

"Ray, you sure?" Dr. Stevens asked.

"Yeah," he said. "I'm sure. If it can't be fixed, maybe I can buy the Rinaldi instead." He rummaged in the violin's compartment for a pencil, wrote his name on the side of the fingerboard.

"Why are you doing that?" Jacob asked.

Even though she'd vouched for Mr. Fischer, Dr. Stevens had told him in the past about dicey violin dealers: "You can't trust them. They appraise, repair, and sell instruments—huge conflict of interest."

"This old fiddle is really special to me, even if it can't be fixed. No offense, but I'll feel more comfortable if I know I marked it. Better safe than sorry."

He'd given Jacob the violin more than two weeks ago. Now, standing in front of the music building where Dr. Stevens had summoned him, he wasn't sure what he'd agreed to. Around them the March wind blew raw and miserable, but Ray could barely feel it.

"Jacob Fischer called me this afternoon," Dr. Stevens began.

"Why wouldn't he call me? What's wrong?"

"He called me because he's known me for a long time and this is a very unusual situation."

"Unusual? How?"

"Ray." She took a breath. "He thinks the violin is eighteenth-century Italian." Three families in Italy were renowned during that time for making the most exquisite, most expensive violins in the world: the Amatis, the Guarneris, and, most famous, the Stradivaris. These violins were worth tens of thousands of dollars—sometimes millions.

Ray waited for her to burst out laughing. She didn't. "What are you talking about? You think it's a Stradivarius?"

"It's a serious possibility."

The entire situation struck him as stupidly absurd. PopPop's fiddle? Seriously?

He sat down on a bench along the path, put his forehead in his hands, closed his eyes. "Look, it's cold out here. If this is your way of telling me I have to practice more, I get it."

"I'm not joking. I've known Jacob for a long time.

He called me to tell me that it might be something special. I want you to take it to a top appraiser. In New York."

She sat next to him, spoke more gently. "Tell me everything you know about it."

Chapter 11

Grandma Nora

3 Years Ago

Everything that Ray knew about the violin came from Grandma Nora, of course. And the bulk of what he'd learned came from a few all-too-short weeks that Ray spent with her when he was a sophomore.

One rainy April evening his aunt Rochelle called to tell him that Grandma Nora had been diagnosed with lung cancer: "Typical Mama," she'd said, voice thick with tears. "They're saying she only has about six weeks, and I just wanted to let you know in case you wanted to come see her."

He hung up and immediately booked the nine-hour bus trip to Atlanta.

When he arrived at his grandmother's house, no walker, no pink housecoat, and no smiling face awaited him as he trudged up the path to the front porch.

He rang the bell and Uncle Larry answered, embraced him.

"How's she doing?" Ray asked.

He shook his head. "She's a tough old lady, but it's not looking good."

"Is everyone here?"

"Rochelle is coming in tonight. Everybody else is here."

"My mom, too?"

"Yeah. She's in the kitchen."

As Ray edged past him into the foyer, Larry put a hand on his arm. "Ray, when you go in to see your grandma, know that she's lost a lot of weight. I don't want you to be shocked."

Inside, everyone hugged him or rubbed his shoulders. Even his mom stood up and gave him a very fake, very tactile hug. "Go see your grandmother. Don't stay in there too long. She needs to rest."

Aunt Joyce, sitting next to the bed, stood up when she saw him. He took her place. Grandma Nora was a shell, the color drained from her face. There was no sparkle in her eyes. He wasn't sure she even recognized him. Even if she did, Ray doubted she could muster the strength to even give him the hug he desperately needed. He sat down, took her hand, careful to be gentle. "Grandma?" the word caught in his throat.

She didn't speak. She didn't move. He tried again. "I came to see you." He was losing the struggle not to cry. He kept blinking. "How are you feeling?"

"Oh, baby, I don't think Grandma is doing too good. They tell me I have cancer, baby."

"Grandma . . . I'm so sorry. What can I do for you?" Ray gave up on trying to hold back his tears.

"All you can do is what you always do. You make me so proud." She took a breath. It hurt to watch. "I'm happy to hear that you're playing your fiddle good."

"I'm doing my best, Grandma. Every day I'm trying so hard to make you proud." His voice broke.

"I know you do, baby. Did you bring it?" A breath. "Your fiddle? You gonna take it out and play for me?"

"Of course." He stood to retrieve the instrument case, which he'd left in the living room.

"I don't think she means right now," Aunt Joyce said softly from the doorway. He hadn't realized she was still there. "Why don't we let her rest for a little? You want to sleep a little bit, Mama?"

"Yes, baby, maybe I'll rest a bit. And then Ray can bring up his fiddle for me."

"Okay," Ray said. He sat back down and reached for her hand again.

He sat with her as she slept.

———

The next few weeks passed in a blur, taking turns at her bedside, and when he couldn't be with her he sat in the hallway, staring blankly at his textbook: **A History of Western Music**. He played for her whenever he could—**The Lark Ascending** and de Falla's **Spanish Dance**—always finishing with "Rhosymedre."

Often, she'd talk, drifting in and out of consciousness. She seemed desperate to tell him as much as she could about her family, especially her grandfather, and Ray was desperate to hear—as if injecting her memories would allow her to live on.

"Whose fiddle is that?" she asked him the first morning he was back, as he opened the violin case. "You said you'd brought PopPop's fiddle?"

"This is PopPop's fiddle," he said, showing it to her.

"Why isn't it in the case? The one with the loose handle? It's green inside."

"You mean the alligator-skin case? It's under my bed, at school. I just wanted something to protect PopPop's fiddle a little better," he explained.

"That's good, baby. That's real good. Sure wish you'd brought it, though." Then she told him what she remembered about the violin—much he'd already heard, but some was new.

Her grandfather Leon had been born into slavery on a Georgia plantation outside Atlanta. She didn't know the plantation's name. He'd learned to play his fiddle as a child, Grandma Nora wasn't clear how. The slaveholders, the Marks family, had come to Georgia a generation before, maybe thirty or forty years earlier, from somewhere in Italy. The Marks family had built the plantation house, bought slaves, and tried to assimilate into Southern culture.

"Is that where you learned Italian?" Ray had never put it together, but he suddenly remembered that, when he was little, his grandma would sometimes say some words in a different language.

"Yes, baby. You remember **pronto**? I'd say that when the pies were finished cooking. You sure loved my blueberry pie."

"I sure did," he said.

By the time Leon was a young man, he would play regularly for his master. "He always told us about playing after dinner and for the parties at the big house. He told me how much he loved playing at them parties." They would dance on weekends and celebrate when the harvest was in. On Sundays after church, if the field slaves didn't have to return to work, he played for them, too. "He knew playing that fiddle kept him and his family alive, baby." The fiddle made him valuable.

Although it had apparently always been in the Marks family, no one had played the fiddle like Leon could. When the master was upset, Leon's playing made him smile. When slaves were exhausted at the end of the day, his playing made them get up and dance. He could soothe crying babies and impress crowded parlors.

Grandma Nora said that Leon and his master were close. Ray wondered if the master was Leon's biological father.

After the War Between the States, the master freed all his slaves. He gave Leon the fiddle, telling him how happy Leon's playing had made him and his family. "That's all PopPop had in the world when he left that plantation, baby. Just that fiddle. He played every chance he could. He played that fiddle every day. Every single day."

Leon was very superstitious and thought his homemade rosin—his Good Luck Dust—made him a good musician and that it was bad luck to wipe it off. Grandma Nora remembered that whenever Leon picked it up, white fingerprints dusted the fiddle's body.

The violin case had an interesting story. The slave cabins were perched on the edge of a swamp—probably to make it harder for the enslaved people to run away. Alligators lived in the swamp, sometimes eating the chickens and the goats that roamed freely around the cabins. One particularly big alligator would lurk offshore, its yellow eyes gleaming in the firelight, drifting lazily in the water until it lunged onto the bank, dragging its prey down. Three or four of the enslaved men caught and killed it—and one of them turned that skin into a fiddle case. He inlaid the case with scraps of dark green velvet brought special from Savannah for the mistress's gown.

When Leon moved to Atlanta, he first supported himself by playing—at local parlors or at musical events, sometimes accompanying itinerant singers or other musicians. When he married Annabeth Wines, though, his days as a musician ended: he spent the next forty years working in a lumber mill. But that fiddle remained his obsession, and he played for them every night. None of his children or grandchildren had any interest in music, so after his death the fiddle sat, unused, in Nora's home. She'd perhaps opened the case a dozen times in the next fifty years.

"He was a good man," she told Ray. "And, oh, he would have been so proud of you! PopPop always had a kind word for everyone no matter how nasty someone treated him. He always said, 'Respect yourself and people will respect you, too. It has to start with you, Nora.' He'd say to me, 'No matter how they treat you, you just remember that you're worthy of respect.' I can hear his voice right now, baby. 'You're worthy, Nora,' he'd tell me." She looked at Ray. "I never forgot that."

Medicine bottles stood like sentries on top of her nightstand; Aunt Joyce, Aunt Rochelle, and Ray were the ones who memorized her medication schedule and knew when to add dolasetron to ease her nausea, or to cut back on FEC-T, the chemotherapy drug, when she complained of headaches.

Aunt Rochelle never tried to make him leave the room: that time a few years ago in the music shop, when the racist clerk had yelled at him, had formed a special bond between them. Ever since then, she'd go out of her way to ask him about music, or get him to play for the family. She was unmarried, a paralegal in a big law firm outside Philadelphia, and Ray wondered if she sometimes thought of him as the son she never had. He sometimes wished he had been.

Almost three weeks after Ray arrived in Georgia, Aunt Rochelle came upstairs with Grandma Nora's lunch. Ray was sitting by her bed. "Mama," Aunt Rochelle said loudly. "Time for lunch. Made you some fresh tomato soup. I know how you like your tomato soup."

"I can feed it to her," he said, taking the bowl.

Grandma Nora opened her eyes, smiled at him.

"Tomato soup," he said, lifting the spoon to her mouth. She kept her mouth closed, just smiled at both of them.

"Don't you feel like eating?" he asked.

"No, baby. I don't think so. Not today."

"Now you eat that soup," Aunt Rochelle told her.

"It's your own recipe and I know how you like it. Joyce made it for you special."

"In a little while then," Grandma Nora said.

"Okay," Ray said. "I'll put it right here until you feel like eating."

"How about I get you some tea," Aunt Rochelle suggested. "We have a fresh pot, and it has honey in it. Good for your immune system. I'll be right back."

When Ray and his grandmother were alone, she smiled at him even more broadly, struggled to lift the arm with the IV in it, brushed her fingers against his cheek. He reached for her hand as she caressed his face. "Baby, one of the best things that I've ever been able to do is to say how proud I am of you. You always bring a smile to my face. You've stayed so sweet, even when you're sad. That's why I love you so much."

Ray was about to speak and lay her arm down when she sighed, the sound loud in the room, deep, as if she were expelling air from the very depth of her being. "Promise me something?" Her breathing got heavy, growling, a deep rumble.

"Of course," he said. "Grandma, you okay?"

"Promise me you'll always stay that sweet boy Grandma loves so much, okay?" The rattle in her chest grew louder.

"Okay. Of course." He went to the doorway.

"Aunt Rochelle? Hey, Aunt Joyce? Can you come in here a sec?"

They were there immediately, Aunt Rochelle clutching the teacup.

"Sit me up, baby."

Ray knew what was happening. She wanted to be ready when it was time for her to go home. "Can somebody do something?" Ray said. His voice came out as a squeak.

Aunt Joyce and Aunt Rochelle were blocking his view of her. "Mama?" Aunt Joyce was saying, leaning over and holding Grandma Nora's hand.

"Mama," she said again, but this time it wasn't a question.

The new silence in the room crashed around him.

Chapter 12

Authentication

14 Months Ago

Dr. Stevens pinched the bridge of her nose, thinking. "So the Italian connection certainly adds to the possibility that this is a Strad. Although it's hard to imagine a nineteenth-century plantation owner giving an expensive violin like this to a freed slave," she mused.

"I always wondered if he was actually PopPop's biological father," Ray said.

"Still," she said. "It's hard to believe. Which is why we're going to New York, to an expert," she said, standing up. "Let's get the violin."

Jacob Fischer smiled when they entered, lifting an off-white case with black leather trim—a Tonareli fiberglass case, which easily cost $300—onto the counter. Ray had never seen a case like that in person before. He pulled it toward him. The case felt empty, as if it were filled with air, or filled with light.

Gingerly he folded back the emerald-colored top cloth, revealing a violin that was at once familiar and utterly, staggeringly, the most beautiful object he'd ever seen. His great-great-grandfather's fiddle was unrecognizable. The beat-up old body, coated with decades of Good Luck Dust, had been buffed to a deep fiery orange. The cheap plastic tailpiece had become an ornately hand-carved ebony work of art. The bridge was handcrafted and placed perfectly beneath the strings. Every crack, every scar, had vanished. Jacob had taken ebony pegs and ornamented each tip with mother-of-pearl. The back was perfectly polished, the red and orange glowing like sunrise.

Dr. Stevens was smiling more than he'd ever seen her smile, and her eyes were bright.

"Why don't you play it a little?" Jacob said. "Check out the improvements. See if you can tell the difference."

Ray played two notes, and stopped. He couldn't breathe.

The sound was unlike anything he'd ever heard before: the notes more resonant, as if reaching into the marrow of his bones. He drew in a shaky breath.

He realized he was crying, but couldn't even wipe away his tears. What a gift his grandmother had given him. How would he ever be worthy? **Promise me you'll always stay that sweet boy Grandma loves so much.** He promised her again, right then, that he would keep working twice as hard. To make her proud.

He took another breath, then played the adagio from Mozart's Third Violin Concerto. He'd never felt such joy before; it was as if his heart were in all his fingers, playing.

When at last he drew his bow over the final chords, the room continued to echo.

"Ray, are you okay?"

He was thinking of his great-great-grandfather. He was thinking of Grandma Nora. He was struggling to find words. So instead he looked at Dr. Stevens, and at Jacob. "Thank you."

"No, son, thank **you**. This was an absolute treasure."

"It's stunning," Dr. Stevens breathed. "May I?" Ray handed it to her. "Were you able to determine the date?"

Jacob shook his head. "The label's long disappeared. My best guess is that it's from between 1720 and 1730."

They talked for a while longer, then Ray paid Jacob—his $1,500 fee and the cost of the new case—and they left, planning next steps. If this were an Italian eighteenth-century violin, it needed to be authenticated by an expert, and probably insured. Janice now informed Ray that he would be making an appointment in New York City with Mischa Rowland, one of the top Italian violin experts in the country, for Monday morning.

Going through Charlotte's airport security was anxiety inducing: he'd seen PopPop's fiddle go through the X-ray machine dozens of times, but this was the first time he'd watched a $300 white case cradling a **Stradivarius**—his Stradivarius—float away into the X-ray machine. Being separated even so briefly from the violin now made Ray slightly nauseated. He wondered if this was how the rest of his life would be: glued unceasingly to this violin, forever. Would he take it into the shower with him? He'd be taking it to the Tchaikovsky Competition, that was for sure. He grinned to himself.

Two hours later, the plane banked for a landing and there was Manhattan, gleaming in the early-morning sunshine like a fairy-tale city, all glass and gold. It wasn't a real place: it was something out of a movie, like these past few days. He was just a Black kid who hadn't wanted to work at a fried-chicken restaurant, and now he was a musician and there, spread out like a Thanksgiving feast, was New York City. He couldn't believe this was real.

After they landed, though, JFK airport's grime coating every institutional beige surface jolted him back to reality.

Dr. Stevens—"Ray, you need to call me Janice now, not Dr. Stevens"—had planned on an hour to get into the city, and they needed every minute of it, sitting in their taxi in bumper-to-bumper traffic nearly the whole way. Ray couldn't imagine how people did this every morning. At 9:04 a.m. their taxi passed Carnegie Hall and a few moments later pulled up in front of a nondescript beige building. ROWLAND'S FINE INSTRUMENTS, SALES & APPRAISALS, EST. 1927 was stenciled in ornate gold lettering across the plate glass window. Inside, a single violin, encased in clear Plexiglas, stood proudly. Their appointment was for 9:00. "Good timing, huh?" Dr. Stevens said.

They had to ring a bell to be buzzed in to the main showroom, where a faded violet couch sat against one wall, a beat-up coffee table covered with magazines in front of it. Instruments hung from everywhere, including the ceiling: violins, violas, and cellos shone with a gorgeous luster like nothing he'd ever seen. These were the instruments of princes and kings, the violins for the best violinists in the world. On the counter rested an old-fashioned cash register. No electronics, no card reader. Behind the counter, a staircase carpeted in red damask led up into darkness. On one side of the steps hung an enormous sign: EMPLOYEES ONLY. On the other: ALL OTHERS KEEP OUT!

The room seemed deserted, but moments after they arrived, a voice boomed from the stairwell. "You have kept me waiting. Your appointment was for nine, and it was a serious inconvenience to fit you in." A very large man descended. "Janice Stevens and Ray McMillian?" He was very intimidating. Easily six feet four inches, with jet-black hair slicked back to reveal a high forehead and bright blue eyes. He did not offer to shake either Ray's or Janice's hand.

"Let me see this instrument."

Ray set the case down on the glass cabinet behind them. Mischa Rowland leaned forward, expressionless, and then lifted out the violin, turned it around—even, Ray could swear, sniffing it. Mischa pulled out a jeweler's loupe and did it all again.

"I will give you ten thousand dollars for it," the man said. He had a thick accent that Ray couldn't place. "Not a penny more."

"Wha—no, we'd like it appraised," Ray said.

"This is an assessment and appraisal," Janice put in.

Rowland shook his head. "Fifteen. Cash."

Fifteen thousand dollars could buy a lot of violins. Could pay travel costs for auditions. Could set him up on his feet. "I'm sorry," Ray said, "it's really not for sale."

"Twenty-five and that is my very final offer."

"It's been in my family for years," Ray said. "I'm not selling it. Ever."

"Excuse us," Janice said, pulling Ray's arm. A few feet away, she said quietly, "You sure you don't want to reconsider? This is a lot of money. Jacob can find you a great violin for that."

Ray turned back to the man, took the violin gently from him. "I'm not selling," Ray said. "I can't sell my grandma's violin. I'm going to keep this for the rest of my life and pass it down to my kids."

Rowland nodded once. "I expected as much. Come." With no further comment he turned, retreated up the red damask steps. They threaded behind the counter and followed him. At the top of the stairs, heavy metal doors glowered. Ray gripped the violin more tightly.

Rowland pulled out an elaborate key; when he turned it, a keypad with numbers lit up. He pressed a sequence and the heavy door opened smoothly. They found themselves in a room that ran the entire length of the building, the space filled with cases, instruments, worktables, tools, and what looked to be a well-equipped scientific laboratory. One table held the back of a cello with electrodes bored into it; on another, a violin lay on its side with six magnifying glasses surrounding it from multiple angles. Although it was just after

9:00 a.m., several people in white aprons seemed to be engaged in important tasks.

"Lay your violin here and take a seat."

Ray placed his case on a table lined with maroon velvet. Rowland put on a pair of white gloves and opened the violin case. "Alexa," he said to the room, "play old-school hip-hop."

Within moments the Beastie Boys' music pumped through wall-mounted speakers around the room.

Under bright lights, on the velvet-lined table, Rowland began his appraisal. Lamps suspended on pulleys from the ceiling lit the violin from every angle as he, jeweler's loupe over one eye, focused on every inch, traced every curve, every corner, pulling down different colored lights, changing the lighting and the colors, flipping through dozens of magnifying glasses of different intensities. Every few minutes he'd pause, write down something, and then resume his examination.

Finally, at about 1:15 p.m.—Ray's stomach was rumbling and he was just about to ask if they could order something from a local deli—Rowland abruptly stood up, violin in hand.

"It is done," he said.

"It is? What do you think?" Janice asked. Ray braced himself.

Instead, unexpectedly, Rowland grinned. His blue eyes lit up. Ray couldn't help smiling back.

"Now that I am done," Rowland said, "I would like to ask permission to play this violin, since you will not sell it to me."

That wasn't what Ray was expecting, but he said, "Yeah, sure. Of course. Go ahead." He and Janice looked at each other. Janice shrugged.

"Thank you, young man." Rowland took out Ray's bow and tightened it so it was just off the wood. "Alexa, stop." From the speakers, Lil Wayne's voice cut off.

Ray had seen videos of bohemian Gypsy and bluegrass players using very loose bows but had never seen it in person. Then Rowland busted out with an incredible display of virtuosity. His fingers flew up and down the fingerboard. Ray was astounded that someone with such large hands could move them so dexterously. The more he played, the more possessed he looked. He drew the bow in one final flourish, stared at the violin for a moment, and then handed it to Ray, bowed slightly. "Jacob Fischer did an exceptional job on this violin. Please pack your instrument away. I will meet you downstairs."

"What—"

Rowland's forefinger waved him silent, then gestured for him to return the violin to its case. Wordlessly he disappeared through a door in one corner of the room. Ray and Janice returned down the stairs.

After about twenty minutes, Rowland's heavy

tread resounded in the stairwell, and a moment later he appeared, carrying a leather-bound folder.

"Jacob Fischer is correct," Rowland told them. "It is an Italian violin, constructed during the so-called golden age of violin making. This is, without question, one of the better examples. This varnish is exquisite. It cannot be duplicated. Even the fingerboard is well preserved. It is pure ebony. The shape of the body is unique and absolutely unmistakable. It is without question a Stradivarius. And a fine example of one. There is no label, however."

"Wha—" Ray's mouth had gone completely dry and his head was pounding. "You were going to offer me twenty-five thousand dollars for it and it's a **Strad**? That is fucked up!"

"I offered you this before I was certain," Rowland said—a bit lamely.

"What's it worth?" Janice asked.

Rowland shrugged. "For sale purposes, I believe it would fetch between 9.7 and 10.8 million dollars. For insurance purposes, I would value it at 10.1 million dollars."

A sharp intake of breath from Janice.

Ray could only nod—his ribs couldn't expand for him to take in breath. His body had grown cold.

"He needs to insure it, then," Janice said casually.

"He does," Rowland said. Twenty minutes later, a thin older woman, her graying hair streaked with blond, had sold Ray a month's worth of insurance for $2,000. A year cost $22,000. Ray had no idea how he would pay for something like that. He slumped back in his chair. Between the insurance, Rowland's appraisal fee, and the travel costs to New York, Ray's credit card was maxed out.

Outside the office, Rowland was waiting for them. They thanked him again. "I am looking forward to hearing great things from you, young man. Now play."

"Wha—what?"

"I want to hear you play. I want to hear from the great McMillian Stradivarius before the world knows its greatness."

"What do you want to hear?"

"Does not matter. You just play."

Ray opened the case and launched into Ravel's **Tzigane**, one of his favorites. The opening adagio starts out rich and full, slightly mournful, announcing his presence with passion and wistfulness; and then it lightens, begins to dance, bob along in the current of life: excitement and great joy competing, soaring, grateful, and alive. The violin took over: he wasn't playing notes, he was making music the way Ravel intended, the way Antonio Stradivari intended, the way he always dreamed he could play. He poured out into the air what he was unable to put into words: his gratitude—for this violin, for Janice, for Grandma Nora, for Mischa Rowland's assessment—a few words transforming his life utterly. **Thank you.**

He ended the piece with its thunderous final note, opened his eyes. The applause echoed in the show-room; from the stairwell, all of Rowland's associates had come down and were clapping as well.

With a violin like this, he would be worthy of the Tchaikovsky Competition. There was no way they could keep him out, no matter his skin color.

Chapter 13

New York City
13 Months Ago

Manhattan's skyscrapers and streets can seem unreal on an average day. Now, as he carried a Stradivarius violin, the sunlight was almost a melody; the taxis and town cars shuffled in a dance he could almost anticipate and join. He was Dorothy in a world new with Technicolor; he was Alice following a watch-checking white rabbit down a hole; he was Neil Armstrong stepping into a lunar landscape and the future. **He owned a Stradivarius violin worth $10 million.** Was this even remotely possible?

On the street, Janice said to him, "You know something? The instrument you played today—not the one you've been using the past four years—has really brought out the confidence in you that's always been there. Nice job with the Ravel."

He ducked his head.

"We're going to the hotel now—I just got a couple emails that I need to deal with—and then we're going for a celebratory lunch. And then shopping. We're buying you a new wardrobe."

"New wardrobe?"

"I was thinking about it in Rowland's. It's not just your violin that's being introduced to the world—you will be, too. You're going to need to step everything up to the next level. Your appearance is going to have to match your playing. People can be cruel, and they're always looking for something to criticize. We won't give them any ammunition. Do you understand what I'm getting at?"

He nodded. Being Black meant being watched— and usually not in a good way. So many times he'd walked into a store and the sales clerks glared at him. He'd been followed up and down aisles in grocery stores. At restaurants, out to dinner with friends, he'd be seated in the back near the kitchen or the restroom. No more. The days of being treated as a second-class citizen would soon be over.

"You need more than your one suit. You'll need a couple beautifully tailored suits, a couple blazers, and some high-quality shirts and trousers. And a new tux. Plus shoes."

"I sure hope my bank account can handle all this."

"I sure hope so, too," she said. "If not, we can

use mine and you can pay me back. You're going to need something nice for the media interview."

"Wha—what? Media interview?"

She explained that this discovery would be news—the university would want to profit from it; this would put the music department on the map. It was an extraordinary story, and she expected even the **Charlotte Herald** would want to run an article. Maybe the local news would, too.

"I'd need to tell my mom," he said.

"Of course. We'll time it so you tell your family and then we'll sit down with a reporter to break the story. But if you tell them now, I'd worry that somebody will leak it all over social media."

This was all happening far too quickly.

His mind was already off, running down the rabbit hole of telling his mother. He was nauseous with nervousness. The rest of the family—Aunt Rochelle especially—would be thrilled, but he wondered how his mother would handle it. The Stradivarius wasn't "noise" now, that was for sure.

The hotel was a few blocks away. Skyscrapers sprang up around them, and everywhere people dashed past, looking determined and energetic. Ray, in his faded jeans, with North Carolina all over him and a $10 million violin strapped to his body, had never felt so out of place. "This is all so much at once. You know?"

"I do, and it's just the beginning." She had been

looking distractedly down at her phone several times. "When we get to the hotel, you check in and I'm going to use their business services for a sec."

"No problem. Is there anything I can do?"

"Department bureaucracy. It'll just take a few minutes. You can go up to your room and have a few minutes to yourself. I'll text you when I'm ready and we can grab lunch. And then go shopping!"

They arrived at the Saint Jacques Hotel. Revolving doors led into a stark white lobby with an artificial fireplace that took up almost the entire length of one wall; on the other wall a concierge desk stretched forever. Janice asked the doorman where the business service center was and disappeared, heels clattering, down the marble corridor.

Ray carried his red duffel and violin case to the enormous front desk, where two clerks stood some distance from each other, both staring down at their computer monitors.

He chose the young blond woman on the right who looked not much older than he was.

"Hey. How's it going," Ray said.

"May I help you?" She looked him up and down.

He checked to see if he'd spilled anything on his shirt. Nope. Clean polo shirt, clean jeans. "Yes, I'm checking in. Ray McMillian."

She punched a few keys. "I don't seem to have you in our system."

"Try Rayquan." He spelled it.

He was dimly aware that a well-dressed couple entered the lobby, taking their places in front of the wispy-haired clerk on the left.

"I see you booked online," his front desk clerk was saying. "I'm afraid that it's late in the day, so all we have left is a single with one twin bed."

"I requested a queen-size bed." He searched for the reservation on his phone. "My confirmation said it was available."

"Yes, I'm sure it did. I'm afraid that this is the last room we have at that price."

"I'm not sure I understand," Ray said. "I'm booked for two nights in a queen room."

"Well I don't know what to tell you. This is all we have available." She stared off into space, uninterested.

"There we are," the other clerk was saying to the couple. The man was wearing a long coat that looked expensive. Diamonds glittered in the woman's ears. "A queen-size bed, yes?"

Ray looked over at the other clerk, then at the blond woman in front of him. She pretended not to notice. "You know what, fine," he said. "I'll take the twin room." He adjusted his grip on the violin case. "What's your name, ma'am?"

"It's Kara. Will there be anything else?"

"No, Kara, there won't be anything else. It really

is a shame that you are so selective on who to give your nice rooms to here. Maybe I'll overlook this when I'm asked to endorse this hotel."

Did that seriously just happen? The elevator went up six floors and he found his room, barely more than a closet, overlooking an air shaft. He put the duffel bag on the leprechaun-size desk, lay down for a minute on the bed, violin next to him. **Ten million dollars.**

Fifteen minutes later, Janice texted him and he joined her in the lobby, violin in tow. They decided to find someplace nearby for a late lunch. The doorman gave a friendly nod. Ray stopped. "Hey, man, have you worked here long?"

"About nine years, sir."

"Please, it's Ray."

"Nice to meet you, sir. I'm Mike."

"Is it me, or . . ."

The doorman chuckled. "You don't even have to finish that sentence. Trust me, it's not you. That happens all the time. They look at you like you don't belong. Like they're doing you a favor. Don't let it get to you."

"Thanks. You know, if I stay here again, I'm going to look for you, okay, Mike?"

"Thank you, sir."

After they'd headed out, Janice said, "Since you're in New York for the first time, and since we have to celebrate, you need to have a real New York experience. That means New York pizza."

It was an afternoon he never forgot. He left the impoverished student behind and stepped into the shoes of a classical music violin soloist: carrying his Grandma Nora's $10 million violin, eating New York pizza, shopping for a new wardrobe at Bloomingdale's: suits, a tuxedo, blazers, and trousers. Everything to be hemmed, tailored, customized.

Two hours later, it was time to pay. He kept worrying about how he would pay for any of this.

"Okay, sir, your total comes to $3,463.47."

Janice handed the sales clerk her credit card. "You'll pay me back," she said to Ray. "I think you're good for it."

The next day was a whirlwind: breakfast in New York, picking up his tailored wardrobe, then the flight back to Charlotte, then meeting Markham University President Suzanne Herz. Ray showed her the violin, the certificate of authenticity in its leather folder. Herz made a phone call, and soon the university's publicity liaison had joined them. Ray again went through his story. They all agreed that an interview with the **Charlotte Herald** seemed like a great first step and that they'd feature a special article about Ray and the violin in the next alumni magazine.

That night Ray called his mother. They hadn't

spoken since Christmas. "Mom, this is very important. Everything is about to change for all of us."

"What are you talking about?"

"I'd like to tell everyone at once. Can you get
in touch with everybody? All your brothers and
sisters. Let's set up a video call for tomorrow night,
seven p.m."

"This better not be something crazy. Ain't nobody
got time for craziness."

The next night, one by one, Ray's aunts and uncles
joined a video call. When they'd all assembled, he
put everyone on mute, glanced over at the violin
case for reassurance. Aunt Joyce was mouthing
something.

"Everyone, I have some news. I found out
recently that PopPop's fiddle is worth a lot of
money. It was made in Italy around 1724. It's called
a Stradivarius. What that means is that my violin
is one of the most rare instruments ever made. It's
been tested and confirmed." He showed them the
certificate of authenticity. "It may even be in the
local news. People will try to buy it. Some of them
may contact you and try to get you to convince me
to sell it. They may make some really good offers,
but I need you all to understand that the fiddle is
not for sale. My plan moving forward is to start
playing concerts and recitals.

"There's a piece that's going to run in the
Charlotte Herald tomorrow, and I wanted to let

you all know ahead of time. I'm going to take you all off mute now."

Ray's mom was first. "How much is it worth?"

"It's appraised at about ten million dollars."

Everyone in the video chat began to scream.

"Are you for real, boy?" Uncle Thurston got closer and closer to his monitor.

"Yes. I'm being serious."

"Oh my god. If this is real, we are rich!" Aunt Joyce screamed.

"Lord have mercy. I can't believe this," Ray's mom said.

"Ray! What did you do with that fiddle? Where is it?" Uncle Larry said.

Ray sat back in his chair and looked up at the Optimus Prime poster on his wall. "It's here with me and I—"

"If we can get ten million dollars for it, we split it evenly," Thurston said, cutting Ray off. "If we divide it by five, since there are five of us, we each get two million dollars. Minimum." He gave a fist pump. "Ray, you can share with your mama."

"It's Ray's fiddle," Rochelle said. "Maybe he should get a finder's fee? You want a finder's fee, sugar?"

Ray put them all back on mute. "Wait, wait, everybody. I don't think you understand. I hope I'll be making some pretty good money from my concerts, but I'm not selling my violin."

He turned off the mute.

"**Your** violin?" Ray's mom said, as if he had invented a new language.

"Yeah, I'm not selling my violin."

"That was Mama's violin. It belongs to the family."

"Actually it doesn't. Grandma Nora gave it to me four years ago."

"Boy, ain't nobody got time for this craziness," his mother said.

"Once I get on my feet, though, and start making money, I'm planning on sending what I can to you all, to divide among you," Ray said.

"I say we sell the fiddle right now and split the money evenly. We can even divide by six, so you can have your own share," Thurston said. "That's a minimum of 1.6 million dollars each."

"That's right," Ray's mom said.

"No," Ray said. "I know this came out of nowhere, but the best thing for me to do is—"

"The best thing for you to do is bring that violin back to Mama's house so we can figure out how to sell it. We finally have a chance to get rich and you are about to fuck it up for all of us?"

"Larry, stop," Aunt Rochelle said.

"You know it's true," Uncle Larry told her. "That boy thinks he's all that because he's going to that white school."

Ray took a deep breath. It didn't help. "I'll tell you who I think I am. You never thought twice about that fiddle."

"What did you say, boy?"

"You heard exactly what I said. My violin is not for sale."

"Well lookee here. Somebody finally grew a pair. Why are you doing this? How can you be so selfish?" Uncle Larry asked.

"Is this how I raised you, to only think about yourself?" his mother wanted to know.

Ray couldn't help rolling his eyes. "I'm not thinking about myself. I'm thinking about Grandma and what she wanted. And she wanted me to play PopPop's fiddle."

"You know what, fuck this," Uncle Thurston said. "I'm calling a lawyer. I don't know who you think you are."

"You know what, I tried," Ray told them. "I'm not selling my violin. Good luck with your lawyer. Oh, and thanks for your support."

He ended the call, stared up at his poster of Optimus Prime. "That went much better than I thought it would. Don't you think?"

The next morning, the front page of the **Charlotte Herald** ran the headline "Markham U Student Discovers Strad Violin," and below it: "Estimated at $10 Million."

At 12:01 a.m.—long before papers reached local front doorsteps, mailboxes, and stores—the electronic edition of the **Charlotte Herald** was posted online.

By 12:23 a.m., Ray's phone was buzzing with numbers he didn't recognize. He received messages, emails, and texts from the **New York Times**, the **Wall Street Journal**, BBC News, the **Today** show, **People** magazine, and dozens of other media outlets.

Janice had thought only the **Charlotte Herald** would care. She was wrong: the world woke up to the story of a young Black violin prodigy who played on his grandmother's $10 million Stradivarius.

The circus had begun.

PART 4

Music Making

Chapter 14

Debut
11 Months Ago

On the night of Ray's debut performance as a soloist, everything that could go wrong for his performance did, indeed, go wrong.

As he opened the doors to the Belk Theater at the Blumenthal Performing Arts Center, a blast of warm air poured out. The June day was already muggy; now, at just after noon, the city streets were thick with exhaust and humidity. He'd expected a cool air-conditioned wave to embrace him, and instead it seemed hotter inside than outside. Janice, for whom he'd held the polished aluminum door, looked back at him and grimaced. "I think the AC is broken."

They crossed the foyer as three workmen carrying a stepladder, big aluminum ducts, and other mechanical parts zoomed from the main auditorium to a side door.

Across the lobby, the Belk Theater's doors had been propped open. Distant banging on pipes and the echo of the Bruch Concerto rattled around them, ricocheting off metal and glass. In the auditorium, the stage glowed—the enormous organ pipes at the back gleamed against the cream walls. When they reached the stage, Ray looked back. Rows of seats, tier upon tier of balconies, flung out in front of him. The theater could hold a couple thousand people, easily. He took a breath to steady himself, tightened his grip on the violin case. His hand was already sweaty.

Onstage, several of the musicians and the conductor were practicing the Bruch Concerto no. 1. As Ray and Janice trooped up the stage-left steps, the conductor waved his arms to cut off the orchestra. "Rayquan! Here's the man of the hour," he said, coming toward them, hand extended. "It's such a privilege to meet you. Janice, lovely to see you again." James Meader was a slender older man with salt-and-pepper hair and a seeming inability to look Ray directly in the eyes.

"It's Ray. Please. It's an honor to meet you, Mr. Meader."

Ray shook Mr. Meader's hand, and then the concertmaster's, who came up right behind them. The principal cellist and principal bassist introduced themselves. Ray was nervous and instantly forgot everyone's names. "You're certainly getting a lot of attention," the cellist said.

He ducked his head. "Five minutes of fame, I guess."

"You sure are lucky," the cellist said. "Can I see the violin?"

"We're really excited to have you play for us," Mr. Meader said, sounding less than excited. "But there's one snafu. We need to play the Bruch instead of the Mendelssohn."

"What?" Janice said. "You don't have the music in your library?" Ray was too startled to say anything.

"I'm so sorry. We don't know what happened. We always rent the major concertos."

Janice sighed. "Ray, take a walk with me." They headed backstage, down a corridor lined with music stands. "Can you play it if you need to?"

"I guess. It's just—" He hadn't practiced the Bruch in months.

"You need to learn how to handle this kind of thing—this is the life of a soloist. Bruch's not your favorite, right?" Max Bruch's Violin Concerto no. 1 in G Minor was a lush, romantic nineteenth-century piece with a lot of intricate fingerings, especially in the second movement. Ray'd always thought it was a little melodramatic and overemotional. It also seemed repetitive—which, come to think of it, was going to be a good thing now, since it had been a while since he'd played it. Mendelssohn's tried-and-true, gorgeous Violin Concerto in E Minor was what he'd been prepping for weeks. "I mean, I can play it—"

"Then you'll do it," she said forcefully. "Turn this into your advantage. When this kind of thing happens again, you'll know how to handle it. You'll warm up with the orchestra anyway so that will give you a chance to refamiliarize yourself with the piece."

Ray tuned up, started practicing. Janice, at his elbow, would whisper corrections: **Slower on the second ascending arpeggio. Really milk that fermata.** The heat from the lights in the already-warm auditorium soon had sweat pouring down his face. His shirt stuck limply to his body.

After Ray practiced alone, he practiced again with the orchestra. It was the first time he'd soloed with a professional orchestra, and the difference was astounding. He'd always loved playing with a full orchestra because he could really cut loose. No holding back. The professionalism of the Charlotte musicians made the Bruch enjoyable.

About an hour or so in, after Ray's clothes were actually soaked with sweat, the air-conditioning boomed to life. A few minutes later the air, bless-edly, cooled. Ray's sweat-soaked clothes soon felt icy. He'd definitely have to retune his violin again, but he'd wait til this was over.

After his part of the rehearsal had ended, he and Janice sat in the audience while the orchestra continued to rehearse. He made mental notes about how to adjust his volume by listening to the orchestra play, and Janice gave him further tips.

Around 4:00 p.m., the conductor called a halt, and the musicians began packing up, heading home for dinner before returning for the evening performance. Janice slipped onto the stage. "Mr. Meader, a word?" she said. James Meader closed his musical score on the podium, walked to where she waited on the edge of the stage, not far from Ray. He also stepped over.

"James," she said quietly, "I'm glad Ray was able to handle the Bruch today, but I also need to let you know that your messing up the music is completely unacceptable. You want to be considered a top-notch orchestra in this area but you can't even get the right piece of music? How am I—or anyone else, for that matter—supposed to take you seriously?

"As compensation," she said, "you're going to offer Ray a fifteen percent increase in his performance fee. And I'd think twice before trying this again, if you ever plan on having a soloist of his caliber playing with this orchestra ever again. This is totally on you."

James Meader stared at her, bug-eyed.

"Come on, Ray, let's get some dinner," she said.

Once they were outside, Ray said, "Wow, you really ripped him a new one."

"Let's hope so," she said.

The advantage of debuting in his hometown meant that Ray could run home and change. He could have stayed in the dressing room, but Janice thought this would ease him into performance life a little more smoothly.

He had just moved into a small two-bedroom house near campus—he'd converted the back room into a practice room. It was run-down, but cheap, and the neighbors were far enough away that they wouldn't be disturbed by his practicing.

Tonight, preoccupied with the Bruch, he pulled open the door and stepped on the mail waiting on the mat: a new offer from the cable company, a flyer from a moving company, a letter from the Fraternal Order of Police addressed to the previous tenant, and a slim white business envelope with his name handwritten on it.

Dear Mr. Mcmillian,

We wanted to congratulate you on your newfound success. As you can imagine, we, along with the rest of the world, have heard about your wonderful fortune. Discovering that you have such a rare instrument must be overwhelming. We are certain that you are getting all the support as well as the admiration you have earned.

It has recently come to our attention, after extensive research, that the violin in question actually belongs to our family. They came over from Italy and their name was Marcello. They changed it to Marks. The violin was owned by my great great great grandfather Thomas Marks. Letters to his family in Italy mention the violin. Stories from our family along with the letters from our families genealogist research confirm our ownership. Imagine our surprise at the wonderful news that you have found the violin! You can imagine how excited we all are in anticipation of the return of our family heirloom.

We would like you to make arrangements to return our violin in a timely manner. We will of course reimburse you for your efforts. We look forward to hearing from you soon.

Sincerely,
Andrea Marks

Just another lunatic, he thought—he'd gotten several dozen letters claiming ownership. But this one knew the Marks name; none of the others had. Could this claim be real? Something about this letter felt different. **We would like you to make**

arrangements to return our violin. Was the violin not Ray's after all?

This Andrea Marks must be nuts, no question. And in the meantime he had to perform the Bruch, not the Mendelssohn. And tonight was his debut as a soloist.

He put the letter in a drawer, shrugged off his clothes, went to take a shower. He tried to make words from the Marks letter sluice down the drain: that terrible pronoun, **our**, as in **their** violin. As in **not his** violin.

Lying on his bed, he checked his phone: a dozen or so texts, many from his family. They hadn't patched things up between them after that last disastrous video call, but all the relatives were checking in regularly with him, seemingly polite and benignly interested in his success. He wondered what they were really plotting.

Uncle Thurston: **Go get em boy**

Aunt Joyce: **Sorry I can't be there for opening night! Break a leg!**

His aunt Rochelle called to wish him luck. "Seems like every channel I turn on, there you are," she said. "It's crazy, that's for sure."

Nothing from his mom. He hadn't heard from her at all.

Dressed in his crisp clean Bloomingdale shirt and trousers, carrying his hand-tailored blazer, Ray headed back to the symphony hall, trying very hard not to think about the Marks letter crouching in the kitchen drawer.

A twenty-minute drive back to the auditorium, waiting backstage. Janice said she'd be there, but she hadn't come in yet. The house opened, and even in the depths of the theater Ray could hear the roar of the mob taking their seats. Full crowd. Everybody wanted to see the new kid with his shiny Strad. He wondered how many of them wanted to watch him make an idiot of himself on the stage: he knew he was just a curiosity, something to tell their friends about later. "Yeah, I heard him play. Shitty violinist. Nice instrument, though."

In a few minutes the opening of Rossini's overture to **La Gazza Ladra** wafted into the room. The stage manager knocked on his open door. "Five minutes." Where was Janice? He made his way to the wings behind the stage.

And then the Rossini was over, and the conductor was coming offstage, smiling broadly, extending his hand, and Ray followed Meader as he strutted out onto the stage, into the rolling applause. James Meader acknowledged Ray, who bowed slightly and nodded in the way he'd often seen big soloists do on YouTube. He'd practiced many times in front of a mirror. Did he look as terrified as he felt?

No time to think. He turned to the conductor, gave a nod. The orchestra burst into the Bruch's opening chords and then a ridiculously bright spotlight beamed directly into Ray's eyes. He couldn't see anything except the light: not the conductor, not the audience, and certainly not the music on the stand in front of him.

His solo began in five measures. No time to ask for a lighting adjustment.

This was it. He closed his eyes because there was no point in keeping them open. He was ready. Did he remember the whole thing? He drew his bow, and the first open G of the concerto rang out, long and sonorous, filling the entire auditorium. He could have sworn he heard gasps. Was it bad? No time to think. He was playing blind. The light thrust itself between his eyelids no matter how he tried to avoid it. So he'd just give himself over to the music. Every long note would leap from his fingers.

The flutes drowned him out.

Back off, he told them, and the violin had the power and resonance to overwhelm, so overwhelm them he did. At last he came to the section where the orchestra played without him. He put one hand to his eyebrow to shield his eyes, hoping the lighting guy would notice. The light remained fixed on him.

He tucked his violin back under his jaw, began to play just as a commotion from the back of the auditorium broke his concentration. How could the audience come in so late? Who'd let them in?

The latecomers whispered loudly and climbed over other audience members to fumble for their seats.

A woman's voice, clear and outraged: "Excuse me?"

He would have recognized her voice anywhere. His mother had finally come to one of Ray's performances. Late, and melodramatic, but she was there.

Silence, finally, from the audience. She'd found her seat. At least she was quiet.

At least she'd come during the second movement: the melody batting back and forth between violin and orchestra, flowing smoothly and organically like a fat snake of a river, undulating into the dramatic last movement. He threw himself into it: his mom wouldn't get to hear something lush and beautiful like Mendelssohn or Brahms, but at least she'd hear everything he could pour into the auditorium. Now, at last, she had to listen to him: and he would make it worth her while.

The last movement of the concerto was the most energetic. Ray liked to play it at a moderate tempo, and they'd rehearsed it at a moderate tempo, but now the conductor took it faster than Ray had ever done.

There was nothing more he could do. He was blind, his mother was pissing off the audience, and he was playing the wrong piece of music at the wrong tempo. Awesome. Did Hillary Hahn ever have to deal with this?

Bring it. Just fucking bring it. Stand tall, Grandma Nora had told him: he would stand tall, with the spotlights shining on his face, and his music would pour into all their ears, and they would understand that no matter what anybody threw at him, he was not going away. He was not stooping to their level. The air-conditioning could go off and he could melt. They could toss any piece of crappy music they wanted at him and he would **play**. He would not be ignored or denied or embarrassed ever again: he was a musician, and music had no color.

When his last note rang out, the audience sprang to its feet, applauding.

His first concert performance with his Stradivarius. He extended his left arm, hand firmly grasping the violin's neck, held out the instrument as if he were showcasing his fellow performer: giving it full credit, extending it like a sword in the spotlight. He kept it there a moment. Not just his triumph, but the triumph of his grandmother, and her grandfather before her, here in front of this white audience where few Black people ever played. They had done it together, and together they bowed.

This gesture of holding out and presenting the violin would come to mark the end of all of Ray's performances with his Stradivarius, no matter how small and melodramatic the salute might have seemed. He raised up his glorious violin in an extravagant, intimate gesture; and he did it for himself, and for the unseen ancestors around him; and onlookers must have sensed this, for the applause dynamited in the hall.

Janice met him in the wings, pounding his back. He'd done it. And suddenly he was exhausted. He leaned against the back wall, the dark gray paint chipped in places. The orchestra finished whatever piece they'd played next—he honestly didn't have any idea—and back onstage he went, up into the light and crowd: audience members and reporters waiting to meet him. Waiting, some of them, for his autograph. Surreally, he signed programs.

He was dimly aware of a large bouquet of red and white carnations blundering on the outskirts of the stage; like a battering ram it forced its way forward, and as Ray was signing the program of a tiny blue-haired woman in a sequined blue dress, he realized that his mother was holding the bouquet.

"Rayquan! Come here, honey!" She was looking good in a white summer dress, and the twins hung back behind her.

"Mama!" he launched himself into her arms.

"Stop that," she said. "You want me to drop this? Here, you take it." Her fake nails were a frosty pink.

"Uh—I can't," he said. "I need both arms free."

Janice was suddenly there, taking the flowers, talking to his mother. In the past four years, throughout college, they'd never met. Ray gave the twins a hug—it had been months since he'd seen them, and his sister was definitely taller. They were twelve now, little carbon copies of Mom: good-looking kids. His sister's skirt was too short, and he wondered if his mom had picked it out. His brother was trying to grow a mustache. Both twins seemed tongue-tied.

Later, back in the packed dressing room, his mother cornered him. "I want to see Mama's fiddle."

He had it strapped to his back, as always. He opened it up, handed it to her.

"Is that PopPop's fiddle? You sure? That fiddle was white."

"Yeah I'm sure. That was the rosin. The stuff that PopPop put on the bow."

"That nasty sticky brown stuff you always left all over everywhere?"

He laughed. "Yeah, that's it."

"Ten million, you say?"

He packed the violin away.

"Hope you're gonna share some of that," she said. "The water bill due?"

She rolled her eyes, sighed, and gave him a look.

He reached out, hugged her. "I love you, Mama."

She was stiff in his embrace, but eventually her arms wrapped around him for a moment. It was more than usual: it was enough. It would have to be.

Later, he drove back to his little house. Exhausted

but still on a high, he showered, lay down, and stared at the flowers his mother had given him.

In what seemed like a few moments later the sun was pouring through the window. He pulled up his banking app. A deposit of $2,000 had been made hours earlier. Money from his first performance.

Online, he found a local report about last night's concert and footage of him onstage. He quickly clicked away. It felt weird to see himself like that. But then he couldn't resist, clicked to the end of the video, heard the reporter say, "It looks like he and his Stradivarius have a brilliant career ahead of them."

Ray lay back in bed, closed his eyes. This was really happening.

He called Aunt Rochelle. "Do you use PayPal or Venmo?"

He had to explain what they were and walked her through setting up a Venmo account. "What's this for?" she kept asking.

He transferred $1,200 into her account—$300 for her to keep and $900 to be divided among each of his aunts and uncles. "Tell them there'll be more coming soon."

She tried to object, but he'd already transferred the funds, with another $300 to his mother.

The next morning, all his aunts and uncles texted him, thanking him. **Can't wait to hear you play,**

Uncle Thurston wrote. **You're doing us proud!**
Aunt Joyce said. His mother didn't write.

Four days later he showed his ID to the security
guard at the VIP entrance of the Greensboro
Coliseum. The North Carolina Symphony's warm-
up poured from speakers lining the hallway. He'd
hoped that Janice would come for this performance
as well, but he was on his own.

Just as he was about to go out and introduce
himself, the conductor called for a fifteen-minute
break. This was the time to go onstage, but he hung
back, suddenly shy. What if they didn't know who
he was? Stupid, but he was okay just standing there,
savoring this moment, watching these musicians
congregating in small groups, others heading off to
the restrooms, or for a smoke break outside. The
concertmaster—whom Ray recognized because Ray's
college studio had come to a performance when
the orchestra had played in Charlotte—was heading
his way with a couple of the other violinists.

"Wonder where the wunderkind is," an older
woman—the third chair—was saying.

"Not sure why they're even letting this guy play."

He backed into the curtains that cloaked the
rear wall.

"I don't even think he's played more than one
concert with anybody in his life."

"It's just a PR stunt," the concertmaster told them. "The only reason he's playing is because he has a Strad. You know how people try to get at least one Black person to play with a major group at least a couple times a year? It covers all the bases."

"At least it's not Black History Month. There's no telling what kind of circus music they'd have us playing." Laughter.

They walked down toward the restrooms. He stood in the curtain, face hot, and waited.

Out onstage the oboe played an A: rehearsal was resuming. The concertmaster and his flunkies headed back to the auditorium and he followed a few minutes behind.

After he was introduced to the orchestra, they prepared to rehearse. He tried to summon up enthusiasm but he was suddenly exhausted. He played mechanically, coldly, not investing in the music, barely paying attention. No fiery runs, no subtle dynamic shifts. No passion. Just notes. At the end of the rehearsal Ray thanked the conductor and walked off, headed back to the hotel.

He knew what he had to do. Play or go home. This wouldn't be the last time people talked crap about him. It's how he dealt with them that mattered. He could give back the $5,000 for tonight's performance, or he could play for Grandma Nora. Always work twice as hard: he would fulfill his promise to her.

Another hour and a half later he was back in his dressing room at the symphony hall. Now roses and carnations leaned in vases on the dressing table and on a couple cabinets, with a huge fruit basket dead center, reflected back in the mirror, so it seemed as if there were two of them glowing on the table.

Ray's performance of Mendelssohn's Violin Concerto in E Minor—the piece he'd been slated to perform in Charlotte—was the first piece in the second half of the concert. He and Janice had sat down to determine a handful of pieces that would be in his standard repertoire for the next year or so, as he eased into a soloist's life, building his confidence and prowess with the violin. The Mendelssohn, while widely performed, was also one of his favorites, with lush rich melodies that he could really dive into.

The North Carolina Symphony opened with two measures, and then the first B he played rang through the auditorium. Each note sprang out, the fast passages zoomed by, the violin dancing above the orchestra, them leaping to meet him as he soared on ahead, a wave pouring endlessly up a beach, the foam bubbles kicking in, the stone crabs dancing in the surf, the tide pouring out until he led it, roaring, up the beach again. When he was learning the piece, Janice had told him, "This cadenza tells a story. If you don't like it, tell your own—use every note." Yes, he was Black. Yes, he was inexperienced.

But more than anything else, he loved to play. He loved this music. He loved this violin. He was bigger than all of them.

And then they were into the second movement. Ray's first five notes were at lightning speed—he was playing this movement exceptionally faster than they'd rehearsed. The flutes struggled to keep up. When they did, the entire orchestra leaned in, hyper focused, making sure they stayed with him. Final page. He decided to increase the tempo even more: the surf crept higher, past the beach, onto the dunes, roaring like a tsunami toward houses sleeping under the moon, unaware of what was pounding toward them. The wave built on itself, gathered like a giant feral cat, about to pounce: and then that final chord. He drew it out as long as possible. The water subsided. The village was safe.

Applause washed over him and again he held up his violin for them. He panted, sweat pouring down his face. The conductor extended his hand, nodded slightly, respect and admiration, and a little surprise, very clear on his face. Ray shook the offered hand.

Then he turned to the concertmaster. Leaning over, he said, "Charity work's a bitch, huh? How's that for a PR stunt?"

Chapter 15

Performance

10 Months Ago

The high of Ray's first major orchestral performance lasted until the following morning, when the hotel phone screeched. The dead mechanical voice on the other line intoned, "Good morning this is your automated wake-up call good morning this is your automated wake-up call good morning this—"

"You know," he told Janice twenty minutes later, pulling out the chair across from her and dropping into it, "you really should have offered a class on the life of itinerant musicians. How am I going to do laundry? How do I keep fit and trim if I'm eating all this high-sodium wack-ass restaurant food all the time? It's really quite stressful, you know?"

She peered up at him over the novel she was

reading. "Poor you," she told him. "It's not too late to cancel. Maybe Popeyes is hiring?"

"Love that chicken," he said.

"If you're going to apply, better get going. And cancel Christopher Newport University ASAP because they'll be waiting for you." Since it was summer, Janice had taken several weeks to go with him to some of the festivals and master classes that they'd set up together.

To earn a living as a classical musician meant that either you got a regular paycheck in an orchestra or you traveled around as a soloist or a featured artist, performing with the regular orchestra or at festivals and giving master classes to less-experienced students. Depending on the festival—Interlochen, Bridgehampton, and Aspen were very competitive and highly sought after—he could make bank as a featured artist, and the more fee-based master classes he taught, the better. More to the point, the more he played, the more chances that bigger venues—Powell Hall, Carnegie Hall, or the Chicago Philharmonic— would want him to solo with them.

The obvious way to get your foot in the door was to apply to the festivals, but nobody ever just sent their application in: it was all who you knew. Luckily Janice had been teaching and performing for the past thirty years—many performers she'd worked with now were festival organizers; many of her students went on to set up classes and teaching programs.

Over the past months, she and Ray had reached out to her network and set him up for the summer to play, judge competitions, and start networking. Janice was a powerful force, convincing them that Ray was a talent not to miss while they could get him. Plus everyone in the industry had heard about the Strad, so his summer was already packed. Flying everywhere and being picked up by drivers or town cars took some getting used to. Janice convinced him it was worth it. He was actually saving money.

Coaching younger players and getting paid for it would be a new experience for him, and he looked forward to sharing what he could, especially with students who didn't have the advantages—the nice instruments, the private coaching, the effortless travel to work with a big-name teacher—that wealthy students often possessed.

On one of his rare trips home, he found another white business envelope awaiting him.

Mr. McMillian,

We are getting concerned that we have not heard from you, and that troubles us. Do you require any assistance setting up our violin's return?

Please continue to take excellent care of our family violin until such time that we or our representatives can retrieve it. I know our great

great great grandfather would approve of your playing his violin for a short while longer.

We would prefer not to hire a lawyer, or go to the media, about this. It's a private matter and we want to work it out among ourselves. Please either call or email us at the numbers below at your earliest opportunity.

Sincerely,
Andrea Marks

He tossed the letter in the drawer with three others from the same woman. **Our family violin.** And: **I know our great great great grandfather:** somehow the specificity of the number of **great**s unnerved him—as if she spent fifteen minutes counting, to make sure she got the number right.

After Christopher Newport University, they were off to four other colleges in the next two weeks, and then up to Michigan's Interlochen Music festival, where he taught three master classes, played a recital, listened to some of the finest musicians he'd ever heard, and earned $9,000.

Later that night, his mother texted him. She rarely texted these days, unless, as now, she wanted something.

Mom: **where u**
Ray: **Michigan music festival**
Mom: **How much you make**

He didn't answer but sent more money to her and to Aunt Rochelle for distribution to the family.

The money he was sending did not seem to appease his family. As the summer stretched closer to fall, emails or texts dripped in regularly from one or another of them, asking how he was doing and when his next big payday would be. He wondered if they were coordinating among themselves, as if they were afraid he'd forget them. Little chance of that. He tried to keep a running tally of how much he was sending them—it was well over $10,000, and easily more than half his take-home pay.

In Goldsboro, North Carolina, he judged the solo festival at the Academy of Performing Arts, where local students from the surrounding area performed solos for ratings, later in the afternoon. Besides judging, he would also give a master class to a handful of students. But first he and his fellow judges were assembled in the auditorium. He introduced himself first to Jessica Deitcher from the North Carolina School of the Arts. He'd seen her perform when he'd been in school. She was a self-proclaimed musical prodigy who always played the exact same program year after year.

The other judge, Henry Mason, the conductor from the Wake Forest University Orchestra, was equally taciturn. He was a short, heavyset man with jet-black hair that smelled like shoe polish.

Ray wasn't uncomfortable sitting on a judging

panel with these two. He was clearly just the Token Black, a guy with no talent and no discernment, and absolutely not worthy of listening to. What a pity that he just happened to own one of the most expensive violins in the world.

After each student played, his fellow judges would mutter a few pointers to the students, and scrawl additional comments on a score sheet. Ray always made sure to end with something positive and encouraging, but his fellow judges—who couldn't seem to wait for him to stop talking—seemed to relish in being brutally unkind. Ray wondered if they were in a secret competition to figure out who could reduce the most students to tears.

The master class taking place in a few hours would consist of the players with the highest scores from the day, so Ray kept track of the scoring, just so he would have an idea of who he'd be teaching later. "I swear," Jessica said to Henry, "I don't know what these teachers are doing to these kids. The standards seem to get lower and lower every year."

"This is a waste of my time," Henry agreed. "These kids are very poorly trained." He checked his watch. "Only another hour till lunch. Thank god."

The next student, a Black teenager, maybe fourteen or fifteen years old, came in with his mother. The boy held his violin and the mother carried a portable CD player. The boy set up and started tuning as the mother fiddled with the player.

"Are you kidding me? He doesn't even have an accompanist?" Jessica said, loud enough for the boy to overhear.

"Can we get this over with, please?" Henry said as he stared out the window.

Ray found the boy's name on the roster. "Hey, Bryce. What're you going to play for us today?"

Bryce mumbled, "I'm playing 'My Heart Will Go On' from **Titanic**."

"Excellent," Ray said.

Jessica sighed.

"That's one of my favorite songs," Ray said. "Your accompaniment is recorded?"

"Yeah, is that okay?"

Before either of his fellow judges could respond, Ray leaned forward. "That's just fine. We're looking forward to hearing you. Anytime you're ready."

Bryce's mom hit PLAY.

Next to Ray, Jessica and Henry began writing immediately, not even listening. Ray leaned forward, engaged. Bryce needed a lot of technical work—his fingering was jumbled and the bowing was choppy—but much of the roughness could be smoothed out pretty quickly. The trick was to keep the kid engaged in playing, not let him get defeated.

Two and a half minutes later, Ray applauded and stood to shake Bryce's and his mother's hands.

"I thought you did a bang-up job," Ray said.

"Keep doing what you're doing. You have a great sound and a killer vibrato. Are you working on any other music?"

"Not really. I can play the Concerto in A Minor."

"The Vivaldi?"

"I think so, yeah."

"Fantastic. How would you like to play that in the master class this afternoon?"

"I'd love to." Bryce grinned.

"Great, you're on the list. You can play the Vivaldi. Nice work today. Keep it up."

After they'd gone, Henry said, "If you teach him today, you're taking a spot from someone who deserves it. I'm going to talk to someone about this. This just isn't right."

"What's not right is that you wrote that kid off before you even heard a note," Ray said, keeping his smile plastered on his face, pulling back his shoulders. "Why doesn't he deserve an opportunity to learn?"

"This is absurd. There's no way he's ever going to—" Jessica stopped herself.

"There's no way he's ever going to what?"

"Can we have the next student?" Jessica said loudly.

For the rest of the hour, none of the judges spoke to one another.

The afternoon master class began at one o'clock.

Each student was given a twenty-minute slot for Ray to work with them. All the white girls seemed like clones, playing the same pieces the same way, until Bryce got up to play and Ray perked up. Whispering from the audience seemed particularly loud. "Vivaldi in A Minor, right?" he said to Bryce.

"Yes, sir."

"Good. We have Ms. Lakeland here to accompany you. Have you ever played with an accompanist?"

"No, this is my first time."

"Great, this is pretty exciting. You can start when you're ready."

Bryce raised his violin. The collar of his dark blue polo shirt was askew as he tucked the violin under his jaw. Ms. Lakeland began, and Bryce followed. This was no virtuoso performance: his instrument was poor, like a school rental; his technique was mediocre; his shifting was awkward because his shoulder rest was the cheapest quality and barely held the violin in place. But Bryce continued to play. After the last notes he beamed at Ray and at Ms. Lakeland. "Wow, that was fun."

"I'm glad you had fun playing that," Ray said. "Thanks for sharing your talent with us. Now I'm going to show you a few things that will make your playing even better. Do you mind?"

"Yeah, okay."

They went through the piece together, Ray showing him how his position affected his shifting and tone. He even let Bryce play the Strad. When Ray handed it to him, the audience gasped. Ray was never more than several inches away. By the time Bryce finished, he'd improved noticeably, and the grudging applause seemed genuine.

After the master class ended, Ray spoke to several parents and was taking photos with the students when Sheila Wallace, the festival director, approached him. She was all of five feet three in her taupe heels, with her hair pulled tightly into a bun.

She led him away from the group. "We so enjoyed having you at the festival this year, but there were several complaints about your giving preferential treatment to some of the participants."

"Who were the complaints from?"

"That's not important, but I do want to remind you that—"

Ray had been waiting all day for this moment. He leaned close to her and spoke quickly. "I was brought here to teach. These students are supposed to be here to learn. Most of them weren't receptive to learning anything. They were here to put on a show. The one student who didn't look or play like everyone else got the most out of my session. That's why I'm here. I gave that young man what no one else here was willing to: a chance. I really appreciate you having me at your festival, but, in the future, please don't reach out unless there is a lot more diversity in your clientele. Now if you'll excuse me,

I'd like to speak to that young man's mother before they leave."

Bryce's mother gave him a hug. "Sir, would you mind if I got a picture of you and Bryce?"

"Absolutely, ma'am. I'd be honored."

Bryce's mother took the picture. "He's been reading about you. I can't tell you how excited he was when he heard you were going to be here today."

"May I ask you a question?" he asked Bryce, who nodded. "Do you take lessons?"

Bryce shook his head.

"Unfortunately, no," said his mother. "We just can't afford to—"

"Summertime's hard," Bryce said. "I have to turn in my violin."

"I can't really afford to get him his own yet."

Tears burned behind Ray's eyes. He fumbled in his blazer pocket, pulled out the business cards that he'd had printed up—just his name, email address, and the word **Violinist**. "Can you email me next week? No promises, but I may be able to do something. Keep it between us, please?"

They thanked him, and Ray shook Bryce's hand. "It was my complete honor to meet you. Never stop playing if you love it."

Two weeks later, he called Jacob Fischer, bought a solid, inexpensive violin, and coordinated having it delivered to Bryce Webster of Goldsboro, North Carolina.

Chapter 16

Family Visit
8 Months Ago

Ray's summer of festivals slid to a close. Janice returned to teaching, and Ray was on his own—performing recitals and teaching primarily on college campuses: Johns Hopkins, University of Virginia, University of Maryland, University of Tennessee at Knoxville, and several others.

One damp late-September afternoon, Ray was back in Charlotte for a week between gigs. He was four hours into practicing de Falla's **Spanish Dance** and Saint-Saëns's **Introduction and Rondo Capriccioso**, repeating the second section over and over to really get the flow of the arpeggios—when someone knocked on his front door. The tapping had probably been going on for a while without him hearing it: he practiced in the back of the house, in what once had been a bedroom right off the kitchen, setting his music stand in the center and stacking his sheet music—arranged according to composer, program, and specific musical passages—around the perimeter.

When he heard the knocking, he turned off his phone—he often recorded his playing, so he could play it back and critique himself—tucked the violin into its case, and stowed it in the closet. This was habit by now whenever he was home; but of course he slept with the violin next to his bed every night.

"Hold on, coming!" he shouted, shrugging into a pair of jeans.

A middle-aged white couple stood on the front stoop. They seemed harmless enough—maybe selling something? was it some kind of holiday religious crusade?—so he opened the door.

"Can I help you?"

The woman spoke quickly. "It's so nice to meet you," she was saying with a smile that creased the powder in her face. Her red lipstick was very red, and seemed to have been applied a little too thinly, not quite coating her lips. Her jowls, covered with fine colorless downy hair, shook slightly when she spoke.

"We are so happy to finally meet you in person," said the man behind her, very heartily. He was bald and potbellied and had one hand on the woman's elbow as if he needed to steer her.

"Can I help you?" Ray repeated. "Would you like an autograph?"

"Mr. McMillian, may I call you Rayquan?"

"Who are you? If this is for a booking, you'll need to go through my website, please. Now if you will excuse me—" He started to close the door.

"We're your biggest fans," the woman said quickly, putting out one hand and taking another step forward. "We think you're just the most talented musician playing these days, and we wanted to stop by and meet you for ourselves."

"Music has always been so important to our whole family," the man said, right at her heels. "When we were children, we all learned to play. Play and sing and make music, the language of the gods. That's what our father called it. Language of the gods. It's almost more important to us than food, it really is."

He wanted to close the door, but now they were so close that it felt rude. So he just stood there, like an idiot, and they kept talking.

"Our niece Holly is a wonderful violinist," the woman said. "When we told her we were going to see you, she wanted to come along."

"She really did," the man said, as if Ray had disputed it.

"Does she want lessons?" Ray asked. "Is that why you're here?"

"Oh, she would be floored—floored!—if you'd

be willing to teach her," the man said. "Would you really?"

The woman said, leaning forward, practically inviting herself inside, "I just knew that you were the most generous young man. I just knew it. I could just tell."

"She's been playing since she was this high," the man was saying. "Wonderful musician. Surely not as good as you, of course, but she's very promising. We're really here for her, you understand."

The late-afternoon sky was gray and lowering; a chill wind blew from nowhere. The woman wore a thin pink sweater with little pearl buttons, and shivered delicately. "May we come in?"

Why didn't he just close the door in their faces? Forever after, when Ray replayed the scene, he would ask himself this. In his mind he closed the door and turned the bolt.

The woman took a few steps forward, as if too weak to stand, and Ray found himself backing up a step to avoid her. She tottered past him and into the house, sat down gingerly in the frayed armchair near the front window.

"To think we got this chance to meet you in person. I can't wait to tell Holly," the man said, following the woman and lowering himself onto Ray's threadbare couch. He was wearing a white seersucker suit, despite the raw September day. Weren't seersucker suits only for summer?

He suddenly realized that they were both now inside, sitting in his house. He stared at the open front door accusingly, as if it were the door's fault. "How can I help you? Do you want to set up lessons for your niece? I'm not sure—"

"Oh, she would be thrilled," the man said. "I can't wait to tell her," he told the woman. "But actually," he said to Ray, "we're here more to talk about the violin."

"What about my violin is there to talk about?" Ray said to the man.

"That's just it," the woman said. "It's our violin, actually. That's why we're here."

"Excuse me?" Ray said. "Who are you? I think you should leave."

"Sorry, we should have introduced ourselves," the man said. "What were we thinking? This truly is an honor. You know, we really do feel a kinship with you. Well, actually, our great-great-grandfather—no, one more **great**—owned your great-great-grandfather. I'm Dante, and this is my sister, Andrea. Marks."

Ray felt himself start to tremble, a quiet vibration in his chest and fingertips. He'd never experienced anything like this. The Marks family. **Our family violin.** It couldn't be them, here. It couldn't be.

"Rayquan, we're really dreadfully sorry to have ambushed you like this, but you haven't responded to any of my letters." She shrugged sweetly. Ray wanted to pop off her little pearl buttons. "We knew that if we met face-to-face we could come to an understanding."

It felt like someone had smacked him in the face with a bottle. "I've gotten a bunch of letters from people claiming either that they own my violin or that they'd like to buy it. The violin is mine."

"And we want to thank you for finding it and restoring it." Dante was a big man, with a very black goatee (was it dyed?) that wrapped around his mouth. His voice was somehow thin and nasal, as well as guttural. He chimed in with, "All my life I've heard stories about that violin, how Sherman's men looted and destroyed Summerland—that's what we called our family's home—and how they took everything—all our family jewelry, and the good silver, and, why, they even rolled up the Turkish carpet and carried it away before setting fire to the house. And now to find that your family rescued it, kept it safe all these years—it's a miracle, a real miracle. We're so grateful." He looked properly grateful, but his gentle closed-lipped smile didn't quite light up his eyes.

"Look," Ray said, "nice try, but you need to get out of my house before I call the cops."

He felt his pockets for his phone as Andrea Marks pulled out her phone, scrolled a bit. "Oh, the violin is ours and we will be taking it with us. If you call the cops, they'll tell you the same thing. Not that we need to prove anything to you, but the evidence is all right here." She looked up at him, then back down at her phone. "This is a letter from Edith Marks, wife of Thomas Marks, to her daughter Adeline. It's dated December eighth, 1884."

She cleared her throat. " 'Your father has been gone for close to twenty years now. I try to continue on in this life as best I can, but there is no joy here. The musicians who played last night could not hold a candle to the' "—she hesitated, cleared her throat—" 'to the niggers your father once owned. Do you remember the fiddle player? He must have been bewitched. His playing was one of the few sources of happiness that your father had before his passing. How I wish I could hear him laugh and clap along to the music the niggers played for him before the dark days made their way to Summerland. I wish that fiddle was still here to comfort me.' "

Ray realized after a moment that he was standing in his living room with his mouth open. He couldn't figure out if he was in shock because of the letter the woman read, or because of the ease and comfort in which she let the N-word roll off her tongue.

"Oh, sweet pea," Andrea said gently. "We aren't here in a legal capacity. We're trying to appeal to your sense of decency and humanity. You people are always so decent and kind. We knew that as soon as we could talk to you face-to-face, you'd understand. Our niece will be devastated if she doesn't get to play her great-great-granddaddy's violin."

"You forgot a **great**," Ray said.

"So here's what we're thinking, honey," Andrea said, fiddling with those pearl buttons. "We know you're between concerts right now, and we're prepared to write you a generous check for everything you've done."

"A very generous check," Dante put in.

"That's not going to work," Ray said. "I'm applying to the Tchaikovsky Competition, and I'll need the violin then. If I win, I'll be booked internationally for most of the next year."

"Oh. Well then," Andrea said, clearly rethinking. "When is it?"

"Next summer," Ray said. "Mid-June."

"Mid-June?" Andrea said, incredulous. "That's nine months from now. That's plenty of time. You can get yourself a fine instrument by then."

"You surely want to do the right thing," Dante said as if it were a foregone conclusion. He, too, leaned forward, his belly hanging between his knees. Ray had to fight not to step back. Dante was saying, "Where is it? Can we see it?"

Ray would not risk a glance toward the back room, as if by doing so the violin would waddle in, waving and bowing. "No, you can't," he said. "And the violin really is mine. My grandmother got it from her grandfather. And my grandmother was the most honest person I've ever met. There's no way we stole it from you. Fact is, my grandma told me that her grandpa was half white. So you're my cousins. How about that? No wonder we both love music so much."

Now they were both standing, glaring at him. Dante had crossed his arms above his potbelly.

"I don't give a flying fuck what that old lady said," Andrea snapped. She had gone very pale, and her hands kept twitching at the buttons on her sweater. "You are not our relative. That violin is ours and we want it back."

"Lady, get out of my house." He moved back to the front door, opened it. It hung on its hinges like an open mouth.

She took a step toward him, but not as if to leave. "We will sue you," she said. "We will sue you and your whole family for every penny you made, and will make, if you don't give it back to us. Are you seriously prepared to spend thousands, tens of thousands, maybe a million dollars, to try to keep it? Because we will spend whatever it takes."

Dante said, "Look, Rayquan, there's no way you're gonna win this thing. Save yourself a lot of time and heartache and just give it back." He fumbled in his breast pocket, opened an envelope, leaned forward and showed him a cashier's check. "Look. This is yours. You can surely buy a nice instrument for that. Let's not fight, and let's make it easy on all of us. Now, where's the violin?"

He turned as if to move deeper into the house, as if the conclusion were foregone, as if he were just picking up the golf clubs he'd mislaid the last time he'd been over at Ray's place, after they'd come back from playing the back nine at their country club.

Something cold had lodged in Ray's throat. Did he have his phone on him? Could he call the police? What would the Charlotte police do when a ragged Black man called them over to report two well-dressed white people pleasantly chatting in his living room? They'd tell the police that the violin was theirs, and the police would give it to them.

Suddenly he stood up straight. He threw back his shoulders. He would not stoop to their level. They hated him; they hated what he stood for. They were not ashamed by their past; they reveled in it. But he would not hate them. He would not become them. He would be tall and respectful and he would command them.

"Leave now," he said, and he didn't recognize his own voice, as if it came from a deep part of his diaphragm, lower than he'd ever heard himself before. "If you leave right now, I won't press charges." He willed them outside.

To his immense surprise, Andrea wobbled out, and her brother behind her. Ray pressed his back against the wall to avoid touching them.

On the doorstep, Dante turned. "Think about it, Rayquan. You can't afford this. You won't win. Do the right thing and give us back the violin." He held out the check again, between two fingers, as if its edges could cut him.

Ray closed the door, gently but firmly, and locked it.

It took all his effort to just keep standing, leaning his forehead against the cool wall. Could this be legitimate? Could they really sue him for his violin? Had Grandma Nora been totally honest about the violin? Was it really stolen?

He fumbled open his phone.

"Hello, Aunt Rochelle? I need your help. Everything is just going nuts."

"Whoa, slow down. What's—"

"They just came in talking crazy! They said he stole it!"

"Who said that? What are you talking about?"

"This brother and sister—the Markses—said the violin is theirs. She read some crazy letter from her great-great-great-great-grandpa or something saying that PopPop stole his violin and—"

"What? PopPop stole his fiddle? Slow down."

He tried taking a breath, then repeated what had happened. "They came to actually take the violin! Just walk in and take it! Now they're threatening to sue me. I don't know what to do. I think I need to find a lawyer. Which is why I called you."

"You need to talk to somebody about this," Rochelle said. "My firm doesn't do a lot of these kinds of personal property cases—we're mostly personal injury. But let me get you a number. Someone who'll make this all go away for you."

"How can I afford a lawyer? I don't need this."

"It's over for now. Don't worry about it. We'll find you a good attorney and we can get this sorted out. Give me a couple hours and I'll call you right back."

After they hung up, Ray tried to play, but ended up just sitting there, as afternoon folded into night. Just cradling the violin and trying to imagine life without it.

Chapter 17

Birdland
8 Months Ago

The offices of Mendel, Panofsky & Levine sprawled over the entire forty-seventh floor of a solid-glass skyscraper just below Central Park. One of the top art-and-entertainment law firms in the country, there was no art hung on the walls: just blank expanses of white, and glass windows with killer views of downtown Manhattan. The receptionist—pale blond hair, wearing a white sheath and white pumps—ushered him into the conference room. Five minutes later, Kim Wach was shaking his hand. She was short, barely over five feet tall, her silver hair cut short in a bob, wearing a beautifully tailored dark blue suit, dark pumps, and a crisp white shirt. She came at him smiling, hand extended. He had the impression that she should be wearing glasses. Her teeth were very square and white.

It was two weeks after the Markses' visit, and he was back in New York, booked to play a recital of Biber's **Rosary** Sonatas at Hunter College. Aunt Rochelle had found him several attorneys to advise him on the Marks situation, and one of them was in New York, so he made an appointment for a consultation.

Now he repeated how Andrea Marks had written him several letters and then how she and her brother, Dante, had appeared on his doorstep. As he spoke he felt almost physically ill. Andrea Marks's chicken wattles swayed gently in front of him, and the slightly distasteful way Dante held out the $200,000 check refused to leave his mind.

"So let me get this straight," Kim said when he'd finished. "These two people show up unannounced, read you some letter off their phone, and tell you they're taking a ten-million-dollar Stradivarius? And you're **worried** about this?"

He shrugged. "I'm just telling you what happened. Do you think there's a case?"

"On the face of it, not much," Kim said. "Stolen property cases are pretty clear. The Markses will have a lot to prove." She thought a moment, then ticked off on her fingers, "First, they're going to have to prove that the violin was actually theirs. It's easy enough to say that they **had** a violin, and you

have a violin—but they need to prove that their family's violin is actually yours."

Ray nodded. "Okay, I can see that."

"Assuming they can prove that the violin is the same one, they're going to have to show that it was actually stolen. Did they supply any kind of proof that your ancestor actually stole it?"

Ray shook his head. "My grandma always said that PopPop was given the violin. That the slave owner—who might actually have been PopPop's father—gave it to him."

"The claim seems very far-fetched, honestly. I bet that's why they went to you directly instead of hiring a lawyer. They hoped they could intimidate you."

"So you're saying I shouldn't worry?"

"If it were me, I wouldn't stay awake worrying about it. They might try filing a claim against you, just so you'll settle with them instead of going to court, but I don't think you're there yet."

"Settle?" Ray said. "How? They don't want money. They want the violin."

Kim shrugged. "We don't know what they want. Maybe they want you to sell the violin and split the proceeds."

"Well, that's not happening."

"That's why I told you not to worry. You're not there yet. At this point, I would ignore them. Don't answer their letters."

"And I sure as hell am not inviting them over for a cookout," Ray said.

She laughed. "Yeah, I doubt they'd bring wine."

"So you think I'm okay."

"From what you've told me and what I've seen, that's what I think. Plus think of the optics—slaveholder's family making a claim against their former slave's family. It doesn't get more bizarre than that. Especially in today's world, where reparation claims are being made by the descendants of enslaved people against the slaveholder.

"Go play your violin and stop worrying." She looked over at the violin. "Can I see it?"

"Of course," he said, opening the case. She duly admired the violin, and he closed the case again, as if not wanting the violin to hear the uproar it had caused.

With a lighter heart, he left the white office and the stunning view and returned to the grimy New York City streets. A yellow-and-red gyro stand on the corner of Fifty-Third and Sixth smelled amazing, so he ordered falafel and rice with extra white sauce and headed uptown to Hunter College.

He had to admit that he liked being out in the world by himself, playing whatever music he felt like playing. He liked jazz clubs and now sought out more of them to keep playing, even when he didn't have classical performances scheduled. He loved the showmanship of the French-Italian jazz violinist Stéphane Grappelli—the loose easy elegance of how the Frenchman would throw out a musical sentence and pick it up again, always seeming cool and utterly engaged. Ray wanted to do that: to bring enjoyment to anyone who would listen.

When he'd first tried his hand at jazz, it was a mess. Like most classically trained musicians who relied on strict training, he was most comfortable following the road map that a composer laid out. Ray would pour himself onto the classical route, which had clear signposts and a yellow line down one side. With jazz, there were no signs; the GPS just said, "Go." Jazz charts provided a simple melody he was just supposed to riff from—he wanted to read every note, lock in on each finger pattern. How would he even begin? He started by listening to the opening melody of a song, then adding a few notes in the same key, then changing the key for a while, then somehow, miraculously, returning to the original key, all while making it seem effortless. This took a lot of practice. When he thought he had it, he had to think again. It was fun, challenging, and exercised new muscles in his playing.

Janice would not have been pleased: Ray was moving up in the world of violin performance and, in her view, he had to make his mark in the classical realm, not dabble in jazz. Doing both would mean that Ray had too many irons in the fire.

Nonetheless, in New York City, he always made time for the legendary Birdland Jazz Club, sitting in on the jazz combos—when they'd let him. The first few times were a bit rough—he'd played a jazzy, bluesy minor Dorian mode instead of a major Mixolydian mode—but he hadn't cared, and the other musicians hadn't, either. Each session improved, and soon he was jamming with several regular standards under his belt.

New York City, Ray found, had many drawbacks: crowds; an often-confusing and daunting subway system; high prices for food, lodging, travel. But all the drawbacks were worth it, Ray decided as he looked out at Birdland's audience, glowing in the red candleholders' dim light: New York City women were, without question, beautiful. Check out the left wall—the tawny-haired woman with the tight dress running her fingers suggestively around her wineglass, or the high-cheekboned Black woman sitting with a pimply faced guy at a table two back from the stage. And those were just the people who leaped out at him—there were dozens more, here and out on the street.

Pity that none of them seemed to want to get to know him beyond buying him a drink between sets, or asking for his autograph outside the stage door, or having a conversation that started with anything other than "How long have you been playing?" The attractive women who seemed to take an interest in him were mostly in the look-but-don't-touch category, and things almost always stopped at looking: Was it them? Was it him? It was probably him.

He looked the part, but had zero game.

He'd been a loner all his life, with few close friends, and that hadn't changed much. He'd imagined the musician's life would be filled with gorgeous women. This might have been the case for huge rock-and-roll stars, but thus far, in Ray's classical and limited jazz experience, he was more likely to trip over a microphone cord than to have an admiring fan invite him for a drink and slip him her room key.

So after the Birdland performance, when a tall slender woman with an extravagant hairdo approached him, he thought he'd struck gold. She wasn't really his type: Her hair, curled elaborately, was clipped with barrettes and dazzled with glitter. Her makeup, too, overwhelmed. It looked like someone had loaded a box of crayons into a gun and fired it onto her face. And oh, her outfit! Her white pants looked spray-painted onto her very long, slender legs, and her crop top—about a size and a half too small—was the brightest shade of electric blue that had ever been manufactured. In her yellow-and-white high heels, she towered over him.

But she was smiling at him—really smiling. He could see her back molars. She was seriously into him.

He didn't even register what she was saying until she touched his arm. "Hey, Ray Ray! You look so good! You look just like your uncle."

Uncle? Now he was totally confused. "Um, hey. Whattup. How you doing?" It took him a minute to realize that she wasn't into him, after all—she was into his uncle. Figured.

"Oh, I'm all right. I was visiting my cousin in Newark and I just caught the train over to see you." She cradled her oversize suede handbag, rocking it back and forth. It was big enough to hold a small rottweiler. "Your uncle said you was playing here tonight. Did I miss it?"

Finally it clicked: this was Uncle Thurston's girlfriend, LeShawnah. He'd only met her once in person, although she'd been equally resplendent then. "Oh, that's nice," he said. "Sorry you missed the show. How's Uncle Thurston?"

"He's good," she said. "You want to grab a drink, catch up?"

He eyed the door. "That would be awesome but I've got to get back to the hotel. Early flight tomorrow."

"Oh," she said, clearly disappointed. "The thing is, Thurston had told me to come see you since I was so close. I have a little favor to ask."

Ray waited.

"Thurston said I should ask you for a small loan."

Ray bit his lip. "Oh, wow. I really don't have any

money to spare. I'm pretty much tapped out. Did he tell you that most of my money goes to him and my other aunts and uncles? And my mom, of course."

"Yeah, he said you was gonna say something like that. Ray Ray, we know you got money. You know I'm just like your auntie. You gonna hook me up?"

"Look, I'll talk to Uncle Thurston, okay? That's the best I can do. I hope you have a safe trip back to Newark. I'm sorry you came all this way for nothing." Before he could change his mind—but how could he change his mind, since he didn't have the money?—he slipped away and left the club, zipping down into the subway stop on the corner.

Next day, when Uncle Thurston texted him: **Got a sec?**, Ray didn't reply. Over the next couple days, Uncle Thurston tried calling and texting, and Ray ignored them all. He was furious that Uncle Thurston would put him in such a position with his girlfriend. He still kept sending his uncle—and the rest of Grandma Nora's children—money when he could.

Outside the family drama, with the Markses' bizarre claim seemingly laid to rest, Ray was able to concentrate on music, and began booking performances for early the following year. In February—Black History Month—he was booked solid, back to back every night. He wasn't good enough to play with certain orchestras during the other eleven months of the year, but would shine in February, where he would play composers like Samuel Coleridge-Taylor and William Grant Still. Still's **Suite for Violin and Piano** was always a crowd-pleaser. Ray was honored to bring music composed by people who looked like him to people who knew nothing about him. The most challenging thing about February was finding a pianist who could actually play the parts. It wasn't regular old Beethoven; it was Beethoven on steroids.

As he continued to schedule, a pattern began to emerge that became clear during a call with the Delaware Valley Philharmonic's music director. They were going over an upcoming program. "We were hoping you'd be really excited about our Gershwin review," the woman said.

"I'm sorry, but why would I be excited about a Gershwin review?" Ray asked, genuinely curious. Perhaps they were just enamored with Gershwin, had a unique arrangement or a new adaptation.

"Well, it's Gershwin."

"Okay . . . and?"

"We just thought that you would really like to play Gershwin."

"And why would you think that?" Ray was trying to remember if he'd ever given an interview or ever said anything to anyone about his secret Gershwinian fixation—nothing came to mind. So he'd asked the question to honestly see if she could jog his memory.

"I just have a hunch that you'd really like to play that kind of music."

"Oh," he said, finally understanding. "Right."

He realized that, in the director's eyes, he would play Gershwin because he was Black and because Black people were not sophisticated enough to master—nor in many instances even capable of mastering—the "real" European composers like Beethoven, Bach, Corelli, Mozart, Mendelssohn, or Brahms. Only people who look like dead white composers would actually interpret them effectively.

A week after the Gershwin call, Ray was setting up, via video call, a performance for the Big Rock Symphony Orchestra in Big Rock, South Carolina. "We're quite excited for you to do a performance of some of your music," said a pudgy spokesperson for the board of directors.

"I'm sorry, I don't quite understand," Ray said, fearing that he did, indeed, understand.

"We are trying to promote diversity throughout our organization—we believe that Big Rock leads South Carolina in being inclusive—so that's why we feel it would be best if we feature someone like you, who plays music he is familiar with."

"Oh," Ray said. "I get it."

"So glad we're on the same page," the man said.

The skin under his jaw jiggled. Ray couldn't see his neck.

"That shit is dope, yo," he told them. "I fucks with some Mendelssohn. Imma rock that shit. Playin' them arpeggios an shit is my jam. Can't wait to come. Anything but that Gershwin shit, yo. Every time I turn around somebody be tryin' to get me to play that fake Black shit."

Sufficiently stunned, the board of directors of the Big Rock Symphony knew not what to say nor where to look; their eyes were all downcast, as if deeply engrossed by something slightly below the camera.

"Now that I have your attention," Ray went on, "I need you to understand something. I am a musician. I happen to be Black. That doesn't mean that I am any less skilled or knowledgeable than any musician of any other race. You might want to invest in some diversity training, rather than paying for a soloist. Get your act together and I may come and play for you one day. Best of luck." He left the meeting.

In the meantime, his following was growing. A group at Northwestern University had developed a web page dedicated to him that had more than six hundred thousand hits. The comments ranged from "You are an inspiration" to "If you ever come to Oklahoma, look me up." Ray had become a minor celebrity, especially within college circles—he was the cool classical guy who could play jazz and everything else.

Only eight months until the Tchaikovsky Competition, and Ray was determined not only to apply but to win. The competition, founded in the 1950s and held every four years, was a cross between the Olympics and **American Idol**: it streamed live to more than five million classical music diehards who could rabidly vote for their favorite in various phases of the contest. Classical luminaries—a mix of musicians and conductors—served as judges.

Although the competition should be judged just on musical prowess—and, certainly, a wrong note or a flubbed phrase could destroy a contestant's chances—Ray realized soon enough that, like all the other broadcast competitions, popularity with the audience could be a huge factor. Lucas Debargue, for instance, the self-taught pianist with brilliant blue eyes, was discovered while working in a grocery store: he won both judges' and audiences' hearts with flare and showmanship.

Ray wanted to win but felt like he had several hurdles to overcome if he got accepted to compete. First, he had to really up his game as a musician, and he was working on that: he and Janice were lining up expert teachers—specialists in Bach, Mozart, Tchaikovsky, and the like—to drill him on the repertoire. Second, he was an American in a competition dominated by Asians and Europeans.

Nothing he could do about that. Last, he worried that he was only a performer and not much of a showman: he wanted the audience not to just connect with his music but to remember him, to really engage with him on a deeper level. Lucas Debargue had been able to do this, and Ray thought he should, as well.

Showmanship wasn't Janice's forte—like Ray, she was a performer. So he started asking the various concertmasters, musicians, and conductors he played with for suggestions on who he could talk to about upping his showmanship game. Fellow musicians gave him names, so he internet-stalked them. One name kept reappearing: Kristoff van Cordan.

Kristoff was a German musical prodigy who had played concerts all over Europe by the time he was six. After several years as first violin in the Berlin Philharmonic (considered one of the very best orchestras in the world), he burned out and turned to conducting, eventually landing a position as conductor for the Netherlands Philharmonic Orchestra for three years. He was known as a showman, spending hours focusing on production value—bright colored lights, elaborate costumes, and staging. Audiences loved him. He made the music dramatic, compelling, interesting, and fun.

Back in August Ray had filled out the Tchaikovsky Competition's multiple forms, sent documentation, photographs, recommendation letters, lists of repertoire, performance schedules, and a video performance: all to prove his worthiness. Now, the last week in September, as he was checking his email right before he headed out to play a recital at Georgetown University, a new email awaited him from the directorate of the competition.

Dear Mr. Rayquan McMillian, We are pleased to inform you that . . .

That's all Ray needed to read—he was in! Euphoria made his head swim.

He called Janice, who offered to reach out to specific teachers and help coordinate his lessons with them. In the meantime he'd make sure all of his performing repertoire would be the same musical pieces he'd be playing in the competition, so each performance would also serve as a means of practicing in front of an audience.

Now he needed to up his showmanship. As soon as his plane touched down at Reagan National Airport, Ray emailed Kristoff—what did he have to lose?

Chapter 18

Demands

7 Months Ago

Two weeks later, Ray was playing at the filled-to-capacity Joseph Meyerhoff Symphony Hall, the audience buzzing about the phenom with the Strad. The first half of the recital was Brahms and Mozart. He played Brahms's Sonata no. 3 in D Minor so passionately that he almost turned to his local accompanist to beg her to give him more support from the piano. She was a good pianist but had a very hard time keeping up with him.

Then he dove into the Mozart. The first movement was smooth and flawless, building to the second movement. The pianist was doing her best to anticipate his rubatos, but Ray kept cranking up the emotion to new heights. The third movement took off like a racehorse, Ray pushing the pianist. The notes flew by, and this time she didn't disappoint, building to a final ritard into the last two measures that left them all breathless. The audience roared its approval.

At the end of the recital, when Ray had apparently signed every program, a short balding man in his midseventies approached them. He wore a stained navy blazer with a red carnation in the lapel.

"Hi," Ray said automatically. "Thank you for coming. Hope you enjoyed the show."

"You need much work," the man told him in a heavy German accent.

"Excuse me?"

"I believe you heard me. You people are good at a lot of things, but not this. I may be able to fix you, but it depends on how well you listen."

"What did you just say? Who the hell are you?"

"I am Kristoff van Cordan," said the man.

"But I—I haven't hired you yet."

"I know. I live not far from here and wanted to watch you before I agreed to provide you with coaching. You are extremely rough, but I will agree to do this for three months. Then we will see what we will see."

Kristoff, quite clearly, was a bigoted ass. But Ray had dealt with people like that all his life—Uncle Roger and the wedding-ensemble debacle being one of the most memorable. It was just something you did as a Black person: you learned to overlook the insults in order to get what was more important to you. And right now the Tchaikovsky Competition was more important. Kristoff was a grade A musician, a grade A showman, and a grade F human being. Ray could live with the compromise.

They went to a local coffee shop to hash out the details of Kristoff's tutelage. Kristoff had very large, very light blue eyes that he would blink slowly at Ray, as if disbelieving or disapproving of everything Ray said. They agreed to try a month and see how the situation developed.

That evening, after Ray left Kristoff and returned to his hotel, Uncle Larry emailed.

Hello Ray. I hope you are well. I'm sorry I missed your performance with the symphony here. I'm sure it was fantastic. I'm writing to thank you again for the money you've been sending. Really nice of you. Can you give me a shout? It's important.

When Ray called, Uncle Larry picked up on the first ring. After they chatted for a few minutes, Larry's voice got serious. "So the reason I wanted to talk to you is that a really great opportunity—really great—just dropped into my lap. I got a tip on a bunch of high-end restaurant fixtures going dirt cheap. It's what I've been waiting for. It'll mean I can finally open my own place."

"That's great," Ray said warily.

"So I wondered . . . with all the money you're making these days, if I could get a little loan? Just to cover the costs."

"Oh, wow, Uncle Larry—"

"It'd really help me out."

"I don't have any more money," Ray said. "Every gig I get, I divide and send to all of you. I don't have anything saved up."

"Yeah I figured," Larry said easily. "But you know, you can get a loan on my mama's fiddle. I checked with the bank. They'll use it as collateral."

"I don't know about—"

"It's really easy. I already talked to a bank and I can set everything up from here. You just have to go in and sign a couple documents."

A pause. "How much do you need?"

"Twenty thousand."

Another pause. Was Ray even hearing him right? "That's a lot of money."

"I can pay it back within the year. Easy. This restaurant is a sure thing."

"Can I think about it?"

"Yeah. Sure. Of course. But the restaurant equipment won't be around too long. I'd really need to get an answer from you by tomorrow."

But tomorrow, Kristoff pushed Uncle Larry's cheap restaurant equipment out of Ray's mind. Before rehearsing again with the Baltimore Philharmonic—

Ray had two more performances left—Kristoff met Ray in his dressing room. It was a tiny cubicle barely large enough to turn around in. A narrow counter with a lighted mirror took up all of one wall, and the other walls were gray corduroy. When Kristoff sat next to him, Ray felt as if four people glared at each other in the tiny space: Ray and Kristoff and their reflections, all sitting side by side by side.

"The first thing you need," Kristoff told him, "is a signature. Something nice, something small, that will get your audience on your side."

"Like what?" Ray said, mystified. "I play for them. That's what they're here for."

"I would not expect you to understand. These subtleties are lost on people like you."

This was going to be fun, Ray thought. Only the first day, and the first words out of Kristoff's mouth were stupid and racist—but the racism didn't seem intentional. Kristoff was just deeply ignorant and impossibly clueless.

"What do you have in mind?" Ray asked.

"Your people are known for their jungle rhythms, no? We carefully choose the first piece you are to play, you come onstage, and you dance the first few minutes."

Ray was speechless. "Are you nuts? I can't do that."

"I would not have expected you could," Kristoff said. "Not dance, but something like dance. A nod to your African ancestry. You need something to make your own."

A nod to Ray's African ancestry? Seriously?

"Well, there's the bow I do at the end," Ray said. "When I hold out the violin."

"That comes too late. Can you start the performance by giving the audience something? A flower, perhaps? To a pretty girl? You're a handsome man. Let's make the audience love you before you play a note."

So that night, when Ray appeared, he bowed like he always did, shook the conductor's hand, shook the concertmaster's hand, and then marched off the stage, down into the audience. He handed a long-stemmed pink rose to an older woman in her sixties.

She blushed. The crowd exploded.

Then, when he played the Brahms, he sensed immediately the difference: he was connecting with them more viscerally; they were rooting for him in a way that was beyond the music but also because of the music.

For the next month he would put up with Kristoff's oblivious racism—Ray could learn from him. The five million eyeballs watching the livestreaming Tchaikovsky Competition awaited.

Back at the hotel, he had three texts, two missed calls, and two emails from Uncle Larry.

"Sorry to keep bugging you, but I really need

an answer," Uncle Larry said. "They're holding the equipment for me, and I need to get that loan signed."

"Uncle Larry, I can't," Ray finally said. "I wish I could. But I can't risk losing my violin. I have a bunch of gigs coming up and I can try sending you more money then, okay?"

Larry's voice was soft and deflated. "The equipment will be gone by then."

"I'm sure there'll be another shot, and at that point we both will have saved more. Okay?"

Larry disconnected the line without responding.

Over the next few weeks, Kristoff took apart Ray's performance. He didn't focus on the music, which Ray found difficult to understand. For Kristoff, music was a show. He drilled into each section of Ray's repertoire, telling him to stand in one place at the beginning of a piece's movement, with a yellow light on him; and then, for the second movement, to glide to the other side of the conductor, under a blue light: think of each musical element as a stage play. As the mood of the piece changes, so too does the lighting, your expression, your posture.

They would arrive early to the concert hall, have elaborate discussions with the concertmaster and the lighting team: "No! The lens for the blue is too small for the Mendelssohn! We need something twice this big!" or "The left light bar only! Only! Are you deaf?"

Working with Kristoff was a lesson not only in lighting design and showmanship but in rudeness and bigotry.

In the meantime, Ray's rejection of his uncle's get-rich-quick scheme didn't seem to dampen Uncle Larry's restaurant enthusiasm: a week later, he found the perfect spot for a late-night dinner club, and would Ray cosign that loan? Every day or two, an email or text pinged on his phone from someone in his family. Uncle Thurston had a new girlfriend with expensive tastes and they were really hoping to go to Bali for a vacation this August; Aunt Joyce's husband had decided to buy a shower-door company that was going cheap—everyone needs shower doors, don't they? Thankfully his mother texted the least of any of them, and only when she didn't receive the money she'd expected. She kept a careful eye on his schedule, so if a payment didn't come into her account within twenty-four hours of his previous performance, sure enough, his phone would chime: **You forget about us?**

He gave what he could, but it wasn't enough. He wondered if it would ever be enough. Of all his family, he looked forward to hearing only from Aunt Rochelle: she never asked for money and was always enthusiastic, asking how he was doing. She, at least, was on his side.

At the same time it seemed, too, that the Marks family had disappeared—Kim Wach wrote them a vicious letter telling them to leave her client alone—but one afternoon Kim called. "When did you last check your email?"

"Uh, I dunno," he said. "Yesterday? Why, what's going on?"

"They've lawyered up," she told him.

The air was suddenly too thin to breathe; he tried to take a breath, and then take another, but nothing would enter his lungs. "What do you mean?"

"The Marks family hired a lawyer. Check your email."

Dear Ms. Wach,

I am writing on behalf of my clients Andrea and Dante Marks pursuant to the violin presently in possession of your client Mr. Rayquan McMillian.

Please be advised that Mr. and Ms. Marks, brother and sister, are direct descendants and statutory heirs of Thomas and Lobelia Marks, of Summerland Manor, Milledgeville, Georgia. The Marks (originally Marcello; see immigration documents, Attachment A) family arrived from Piacenza, Italy, in or about 1793. In their possession was one "violino di cremona," or "violin from the city of Cremona" (see Inventory of Summerland Manor, 1806, Attachment B). This violin was the cherished possession of Thomas Marks and went missing sometime during or after December 1864. The Marks family has diligently sought its repossession ever since.

Mr. McMillian has clearly indicated in media interviews (Attachments C and D) that his ancestor Leon Marks was at one time property of the Marks family and that the violin has remained within his family's possession since Leon Marks either obtained or was granted freedom.

Therefore, please be advised that it is my client's contention, pursuant to well-established case law most recently upheld in **Reif v. Nagy,** 175 A.D.3d 107 (2017), as follows:

- The Marks family's original ownership of the violin is undisputed;

- Leon Marks unlawfully obtained possession of the violin;

- Because the initial transfer of the violin was involuntary, all subsequent transfers of the violin, i.e., to Mr. McMillian, are null and void; and

- Thomas and Lobelia Marks remain the true owners of the violin.

The Marks family is not unsympathetic to Mr. McMillian's situation, however, and is willing to settle at an agreed-upon sum if I hear from you within the next ten (10) days.

If I do not hear from you within the time frame set forth above, please be advised that my clients have authorized me to file suit in the relevant jurisdiction, as necessary.

Sincerely,
Albert Bonavincenzo

He called Kim back. "They're not going away," he said.

"It doesn't seem so," she agreed. "They're willing to spend serious money to keep this going. I have to warn you that this is going to get expensive."

"How expensive?"

"Not sure yet. But our firm will ask for a thirty-thousand-dollar retainer if they file suit."

Thirty thousand dollars, Ray thought. How could he come up with $30,000? As he was trying make his mouth work and respond to her, Kim went on, "There's one piece in the letter that sticks out to me. The violin 'went missing sometime during or after December 1864.' That feels very precise, doesn't it? This was around when the Emancipation Proclamation was being issued. That was in 1863, and the Thirteenth Amendment was ratified at the end of 1865. But I'd think if the violin went missing, and if they'd 'diligently sought its repossession,' they'd have included some kind of documentation that shows this, wouldn't they?"

"So you think there's hope for me?"

"Again, too early to tell. Stolen-art cases can get messy."

"Okay," he said, not sure he understood. "What's next?"

"If you agree, I'll write this lawyer a letter asking for more information. Let's see what we can uncover. Let's see if we can buy you some time before they file a lawsuit. If they file in North Carolina, we'll need to obtain cocounsel down there, and that will be even more expensive for you."

He closed his eyes. Somehow it was easier to not see the world right then. "What should I do in the meantime?"

"Talk to your family," she said. "See if you can get any further information on the violin's history."

"Wait a minute," he said, slowly. His tongue suddenly felt thick in his mouth, as if it were difficult to speak around. "Hold on a sec. There might be something."

"What do you mean?"

"Back when I was in high school, I found something up in my grandma's attic." He flashed back to that enormous attic and his systematic search: buried in boxes under one of the eaves, a yellow dresser with round shiny green draw handles, like eyes. "There was an envelope that had the name Leon Marks written on it. I took it downstairs and gave it to my grandma. I thought she'd want it."

"What happened to it?"

"No idea."

"Well, this is great news. Documentation might make the Markses go away forever," Kim said.

That night, Ray called Aunt Joyce. He seemed to remember that she was the keeper of family documents and that his mom had called her the family historian. When she answered, he said, "I don't want to bug you too much, but I need a favor."

Canned TV laughter roared in the background and then grew muted. She must have turned down the volume. "Is everything okay? What do you need?"

"I'm trying to track down any letters or any documents about PopPop and the fiddle. Do you have anything?"

"I don't think so," she said slowly. "I have Mama's and Daddy's birth certificates and some letters and papers, I think. I don't think I have anything about PopPop. I can look, though. What do you need it for?"

"It's really important. Anything you can find will help me. I think I saw an envelope when I was in Grandma's attic—I gave it to her and didn't see it again. It had the name Leon Marks written on it."

"Oh, okay. I'll look. Is everything okay?"

"These crazy people are threatening to sue me for the violin. They're saying that PopPop stole it from their family. And that it really belongs to them."

"What? You have got to be kidding me."

"Yeah, so I need any type of documentation that proves it belongs to us."

"Wait. You're telling me the slave owners' family are saying that PopPop stole the violin from them?"

"Uh, yeah. That's what I'm saying."

"That is totally fucked up," Aunt Joyce said firmly. "Typical crazy white folks. I'll see what I can dig up. Mama used to keep a bunch of old papers in boxes. I haven't even opened them since she passed. I'll find you something."

A few minutes later Ray hung up, feeling optimistic for the first time in days. His family, as defective and maladjusted as they were, was behind him. He was not alone.

His mood continued to improve throughout that day and the next, so the following afternoon, when Kristoff told him he needed "a costume," Ray just went with it.

"A costume? Like what, a clown?" By now he could keep a completely straight face, so Kristoff never knew he was kidding—he just thought Ray was stupid, and Ray found that to be even funnier.

"No, not a clown." Kristoff sniffed. "I would not imagine that you would understand this. But you need people to look at you more."

"They're already looking at me."

"A cape," Kristoff said. "Black on the outside, and dark red velvet inside. Very dramatic."

"Yeah, for Dracula, maybe," Ray said. "Or for somebody who's ninety. Not for me, though."

They spent the next few days going around and around with costuming possibilities before deciding on black sequins for the tuxedo lapel and a colored tuxedo shirt instead of a white one. (Kristoff had tried to put Ray in ruffles, but that was seriously not happening.)

"You'd look good in brighter colors," Kristoff said. Was it a compliment? "How about your wearing a red tuxedo shirt?"

"If I were playing **Carmen** and I was the bull, maybe," Ray said.

"Yellow then. Yellow would set off your skin color nicely."

Ray tried on a yellow tuxedo shirt, decided he looked like a pineapple.

Eventually they settled on Ray's suggestion of a pale pink to match the rose that he now handed to an audience member each night before the performance. Kristoff thought the color was simply to match the rose. In truth, Ray's choice of color was a nod to Grandma Nora's housecoat, a private moment that only he appreciated: it was as if he were performing with her every night.

Kristoff's staginess was paying off. The crowds were huge; most of the shows were selling out. Despite the crazy Marks family and his own family's general greediness, everything seemed to be getting better and better.

And then he flew to Baton Rouge.

Chapter 19

Baton Rouge
6 Months Ago

In mid-November he was booked to play a recital at Louisiana State University. He flew in and was enjoying the drive in his rented Toyota on a late-autumn afternoon, down a lazy southern highway. He blasted Eric B. & Rakim on high. He had an hour before he had to be there, and the GPS showed him only twenty minutes away. It was a Sunday evening and the roads were pretty empty.

He pulled off the highway and onto a divided road lined with fast-food restaurants and big-box stores. A mile on, the GPS alerted him that in five hundred feet he would need to make a left turn. He was in the right lane. Checking his mirrors, Ray put on his signal and turned left.

A few minutes after, he noticed a police car

behind him and began the universal prayer that all
drivers intone when a police officer follows them:
Please let him pass me, please let it not be me.
He wasn't speeding. He was wearing a seat belt. He
waited.

Blue lights flickered behind him. Ray's pulse
quickened. It's always nerve-racking to be pulled
over by police, he told himself. But he knew it was
more than that: he was a Black man in the Deep
South driving a nice car. He'd seen too many news
reports of Black men having awful encounters with
police. **No way,** he thought. **I haven't done anything wrong.**

Plus he had a $10 million Strad sitting on the floor
of the passenger seat. He was a big-time performer
now. He'd explain everything calmly and be on his
way. He pulled into the parking lot of a boarded-up
convenience store. The sun was beginning to set.
Hopefully this wouldn't take too long. Maybe it
was just a taillight. The police car sat behind him,
lights flashing. No sign of the officer yet. He turned
off the Eric B. & Rakim, put both hands clearly
visible on the steering wheel.

The police car door opened. One booted foot
touched the ground.

"Step outside your vehicle." The guy was using a
bullhorn. "You. Step. Out. Of. The. Vehicle. Now.
Are you deaf? Do it now!"

Ray's heart was hammering. He got out of the car,

both hands in the air. Yeah, sure, white cops beat Black guys up, or shot them. But he was a college grad on his way to a classical music performance. That kind of thing couldn't happen to him. He'd just stay calm and do whatever the cop asked him to do. Sweat slid cold down his back.

"Turn around and keep your hands up."

Ray turned around, kept his hands up. Every movement was slow, deliberate, as if in a vat of engine oil.

Boots crunched closer. The snout of a gun wavered into view. Had the guy actually drawn his gun? On Ray?

"Get down on the ground. On your knees."

Ray's heart threatened to pound out of his chest. The asphalt pebbles dug into his knees as he slowly lowered himself. He wanted to speak but couldn't.

"Show me your ID."

"It's in my wallet. I'm going to reach into my back pocket and pull it out." He moved his right hand to his rear pocket. The wallet wasn't there. Damn—it was in the center console. "It's in my car, Officer. In the middle. Between the seats."

"Stay where you are. You make one move and I'll blow your fuckin' head off." The cop looked to be in his late forties, a meaty blond man with a reddened face, scraggly goatee, and receding hair barely visible beneath his deputy's hat. His gut hung over a wide black belt. When he bent through the front door, his shirt rode up, revealing a white back covered in coarse hair. He stood up, holding Ray's wallet. He pulled out the driver's license, stared at it, put it back. The name on his badge: **E. Bocquet**.

Officer Bocquet looked at the front passenger seat. "Well, well, well. What do we have here?" He reached for the violin case.

"No, that's my—"

"Shut the fuck up!" Bocquet pointed his gun at Ray's forehead. Ray bit the inside of his cheek. The muzzle of the gun was the blackest color ever. The metal around it gleamed with an oily sheen. He'd never been this close to a gun before.

Officer Bocquet pulled the case out of the car, fumbling and dropping it on the ground. Reflexively Ray lunged forward. "Officer, please, that's a very expensive—"

The gun came back up into his face. "Keep your mouth shut. Stand up. Hands behind your back."

Ray stood. A hand pressed between his shoulder blades, and then a jingle, and the cool metal of handcuffs embraced his wrists, rattled shut.

"Wait, what—what did I do?"

"Didn't I tell you to shut up?" He slammed Ray's head against the hood of the car.

Ray struggled to keep his balance, his left leg stepping back onto the man's foot.

"Now I got you for assaulting an officer."

"I didn't do anything—I'm sorry, I didn't mean

to step on you. I need to get to LSU—I'm doing a performance there at—"

"The only place you are going is to the county lockup, boy. Stolen property and assaulting an officer." Officer Bocquet turned him around. The officer's blond goatee, in need of trimming, glistened with sweat.

"Wait, Officer, you need to call LSU, my name is—"

"You have the right to remain silent. Anything you say can and will be used against you in a court of law. . . ."

Where was his violin? He thought suddenly of Grandma Nora, felt unaccountably that he was failing her. Would he live to see the morning? He closed his eyes, opened them. Tried to take a breath, but his lungs couldn't grab air. Of course he'd live to see tomorrow—of course he would. He'd done everything right. He hadn't broken any laws. He was being polite and respectful. This was nothing more than a stupid misunderstanding. With a phone call, it would all be sorted out.

"Officer, can you please just call LSU's music department?"

"Watch your head, boy."

Ray was in the back seat. The violin was in the passenger seat. Where were his car keys? "Officer, please. What did I do?"

"Do me a favor and shut up."

"But I've got to get to LSU. I'm supposed to be playing a recital there and—"

Officer Bocquet slammed on the brakes, throwing Ray forward. Ray bashed his nose on the back of the passenger seat.

"Oops, you should have buckled up. Last warning."

Ray's eyes stung with pain. Blood slid down his face, dripped off his chin. His pants were spattered. With his hands behind his back, he couldn't wipe at it. He rubbed at the blood with his shoulder, but that didn't help. How could he play now?

He said nothing further. Eventually the blood stopped flowing, caking his chin.

Fifteen minutes later they pulled up in front of a brick-fronted police station. Inside, Bocquet, carrying the violin case, said to the clerk, "Book this one for an illegal lane change and assaulting an officer."

The violin disappeared into a back room.

"Hey, I'm supposed to get a phone call." Ray's phone was still in the rental. Nobody knew where he was. Another cop grabbed him by the elbow, took him into a back room with file cabinets, paper everywhere, and some desks and desk chairs. On the walls were wanted posters. The floor was a grimy yellow.

"Give me your right hand," the man said. He was short, with a shaved head and muscles that bulged beneath his shirt. His thin moustache made him look like former military.

"Could someone please tell me what's going on? Am I being arrested?"

"You got it, genius." The officer took Ray's hand and rolled each finger in ink, pressed each tip onto cardboard.

"Why am I being arrested? Is there someone I can talk to? Am I supposed to get a phone call?"

"Shut up and give me your other hand."

"My name is Ray McMillian and—"

"I don't care if you're Ray Charles. Shut up."

Mustache walked him to a holding cell that smelled like pee and cleaning solvent. Where was the violin? He turned to look for it, but a hand between his shoulder blades pushed him through the doorway. On the bench sat an older white man in a tattered tank top. The ripe aroma of at least four types of liquor bathed the air.

"I'm late for a recital at LSU—look, I just need to call LSU's music department and they'll straighten all this out."

Mustache had already strolled off.

"Ha, yeah, that's all it takes," his cellmate said. "If a cop says you did it, you did it. May as well settle in."

"Oh my god. I can't believe this." Ray sat down as far away from the stench as he could. But he realized he wasn't much better—the entire front of his shirt was covered in blood and sweat. His violin could be anywhere right now. Where had they taken it? He tried to remember the details of the insurance policy. How could he live with himself if something happened to it?

Five hours later, near midnight, he was allowed to make a call from the police station's phone. Janice's was the only number he knew by heart.

She answered on the first ring. LSU had called Kristoff, who'd eventually called her.

At least he was safe, she told him. It would all be okay. She'd make some calls, wake up the president of LSU if need be. Sit tight.

Around two in the morning, Mustache came for Ray. By then his cellmate had taken over almost the whole bench and was snoring and drooling inches from Ray's leg. Ray stood up.

"Well, boy, guess you have some friends somewhere." He led Ray back, more gently now, to the front desk, where two people were waiting for him: an overweight woman in khakis and a sagging pink blouse, and a young heavyset kid with bad acne and a worse haircut. Pink Blouse ran to him as soon as he appeared. "Mr. McMillian, I'm Monica DeLongue, I'm the dean of music at LSU, and I can't begin to tell you how sorry I am—"

"I need my violin," Ray told her. "They took it from me."

The violin reappeared. He examined it carefully. It seemed fine.

He didn't look back as he left.

Professor DeLongue led him to her Audi, the student following behind. They'd drop the student off to pick up Ray's car, but she'd take Ray right now to his hotel so he could get cleaned up and get some rest. His clothes and car would be there in no time. She couldn't stop apologizing. He barely spoke, just hugged the violin case tightly.

Suddenly he was exhausted—he felt as if the blood had stopped moving in his veins. Officer E. Bocquet—all those cops—had treated him like he'd murdered the Pope. Why did it keep happening?

He knew the answer, of course.

Later, after the check-in and the shower and the delivery of his suitcase and the throwing away of the clothes he'd been wearing and the wrapping of himself in the thick white terrycloth of the Best Western's bathrobe, he called Janice again.

After reassuring her that he was fine, and thanking her profusely for helping free him, he told her what he wanted to happen next.

Later that morning, at 11:00 a.m., Ray entered the conference room of the Best Western in West Baton Rouge Parish. Janice had flown in earlier and now sat in the front row. There were a dozen or so people in the room, and flashbulbs were going off as he threaded his way to the podium, unfolded the paper he'd printed out an hour ago, and leaned into the microphone.

"Good morning, ladies and gentlemen. I would like to begin by offering my sincerest apologies to everyone who expected to see me at last night's recital. I never made it to the recital hall at LSU. While I was on my way, I was pulled over by Sergeant Ezra Bocquet of the Baton Rouge Police Department. That's **B-O-C-Q-U-E-T, E-Z-R-A**. He made me get out of my car and get on my knees with his gun pointed at my head because I made an illegal lane change. I was demeaned, demoralized, and treated like a criminal as I was taken to jail in handcuffs because I changed lanes. The people of Baton Rouge are some of the luckiest people on Earth to have policing like this. I accept full responsibility for signaling and making a left turn from a right lane. I truly hope that you good people of this city let your police department know how you feel about it as well. Questions?"

The room erupted.

Ray hadn't realized, but Kristoff had come after all. He hadn't even reached out to Ray ahead of time. Now he leaned against the back wall, expressionless.

"Are you saying the police department is racist?" one reporter asked.

"I'm not saying anything of the kind," Ray said.

"Have you faced racial discrimination before?" asked another.

"Constantly," Ray said.

"Did you provoke the officer in any way?"

"No," Ray said.

"Do you feel you are owed an apology?" "What will you do now?" "Do you have any plans to return to Baton Rouge?"

Ray answered the last question: "I can say with all certainty that I will never return to the city of Baton Rouge under any circumstances."

Twenty minutes later, he thanked the reporters for coming and left. Janice met him outside.

"Well?" he asked her.

"You were wonderful."

Kristoff strolled up as they were getting into a town car. "You certainly messed this up. You should have been apologetic to all the people that paid to see your Stradivarius. This is going to take some serious damage control."

Janice opened her mouth to speak, but Ray held up his hand. He leaned forward and looked up at Kristoff, who was about to get into the passenger seat. "Kristoff," he said, "you're a joke. You are a complete and total joke. How I've managed to tolerate you as long as I have is a miracle. I'll pay for the rest of this month and a one-way plane ticket back to DC. In other words, your sorry wack ass is fired, bro."

Kristoff said nothing for a moment, his mouth working. "You can't fire me, you arrogant son of a bitch." He pointed at Ray. "You'll never make it as a soloist. You can't play your way out of a paper bag. That violin is the only reason you are even in my presence."

"You're right, Kristoff. Never mind about the plane ticket. Let's go."

As they drove off, he and Janice burst into laughter.

"You know what?" Ray said. "That really felt good. Today is a new day. I think I just became a man."

"Welcome to manhood, kid," Janice told him.

"And my first job as a man is to apologize to you."

"You have nothing to—"

"Yes I do. I'm sorry. I was trying to figure out how to be a better showman to have a leg up for the Tchaikovsky Competition, and I thought I needed someone like Kristoff to teach me. I think all I learned is that I just have to trust my gut and do what I do, and that means play."

"For the record," Janice answered, "I think it was smart of you to want to stretch your wings. I'll help you find other teachers, people who I think will be a better fit than Kristoff."

The media story lasted for several days, and interviews continued to pour in as an investigation of the Baton Rouge Police Department followed. Months ago Ray had been a curiosity—a Black kid with a priceless instrument. Now the media was interested in him because he was becoming a seasoned, strong performer who was regularly headlining sold-out shows across the East Coast, whose career was on the verge of taking off. It was no longer just the Strad, either—it was Ray himself who drew them. He was handsome and well spoken; the media loved him. When he performed, the energy thrummed through him, so bright that he thought sometimes he would burn himself out with excitement.

And then the next shoe dropped—this one in another email, labeled "Urgent," from Aunt Rochelle, who had never asked him for money.

Ray, I'm sorry to be the one to tell you this but my crazy brothers and sisters are officially suing you for mama's violin. They're worried about the other lawsuit and they think you'll lose the violin so they want to get it first. When you get an official letter from a law firm that's what it's about. I want no part in it. I'm sorry this is happening sugar. Good luck with your performances.

Love, Rochelle

PART 5

Starstruck

Chapter 20

Nicole
6 Months Ago

The day after Ray and Janice returned from Baton Rouge, she told him, "I'm going to see what kind of favors I can call in." He'd thought she'd already called in every favor she could, to get him into festivals and master classes, but apparently her connections ran deeper. They didn't discuss it, but he thought she was shocked by his spending the night in jail—perhaps it reminded her that Black people struggled not only in the music world but in America as a whole.

A few days later, Janice reached out while he was practicing. "Hi, do me a favor and put your violin down."

"Why? Is something wrong?" His pulse immediately started hammering in his temples.

"Have you put the violin down?"

"Hold on a sec." He put the violin down. "Yes. It's down. What's wrong?"

"Do you have anything booked yet for December third?"

"Jeez, you scared me." He had a master class at Ohio State University in Columbus.

"You're going to need to cancel that."

"Why? What's going on?"

"I just got a confirmation that on December thirteenth you'll be soloing with the Chicago Symphony Orchestra. Riccardo Muti."

Ray had clearly misheard. The Chicago Symphony Orchestra was, arguably, the top orchestra in the world—it was certainly in the top five. Riccardo Muti held two directorships: one in Chicago and one in Italy. He was perhaps the best-known conductor in America. A multiple Grammy winner, he also promoted diversity in every program he developed.

If this was affirmative action, if Ray was getting ahead only because he was Black, then he'd take it: this was the opportunity of a lifetime. Possibly of several lifetimes. "How the hell did you do that?"

"Charm and wit, my dear. And a whole lot of promises we gotta keep. This is gonna be fun."

A month before the Chicago Symphony performance, Ray would be playing an afternoon recital at Carnegie Hall. Janice tamped down his expectations: it wasn't an evening performance, and it was one of the smaller auditoriums, and there probably wouldn't be a lot of people in the audience. But it was still Carnegie Hall—one of the most famous concert venues in the world.

But two days before Carnegie Hall, Ray had been booked to play with the Erie Philharmonic. Janice charitably called it an "aspirational orchestra." He took a late flight, and the orchestra's town car deposited him at the auditorium just in time to catch the run-through of Tchaikovsky's **Marche Slave**. The orchestra had clean technique and seemed very well prepared.

He was used to the drill now: he met with the orchestra, ran through the rehearsal, did his solo with the Tchaikovsky Concerto.

Halfway through the second movement, the conductor stopped—as he'd done several times already and as was typical in these rehearsals. "Okay, violas," he said, "this isn't working. We need more finesse in your melodic line here. It's very choppy."

On the first stand in the viola section, a young woman with auburn hair and wide-set hazel eyes was nodding almost before the conductor got the words out. "You're absolutely right," she said, turning around to the violas behind her. "We need to imitate what Mr. McMillian's doing. Play it in the upper part of the bow." She demonstrated, the phrase pouring out beautifully, elegantly.

"That's exactly right," the conductor said. Ray agreed.

The rehearsal continued, Ray finishing his solo, then they took a break and he met individual orchestra members, all of whom seemed elderly, many of whom wanted to see his violin.

And then he found himself in front of the second-chair viola, the young woman who'd spoken up earlier. Her left arm had a single eighth-note tattoo right above her wrist. She had a seriously athletic body, too. "You destroyed that Tchaikovsky," she told him. "I don't think I've ever heard it played that fast."

"You liked that?" He had trouble meeting her eyes. He didn't know why.

"I certainly did. Nice work."

"Thanks. I'm Ray."

"Uh, kind of figured. I'm Nicole. I'm in the—"

"Viola section. Yeah, I noticed you. I mean, I saw you there." Ray McMillian, suave ladies' man.

"Well, I noticed you, too. Kinda rare to have a cute violinist around here."

He had never actually played with someone his own age—someone attractive, of the opposite sex. Someone who was, in many ways, his equal. His mind started spinning, and he was unable to rein it back. Why did she have to live in Erie, Pennsylvania, of all places? What was her name again? Natalie? Natasha? Should he give her his card—was that too pretentious? He suddenly started getting visions of taking her out to dinner, going for long walks on a beach, holding hands. Did Erie have a beach? Wasn't it near a lake?

"So what do you do around here?" he asked.

She looked him up and down. "Uh—I'm doing it. I play music."

Mercifully, the conductor, Kevin Fiore, called the orchestra back to continue rehearsal. Ray was done for the night, which fortunately meant he was done making a complete idiot of himself. "What's your name?"

"I'm Nicole, remember? I told you a couple seconds ago?"

"Right, right. My bad."

"I'll see you tomorrow. Get some rest. You look like you could use it."

Ray went back to the hotel in a daze. The performance would go fine, he thought. That Nicole, though. Damn. Not only was she pretty, but she played well, and she thought he was cute. Ray was beside himself. College had been a single-minded pursuit of music, and although he'd gone out a few times with a few girls, he'd always been more focused on playing than being in a relationship. It didn't help, either, that all the women at school had been white and that they had somehow seemed off-bounds to him. And after graduation, of course, he'd been swept up in the whirlwind of the Strad.

Now he couldn't get the image of that young woman's hazel eyes and eighth-note tattoo out of his head.

Later, at the Shea Center for Performing Arts, he warmed up in his dressing room. The yellow walls seemed to shine in approval as the sounds of the Tchaikovsky Concerto bounced off them. He was ready. Tonight's performance wasn't for the thousand patrons that came to hear him. It wasn't just another warm-up for Chicago. It was for Nicole. He shook his head. How could a forty-five-second conversation make him feel this way? When Glinka's **Ruslan and Ludmilla** overture began, he headed up to the stage, lurking in the wings for a glimpse of her: a delicate gold chain around an elegant neck, below a dark red French braid.

When he finally came onstage, he did everything he could to avoid looking at Nicole, but she caught his eye anyway, lifted one pencil-thin eyebrow. He nodded imperceptibly, an upward tilt of his chin, and focused on the conductor, the shaking of hands, the brief bow. For a moment he thought of giving her the pink rose (why was he such an idiot? he should have brought two!) but instead scurried offstage, handing the rose to a twelve-year-old girl sitting in the third row.

The night's Tchaikovsky Concerto bloomed full of energy, and he followed it with the Massenet encore. He was playing so easily, so comfortably, that he dared to let his head turn to the first stand in the viola section. Nicole was smiling as she played and looking at him.

And then he lost his place. Couldn't remember at all what came next. He'd been playing from memory and had not bothered to even bring out his music.

Janice, as usual, had been right: all the recitals and concerts under his belt kept him from panicking now. He felt the conductor's glare and picked up at the next phrase.

After the curtain call, while the players were mingling, he searched for Nicole but didn't see her. He looked for her backstage, lingered in the dressing room, thinking she'd find him. The conductor came in, shook his hand, led him to the back door and a town car outside, where two dozen people were waiting for him to autograph their programs. "Glad I got to hear you today," one elderly man told him. "You're going somewhere. I'll be able to say I knew you when."

Nicole wasn't outside, though. Where had she gone so quickly? He hadn't given her his card, and now it was too late to go back inside. He signed every program, waiting for her to appear. He could email Kevin Fiore about her, he supposed, but that seemed too intense. Maybe she was listed on the orchestra's website and he could track her down through social media? Would that make him look like a creep? Besides, he reminded himself, she lived in Erie, Pennsylvania—who knew when he'd be back. Long-distance relationships never worked. An itinerant musician on his way up the musical ladder didn't have time for a relationship, anyway. What was he thinking? He had to get ahold of himself. Relationship? He didn't even know her last name. Why was he thinking about a relationship?

Enough. He would put the eighth note and the auburn hair behind him. Goodbye, Erie, Pennsylvania. Good riddance.

Back in New York, he always stayed at the same hotel—the Saint Jacques—where Janice had booked them when they'd flown in to have the violin authenticated. Despite his first experience there, it was familiar. He'd requested it from Carnegie Hall, and luckily it was on their list.

After checking into his room—which went off without a hitch, queen-size bed and a view of midtown—Ray showered and curled up in bed. He couldn't fall asleep right away, brooding about the girl back in Erie. Nicole. Why hadn't he gotten her last name?

He needed to focus. Carnegie Hall. This was his big chance and he couldn't mess it up. Time to leave Erie, Pennsylvania, behind.

Ray got out of bed, attached the practice mute to the violin, and played for the next hour and a half. He must have practiced the same up-bow staccato run in the de Falla for forty minutes. The constant repetition soothed him and he fell asleep, thinking only passingly of Nicole.

The next day, Ray arrived at Carnegie Hall three hours before showtime. He took a moment to look around at all the splendor that surrounded him: the gilt, the crystal chandeliers, the famous stage. Backstage, his feet walked where the feet of some of the greatest musicians—Jascha Heifetz, Yehudi Menuhin, Gil Shaham, Itzhak Perlman—once walked. He introduced himself to his accompanist, an older woman named Grace who did not seem particularly happy to be there. Normally during a recital, the soloist calls the shots—setting tempos, figuring out timing, and so forth. Grace, however, knew better than Ray. She made it a point to let him know how many big-name performers she had accompanied. Ray thought better of asking her what the soloists were like to work with. Instead, he just smiled and told her, "This movement needs to go faster. I appreciate that you're holding true to the set tempo, but I'll be playing it much faster. If that's going to be an issue, we can see about find-ing another accompanist for this piece. I'd much rather have you play with me, of course. I can't wait to add my name to your distinguished list."

Grace relented, and the rest of the rehearsal went more smoothly.

An hour later, Carnegie Hall began to come to

life. Soon the 250-plus-seat auditorium was nearly full; the New York music scene was eager to learn just who this Ray McMillian was. Tickets had sold out shortly after Ray's performance was announced.

Claude Gilliam, the executive artistic director, introduced him.

The moment came. The crowd rustled expectantly, and Ray walked onto the stage, bowed. Applause. Handed out the pink rose to an elderly woman halfway up the right aisle. More applause.

De Falla's **Spanish Dance** was energetic but also languid and sensual, with a deep romantic passion. The music was originally part of an opera in which a Gypsy girl—for an instant, as he visualized the music in his head, the Gypsy girl reminded him of someone: Nicole—fell in love with a man above her social class. Ray had played this piece several times for his grandmother, and she'd loved it. Now it felt like a fitting tribute to her, but also to the violin. His pizzicati were forceful and bold, passionate and rich. His nerves fell away, and the rich acoustics of the room took over, thundering around him. Seemingly moments after he'd raised his violin to begin, he was taking his bow, holding out the violin for its own adoration.

On to the encore: Massenet's "Méditation" from **Thaïs**. Perhaps standard encore fare, but Ray loved this piece, a lyrical gem that starts off with nostalgic yearning, plummets to insecure agony, and then triumphs with peace and joy. He poured himself into the song's desperation, its dark misery, its sun-lit final passages. Too soon, the last harmonic rang out and he kept his bow on the string until the final echoes blurred away. The audience was silent. He lowered the violin.

The audience rose to its feet.

He had done it. He shook Grace's hand.

The crowd came up onstage to meet him, con-gratulate him. It was one of those moments that he honestly couldn't believe was happening. Finally, just before 7:00 p.m., he slipped out the rear door onto Seventh Avenue. A huge crowd waited for him, and he signed programs.

"Not bad for your first time, cutie," said a familiar voice. Nicole, her dark auburn hair loose around her face.

He couldn't help himself: he grinned. He could feel himself lighting up. "Hey," he said. At first he tried to sound casual, but he quickly just gave in. "What are you doing here?"

"I figured it would be stupid of me not to wit-ness Ray McMillian's Carnegie Hall debut. I expect to be telling my grandkids about this. You were incredible, by the way. The way you played de Falla was insanely good. The spiccatos on your arpeggios were really impressive. I don't think I ever saw your bow leave the string. I honestly don't know how you did it."

"I really appreciate that," he said. Many people had complimented him on his arpeggios, but none of them was gorgeous or made his heart hammer in his rib cage the way she was doing. He liked it. A lot. The moment stretched. What was he doing? Why was he so terrible at talking to this woman? She was violin-shaped, right? So why was this so hard? "Are, um, you staying in town?"

"I got this sick deal," she said enthusiastically. "Amtrak is so expensive, but I figured out a way from New Rochelle that's, like, half the price. It doesn't leave till nine thirty, though. That gives me time for dinner. I've already seen the show."

"Yeah, I saw it, too," he said. "No, wait, I was there." **Smooth, Ray.** "Glad you liked it." He looked for something to lean against, but it was just him, this woman, and the sidewalk.

"Look," she said, "you want to grab dinner?"

"Me?" he said. Sometimes he honestly could not believe the stupidity that poured from his mouth. "Um, yeah. I'd love to."

"Good," she said, and confidently headed a few blocks over to a tiny Indian place, on the second floor of a building, above a wig shop. It was cheap, and some of the best food Ray had ever had in his life.

They talked about music and orchestras, about her growing up in a middle-class family that didn't quite understand her love of music but didn't actively try to thwart it the way Ray's mother had.

"The worst thing is that it always felt like there was that one kid who always played better than me, you know?" she said. "The one who always got the private lessons and always got the solo at the end-of-year concert?"

"I know exactly what you mean. For me it was this one guy. Mark Jennings. Racist asshole, but he had seriously fast fingers," Ray said. He hadn't thought about Mark Jennings for years. Did he still play?

"Kyle Rasmussen. I hated Kyle Rasmussen." She laughed.

Her experiences mirrored his own. She could understand him. She was a performer, like him. She was a musician. Even without her figure and her great laugh, he would have picked her out of a crowd. How could he make this into something more than just dinner, more than just—maybe— a one-nighter? He toyed with his vegetable tikka masala and wondered if he could move to Erie. It had an airport, right? He didn't need to be in Charlotte.

But it didn't seem like she'd be in Erie for long, anyway. Erie was her first gig out of college, but she was ambitious. She'd been doing some substitute viola work in the Cleveland Orchestra, for starters, and that might lead to something more permanent. She really liked Cleveland—it had a vibrant musical scene. "I've also been volunteering there," she confided, as if it were a secret.

"Doing what?"

"There's a program where we play music in soup kitchens. First you serve the guests, and then you serenade them. It's pretty awesome. I'm way better with the viola than I am with the mashed potatoes, though."

"Wow," he said. "That sounds really awesome. I'd love to do that sometime."

"You should come," she said casually.

"I'd love to," he said. "We just have to figure out when. Let me know when you're there and I'll rearrange my schedule." Yes! He had an excuse to see her again. He'd impress her with how well he could ladle out the gravy to pour over her mashed potatoes.

Two hours flew by. Nicole glanced at her watch. "Oh, man, I've got to get going. The Metro-North train leaves in, like, twenty-five minutes."

There is a desolation like none other when a beautiful woman sitting across from you has to catch a train in twenty-five minutes. This was a far cry from eating alone in a hotel restaurant or picking up some fast-food takeout and gulping it down in his room. "Isn't there a later train?"

"Not for the twenty-three dollars I found," she said. She pulled out her phone, thumbed through a couple apps. "There's another at six thirty-two a.m. for thirty-two dollars, but I don't want to sit in the Poughkeepsie train station for three hours."

"Oh," he said.

"Plus where would I hang out for the night?" she said.

The energy pulsed between them.

"I guess I could take the train at twelve thirty-two," she said. "It costs forty-six dollars, though."

"I think you should. We can grab a nightcap."

"Yeah, sure. If you want."

They headed back to the Saint Jacques. Mike held the door for them. "How did the concert go?"

"Pretty good," Ray said.

Nicole said, "He was terrific."

"Sorry I missed it."

"Thanks, Mike," Ray said.

Nicole smiled, grabbed Ray's arm, and led him to the hotel bar.

Three beers later, it was almost 11:45 p.m. and time for Nicole to head to Grand Central for the train. "I wish you didn't have to go," he said.

"I don't," she said. Before he could mess up the situation, she leaned over the table, bumping into one of the beer glasses, and kissed him.

The kiss lasted a very long moment.

He stood, reflexively swinging the violin case

onto his back. "How would you feel if I asked you to come up to my room?" he said.

"I would feel like what took you so long to ask me," she said.

He led her to the elevator.

At 5:00 a.m. he woke up to an empty bed, turned on the light. Her clothes were gone. He sat up, pressed his back against the padded ivory headboard. He knew it was too good to be true. She was gone. There's no way a pretty girl like that could be interested in him.

He dove back under the covers just as the room door clicked open. She was back, carrying two coffee cups and a brown paper bag.

"Hey, uh, morning," Ray said.

Nicole sat the items down and kissed Ray. He worried about morning breath, but she didn't seem to mind. "Morning, handsome. Sorry to wake you up. I was hoping I'd be back before you noticed I was gone."

"I—"

"Thought I ditched you, right?" She grinned. "Not a chance. I picked up an early breakfast for us. I have **got** to catch my train at six thirty-two, though."

"Oh."

"I hope you like egg on an everything bagel."

"Oh man. You actually remembered that?"

"Of course I did. Here, this one's yours." She handed him one of the coffee cups. It was cool. Orange juice. He'd told her last night that he didn't drink coffee.

He took a swig, kissed her again. "How much time do we have?"

"I need to leave here in forty-five minutes, tops."

"Plenty of time," he said.

Later that morning, hours after she'd left and he'd fallen back asleep, his phone rang. A 212 number he didn't recognize. "Mr. McMillian? I'm David Talbot. I'm an executive producer at **60 Minutes**. I was in the audience yesterday afternoon at Carnegie Hall," the man went on. "I was very impressed. That was a sold-out crowd. Not bad for a Thursday-afternoon recital."

"I guess they liked my playing."

"Which is why I'm calling. I wonder if you'd be interested in having us do a piece about you? I've been following your career for a while, and yesterday's performance wasn't an anomaly. We'd like to explore that on the show."

"So," Ray said. Took a breath and said again, "So. You want me to be on **60 Minutes**." He tried to wrap his head around the conversation.

"Yes, we do."

Chapter 21

60 Minutes

5 Months Ago

Twenty minutes until he performed with the Chicago Symphony Orchestra. The Chicago Symphony Orchestra! He thought his head might explode. He'd asked Anderson Cooper (Anderson Cooper! When he met Anderson Cooper and Anderson Cooper had introduced himself as "Anderson Cooper," Ray thought he was having an out-of-body experience) and the cameramen to give him a minute. Now it was just him, and the violin, and the panic that was threatening to overwhelm him.

Nicole had flown in and was sitting with Janice in the audience. Although he'd seen Nicole only twice since their time together in New York (once he'd flown to Erie, and the other time she'd met him after a performance in Ann Arbor), they were talking and texting regularly. When he'd called to tell her that David Talbot of **60 Minutes** told him the show wanted to film him performing with the legendary Riccardo Muti, Nicole had screamed and actually dropped her phone. When she'd picked it up and called him back, she'd asked him, "Can I do anything? I know you must have everything set up, but if I can help, I'd love to. Want me to pick up your dry cleaning?"

"I want you to come," he'd said impulsively. "I can get you a ticket. Will you? It would really mean a lot to me."

Both Janice and Nicole had asked if he wanted them backstage, and he said of course they should sit in the audience, he got free tickets and someone should use them. Now he regretted it. Should he ask them to come back now? No, of course not. There wasn't time.

More than anything else, he worried about letting everyone down—Nicole, Anderson Cooper, Grandma Nora. And especially Janice, who had called in every favor she had to get him here. What if his bow slipped? What if his harmonics didn't sound? Or worse, what if his coordination was just off? What if he just played notes instead of making music?

He called Janice.

"Is everything all right? Where are you?" Her

words were a little hard to hear above the hum of the crowd.

"Everything's fine," he said, unconvinced.

"It's Ray," he heard Janice saying, probably to Nicole.

"I just called to say thanks for everything." And then, unprompted, "I'm just so worried about screwing up tonight."

The silence stretched. Had she hung up? But then her voice poured over the line, golden. "What was that piece you auditioned with?"

"What are you talking about?"

"When you were in high school. You played Vivaldi, right?"

"Why are you bringing that up now?"

"Because I think you should remember it yourself. You were so nervous and you outplayed everyone. On that rental instrument. Remember?"

"Yeah, I remember. I had no training. I was a mess."

"You were a seriously talented mess," she said. "It wasn't your grandmother's violin that got you here. It's your own talent. Remember that, okay? And remember why you're doing this."

Her words echoed between them, and he found that he could take a breath. And then another.

He could hear Nicole's voice in Janice's phone. "Can I talk to him?" and a moment later: "Ray? What did you eat at that Indian restaurant we went to? After the Carnegie Hall performance?"

"Huh? What—vegetable tikka masala. Why?"

"You're the only guy I've ever met who can casually eat vegetable tikka masala after totally slaying them in Carnegie Hall. And now you're playing with the Chicago Symphony. You totally got this."

Janice took the phone back. "Just remember how much you love playing. That's all you need to do. Stand up there and hold that amazing gift your grandmother gave you and just love the music you're playing. Nicole is right. You've got this."

For a moment, Anderson Cooper wasn't outside and Riccardo Muti wasn't conducting the Chicago Symphony fifty feet away. "I'm glad I called."

"I'm glad you called, too. We'll see you after the performance, okay?"

The monitor in the dressing room showed he had six minutes till he had to be onstage. Only six minutes? Would his mother watch when it aired? Would she be proud of him? Would she even know?

One more check in the mirror. He lifted the violin from its case, triple-checked to see if it was in tune, played a quick G-major scale.

He picked the pink rose out of its glass of water, opened the door, and walked out into the lights.

A week before Christmas, the **60 Minutes** piece ran. He was the final segment.

Janice: **I JUST SAW YOUR FACE ON MY TV**

Aunt Rochelle: **Sugar this is so exciting!!!!!!!!**

And dozens of others who'd seen the teasers and were sitting at home, waiting. He was in Erie, holding Nicole's hand, about to watch himself on her TV while a half dozen of her friends and a couple other orchestra members perched on chairs, leaned against the walls, or sat cross-legged on the floor.

He'd had no performances booked for most of December and had spent the time in Erie with Nicole. When he'd learned the airdate of his segment, Nicole asked if she could throw him a watch party. It was a chance to meet her friends, too, so he agreed.

The trademark ticking clock of **60 Minutes**: 7:42 p.m. Anderson Cooper's face, and Ray recognized the background: the Chicago Symphony auditorium, lights ablaze, seats empty.

"When you think of classical music," Anderson Cooper began, "you might think of bewigged men in frock coats playing to ladies in hoop skirts in nineteenth-century drawing rooms. Nothing could be further from the truth today."

And there was Ray's face, on the screen, eyes closed, violin uplifted, playing the Mendelssohn Concerto. The camera panned back. The tuxedo twinkled.

"Ray McMillian—his full name is Rayquan, but don't ever call him that—is one of the most unlikely musicians today," Anderson Cooper said. "It's hard to understand his rise to stardom. Most musicians who are in the top ranks learn classical music from a very early age, with private lessons and special tutors. They go to rarified schools like Juilliard or the Manhattan School of Music. Most of them are not people of color. Ray is an exception."

The piece went on, talking about how Janice had offered him a music scholarship, about how his single-minded devotion made him the top violinist at Markham University, playing doggedly on a beat-up fiddle that his grandmother had given him.

Cut to Anderson Cooper's interview with Janice as they walked around the Markham grounds.

Anderson went on, "What makes Ray even rarer is that he's Black. Go look at any orchestra in any city in America and you'll see the faces onstage are overwhelmingly white."

Close-up shots of various symphonies, of white musicians.

"In fact, in all major American orchestras, only 1.8 percent of musicians are Black. The number jumps to about twelve percent if you include all people of color. Ray's story is unique only because he's more talented, and more single-minded, than many others—and he found a teacher who nourished and supported him."

The crowd in Nicole's apartment roared with sympathetic laughter, clapping Ray on the back or high-fiving him.

Cut to a heavyset guy walking down a Charlotte street. Ray didn't recognize him. "Yeah, Ray and me were buddies," the guy said. His voice sounded familiar. "We bonded over the violin. That guy couldn't get enough of it. He loved it. I used to give him pointers."

Anderson Cooper's voice-over: "Growing up, he had few friends—except Mark Jennings, another violinist in orchestra, who told us how devoted and disciplined Ray always was."

Mark Jennings? The racist? Before Ray even had a chance to process this, the piece was moving on.

"And then something unlikely—one of the most extraordinary events in recent music history—occurred. You've probably heard the story, since it made headlines. It turns out that the old fiddle he played, the one his grandma had given him, was actually one of the rarest instruments ever made. A Stradivarius violin."

Shots of Cremona, a brief discussion of Stradivarius violins: "Experts tell us that Antonio Stradivari made about 650 violins, but only 244 have been accounted for—make that 245."

Interview with Ray, which he'd done in the Chicago Symphony dressing room, trying to look relaxed and calm with the lights glaring in his face and Anderson Cooper sitting across from him asking questions. The makeup woman had to stop the interview several times to blot at the sweat on Ray's hairline; afterward, under his tuxedo jacket, his pink shirt had been soaked.

"The violin is valued at somewhere between ten and twelve million dollars," Anderson went on. "It's a Cinderella story—or it should be. Instead, Ray McMillian has found himself mired in lawsuits contesting his ownership of the violin.

"The first is from his family, who believe that the violin should rightfully belong to them." Shot of four people: Thurston, Larry, Joyce, and his mom, sitting in what Ray recognized as Joyce's living room.

"That fiddle was my mama's," Thurston said. "It's been in our family for a hundred years. It should've been ours, not Ray's."

Joyce said, "Mama didn't really know what she had. We think she may have had dementia. If she'd known what it was, she would never have given it to him. And the Ray I knew and watched grow up would never have done this to us. He's really changed in the last few years."

Thurston, Joyce, and Larry sat uncomfortably on Joyce's brown sectional couch. Ray's mother, in a yellow minidress, was perched on a faded tan armchair next to them.

Anderson Cooper asked, "So you think all this new fame has gone to his head?"

"You damn right it has," Larry said.

Thurston said, "Our mother would tell us stories

of how her grandfather would play that fiddle and how one day it would be passed down to **us**. Ray knew that. All we want is for him to do what's right."

Cut to Anderson Cooper. "And so Ray's family filed a lawsuit against him, claiming that the violin is rightfully theirs. They didn't know, however, that another family also has a prior claim to the instrument: the Marks family.

"The Marks family are descendants of the slave owners who owned Ray's great-great-grandfather. Ray's family maintains that Thomas Marks gave the violin to their great-grandfather and that it has remained in their possession ever since."

Cut back to Anderson, now onstage in the Symphony auditorium.

Dramatic pause.

"The Marks family, however, disagrees."

A familiar man and woman filled the screen, walking down a garden path. "Andrea and Dante Marks maintain that the violin is theirs and that their ancestor never gave the violin away. They're suing Ray to get the violin back."

Ray found himself standing. He'd been holding Nicole's hand, leaning forward, and now he clenched his fists, unable to breathe.

Andrea Marks—gray haired, gray eyed—said earnestly into the camera, "We feel for Mr. McMillian, we do." The makeup and the lighting made her look hard and gleaming, like polished steel. "It's just that this was our property."

"The Markses have filed their own lawsuit claiming that the violin belongs to them, not to Ray or his family.

"The Marks family immigrated to America in the late eighteenth century," Anderson went on, "where they built Summerland Manor outside Milledgeville, Georgia. They farmed three thousand acres. They grew cotton, corn, tobacco, and wheat. They owned many musical instruments, including a violin from Cremona, Italy. And they enslaved, at the height of their economic prosperity, one hundred seventy-two human beings—including Leon, who may have been the natural son of the plantation owner and who was Ray's grandmother's grandfather."

"We thought the violin went missing during Sherman's March to the Sea," Dante said. "But when we heard about the violin that Mr. McMillian is playing, we realized it was our family's."

"Did you reach out to Ray?" Anderson Cooper asked.

The brother said, "We did, we surely did."

"He wasn't interested in talking to us," the sister said.

Cut to Anderson Cooper. "So what are you going to do? Are you going to sue Ray for the instrument?"

"We don't want to," Dante said. He and Andrea were now sitting on a garden bench, dark green bushes massing behind them. The sky was a clear pearl gray.

"Seems to me that you didn't even notice the violin was gone," Anderson Cooper said, "and meanwhile it's been a godsend to Ray McMillian. A gift from his beloved grandmother."

"It's not his!" said the sister. "His family somehow appropriated it during the war, during Sherman's March, or afterward, during the Emancipation."

"Does it feel a little awkward, asking the descendant of a man your family once owned to give back your property? After all, there are those who would say the violin is a means of compensating Black Americans for what they suffered as slaves. That even if Ray's ancestor did take the violin, he and his family are actually owed much more by your family—that it's from his family's labor that your family was able to prosper. It's even possible that Ray's family actually built Summerland Manor to begin with."

Again the shot of the brick mansion.

"Well, I don't know about that," the sister said. "It's ours, and we're glad to come to a settlement arrangement for it."

Back again to Anderson Cooper, standing in the empty Chicago Symphony auditorium, and then a voice-over as Ray silently played onstage. "And that's where things stand today," came Anderson Cooper's voice. "A priceless violin, a battle over its heritage, and a Black musician who, more than anything else, just wants to play it."

Ray faded from the screen and the ticking clock returned: 7:55 p.m.

Around him the room erupted in shouts. People—he was barely aware of who they were— trying to hug him, telling him what an amazing piece that was, how great he looked. Calls—Janice, Aunt Rochelle, others—were coming in. He shook everyone off, slid out of the living room and into the small bathroom off the kitchen, shut the door behind him, sat down on the closed toilet-seat lid and took out his phone.

He thumbed through his email, found Kim Wach, associate of Mendel, Panofsky & Levine, 666 Fifth Avenue.

Hi Kim I don't know if you saw the **60 Minutes** piece that just aired about me but it sure doesnt look like the Markses are going away. Can you call me ASAP?

He put his head between his legs, trembling. Sat up. Next to him, in a pile on a shelf, rested several random magazines: **People**, **Cosmopolitan**, **Men's**

Health. He pulled down the **Men's Health**, opened it blindly.

A knock on the door. "Ray?" Nicole's voice. "Hey. You okay?"

He returned to the party, tried to smile and join in the celebration, but his stomach churned with nausea.

Next day, Kim Wach gave him a call. "They're going to try playing this in the media, clearly. I heard from the lawyer yesterday that they're getting ready to file the case in federal court. He said that they have more evidence, but he hasn't sent it over to me yet. The lawyer insinuated that they'll just keep grinding you down until you give in."

"Yeah, that's what I thought," he said.

"And you still weren't able to track down anything from your family," Kim said.

"They're not speaking to me now," he said. "They're filing a suit against me, too."

"What about your cousins?"

He'd reached out to distant cousins; they knew nothing about any envelope with the name Leon Marks written on it and didn't know anything about the violin.

"Let's see what the Markses' evidence is," she said. "Maybe it's not that bad."

They hung up, and he tried to hold on to the hope that things weren't that bad—that everything would work out.

Maybe the Markses would just slither back under their flat rock.

Or maybe not.

Chapter 22

Boston
4 Months Ago

The **60 Minutes** interview, coupled with the Chicago performance, generated invites from orchestras across the United States—his star was definitely on the rise. He was starting to make money and was saving every penny, terrified of the upcoming legal bills from two lawsuits. He should just cut the violin in half and give each of them their own piece, just keep the alligator-skin case for himself.

Nobody except him cared anything about the violin: to them it was a dollar sign, or a sign of prestige. He tried to tell himself that it was just a precision instrument, chunks of wood carved and glued together. And yet sometimes—no, often—as he was playing, it felt like it wasn't just **him** playing: it was the instrument itself, singing with joy and, yes, with gratitude—grateful to him, grateful to the world. How could he betray it?

He flew to Boston for a recital in Jordan Hall, on the campus of the New England Conservatory of Music, playing Dvořák and Mozart. He was especially happy with his performance of Dvořák's Romance in F Minor. The piece grew on him the more he performed it, reminding him of taking walks in the summertime with Grandma Nora, the Georgia heat thick and soft against his skin. He felt like she would have loved the piece.

After the performance was over, he ducked out the back entrance. He was tired and very hungry. He definitely needed to schedule his recitals earlier in the evening.

The cold night air cut through his shirt and jacket—he put on the large sweatshirt he'd brought. He should have packed a better overcoat, but the sweatshirt was easier to fold and more portable. He pulled up the hood, but it didn't help. It started snowing. Welcome to Boston.

The wind attacked like a hawk after a mouse. He'd heard Aunt Rochelle say, when he'd visited her in Philly, "Ooh-whee, that hawk is biting" when the wind would drive into their faces. Now he understood: the hawk was certainly biting tonight. He pulled his black baseball cap farther down over his face. Definitely doing Boston recitals in the summertime from now on.

A diner beckoned, perfumed with the scents of roasting meats and grilled onion. He thought of sitting at the counter but decided to eat back at the hotel. "Whatcha havin', hon," said the thick-waisted, thick-accented woman at the counter. He ordered tater tots, Cobb salad, and a slice of apple pie to go.

While he waited, he called Nicole. He hadn't talked to her since early that afternoon, and he wondered how her own performance that evening had gone: she was playing a chamber music recital, Brandenburg Concerto no. 6, which featured two viola soloists. She'd been very excited about the performance, and he regretted having to miss it.

But she didn't pick up: his call went straight to voice mail. "Hey. My recital went well—how did yours go? Did the cellist get the rhythm right? I'm going to get something to eat before I head back to the hotel. I'll call you later."

A few minutes later, takeout bag in hand, he shouldered open the diner's door and the cold Boston night blew around him. He wasn't really aware of the people standing outside on the sidewalk until one of them spoke.

The voice was terrifyingly familiar: high yet gravelly. "That was just the most amazing performance I think I've ever heard!" Dante Marks and his sister stood not five feet away, their hands in their pockets, their eyes bright beneath ski caps pulled low across their foreheads. Behind them was a very tall man wearing a tan overcoat. He kept looking left, then right, then at Ray.

"What the—"

"You did such a fine job tonight," Andrea said. She sounded earnest, but he somehow thought she was mocking him.

"Why are you here? Are you following me?"

"We know you're often traveling, so we just wanted to see for ourselves that you're taking good care of our violin," Dante explained.

Heat surged through Ray. **Our violin.** The words lay on the pavement, cold and dead, like something run-over. He took a step forward. "I don't know what drugs you two freaks are doing that make you think you can follow me around, but let me make it clear to you: This is my violin. I'll say it again. **My violin.** It belonged to my great-great-grandfather and now it's mine. You're out of your fucking minds if you think you're getting your dirty fingers on it."

"Rayquese, or whatever the hell your name is," Andrea said, "we are getting that violin back. If you think you have a chance in hell of keeping it, you better think again."

The tall man loomed over all of them, glancing around as if waiting for something.

"You know damn well what my name is, lady. If you think I'm giving you my violin—"

"Our violin," Dante said. "See, we tried to be

nice and give you a chance to give back our violin without getting lawyers involved, but you had to try to be Billy Badass and act all tough. You're not gonna win this one."

Our violin. Ray could hear only those two words. Something cut loose inside him and he was suddenly yelling. "Shut your fucking mouth. I swear if you say 'our violin' one more fucking time, I won't be responsible for what happens next. Your rapist great-great-great-grandfather gave that fiddle to my PopPop. He didn't steal from you or anyone else. If it was so important to you, why the fuck didn't you try to get it back thirty years ago?"

Passersby turned to look at him. He didn't care. Both Dante and Andrea seemed, maddeningly, to be smiling. The tall man looked off to the right, behind Ray.

"Stay the hell away from me. If I see you again, I swear the cops—"

"The cops what?" a deep, thick Boston accent said behind him.

And another voice: "What's going on over here?"

Ray turned: two big-bellied police officers, hands on their belts, stood splay-legged on the sidewalk. Steam seemed to snake from their nostrils and form a plume above their heads. The one on the left was in his fifties, a little heavier, with a clean-shaven face that looked scraped raw. The one on the right was younger, with a thin dark mustache and the promising beginnings of a paunch to rival his partner's.

"Officers, thank goodness you're here," Andrea said. Ray would have sworn she batted her eyelashes like some kind of geriatric Miss America contestant. "We were simply asking this young man to return some property when he started threatening us."

"What?" Ray said. "That's not—"

"You got some ID?" the cop on the left said.

Ray let out a breath. "Officer, this isn't what it looks like. These people are basically stalkers. They showed up at my house. They showed up here, and—"

"ID. Now," the older officer said. He shifted his hand from his belt to his holster.

Dante's smile broadened.

Ray glared at both Markses as he reached for his wallet.

"Whoa there, chief. Slowly," said the younger cop.

"My name is Ray McMillian. I'm a concert violinist—see, this is my violin? I'm here from out of town and I'm just trying to get some dinner before I go back to my hotel."

"I didn't ask you any of that, chief. I just need to see some ID. Now."

"I'm going to reach into my back pocket, okay?" Slowly he reached into his back pocket and pulled out his wallet. He was fumbling for his driver's license as another police car pulled up. Several bystanders and people inside the diner held up their phones, filming him.

"Thank goodness you showed up when you did, Officer," Andrea gushed, as if she had just been rescued from a serial rapist. "I was worried he was about to get violent."

"Fuck you," Ray said to her.

"You see, Officer? All we want is for him to return some property that belongs to us and he goes off and calls us names and threatens us."

"I need you to put your hands behind your back while my partner runs your name to see what your deal is," the older cop said.

"What? See what my deal is? You don't ask these three nutcases for their IDs. I didn't threaten them. Why am I being cuffed?"

"Because you are being very aggressive and these people seem to fear for their safety. Now put your hands behind your back."

"Oh, I get it. Angry Black man dangerous. Protect innocent white folk. This is bull."

"I suggest for your own good that you keep your mouth shut." Metal cuffs, warmed from the police officer's body, curled and wrapped around Ray's wrists. Nervously he kept reaching up with a finger or two to touch the violin case on his back, as if he needed extra reassurance that it was still there. The younger officer took Ray's wallet and retrieved his driver's license. Two more patrol cars pulled up. "Gentlemen, ma'am, why don't you go inside and give this officer a statement while we check this guy out."

"Thank you, Officer. Come, my dear. Are you okay?" Dante asked his sister, and then smiled toothily at Ray.

He stood in the cold as the Marks siblings and their tall companion were coddled in the diner, probably ordering coffee and onion rings. Ray kept touching the violin case to make sure it was closed. Inside, Dante, Andrea, and the tall man were talking to the younger officer, pointing and glaring at Ray.

A few moments later, the police officer came out of the diner. "Those people claim you have their stolen property. What's that on your back?" The officer stepped forward. Ray's fingertips instinctively reached for the case.

"It's my violin. I'm a musician. I was just on **60 Minutes**—go google me. My name is—"

"Open it up. Let me see."

"Take off these cuffs and I will." He was trembling from rage and impotence. He kept saying to himself that one word over and over, his mantra: **respect.** No matter what. He'd gone overboard with the Markses. Right now he just had to get out of this situation before it escalated further, became Baton Rouge all over again.

"Officer, I'm a musician. I just played a recital at Jordan Hall. My violin is inside. I don't want to take it out on the sidewalk. Exposure to this cold isn't good for it. It's very fragile and very valuable."

"Got it," said the fat cop. "Open up the case, sir, or we can do this down at the station."

"Okay," Ray said. "Take off these cuffs and I'll open it right up. Let me just confirm, though, that you want me to open a ten-million-dollar instrument in the middle of a city street while it's snowing?" A few fat flakes drifted down. "Are you sure that Boston wants this kind of lawsuit if something goes wrong? Not to mention the publicity? This violin costs more than your whole department. I just want you to confirm this first, **chief**."

The cop eyed him, then the diner. "I guess we can go inside if you don't interact with the individuals who are already there?"

"Sounds great," Ray said. He stood, handcuffed, in front of the glass-and-metal door, waited for the cop to pull the door open. He waited again at the inner door.

Dante, Andrea, and the tall guy were standing near the counter, and they all stepped back as if terrified to be in the same space with Ray.

"Oh please," Ray told them. "Spare us the dramatics. You're not getting my violin. It took me a minute, but I figured out what you are trying to do. It's not going to work."

"I'm sure I don't know what you are talking about," Andrea said, her accent suddenly thick and Southern and nothing like her usual voice.

Ray marched left, between a double row of maroon booths that ran the length of the restaurant. All the patrons were turning to look at him, handcuffed and flanked by three of Boston's finest. At the far end, in front of a busing station where dirty plates poured from black plastic tubs, he said, "If you'll remove these cuffs, I'll show you the violin."

The police officer grabbed Ray's arm, fumbling with the cuffs, and one of the other officers strolled up. "This guy checks out. No warrants."

"Looks like it's your lucky day, chief." The handcuffs fell away, and Ray ostentatiously massaged his wrists as if they'd cut off his circulation for hours. The cop was saying, "Now, these people say you have their property. Can you prove that instrument is yours?"

Ray looked at the cop like he had just grown an extra head. "Are you fucking kidding me? I literally just told you I played a recital at Jordan Hall."

"And I just told you to prove it."

Ray knew the look in the police officer's eyes. The man was looking for any excuse to take him down to the police station.

"Well, it's nice to know you guys are consistent. These people stalk me, accost me out in the cold, pretend I'm about to beat them up, and here you guys come to the rescue. The darkest one in the crowd has got to be the guilty one. I have to prove my innocence while they just sit inside and need protecting, right? That's how this works?"

"You got it, chief," the fat cop responded, to Ray's surprise. "Right now they look far more credible than you do. Your next move better be showing me what's in that case. Otherwise I'll be confiscating it until you prove to a judge that it doesn't belong to these nice people."

Ray unclasped his case. As he took out the instrument and the bow, he asked the younger cop, "You have any requests?"

"Just play, smart-ass."

"Right," Ray said as he continued to stare daggers at the Markses and their accomplice.

Ray put his bow on the D string and looked as if he were preparing to launch into the most lavish concerto ever written. Instead, he played a two-octave D-major scale. It was nothing special, just a simple scale, but played beautifully. After his last note, he looked directly at the Markses and said, "You don't deserve to hear another note from my fiddle." Then he turned to the officer and said, "Satisfied? I can show you dozens of photos online of me playing this violin," Ray said. "I can call dozens of people to vouch for me. Just google my name."

This time the officers listened, pulled out their

cell phones, read, glanced up at him, read again. "This is the Stradivarius?" the younger one said. "Holy shit."

"Yeah," Ray said. "It's mine. These nutjobs have come up with some crazy idea that it's theirs, but they're just lying." He spoke loud enough to be heard at the counter.

Andrea rose to the bait. "We are not," she yelled back. "It's our family heirloom. Our niece is going to play it someday." But she sounded hopeless and definitely crazy.

"Ma'am, sir, you're going to have to take him to court for this one," the older cop said. "I don't think any of you are in any physical danger. If you have further issues, we can take this down to the station." The Markses shook their heads, and soon the police officers left. The tall goon behind them still hadn't said anything. The people in the diner and the people outside continued to hold up their phones, filming them.

As Ray packed up the violin, Andrea inched over to him, hissed, "Don't think this is over. We tried to let you off easy."

"Lady, go home. Stay out of my face. You'll be hearing from my attorney."

He was so angry that he left the diner without taking his tater tots, salad, and pie. Now the Boston hawk didn't seem nearly as cold.

Chapter 23

Settlement

4 Months Ago

No phone call or high-res video could take the place of standing in front of Aunt Rochelle and talking to her. So that's what Ray would do. Now he was half sitting, half leaning on the hood of her car, hands jammed into the pockets of his puffy coat. He'd been standing outside her Philadelphia condo waiting for her since 7:00 a.m.; he knew she sometimes left early for work.

At about 7:40 she came into sight. When she saw him, her shoulders lifted and her head rocked back on her neck, her body language projecting surprise at seeing some Black dude sitting on the hood of her car. Her hand came up to her throat. Then she recognized him. "Ray?"

"Hi, Aunt Rochelle."

"Oh my lord, you gave me a fright," she said. She bounded forward and hugged him tightly. The hood of her car jammed into the back of his leg. "What are you doing here, sugar? You okay?"

"I wasn't sure if you'd talk to me," he said, hugging her back, breathing in her familiar perfume. "So I figured I'd just show up and say hello."

"Not talk to you?" she said. "Why wouldn't I talk to you? Because of all that foolishness with your violin?" She shook her head. "I don't know where their heads are sometimes, and that's the god's truth. Of course I'll talk to you. How are you? What's been going on? It's been forever since I've seen you. Except on TV." She hugged him again.

He started telling her about the concerts, about playing all over the country, about the media interviews. She cut him off. "You know, I'm not going to stand out here in the cold and listen to my favorite nephew, who just happens to be a famous musician. We're going for breakfast. Have you eaten?"

"Don't you have to go to work?"

"Screw 'em," she said cheerfully. "I feel a sudden sore throat coming on. Hold on a sec." She pulled out her phone, tapped an email. "I got some sick days coming anyway. Where you want to go for breakfast? There's a Bob Evans down the street that makes a mean sausage biscuit."

Ray had forgotten Aunt Rochelle's love of biscuits. "That sounds great," he said.

She drove, her car immaculate, with a lemony air freshener that surprisingly did not smell like some kind of chemical spill. "Tell me everything," she told him. "I can't believe I'm sitting here with my world-famous musician nephew," she said. She looked in the rearview mirror. "And a billion-dollar violin in the back seat."

So he talked—in the car, and in Bob Evans, as they sat in the booth and ordered. It had been months, he realized, since he'd had a conversation with someone in his family, and family really was special; the relationships were unlike any other. Fraught and perilous much of the time, but sweet as well. He told her about touring, about Baton Rouge, about Kristoff, about performing in huge concert halls and in school gyms.

In the meantime they wolfed down eggs and biscuits with bacon and vegan sausage.

The waitress brought over more orange juice for Ray and refilled Rochelle's coffee. She cleared their plates.

"You see this handsome man here," Rochelle told her. "He's a famous musician. He was on **60 Minutes** last month."

"Aww jeez, come on, Auntie," Ray said, embarrassed.

The waitress, hands full with dirty plates, was properly appreciative.

After she left, Rochelle said, "Speaking of **60**

Minutes, what's going on with those people? The ones who said they used to own PopPop's fiddle?"

"That's one of the reasons I wanted to meet you," Ray said. "I had to hire a lawyer. To fight them and—well—the family."

Up until now, neither had directly acknowledged the family's lawsuit against Ray, of which Rochelle wasn't part.

"I can't tell you how sorry I am about all this," she said now. "It wasn't my idea. I told them that Mama wanted you to have that violin and it was criminal to say otherwise. Mama would be turning over in her grave if she knew."

"Yeah," Ray agreed, "I think she would. It's really rough. And now that they have this lawsuit, I can't even talk to them. Which makes this next part harder. My lawyer asked me to see if I can get any information about how PopPop got the violin to begin with."

Rochelle stared down at the tabletop, then up at Ray. "Mama's the only one who really knew. But seances aren't admissible in court," she said with a laugh. "So getting an affidavit from Mama won't really help."

"I asked Gene and Rita," Ray said, referring to distant cousins. "But they weren't even born then and didn't know anything. The thing is," he went on, "I actually may have found something." He told her about the big clasped envelope with the name Leon Marks scrawled across it that he'd found in his grandmother's attic. "I remember where I found it—it was in a yellow dresser that was wedged under the roof, in the back right corner. I asked Aunt Joyce about it a couple months ago and she said she'd check in Grandma Nora's other papers, but I never heard back from her. And now I can't ask her directly. I'd really like to see what was inside that envelope."

"Did you open it?"

"I think so?" he said uncertainly. "I honestly don't remember. I was looking for a fiddle. I think I remember seeing some folded-up paper, but I could have invented all that by now."

"I have no idea where it would be," she said. She reminded him of how, a few months after Nora's death, the five siblings had met in Georgia to go through the house—picking out what they wanted, selling or donating or throwing away what they didn't. She didn't remember seeing any envelope, but the house had been packed with sixty years' worth of family life, and she'd seen only a portion of it.

"I thought Joyce had all the paperwork, but I can ask everybody for you."

"They won't be very cooperative. But if the Markses' lawsuit goes away then I guess maybe their own lawsuit has a better shot?" He laughed humorlessly.

"I don't have to tell them it's for you. I can say I was just curious."

"That would be awesome," he said. "Thank you. Do you know who bought her house?"

"No idea. We just hired a realtor and sold it. But if you're thinking we left stuff up in the attic, you can think again. I know Thurston and your mom spent days up there, dragging everything out. I think your mama was convinced there were family jewels hidden in the walls. We ended up hiring a dumpster and throwing almost all of it away. The house was totally empty when we sold it."

He had a mental image of that yellow dresser lying on its side, green eyes staring up at the sky, surrounded by moth-eaten winter coats and old Stevie Wonder albums.

Rochelle and Ray talked for another twenty minutes or so, then finally slid out of the booth. "What are you up to today?" she asked.

"Just wanted to see you," he said, slinging the violin onto his shoulder. "I'm leaving for Des Moines tonight, but my flight doesn't leave until six o'clock."

"Good," she said. "Let's play hooky. Let's go to Reading Terminal Market and wander around the city some. I never get to go places like that and I've been wanting to." She eyed his violin. "Are you taking that everywhere?"

He shrugged. "When I'm traveling, I don't leave

it behind. The case is indestructible, and honestly I don't even notice it anymore."

"Okay, well, we'll make a tourist out of that fiddle," she said.

They spent the day wandering around central Philly—the stalls and great food of the Reading Terminal Market, down into Chinatown, over to the Liberty Bell.

They were crossing Franklin Square when Aunt Rochelle nudged him and pointed with her chin. "Look, look," she said.

"What? What's wrong?"

"Look at her," she said. "Don't you think she's cute?"

A young athletic woman was crossing in front of them, her toned ass bouncing with every step in her black leggings. She had her hands jammed into the pockets of her red puffy coat, hair pulled back in a ponytail. She wore red earmuffs.

"What? She's aiight."

"I'll give you a dollar to talk to her."

He stopped in the middle of the street. "Are you serious? I'm not doing that. I have a girlfriend."

Now it was her turn to stop. "What? When did you find a girlfriend?"

"We've been together for a while now."

"You have? How long? You have a picture? Let me see. I can't believe you didn't tell me you got a girlfriend."

So he told her about Nicole—how they met, how often they could see each other. Relaxing and chatting with his aunt was the most fun he'd had in weeks. He was sad when she drove him back to her condo to pick up his rental car to head out to the airport. But they promised to be in closer touch. It was a good day.

A few days later, true to her word, Aunt Rochelle emailed Ray.

Hey sugar, still thinking about that philly cheese steak I got at Central Market! I need to find an excuse to go back again lol. So I asked all the sibs about any paperwork and they all said they'd look. Your mama kept asking why and I told her I was curious about family history. Not sure if she believed me or not but we'll see what they come up with.

A week later:

Just wanted to give you an update, which is no news. Joyce did have mama's and daddy's birth certificates but nobody can find anything about PopPop. They promised me they'd keep looking but they think they probably threw it out.

Two weeks later:

Sorry sugar nothing new to report. They say
they don't have anything. When you coming
back to Philly? There's a new restaurant
that opened near me and I want to take you.

He called Kim Wach. Told her how he'd reached
out to his cousins, and they knew nothing about
Leon Marks and the violin. Told her how his aunt
Rochelle had asked his family to see if they'd seen
the envelope, and how they told her they hadn't.
"The thing is," he said, "I don't know how hard
they looked. I seriously doubt my uncle Larry or
my mom would even bother looking, even if they
did have it. There's nothing in it for them, so
they won't bother lifting a finger."

And then Ray told her his plan: a stroke of genius
that killed two birds with one blow. His plan would
resolve his family's issues and get him that missing
envelope.

Kim Wach did not think it was a stroke of genius.
"That is the dumbest thing I've ever heard," she told
him. "You are seriously not going to do this."

He ignored her.

A week later, in a Sheraton outside the Baltimore/
Washington International Thurgood Marshall Air-

port, Ray seated himself at the head of a conference table, his back to the brown vertical blinds, a sheet of paper with his notes in front of him. He'd arranged with the hotel staff for two video screens, and he booted up both: on the first was Kim Wach, his lawyer; on the second was Colin Handzo, who collectively represented his family—except for Aunt Rochelle—in the lawsuit against him.

En masse, his mother and her siblings poured into the room. No significant others or kids. Aunt Rochelle, who didn't have to be there but wanted to back him up, hugged him. Uncle Larry shook Ray's hand, told him he looked good. The others nodded and smiled insincerely. His mother glared at him from the far end of the table.

"Thank you for coming," Ray said. "I hope you all had good flights or drives in. I know how bad the traffic can be. I tried to find a place that was central for all of you."

"Woulda just been better to pick someone's house and we all could go there," said his mother. "I got to pay for a hotel room tonight." She'd dressed up for the occasion in a tight salmon-colored dress, with fake nails and lipstick to match.

He ignored her. "Anyway, I have a proposal for you, and I wanted to talk to you about it in person."

"Ray," Kim Wach cut in from the video monitor, "can I just say for the record that I think this is a terrible idea?"

He ignored her, too. "I'd like to settle the issue of PopPop's fiddle. Kim here"—he nodded at the screen—"says that if you end up actually going to court, and not just writing me threatening letters, that the case will get thrown out as frivolous and that you'll have to pay her attorney fees. She thinks you're doing all this because you want me to settle and you want to make some money, even if you don't have a good claim to my violin."

He took a breath, waiting for a contradiction. But no one spoke. "Let me start by saying that there is no way that I'm getting rid of PopPop's fiddle. Grandma gave it to me. It was important to her and to this family, and it's going to stay with me. If I have kids someday, I'll pass it down to them.

"But I do want to settle this, and I want us to be a family again. I also got accepted to compete in the Tchaikovsky Competition, which is pretty much the biggest competition in the world. I need to be able to practice without all these distractions.

"So here's my proposal. When I'm done talking, I'll leave the room and let all of you talk to your lawyer and figure out if you want to do it. Just know that this is the only settlement offer I'll be making. If you go to court and lose, you won't be getting anything, and you'll be stuck with Kim's attorney fees, too—which are pretty steep, let me tell you.

"Here's what I'm offering." He looked down at his notes, looked back up. "Starting next year, I will pay each of you a hundred thousand dollars over the next ten years. That's five hundred thousand dollars total. I know you think that's nothing to me, but let me tell you: for a working musician, it's a lot of money.

"I'll also list the five of you as the primary beneficiaries of the violin's insurance policy in case something happens to the violin. But let me be super clear here: if the violin gets damaged or stolen, or if I get injured in any way, and if there's the slightest evidence that any of you or any of your friends or relatives are involved, you'll get absolutely nothing. And to make sure this happens, the insurance company will be instructed to hold the money in escrow for five years, so you won't see an immediate payday if something happens to the violin. So it'd be better for you if you kept me alive." He smiled. Nobody else did.

"This is the last thing: I want all papers from Leon Marks. From PopPop. I know there was an envelope that had some papers in it—I found it in the attic and gave it to Grandma—but I don't know what happened to it. So if by June first you find that envelope or those papers, I'm willing to give you all another five hundred thousand dollars that you can split however you want.

"So that's my offer," he said, standing and folding the paper with his notes on it. His hands were shaking, but he clenched them into fists. "A million in cash and you're listed as beneficiaries on the insurance. Think about it and let me know. I'll be outside in the lobby."

And he walked out the door.

Fifteen minutes later they texted him to come back: they would take his offer.

Within the next two weeks, the lawyers wrote it all up in nice legalese and the deal was done.

Ray heard later that his family tore their houses apart looking for documents about Leon Marks. They contacted the Georgia Historical Society, the ACLU, and everywhere else they could think of. They knocked on the door of Grandma Nora's old house, went up to the now-barren attic, pounded on the walls, and searched the insulation.

But Leon Marks's papers had disappeared— probably thrown out with so much of Grandma Nora's life.

Chapter 24

Theft

In the meantime, the Tchaikovsky Competition, slated for mid-June, was bearing down upon him. Practice and lessons dominated Ray's life. Both Ray and Janice had their own thoughts about his strengths and weaknesses; the trick was to find teachers who not only could build on his strengths and improve his weaknesses but who also had the availability—and the willingness—to teach him. Janice had pulled many strings, and the strings of strings, because that was how the game was played. And she was good at it.

From January to June, Ray would divide his life into three blocks. In the first, he'd focus on Bach and Ravel; in the second, on Mozart, Kreisler, and Paganini; and finally, in the few weeks before the competition began, on Tchaikovsky. Once a week

Ray would fly to take a lesson with the instructor, then fly home to practice, practice, practice. Money would be very tight for the next six months. It was a big gamble, and Ray hoped it would pay off.

By early January he'd finalized his schedule—and it was grueling. Block one was with Rachel Vetter in Chicago (he'd already met her briefly, when he played with the Chicago Symphony) and focused on the Bach Chaconne and Ravel's **Tzigane**. She was considered one of the foremost Bach experts in the country. Ray had once heard her perform the **Tzigane** and was completely astounded at how she balanced power and precision. Such a petite person playing so fiendishly well, as though she summoned Gypsy spirits when her bow touched the string.

Rachel drilled him on the Bach and the **Tzigane** for five hours at a time, and then he flew home and practiced until his brain and fingers gave way. He practiced so much that he began making simple mistakes. Miscounting, playing wrong notes, ignoring accidentals. This was a sure sign that he was beginning to overdo it. His brain was experiencing serious fatigue.

Every week or so, Nicole would fly down to Charlotte—she was a virtuoso with flights and found the cheapest offerings possible, so that meant she was often showing up on Ray's doorstep at 2:00 a.m. or leaving for the airport at 4:00 a.m.

March and early April were slated for block two

with Ben Amundsen in Los Angeles, who focused on Mozart, Kreisler, and Paganini. Amundsen was heralded for his interpretation of Mozart concertos and sonatas—he was also a very good friend of Janice's, so that was an easy choice to make.

In Charlotte, between lessons, Ray buried himself in the music, with a strict practice routine that didn't vary. Up at 7:00 a.m. for breakfast and a quick workout; then, at nine thirty, an hour of scales and arpeggios—starting off with every major and minor scale, using several different bowings, focusing on making each scale a work of art—and then on to harmonic, melodic, and natural minor arpeggios, concentrating on the fingerings and the bowings.

At eleven o'clock he'd start in on Mozart, his long fingers effortlessly jumping into the intricacy, like a puzzle he'd manipulate in the air. Since he'd worked on these pieces with Janice when he was in college, he'd sometimes stop and call, ask her about a specific fingering. If she wasn't teaching they'd sometimes do a video call and she'd watch him, critiquing as he went.

No later than 1:00 p.m., he would turn to the Paganini Caprices nos. 24 and 6. These pieces worried him: they were in the compulsory round of the competition, and he'd have to do something to stand out. Janice suggested that he play them at lightning speed, so he was trying hard to do that.

At 2:00 p.m. he'd drill into the simple, beautiful **Valse-Scherzo** in C Major by Tchaikovsky—even though he'd be focusing on it during block three, he still wanted to play it every day, since that way even his muscles would follow and anticipate the flow of the competition. Besides, he just liked playing it.

Three p.m. and time for a late lunch. He was always starving. If he and Nicole were in different cities, he'd give her a call and her voice would pour out, warm and honey gold, making a knot loosen in his chest. "How is practice going?"

"Okay. The **Scherzo** feels better. I think I got a handle on it."

"I love the way you play that piece. It's like Tchaikovsky wrote it for you."

"It felt pretty good at the end."

"Of course it does. Now get back to it. You have a competition to win."

After lunch, he drilled into Mozart and Kreisler for the next three hours, playing each piece from beginning to end as if in a concert performance. Before he knew it, 10:00 p.m. had barreled past, and he staggered into the shower, and bed.

In May—only a month before the competition—Leonid Molchalin, one of the world's foremost Tchaikovsky authorities, had deigned to bestow his insights upon Ray: Molchalin's teaching schedule at Juilliard meant that he would be available only once school was out, in mid-May. Ray would stay in New York to work with him.

Later, the FBI and Alicia Childress would tell him that his regimented schedule made it easier for the thieves to track him, so he could blame himself for his own stupid predictability; but on May 16, the day of the theft, Ray was still pointlessly unaware, still believed that a strict schedule would help him. He'd practice ten to twelve hours a day, minimum, with lessons in the late morning every other day. He wanted to practice more, but physically he knew he couldn't: carpal tunnel syndrome could kick in, or tendonitis. It wasn't worth taking the risk.

May 15—a month before he was slated to fly to Moscow—was Ray and Nicole's last full day in Manhattan. The morning's schedule would be identical to the previous five days. Only the late afternoon and evening would be different—a celebration of his last lesson. They were scheduled to leave New York the following day.

So he woke that morning before the 6:00 a.m. alarm, crept out of the room, down to the hotel gym, and worked out for an hour. When he returned at seven, Nicole was awake. He poured the last bowl of cereal, drizzled the little bit of milk that was left in the hotel refrigerator, and then practiced till eight thirty. He slid the violin back into its case, kissed Nicole goodbye, and headed out into the Manhattan morning. Commuters in long tan overcoats swam along the sidewalks, staring at their phones. Garbage trucks roared past. He headed down Fifty-Third, turned up Seventh Avenue toward Lincoln Center and Juilliard.

One of Leonid Molchalin's earliest teachers actually studied with Adolph Brodsky, who worked with Tchaikovsky himself on the famous Violin Concerto. Russian-born, with decades of experience as a performer and a teacher, Molchalin had been a student of Ivan Galamian and Isaac Stern and a member of the Moscow Philharmonic Orchestra. It was pure luck, and a lot of Janice pulling strings, that Leonid agreed to meet with Ray—and they only had a few weeks together. Molchalin was heading to Europe soon to play with the Royal Stockholm Philharmonic Orchestra.

Now above Ray loomed Juilliard's dramatic steel and glass. Inside, he breathed in its aroma of Pine-Sol and air-conditioning. Most students were gone, and the halls echoed as he ascended to the practice rooms on the second floor. He started warming up. Leonid—a short man in jeans and a shapeless dark green polo shirt—arrived a few minutes later.

On this final morning of Ray's lessons with Leonid, they practiced the Tchaikovsky Concerto over and over again, Leonid drilling Ray on the interpretation in the third movement. Finally Leonid nodded. "From now on, you must just practice and make it your own. Even more your own. Your sound is very pure, very Russian."

Very Russian. It didn't get better than that. Ray packed up the violin, slung it over his shoulder, headed out and down Sixty-Fifth to Central Park, weaving past bicyclists and a waffle stand toward Seventh Avenue, and then back to the hotel. It was 1:30 p.m.

Nicole reappeared around two o'clock—she'd been shopping for her niece whose birthday was next week—and set her packages down just inside the door. She kicked off her shoes and lay back on the bed, listening to him play, or reading her novel, or both.

A little after 3:00 p.m., he set the violin back in its case and spooned with Nicole on the bed for an hour, exhausted, the music of Tchaikovsky and Mozart in his veins. He got up and practiced again until just after 6:00 p.m.

Then, a little after six—he later told the investigators between 6:05 and 6:15 p.m.—he put the violin back in its case for the last time, closed the clasps, put the case on the bureau, below the TV, where he always set it. He shucked off his T-shirt and jeans, padded naked into the bathroom for a shower before dinner. Nicole, who'd showered, was right outside, putting on her makeup in the bathroom mirror.

They were meeting Leonid Molchalin and his partner, Gary Broussard, a science writer for the **New York Times**, for dinner on the Upper West Side. They would rather have taken the subway—cheaper, and faster during rush hour—but Ray was always very conscious of the violin and would rather take a car instead. If he had only taken the subway, despite his own instincts.

Dinner at a fancy Indian restaurant: Ray sat on the banquette, his back to the room, violin next to him. They talked about music, of course, and the Tchaikovsky Competition, and Gary held forth about some theories about what gave the Stradivarius its unique sound—some thought it wasn't the wood or the perfect proportions but actually the varnish that coated the instrument.

Ray, several glasses of wine in, asserted that it was none of those physical characteristics—that Antonio Stradivari had, magically, somehow managed to imbue his instruments with a life of their own, with soul. They could laugh at him all they wanted, but he was convinced of this—his violin was vastly more than the sum of its parts.

The four of them together polished off three bottles of wine—they were musicians, okay? everyone knew musicians like to drink—as well as assorted cocktails, so that when they staggered out into the balmy May night, the streetlights spun slightly, and

Leonid barely avoided a delivery guy biking on the sidewalk without headlights.

"Watch it, buddy!" Gary yelled after the cyclist, who zoomed off, unconcerned.

Ray couldn't remember ever being parted from the violin case the entire time they were at the restaurant. He did indeed take it with him when he went to the bathroom (twice). The police and CCTV further confirmed the route they took after dinner to an Irish pub on the corner of Eighty-Third and Columbus, where Ray tucked himself into a booth, the violin in the corner, and where they continued to drink until almost midnight, when Ray and Nicole caught a cab south to the hotel.

No, he didn't open the case when he was out at the restaurant or the bar or in the cabs. At least he didn't think so.

Had he opened it back in the hotel? There was that one bit of fingering that Leonid kept drilling him on: Had he practiced briefly before putting the violin back?

He'd had too much to drink. He didn't think he'd opened the case. He wasn't sure. He never locked it when it was with him. It was always with him. The keys to the lock were on his keychain. He had his keychain. The case had not been locked when he opened it in Charlotte.

The next morning they woke after 7:00 a.m.

Both their flights were around eleven o'clock, so they ordered room service, and a woman named Pilar Jiménez set out their breakfast on the small dining-room table, inches from his unopened violin case.

She left, they ate, they packed, they took cabs to the airports—Nicole flying out of Newark to Erie and Ray heading to Charlotte via LaGuardia.

That afternoon, back in Charlotte, he'd opened the violin case for the first time in twenty-four hours and, instead of his violin, found only a white Chuck Taylor tennis shoe and a ransom note.

How do you remember to keep breathing when the most important piece of your life—a violin-shaped marvel that defines who you are, that organizes your day, that completes you as a human being—is stolen? How do you keep the blood moving in your veins? How do you make sure your eyes blink, your throat swallows?

You just do. You lie on your bed for hours, you pull out the Lehman that you have to practice on. You try to recapture the magic of music, the emotion of the moment, the days and weeks of practicing. You try because, after all these years of practicing, you're hardwired to try.

The world swims in unreality, and for a moment you believe that your violin is in its case—you only have to open it. The next moment, reality crushes you: the case is empty, miles away, in some police warehouse somewhere.

This happens all day, forty or fifty or two hundred times: opening a door or pouring a bowl of cereal or flushing the toilet. A knock on the door is someone returning the violin: no, it's the mailman with a Bath & Body Works coupon. You open your closet and expect to see a violin hanging from a hook or propped on a shelf. You turn on your TV and anticipate that the newscaster will talk not about the latest stock market updates but about a violin miraculously restored to its owner.

You convince yourself that you're going to get it back, but the voice that tells you you're going to get it back is also the voice that tells you, a half breath later, that you'll never see it again. No matter what anyone says. No matter how often your girlfriend hugs you and holds you. No matter how many bouquets of flowers—or teddy bears—fans send you, or casseroles that your beloved mentor, friend, and teacher drops off, it doesn't matter. It doesn't help. The teddy bears pile up in a corner and you throw a sheet over them so you don't have to encounter their accusatory glares, them telling you that it's gone. **It can't be gone, it was just here. It's gone.**

Because here is the heart of it: it wasn't about the money, or the prestige of playing a Stradivarius, or the looks people gave him—envious and impressed—when they learned who he was and what the violin had been. His loss had nothing to do with any of these things, and the wealth and fame were distractions that he shrugged off.

Here is what he realized in the gray shadows of his 3:00 a.m. vigils: He was alone now. He was desperately, terribly, alone. Until then, he'd been a solitary, lonely kid—and then a solitary, lonely man—who had had one special person in his life, dressed in a pink housecoat and smelling of lavender and bluing solution in her hair. She had gone, but she had given him music, and music had filled his world, had allowed him to connect with people in a way that he sometimes could not believe could ever be real. But now she was gone, and the violin had gone, and the music had gone, and he felt so lonely and guilty now that he often thought the misery would paralyze him and he would simply, suddenly, stop breathing under the weight of it.

He obsessed over who could have taken it. After the initial flurry of police activity, the FBI did not call that often, Alicia's texts pinged his phone less frequently, the updates only trickled in. So he pushed them all—Bill Soames and Alicia Childress and the NYPD—to investigate every lead.

Nicole was convinced it was his family who wanted their half of the insurance money—and figured it would be better to wait the agreed-upon five years for it rather than have Ray dole out their money in tinier increments.

Ray, however, was convinced that it was the Marks family. They were crazy. They were also unscrupulous and obsessed with the violin. They seemed less interested in money and more interested in owning the violin itself, or in punishing Ray for his existence. The only thing that made him doubt his own theory was the ransom: the Marks family would have no intention of returning the violin for whatever price. But perhaps that, too, was part of their plan—to take the violin **and** an extra $5 million. He wouldn't put it past them.

Chapter 25

Day 17: Raising Money and Hope

Here was the thing that Ray knew about himself: he was hardwired not to give up. The violin was gone, and its loss paralyzed him, but paradoxically, its loss also spurred him to control the two areas in his life that he could control: practicing his ass off and raising money for the ransom.

By the last week of May he had resumed his regular practice schedule: up at 6:00 a.m., exercising, and beginning practice by seven. Every morning he'd awake and expect the violin to be returned, and every day its loss punched him like a bowling ball to the face, but he would draw a breath—or two, or three—and reach for the Lehman. More than ever, he would not let the loss destroy him. He could still make music. He could still stand tall. He could still be worthy of respect.

He'd practice maniacally until early afternoon, until his legs wouldn't hold him or his fingers had gone numb. Then he'd grab another bowl of cereal—cereal was pretty much all he was eating these days—and open his laptop.

He spent every afternoon trying to raise $5 million. Six days in, his crowdfunding campaign had raised a whopping $143,228. "That's an awesome beginning," Nicole told him that afternoon on the phone. They were both in their respective cars: she driving to a last-minute substitute performance in Cleveland, and he in Charlotte, heading over to meet Wells Fargo's wealth-management team to discuss possible benefactors or investors.

"That's so far from five mil that it doesn't even count," he said.

"Will you stop? It's a start, and a great one. These things take time. You have over a month to raise the money. And it always snowballs." When he'd decided to raise money using crowdfunding, she'd helped him with a lot of the research, even edited his plea for money.

"I should have started it right away," he said. "I should have gone on TV shows. I could have said something and millions of people would have heard me."

"They wouldn't let you, remember? The FBI didn't want you on TV."

"Well, they ain't got shit done," he said. "Pilar

Jiménez is probably partying every night, playing merengue on the violin to her family."

"You have time," she repeated. "It hasn't even been a week. You've raised almost thirty thousand dollars a day. That's incredible!"

"It's been almost a week. At this rate it'll take me five months to raise five mil. I have less than five weeks. And the comments are fucking me up."

"Call Benson again," she said. She was convinced that the insurance company was to blame: all it had to do was pay the ransom, or pay out the insurance policy before the ransom date, and Ray would have his violin back. Simple. The insurance agent had tried to explain to both of them that the company had a strict policy not to pay ransoms and that there was also a waiting period before any payment would be issued—let alone the delay required by his family's settlement—but Nicole told them that their "strict policy" about ransoms wasn't written anywhere in any of the paperwork. She'd checked. So now she hounded Ray to make them pay.

"It doesn't do any good to call them," he said. "They're not paying more than the twenty-five-thousand reward."

Benson was no help—neither were the investors. Trying to convince wealthy investors to cough up some of their hard-earned cash to invest in a small percentage of a stolen Stradivarius violin wasn't quite as easy as it might sound—especially when

Ray had no proof that the violin still existed. And of course these investors were savvy enough to understand the implications of the Markses' lawsuit: Even if Ray did get the violin back, he might not actually own it. He might have to give it to the Marks family.

When the violin had been stolen, it had seemed that there were a half dozen very possible leads—Pilar, Ray's family, the Marks family.

Pilar had turned out to be a dead end. Alicia had talked to her, then the FBI had flown down. She'd refused to say anything, and they could find nothing in her movements or actions to tie her to the lost violin.

Ray's family continued to be scrutinized, Bill Soames reported, but their bank accounts remained consistent (**Consistently low,** Ray thought), and none of them had acted suspiciously. Until someone made a move or slipped up, nothing could be done against them.

The Marks family, by their very existence, was the most frustrating. If they hadn't stolen the violin, they **should** have—and in any case they should take the blame. That said, the Markses had been very quiet since the theft: their lawyer had never coughed up additional evidence of the Markses' legal claim. "Why should they," Ray told Alicia, "since they already have the violin? Their niece is probably practicing on it right now." Maybe the niece and Pilar Jiménez would start a chamber group.

So Ray had lost faith in the FBI and in Benson's crack art detective, Alicia. If he was going to get the violin back, he was going to have to do it himself.

He'd tried to find investors to pay the ransom, but the money hadn't materialized. So he'd tried to raise the money himself, spending an hour a day on his crowdfunding site, answering questions or reaching out to music lovers, violin aficionados, fan groups. By the first week of June, he'd raised $1.2 million.

So he hit the talk shows. Going to New York seemed intrusive and would derail his daily practicing, so he reached out to the TV and radio producers he'd met over the past year and invited them to film him in Charlotte. Several syndicated radio shows aired interviews across America. **The New York Times** unveiled an enormous photo of him on the first page of the Style section. By June 15, the day before he was leaving for Moscow, he'd raised $2,330,285: $1,349,775 from wealthy donors, $683,510 from crowdfunding, $52,000 from the bank. Janice had taken out a second mortgage on her house and given him $245,000. His family had been disinclined to assist. Why would they? They'd get $5 million shortly.

The Tchaikovsky Competition loomed. Ray couldn't forget those millions of online viewers who would be watching the contest. All rabid classical music fans. Many wealthy. If half of them donated one dollar, he'd have the ransom money.

Win or lose, gold medal or none, the Tchaikovsky Competition—which he'd spent the last eight months practicing for—took on a whole new meaning: it would be his road to recovering the violin. The longer he survived in the tournament, the more people would see him and, hopefully, want to contribute to the crowdfunding campaign.

Ray couldn't wait to get to Moscow.

Chapter 26

Day 32: Departure

On June 16, the day that he, Nicole, and Janice were heading to Moscow, Ray was packing when Kim Wach called. "Hey," she said, "glad I caught you."

"I leave in three hours," he said. "Please tell me you're calling with good news? The Markses dropped their suit?"

"I wish," she said. "I'm actually calling with bad news. I wish I didn't have to tell you before you leave for the competition, but there's no way around it."

His heart hit his throat. "What is it? Is it them? The Marks family?"

"Yes," she said. "They've altered their claim. Since the violin has been stolen—allegedly through your negligence—they're now going after the insurance money. All ten million dollars. They're claiming it's theirs. Their lawyer sent a raft of paperwork over to me—I'll email it to you if you want to read it on the plane. But it's fine by me if you just want to wait until after you're back."

He slumped against the wall. "You know that the Tchaikovsky Competition is supposed to be the biggest pressure cooker in the classical music world? I was reading over the guidelines last night. Before I head to Moscow, I'm supposed to get at least eight hours' sleep and not panic about all the music I'll be playing. There are websites with meditation suggestions. I'm pretty sure this wack-ass lawsuit isn't in their rules."

"Glad you haven't lost your sense of humor," she said. "There's one more thing. It's not hugely urgent, but I figure I might as well tell you."

He waited.

"The lawyer is asking that the original violin case be examined and documented. Photographed, appraised, etc."

"Holy crap, are you serious?"

"It's not a big deal," she said. "You just have to take it to a mutually agreed-upon appraiser who'll photograph it and appraise it. Easy."

"Can I do it when I get back?"

"Of course," she said, "But I've talked to the attorney, and they're okay using the people who restored the violin in the first place. They may want a second opinion if they contest the value, but this feels a bit pro forma at this point. The case is probably only worth a couple hundred dollars."

"So Jacob Fischer can do it?"

"Yes," she said. "If there's time, you can drop it off before you head to the airport. If not, you can take it after you get back. I'd love to get this sorted sooner rather than later, but in any case that's all I need from you for the time being."

"Okay," he said. Ray had almost forgotten the case, stuffed in a garbage bag under his bed. Now he dug it out from under the bed, wiped the dust bunnies off the garbage bag, and carried it, still in the bag, to Jacob's for photographing.

What a waste of time and money, Ray fumed as he tossed the case into the back of his car. Whatever. Everything with the Markses wasted his time and money. He should be getting used to it by now. He'd drop the case off with Jacob, since the shop was on the way to the airport.

PART 6
Competition

Chapter 27

Day 33: The Prequalifying Round

Six stories of ornately clad windows glared at Ray as he emerged from the taxi. The Moscow State Tchaikovsky Conservatory brooded down: an enormous Greek Revival building, with ionic columns flanking an austere pediment.

On the other side of the driveway, a colossal bronze statue of Pyotr Ilyich Tchaikovsky, conducting a silent symphony, gleamed in a small park, the reds and yellows of the roses, marigolds, and dozens of other flowers glowing in the late-afternoon sunshine. Quite a sight for a Black guy who'd never been out of America before.

He'd made it. The Tchaikovsky Competition. The Music Olympics: ten days of arguably the most grueling performances in the classical music world.

Three hundred sixty candidates had been selected

for the live preselection/qualifying round, with sixty each from the following categories: violin, cello, brass, piano, woodwind, and voice. Two days from now, the numbers would be cut: there would be twenty-five violinists in the First Round, then that number would whittle down to twelve in the Second Round, and finally to six in the Third Round.

Only a handful of Americans had ever made it to the First Round, and only one had actually won. Now, Ray vowed, it would be two.

Nicole and Janice were back at the hotel. They'd flown over with him on the sixteen-hour flight, and they'd all staggered gratefully to their rooms at the flamboyant National Hotel, near the city center. Despite his weariness, Ray was charged up. "I'm going to go over and register," he told Nicole.

She was sitting on the bed in a daze. "You want me to come? I'll come if you want."

"Nah." He grinned at her. "You have a lie-down, as they say on this side of the pond. I'll check out the Moscow hotties and report back."

He grabbed a taxi outside and went to check out his competition—not the Moscow women (although, to be fair, there were several head-turning young women on the drive).

The press photos of the Conservatory's auditoriums were dauntingly impressive. Soaring ceilings vaulted over intricate plasterwork, rows of theater seats encircled perfectly proportioned half-moons of stages. Everything in the pictures gleamed gold and blue and white, stunning in its magnificence.

Reality was, as usual, less enticing. Outside the main hall and the smaller performing halls, the classrooms, offices, and practice rooms were decidedly more run-down and pedestrian. The stone floors and the off-white paint on the walls seemed slightly exhausted—just a bit grimy, as if the building had been waiting for an enormous hand wielding a mop dipped in a truckload of industrial-strength bleach, to make it sparkle. The public glamor and private grubbiness made him feel welcome and immediately helped him get his bearings. Despite the Cyrillic signs everywhere, this place was similar to all the other theaters he'd played in over the past year.

He felt similarly about the other competitors. Before he'd arrived, and even though he'd watched a lot of the internet footage of previous competitions, he'd somehow expected everyone to be wearing tuxedos or ball gowns and to be dignified and austere. He imagined a lot of bows and curtsies, the kissing of gloved hands. He knew, of course, that this was a competition for the young, but seeing many kids younger than himself—seventeen or eighteen—dressed casually in jeans and sneakers, complaining about waiting in line or wondering if they could get a cup of coffee, made him feel like he belonged. He was as good as they were. No one was Black, but he didn't expect that. Besides, he'd gotten used to being immediately distinguishable from the crowd: people knew who he was just by the color of his skin.

When he'd first pulled open the enormous doors into the towering vestibule, he thought that the people were looking at him because he was the only Black guy in the crowd, but when an older woman with tired blue eyes and a gentle handshake immediately approached him, telling him in a heavy French accent how sorry she was to learn about his Strad, he realized that the heads turning had little to do with the color of his skin and everything to do with the loss of the violin. In minutes he was surrounded—dozens of hands reached out to pat him on the back, and he heard what he thought was "sorry" in dozens of languages.

The crush of people scared him for a moment, but then he realized that this was his tribe, people whose lives centered around music—who would understand like no one else what losing his violin meant to him.

He stood in line for registration. People were still constantly tapping him on the shoulder, talking to him in heavily accented English, Russian or other Eastern European languages, or French, German, or Japanese. Sometimes he could distinguish only the words "sorry" or "Stradivarius."

Then he caught sight of not one but two camera

crews from medici.tv, which would circle the hall, streaming the performance live to its five million viewers. The lights were disorienting, casting unexpected shadows. He needed to be interviewed, so he could appeal to its listeners to go to his crowdfunding site. As soon as he was registered, he'd introduce himself to one of the camera crews.

Many kids had come with their parents, luggage in tow, straight from their flights. A tall, slender guy, two contestants ahead, carried a cello case. A CANADIAN A bumper sticker with a maple leaf on it shone red and white against the black fiberglass.

A tall Slavic woman with acne scars on her cheeks and a bloom of pimples on her chin said, "Excuse me, you are Ray McMillian, yes?"

"Hey. Yeah," Ray said, holding out his hand. "Violin. And you are . . . ?"

"Svetlana Svotsolov, voice," she said. "So sorry to hear about your violin," she started, and Ray got ready with his standard "Thanks, I haven't given up hope" response; but she went on, "My friends and I have bet that you would speak with Mikhail and I won this bet. So thank you."

"What bet? Who's Mikhail?"

"My friends"—she indicated the two girls with her—"bet that you would speak to him, and I bet that you would not. I have won this bet, and they must take me to special dinner, so thank you."

He shook his head, bewildered. "I don't understand. Who's Mikhail? Why would I talk to him? Is he American?"

She laughed, and her friends laughed, too. "Mikhail Lezenkov," said the short dark-haired girl next to Svetlana, like it was obvious. "Mikhail Lezenkov from Serbia," she repeated, like maybe he was teasing her.

Ray stared at her blankly. "Sorry, miss, I'm not following you. Is he a judge?"

"He is—how do you say?" They talked among themselves for a moment. "He is your rival," Svetlana said. She fumbled with her phone, pulled up a page, handed it to him.

It was in Cyrillic. He handed it back. "I can't read this. And I honestly don't know what you're talking about."

The third girl was pulling up a translation: "Who will win the Tchaikovsky Competition, America or Serbia?" He scanned the blog post. Apparently cyberspace was taking bets about the outcome of the competition, and there were two crowd favorites: the Serbian Mikhail Lezenkov and the American Rayquan McMillian. He wasn't sure if he should be flattered, embarrassed, or surprised.

"I didn't even know about this," he said. "I haven't really been focusing on social media." Ray had spent the last month online dealing with crowdfunding. He'd studiously avoided looking at the other potential competitors; for him, this was all about the music, about playing the best he could, and he knew that if he spent a lot of time studying other people who potentially would be competing against him, it would only undermine his confidence and psych him out. Besides, up until a few weeks ago he'd had one advantage that none of the rest of them possessed: a magical violin that made every note sound perfect.

"Mikhail is right there," the dark-haired girl said, pointing with her chin. "He keeps looking at you, you did not see?"

Ray hadn't noticed, but now he turned, like a moron, and locked eyes with a handsome blue-eyed blond guy about his age standing in another line a few feet away.

"Stop!" Svetlana said, grabbing Ray's shoulder. "Now he knows we are talking about him!"

The damage was done. All Ray could do was give a cool **What's up?** nod and turn back to the group. "I guess this hasn't really hit the States yet," he told them.

"Are you going to talk to him?"

"Probably later," he said.

He wished them luck—only Svetlana was competing, the others were there for moral support—said goodbye, and his turn came at the registration desk to pick up his badge and registration materials.

Afterward he'd planned on introducing himself to the medici.tv people, but a thought had struck him and now he couldn't shake it loose. He wandered outside, thinking about **Mikhail Lezenkov from Serbia.** He tried out the name a few times. How awesome that he had a rival, that a bunch of strangers would create his own personal duel. Typical media hype.

His brain felt like a Ferris wheel, spinning—catching a glimpse of a farther shore, and then whirling on and down. He decided to walk back to the hotel, since it wasn't far. He checked out a few shop windows as he passed, enjoying the exotic alienness of an early Moscow evening. Maybe he'd pick up the gorgeous silver filigree necklace, set with blue-painted porcelain beads for Nicole. That amber bracelet, in the next shop window, would look really good on Aunt Rochelle. **Mikhail Lezenkov from Serbia.** He didn't have a lot of money left—especially with the Markses' lawsuit—but he thought a little splurging wouldn't hurt anybody. To celebrate his arrival in Moscow, he bought a sweet braided-dough **kolach** from a tiny bakery, ate it as he walked.

Mikhail Lezenkov. He couldn't shake the name. It resonated, echoing.

Now a wild, irrational thought kept bouncing around his head: Could Mikhail Lezenkov have had anything to do with his Strad's theft? Of course not: Ray was seeing suspects everywhere. It was only natural.

But he couldn't shake the possibility, and the more he mulled it over, the less irrational it seemed.

He pulled out his phone and googled **Mikhail Lezenkov**, but it was too hard to walk, eat, and read. Besides, the hotel was only a couple blocks away now.

The blinds had been drawn in the hotel room. Nicole breathed, rhythmic and faint. He showered—she'd unpacked and left his toiletry bag in the bathroom, what a goddess!—slipped into bed, pulled up the website he'd been looking at on the street.

The alleged rivalry between Lezenkov and McMillian was all over the internet, on all social-media channels that covered the Tchaikovsky Competition—which, to be fair, were mostly European. But still, he hadn't touched social media for the past six months. He also never googled himself—it was too weird. He wondered why nobody had mentioned this rivalry to him before, and he had a vague recollection of Nicole—or was it Janice?—mentioning that one of the other competitors was really great, but honestly he hadn't been paying much attention, caught up in the loss of the Strad and the pressure of practicing.

So, Ray thought, let's just say that you're a young ambitious Serbian violinist who everyone says is a shoo-in for winning the Tchaikovsky Competition—except for one other competitor, some Black dude who happened to luck into a Stradivarius. Without it, the Black dude is just a really good player. With it, the Strad could put him over the top. Is it inconceivable to believe that you'd figure out a way to steal the violin? Find a housekeeper in a hotel where the Black dude is staying, pay her a few thousand dollars to take it?

Ray was crazy. Stupid. Paranoid.

He slipped out of bed, into the bathroom, texted Alicia.

Ray: **Hi I'm in Moscow theres a serbian violinist who ppl say is my big rival here. Mikhail Lezenkov, google him. I just learned this a few minutes ago or i wouldve said something sooner. You asked about people with a motive, he has a big one**

Alicia: **Just to win the competition? I know it's a big deal but is that really a motive?**

Ray: **I seriously think it is. Can you at least check it out?**

Alicia: **This is really interesting. There's a violin rumored to be for sale in Serbia. Black market. I was having contacts check it out but its one of several leads. Now will dig in more thoroughly asap**

Ray: **Theres a black market violin in Serbia????????? Seriously??**

Alicia: **Dont get your hopes up. I heard of violins for sale in Qatar and China too**

He lay awake for another hour, vibrating with exhaustion, listening to Nicole's breathing, unable to stop thinking about Mikhail Lezenkov, those knowing blue eyes. Would his family steal the violin, sell it on the black market, **and** get the ransom money? And their son would win the competition to boot. Why hadn't Ray thought of it himself?

Finally he wrapped himself around Nicole and at last fell asleep, not waking until the alarm went off three hours later.

The day was slated for practice, with a schedule and practice room assigned before the prequalifying round the next day; but at the Conservatory all the musicians distracted him, and he ended up returning to the hotel and running his prequalifying program with Janice and Nicole. In the afternoon he returned to the Conservatory to look for Mikhail Lezenkov but couldn't find him.

He did find the medici.tv camera crews, however. The Russian classical music scene was on an entirely different level from America's. Both up-and-coming as well as established musicians held rock star status, primarily because medici.tv broadcasted all types of classical music performances: opera, small ensembles, choral, soloists, orchestras. The station's logos and banners were prominent in the hall and in the programs.

An interview couch sat right inside the small auditorium's foyer. On it, a correspondent interviewed one of the piano contestants. Ray lingered. The young Japanese pianist batted her eyes at the camera and at the fans who loosely circled them. She was really excited to be playing the second Ravel Piano Concerto: "I feel the second movement will really speak to the souls of anyone who has ever been in love." Okay then. Sure.

Here goes nothing, he thought.

He straightened his blue blazer, waded through a group of Russian and Asian fans, made eye contact with the interviewer as the pianist's interview concluded. The Japanese pianist was barely off the couch before the interviewer—a young woman with shaggy hair and round John Lennon–style glasses—was up and shaking her hand, her smile as wide as the couch she'd been sitting on. "Rayquan McMillian, welcome to Moscow! How are you feeling? Are you ready to take on the competition? Do you have a few moments? We'd love the chance to talk to you."

Ray was careful to smile as he shook her hand. The camera's enormous eye glittered at him, but he'd done his share of media interviews: after **60 Minutes**, this didn't seem particularly terrifying. "I'm really happy to be here. I'm so excited to be a part of the competition."

He was focused on the camera and the interviewer, but could sense the crowd around and behind him: people were gathering, listening.

"Rayquan, you have such an interesting story—so inspiring and so heartbreaking."

"Please, call me Ray."

"We've all heard about the devastating loss of your instrument, but we'll get to that in a moment. What made you decide to enter this competition?"

The trick, he knew, was to first make your audience sympathize with you. Then you could make the ask. "I've always loved music," he said. "I've always loved playing. This is the most prestigious musical competition in the world. Of course I want to be part of it."

"The world is glad you are a part of it. We have all been following your journey, which is so unconventional and so inspiring. No formal instruction until college, I believe? And you play at jazz clubs? How have you managed to balance these aspects and make it this far in the classical music world?"

Ray talked about how music was a strong influence in his life, how he'd made music on a cheap school rental, how people surrounding him had supported him, saw something in him that he hadn't even known existed. "I learned to accept help and encouragement in every form it comes in," he said.

The crowd let out a collective "Awwww."

This was his chance.

"Which is why I'm hoping your viewers can help me. As you know, my violin was stolen a month ago."

"We've heard. So terrible. And it hasn't been recovered."

"No, it hasn't been recovered. Yet. But your viewers can actually help. You may know that there's a five-million-dollar ransom, due in less than a month. July fifteenth. I don't have the money but I'm trying to raise it myself. So part of the reason I'm here, part of the reason I'm actually competing, is to make an appeal to your listeners to help me get my violin back."

"How can we help?"

"I'm doing everything humanly possible to raise the money. I know there are millions of people watching this competition right now. Imagine if five million of you sent me one US dollar. I could pay the ransom and get my violin back. Everyone would have a chance to hear it."

He looked directly at the camera, imagining that it wasn't a cold round lens but the face of a little old Black lady in a pink housecoat, her blue-tinted hair in curlers. "Please," he said, and the emotion was raw in his voice. "Please help me get my violin back. My crowdfunding page is Ray's Fiddle. Please help me."

Silence for a moment, both from the woman across from him and from the audience. Then the woman cleared her throat. "Well then, there you have it. A very heartfelt plea from the American violinist Ray McMillian for help in the return of his violin. Ray, will you join us again in the coming days to update us?"

Ray leaned in and smiled. "Absolutely."

He spent the afternoon talking to audience members, providing further information about the violin, checking the GoFundMe page: the donations had immediately spiked by another $10,000 and were steadily increasing. He just needed it to go viral.

Next day, after an early workout and a quick practice, Ray, Nicole, and Janice returned for the live prequalifying round, which started at 9:30 a.m. He caught sight of Mikhail Lezenkov, who appeared right before they all went off with their different groups to separate parts of the building for the next five hours.

Ray had chosen a grueling twenty-minute program: **Tzigane** and **Dance of the Goblins**, with Tchaikovsky's obligatory **Sérénade mélancolique** thrown in. Janice tried to give him last-minute suggestions backstage, but he didn't really hear her. He was itching to be in front of the orchestra, show them what he could do. He was in a group of fifteen, performing for judges and a packed audience of rabid music lovers who stomped and cheered for each contestant. As he stepped onto the stage, the press in the balcony lifted cameras, the audience clapped and held up phones to record him. The air was electric. The crowd thundered—he couldn't believe that even in this preselection round there would be an audience of such rabid classical music fans.

Marathon runners train for months, gradually building up endurance and strength—both mental and physical—to withstand hours of running. A few weeks before the race, they taper down to shorter, easier runs, scaling back on their mileage to be fresh for race day.

All Ray knew, at the start of the competition, was that he hadn't really picked up his violin to play seriously for well over a week. He hadn't the heart, so he'd focused on the theft and trying to raise money for the ransom; and then there was the travel to Moscow. So now, as he jumped into his beloved **Tzigane**, which he'd practiced endlessly for the past six months, he was playing it fresh—the Gypsy themes, light and bold, poured from the violin, and he threw himself into its lushness.

The ten minutes of Ravel flew by and then he was on to the Bazzini, and all too soon Tchaikovsky's wistful, elegant, **Sérénade mélancolique**. He realized only when he had finished that it was over. He bowed and the crowd again roared approval, palms hammering against armrests and feet stomping. He'd never played for such an enthusiastic audience before—despite the pressure, it really was fun. He gave a thumbs-up to the judges and the crowd collectively "lost their shit," as he told Janice afterward.

That evening, the judges read out the names of the twenty-five performers who were officially competitors and, the next day, would begin the First Round. Ray was one of them. So was Mikhail Lezenkov.

The competition had begun.

Chapter 28

Day 36: First Round

The next morning he didn't much feel like eating. Nicole made him choke down some **kasha**, a kind of Russian oatmeal that really wasn't so bad after the first few spoonfuls. He worked out hard in the hotel gym—the weights were all marked in Cyrillic, which was disorienting, but the weight machines were familiar enough.

At 9:00 a.m., the twenty-five violinists for the First Round assembled in the Small Hall, its white and gold glowing brighter than ever, to draw lots for the order in which they'd play throughout the competition: Ray drew the number six and would play on Day One. Mikhail Lezenkov drew number thirteen and would play on Day Two. After that, twelve musicians would move on to the Second Round, and a final six to the Third Round.

Ray had two hours to rehearse with his accompanist in a practice room, then, that afternoon, he'd rehearse with her onstage in the recital hall.

After about twenty minutes of warming up alone, a knock came on the practice-room door. A middle-aged horse-faced lady, hair tightly pulled back in a bun, introduced herself: Mariamna Gaevscaya.

She took a seat. Her fingers flexed dangerously above the piano's keyboard as if intending to inflict harm. The next hour felt deeply unsatisfying as they stopped periodically to adjust phrasing and timing. She was a pro, a Russian playing in Russia—the fault, clearly, was his. Her piano couldn't be out of tune, could it? No, of course not. Maybe it was his violin? He hadn't had the Lehman long enough. He was trying to make the Lehman do what his Strad had done—with his own violin, it had been effortless. Now, with this one, he still had to focus on every bow stroke, every position. It was work: he wasn't playing music, he was working at playing music.

She could tell how miserable he was; she was very disapproving. But maybe that was just her regular expression. They would have a final rehearsal onstage, she reminded him, and it sounded like a threat.

His First Round repertoire: Bach's Chaconne from Partita no. 2 in D Minor; Paganini's Caprices nos. 24 and 6; Tchaikovsky's **Valse-Scherzo**; and, again, Ravel's **Tzigane**.

After Mariamna had stomped out—no doubt in search of better musicians to accompany—he skipped lunch and stayed in his practice room, woodshedding: going over and over the same phrasing until he got it right, trying to recapture the music. No wonder she was so pissed: he sucked.

He realized that up until today—until he was actually playing with his accompanist—he'd just been practicing: with his teachers, alone at home, in the hotel rooms. He'd been learning the notes. The time for practice had ended, and now it was time to perform, really perform—time to connect with the audience and make them feel about this music the way he felt about it. But he wasn't performing. He was just playing notes, almost randomly.

He wondered if it was too late to back out altogether. He'd thought that when he arrived in Moscow, being around all the other competitors would renew his laser focus, but in reality the opposite was true: he couldn't concentrate for more than fifteen minutes. He was constantly checking his phone between pieces, watching the numbers climb on the crowdfunding site and hoping Alicia would call with news. His phone's voice mail continued to fill with media inquiries and questions from possible donors who could fund the $5 million ransom.

Around 2:00 p.m. came a light tapping on the

door: Nicole. He let her in. "Did you eat?" she asked.

"Um—well, I thought I should practice."

"I figured," she said, and handed him an apple and a granola bar.

"Where the hell did you find a granola bar?" he asked her.

"Never underestimate a girl from Greenwich," she said. "I'm not giving up my secrets. Sorry, dude."

He took the granola bar, tore open the wrapper.

"How's it going?" she asked.

"Okay. It's aiight."

"Really?" She was staring at him as he chewed.

"Yeah, it's fine. Why?"

"Because you seem really wired. Really tense. You're usually much more relaxed when you're practicing."

"This is the Tchaikovsky Competition, remember?"

"Yeah, I remember," she said. "All sixteen hours on the plane. Come here." She gently grabbed the back of his neck, pulled his forehead until his touched hers. He was still chewing the granola bar. But as soon as he felt the light pressure of her skin, he could feel himself relax—as if her serenity, her calm, was flowing into him. Giving him strength. "You can do this," she said. "You're doing it."

"Yeah," he said. "I know."

"Well, it never hurts to be reminded now and

then." She kissed him lightly. "You get back to work. There's this hot Russian guy that was checking me out on my way over here and I want to make sure he got my number right."

"Good one," he said.

She left him to practice.

By late afternoon, self-doubt had bloomed into all-out self-disgust. He decided that coming to the Tchaikovsky Competition was the dumbest thing he could have done. The rivalry with Mikhail Lezenkov was stupid, because of course Mikhail was a better player. One minute Ray was blaming himself and the next minute he was blaming the Lehman. The Strad's absence throbbed in the air. Playing with this other violin was like playing with a prosthetic arm; it worked but was not the same. It felt lifeless. It was all the Lehman's fault that he was fuckin' up Christmas.

There was no use in more woodshedding. He was not getting any better and wasn't going to get any better. He gave up. He wandered around the halls but felt like an endangered species on display. Stares from every direction. One young man actually came up and tried to touch his hair.

"Come on, man. Not cool."

Press and fans circled him, and again he spoke to as many media outlets as he could: "If you're watching this, know that I'm trying to get my violin back. It was stolen a month ago, and the kidnappers want five million dollars. That's what I'm trying to raise. I can't do it alone. I need your help."

The afternoon rehearsal onstage went no better than the rehearsal in the practice room. If he'd held out hope that Mariamna was not deeply disapproving of his existence, that hope was dashed: he was sure she thought that his survival this far in the competition was due, without question, to a clerical error. He suspected that she was right.

Back in the hotel, he changed into his tuxedo, which felt too tight. He was probably getting fat. It would undoubtedly split open in the middle of the Paganini. He waddled up to the warm-up room to await his imminent debacle, figured he might as well warm up. Because playing for the past ten hours hadn't warmed him up, right?

In the practice room, the Bach Chaconne awaited—one of the most difficult pieces, period, to play, because of its extensive polyphony and implied counterpoint. It was mathematical, precise, dizzying—and that's what he'd heard all the other contestants focusing on: making the piece precise, vital, energetic. Rachel Vetter kept drilling emotion. "Never forget the rich emotional core of the piece," she had told him.

And there, fed by the listeners, he felt himself thawing into the way he'd played for all those months of practice. Reached deep inside himself, summoning up strength and emotion and assurance. It was the audience that he tapped into. The music he knew; it was all muscle memory, and his muscles were ready. He could feel the Bach reaching out from his shoulders like wings, or a cloak, lifting into the corners of the room.

Dimly he was aware of Mikhail Lezenkov in a corner, watching coldly, and Ray could not have cared less.

He was ready. His Bach was sounding exactly the way he wanted—like himself, like all the work he'd put in, to be distinctive and original. A few heads turned as he practiced. Mariamna was there, and together they walked out onstage. He held the emotion close to him, looked out at the sea of white faces, so different from his own, and vowed that he would connect with them: if nothing else, he would connect.

Those fifty minutes he played seemed more like five. One after the other, the music spooled from him and his instrument: the Bach, the Paganini, the Tchaikovsky, the Ravel.

He fucking belonged up here.

He didn't want to leave the stage. Ever.

This audience was like nothing he'd ever experienced. He knew that the online component was following the competition by making lists and tallying scores. Dozens of cameras stared into him to remind him that five million people were watching, sending money to his crowdfunding site.

But now, here in the recital hall, it was the live people, the people in front of him, who gave him a boost. With every pull of his bow, the audience leaned one way or another, like they were sledding, pounding on the seats at the end and standing up and shouting. It was electrifying, terrifying, and reminded Ray of a gospel choir.

When they finished, Mariamna smiled at him—or maybe it was a wince, it was difficult for Ray to tell. He was dripping with sweat but barely noticed. So that's what playing in a perfect concert hall, with hordes of passionate music lovers, was like. Could he do it every night?

After his performance came an intermission, and the crowd swarmed him. One man, a very tall Russian, extended his hand. "You played well for your kind. We have not seen this. I did not think this possible." Ray knew already—how could he not—that there was an obvious Russian bias in the judging: the question was, what was Ray's "kind"? Being Black? American? Non-Russian? All of the above? He wasn't sure if it was a compliment or an insult, and decided to just ignore it.

Another media interview: "I'm not asking for myself, to get my violin back. You're making an investment not only in me but in your future. I'll be making music for many years to come, and I want to make sure that everyone can enjoy it. Just a dollar's donation can make an enormous difference."

There was a seat for him to watch the rest of the performances, but he obstinately decided instead to head for the hotel and get ready for the opening-night gala. That evening, at 7:00 p.m., the competition was officially inaugurated with a "Grand Opening" in the "Great Hall": these Russians did nothing by halves.

Press people surrounded him in the lobby. Asked him about his chances as an American to win a prize that no American had won since the first competition in 1958, when a twenty-three-year-old Texan named Van Cliburn won the heart of Moscow and took home the grand prize and international adulation that lasted the rest of his life. Ray answered their questions until the lights flickered and it was time to take their seats. He sat next to a scrawny cellist.

The kid introduced himself: "Annyeonghaseyo, Kwon Jungho-rago hamnida." Ray must have looked blank because the kid laughed, said, "I'm just fucking with you," and told Ray to call him Josh. He was Korean and had been playing since he was four. He'd spent a year studying in Japan and then two years in Italy. By eleven, he'd won several prestigious awards in Korea, then spent a year at the Manhattan School of Music, which was why his English was so good.

All this came out in a few minutes. These

competitors wouldn't just introduce themselves, Ray soon realized; they introduced their résumés.

Ray's résumé: Pretending his bed's headboard was the violin's fingerboard. Taking a beat-up old fiddle for repairs in an Atlanta suburban mall, where a racist clerk told him to pull up his pants. Begging for rides to a jazz club just so he could play for an audience. And now he was here, surrounded by the best young musicians in the world, in the grandest music hall in Moscow, with the Russian prime minister slated to appear and say stuff. Not too shabby.

At last it began. Fanfare. Speeches. Music, much of it by Tchaikovsky (this could not be a coincidence, given the enormous portrait of the composer that loomed over the stage). Performances by grand prix winners, Grammy Award winners. More speeches. Much self-congratulatory back-slapping. Ray wanted to savor each minute, but honestly couldn't wait for it to be over.

Then there was the gala, with champagne in tall flutes and vodka in shot glasses. There were hors d'oeuvres, mostly unidentifiable pastries with unknown meat-like fillings inside; Ray skipped them and dived into the grapes and cheeses.

Now that he was aware of Mikhail Lezenkov's existence, he saw him everywhere. They circled each other like hermit crabs, claws extended, holding champagne glasses, hiding behind the crowd like rocks in the sand. Neither made a move to approach.

In the meantime the mob swarmed him, thrusting out programs for autographs, posing for selfies, asking him how the crowdfunding was going. Who would win, the classically trained Eastern European aristocrat from a strings-playing dynasty? Or the Black kid who'd rented his fiddle and had no private instruction, no family support, and had gained and already lost a Stradivarius? Tune in at eleven o'clock.

This audience and this media saw him the way that all the kids saw him in college, the way orchestras saw him when he set foot on the stage: as a PR stunt, as something good for ratings, a nod to diversity. **Look at the darkie playing the violin like a human being.** They loved him not for his musicianship but for his facade. Because he was cute, and Black, and different. He smiled and smiled and couldn't wait for tomorrow, when he could show them what he could do in a competition based on musicality, not on backstory.

And in the meantime he'd play on their sympathy—he'd get their donations. He'd get his violin back.

Because he'd played on the first day of the competition, he had the next two days off—to practice for the Second Round, if he made it.

Instead he stalked Mikhail Lezenkov. That afternoon, at 2:00 p.m., he watched Mikhail perform. Mikhail was, in a word, brilliant. A crisp, almost machinelike technique, combined with a sound that reminded Ray of a young Isaac Stern, made him a very formidable opponent. Mikhail performed a wild Shostakovich sonata that Ray had never seen anyone perform live. Mikhail played with crazed virtuosity, his fingers flying up and down the fingerboard, every note crystal clear. He made playing Shostakovich look easy. He must have been playing that piece since he was five. It was, Ray admitted, wonderful to listen to him: Mikhail brought such a spark to the music, such an extraordinary energy. They played very differently: Ray was all passion and fire; Mikhail was electricity and light, with a sweetness that was endearing and impressive.

After Mikhail's performance, he came back into the warm-up room, his coach and friends backslapped him, and Ray edged toward him. But Mikhail's coach put an arm around his shoulder and, heads bent together, led him away.

Ray followed, finally cornering him in a back corridor behind the practice rooms, without many people about. He lunged forward, extending his hand. "Mikhail. I've been wanting to meet you."

"Hello, American."

They shook hands.

"Your Shostakovich was insane," Ray said, meaning it. "I had no idea it could be played like that."

Abruptly and unexpectedly, Mikhail pulled Ray in and whispered in his thick Eastern European accent, still fake smiling, "You will not win."

"Probably not," Ray said easily. "I'm a Black American. The judges will say that I don't have Russian in my veins the way you do. But that's cool. It's pretty awesome just to be here."

"You do not care that you will lose?" Mikhail seemed unconvinced.

Ray shrugged. "Of course I care. But I made it this far. I think both of us will make it into the next round, and maybe even to the finals. That's pretty historic for me, and for the US. I'm not going to complain." Finally he arrived at the point of the conversation he'd been planning for three days: "Especially since I don't have my violin." **Say it casually, Ray. So casually.**

"Ah," Mikhail said. "I hear of this. Your violin, she was stolen, I am sorry of this."

As they were speaking, Ray carefully and deftly steered the big blond man over to the back wall, away from the doors leading to the auditorium, where it was quieter. "I'm thinking more about my violin than I am about this competition, to be honest."

"It seems to me you are thinking very much about this competition."

"I'd walk out right this second if someone told me he knew where my violin was."

"You would do this? For a violin? Well, it is a Stradivarius." Mikhail guffawed. "Probably many people would do this."

"I would do it in a heartbeat," Ray said earnestly. "My grandmother gave me the violin. It means everything to me."

Mikhail laughed again. "I wish I could tell you where your violin is then. I would for sure win gold."

"You're from Serbia, right?"

"Yes. Belgrade. Why do you ask?"

"I heard a rumor that the violin was actually in Serbia."

"Really?" Mikhail seemed genuinely surprised, but he was a performer, after all. "I know nothing of this."

"Would you know people who might? Your family is really tapped into the music world, right? Would they be able to ask around? I'd pay to get it back. The insurance company would pay."

Mikhail looked around the crowded hall, the people eyeing them. "This is not the conversation I expect to have with you, American."

Ray shrugged. "I've been trying to find you for the past two days, but you've been hard to track down."

"Let me see what I can find out," Mikhail said.

"My father knows all the important people in Belgrade."

Ray handed him the business card that he'd been carrying in his pocket for three days. On it he'd written his hotel and the room number; his email address and phone number were already there. "Seriously, man," he said, "if you hear anything, let me know. I'd be on a plane to Belgrade in seconds. I'd forfeit without even blinking."

"I do not wish you to forfeit," Mikhail said.

Ray shrugged.

"But I will ask my family. My parents, they are here tonight, of course. I will have them talk to their friends."

"Thanks, man." They shook hands again, and this time they meant it.

He texted Alicia: **Any news? Talked to the Serbian guy and hes going to ask around**

A few hours later Alicia messaged him: **Looks like your source was accurate. Following a lead on a violin in Belgrade. I'm flying there immediately. Ill keep you informed. Stay focused.**

The next day he again holed up in the practice room. Nicole came in a couple times but spent most of her time prowling backstage and listening from the wings. "That Mikhail guy is good," she said. "Really good. You should listen to him." He didn't go. Instead he threw himself into the music in a way that he hadn't before the First Round's performance. That evening he got takeout from a restaurant between the Conservatory and the hotel and ate it in his room, watched TV and fell asleep, exhausted.

The next night, Ray, Nicole, and Janice joined the other contestants and their fans in the main hall for the announcement of who would be among the twelve to move on to the Second Round. Each name was met with thunderous cheering and applause. When the elderly judge on the left—one of the top violinists in the world—called Ray's name, the crowd roared even louder. It was kind of cool to be the favorite. They called Mikhail Lezenkov's name two slots after his.

He could feel eyes upon him and involuntarily looked over. Mikhail Lezenkov stared back, smiling slightly.

Chapter 29

Day 40: Second Round

The evening's festivities were still moving forward when Alicia texted. His phone, muted, buzzed lightly. He stood up, apologized as he stumbled over the people seated down the row and out of the hall.

Alicia: **Confirmed a black market violin in Serbia**

Ray: **Will let you know if I hear anything**

Alicia: **OK am pursuing leads. Will keep you posted**

Ray lingered in the ostentatious vestibule while the rest of the program finished inside—it felt rude to go back in. Once the final applause had washed out with the opening doors, the crowd following a few minutes later, he tried to find Mikhail, to ask him if he'd heard anything from his family yet.

It had seemed like every time Ray had left the

practice room that day, or the previous days, there was Mikhail, glowering. But now, true to the way the world worked, as soon as Ray wanted him, Mikhail had disappeared. He circled the hall several times. He asked Nicole to look for him, too—no luck. After a while the crowds wore him out. Ray went back to the hotel and went to sleep.

The Second Round followed the same order as the First Round, but now the number of contestants had been cut in half, to twelve. Ray was third on Day One, and Mikhail was ninth on Day Two.

He arrived at the Conservatory early that morning, hoping that Mikhail would already be there, just loitering outside in the Tchaikovsky garden, but Mikhail apparently hadn't gotten the memo and did not appear. He was probably hidden away in a bunker somewhere, plotting Ray's destruction.

The rehearsals with Mariamna went better this time. He'd clearly won her approval, or at least thawed the coolness of her disdain. Twice it seemed that she almost smiled—but perhaps it was just gas, or a finger cramp.

The grueling fifty-minute lineup for the Second Round: Mozart's Violin Sonata no. 21, Pablo de Sarasate's **Zigeunerweisen**, Kreisler's **Preludium and Allegro**, and Tchaikovsky's **Sérénade mélancolique**.

He couldn't get to the stage fast enough.

His goal, again, was to come out swinging and

make the judges notice him, and his focus was razor sharp. Mozart had written his sonata in 1778, just when he'd started as a freelance musician. It had a brilliant opening that shifted to restless agitation: there was a world of possibility in front of Mozart, in front of Ray, and they were eager to see it through, eager to get on with life, eager to rise to whatever challenge was in store. Ray felt like he owned every note, breathed life and possibility into each passage.

In the final movement, Mariamna wasn't quite behind him the way she should be. Was it on purpose? She was Russian, after all, and not Austrian. No matter, the judges were paying attention to him, not to the piano; and, in any case, he was having the time of his life.

The **Sarasate** was just fucking fun—a Gypsy delight that began slowly and stately and soon progressed into something so fast that he thought poor Mariamna might have a coronary trying to follow him. Guess these Russians have to work harder to hang with the homies, eh?

He played his Kreisler with flair and elegance. The piece had so much personality to it that there was no way a listener could not be charmed. The allegro section was incredibly fast—so much so that Ray actually impressed himself. Every note sounded even and true. Playing was like the first big drop on a roller coaster that just kept going down, endlessly, the thrill nonstop.

And finally—finally!—Tchaikovsky, of course. Let's be clear here: Ray may have looked like a Black American, but secretly—secretly!—he was Russian. Secretly he'd spent his life ladling borscht and nibbling pelmeni. Vodka, not blood, surged through his veins. He was melancholy because it was always winter in St. Petersburg, and jovial because Muscovites are a good-hearted people who love to laugh. He killed the Tchaikovsky. He left the **Sérénade mélancolique** bawling its eyes out onstage. He bowed.

He never held the Lehman out the way he'd held PopPop's fiddle.

Whether or not he made it through to the next round, he knew that he could have done no better, and that would have to be enough.

That night, in the grand hall, he and Mikhail sat next to each other, waiting for that final list of names to be called.

Silence fell as a world-class pianist stepped to the microphone, began to speak in Russian. Above him, three enormous monitors with close-captioned English translated in real time.

Ray couldn't read the words on the screen. He was suddenly, stupidly, conscious of Mikhail's tuxedo-clad shoulder so close to his: Mikhail's arm on the

armrest, the satin cuff of his sleeve, and the glitter of his opal-and-silver cuff links. How had he
gotten the armrest? Ray hadn't even realized it was
a competition but now wished that he could put
his own tuxedo-wrapped arm—with the good-luck
cuff links that Janice had given him last Christmas,
picked up from a mall in Charlotte—on the
armrest, claiming it as his own. Too late, and now
Mikhail, next to him, seemed twice the size of Ray,
looming blackly and confidently next to him like a
tuxedo-covered cement truck. How could Ray even
begin to compete with a cement truck?

The elderly judge with the quavering voice called
Mikhail's name, and a moment later Mikhail's
name flashed golden and enormous on the screen:
Mikhail Lezenkov. There it was. Ray was sitting
next to a finalist. Ray could feel eyes on him and
felt flattened by them. As the crowd roared out, Ray
couldn't help nodding, agreeing with the judges'
choice. **Of course** Mikhail was chosen. Ray reached
over and pounded Mikhail's back, and Mikhail
gripped his hand. Both their hands were sweaty.

The applause was dying down, the ancient pianist
judge was moving on, saying stuff, but Ray felt like
he was underwater, the sound blurred and ragged.
The closed-captioned letters flashed like fish in an
aquarium, wriggling away before he could read them.

And there it was, his name, alien in the judge's
foreign mouth—so alien that if he hadn't seen his

name snap into glittering gold on the screen, he might not have believed it.

Rayquan McMillian.

He wanted to jump up, fist-pump, scream "Fuck yeah!" as loud as he could. Instead he clenched his hand on the armrest—the hand inches from Mikhail's arm—and watched his dark fingers turn almost white from the pressure. **Fuck yeah.** Dimly, as if in another room, he could hear the crowd roaring his name, but sounds filtered in dimly, as if from underwater, or from space.

Was this real? Could it be a mistake?

And then Mikhail was turning, shaking his hand, and Nicole was pounding his back and he was hugging her and, fuck no, it was not a mistake. It was real. He was a fucking finalist in the Tchaikovsky Competition.

Chapter 30

Day 42: Serbia

Third Round: the honor and the pressure were immense—the media clamoring for interviews, programs being shoved at him for autographs, three record companies calling to ask when he'd have "five minutes for a quick conversation."

He knew he should milk it for everything he could. He should plaster his face over every media opportunity with a link to his crowdfunding page and a plea to donate just a dollar/euro/ruble so he could ransom back his violin.

And he had every intention of doing just that.

Then, late that night, after the latest round of gala cocktails and glasses of champagne and vodka floated past, after the chatting and the backslapping and the adulation, Alicia texted: **Hi I'm in Serbia.**

Theres a violin that's going on the black market. Will let you know when I learn more.

Serbia? Black market? No time to text: he called her. "So it's there?"

"Calm down," she said. "There is a violin here. I haven't seen photographs yet." A few weeks ago, she told him, one of her informants in Italy mentioned a violin somewhere in the Baltic states, newly up for sale.

A few other similar rumors floated in: It was in Montenegro; no, Croatia; no, Serbia. It was in Serbia's capital, Belgrade. Alicia's contact had reached out to the Belgrade police. A week ago, just after the start of the Tchaikovsky Competition, the chatter grew louder: a wealthy Serbian family of musicians was interested in purchasing a high-end violin. Money was no concern. Were any such violins available?

"Mikhail Lezenkov's family," Ray said.

"Quite possibly," she said. "Whatever you said to him seems to have shaken things loose."

"I'm coming," he said. "I'll be on the next plane." He was sitting on the edge of his hotel bed with Nicole hovering somewhere in front of him.

"Absolutely not," she said. "No. Don't even think of coming here."

"But if I see it, I'll know immediately if it's mine or not."

"So will I," she said. "I have enough photos to identify it in the dark."

"You need backup," he said.

"What are you going to do, serenade them to death?"

"I'm serious," he said. He worried that he sounded like he was whining.

"Look," she said, "I could be here for days. Weeks, even. This kind of thing takes time. I'll let you know how things go. You just go practice your Tchaikovsky and win a gold medal, will you?"

"Okay," Ray said, already pulling his suitcase out of his closet. "Keep me posted, will you?"

They hung up, and Ray packed.

Nicole begged to go with him, but he thought it would be better if he went alone. She and Janice could stay at the hotel, tell people that he was holed up in his room with a stomach bug. She could run interference for any competition officials who came to check in on him. Besides, he told her, he needed her and Janice to rearrange his practice session with the Moscow Philharmonic. He needed her in Moscow.

At last she relented. "We Greenwich girls hold it down for our men," she told Ray, sending him off with a hug and a deep kiss as he went to catch the first flight out to Belgrade.

After a three-hour flight, as soon as he had a cellular connection, Ray texted Alicia: **Hi where r u**

No immediate response. Was she still asleep? It was almost 9:00 a.m. Was she in the shower? Still, he was illogically disappointed. After he collected his suitcase and waded through customs, he took a cab to Belgrade's city center, passing a motley collection of ornate nineteenth-century buildings interspersed with blocky Soviet concrete monoliths. Alicia was staying at the Sky Hotel, she'd told him. He arrived and checked into an ultramodern mash-up of open white spaces and slanting plate glass.

He unpacked his Lehman and started practicing, his phone propped on the narrow hotel desk.

She didn't reply till almost 11:00 a.m.: **Sorry still no news**

Ray: **where r u**

Alicia: **Belgrade**

Ray: **where**

Alicia: **?? coming back from Dedinje**

Ray: **coming back to hotel?**

Alicia: **Yes. Why?**

Ray: **I'm at Sky Hotel, rm 409**

Alicia: **WHAT**

Ray: **Yeah I know you said not to come**

Alicia: **YOU WILL BLOW MY COVER**

Ray: **Meet me in my hotel room?**

Twenty minutes later, she knocked on his door. "What are you doing here?" She was not pleased.

"I couldn't sit there waiting," he said. "I'm sorry.

I promise I won't be seen with you. I'm just a tourist wandering around Belgrade."

She glared at him. "Shouldn't you be rehearsing? Don't you have the finals to get ready for?"

He shrugged. "I have three days. I had to move around one practice session, that was it."

He didn't mention that it was the practice session with the Moscow Philharmonic Orchestra, rehearsing in the Zaryadye Concert Hall—arguably the best concert venue in the world—and that he'd heard from Nicole that the Tchaikovsky Competition organizers were furious with Ray's last-minute change of plans. It didn't matter. Being physically present when the violin was recovered meant everything to him.

"You might as well tell me," he said.

She sighed, relenting. The surprising—or, come to think of it, not surprising—thing about $10 million Stradivarius violins is that they're not that easy to sell. It's a distinctive instrument, everybody knows what it looks like, and nobody wants to risk being the one caught holding it. Meanwhile the original thief has it. He tries to ransom it, but if the ransom plan doesn't succeed—as thus far it hadn't succeeded with Ray's, since the insurance company refused to pay immediately—the thief could try to trade it on the black market, working with various fences to exchange the instrument for cash or drugs. Then some other lowlife will have it and again swaps it for drugs or guns or a few thousand dollars. Each new owner optimistically takes the chance to resell it, hoping to find an unscrupulous collector who will pay a couple million for it, stuff it in a vault, and never pull it out again. Unless, that is, the thief disappears with the violin. He might simply decide to hold on to it, use it as a get-out-of-jail-free card: if in the future he is picked up for another crime, he could trade the Strad's whereabouts as a bargaining chip for a lighter jail sentence.

Alicia now believed that Ray's Strad was somewhere in this chain, being passed around from one crook to another—the ransom was just a red herring, a means of generating additional income. Finding the violin itself was the best way of ensuring its recovery.

"You think the Lezenkov family stole it?" Ray asked. "Hired people to steal it, I mean?"

Alicia was sitting in the armchair near the window, looking out over Belgrade's blank-fronted buildings, which looked like warehouses. "So their kid would win the Tchaikovsky Competition?" She shook her head, playing with the gold necklace around her neck. She was dressed in some sort of long flowing skirt and turquoise scarf—she looked very European. "Seems like a long shot, honestly, but the father is very competitive. Apparently he really forced the kid to play all the time. Didn't seem like much of a life, honestly."

She went on to tell him that a wealthy Serbian dealer had reached out via several intermediaries to let people know that, along with the Lezenkov family, he, too, had a client who was in the market for a very nice violin, no questions asked. This client would pay up to 1.3 million euro—vastly more than the thieves would get just from passing it off as collateral for guns or drugs.

"Who's the client? Do you know him?" Ray asked.

Alicia fumbled in her purse, handed him her passport. "Me," she said. "I'm an intermediary interested in purchasing a very nice violin for an anonymous client."

"You? Seriously?"

She took back the passport, opened it. Marie Hodges of Galveston, Texas, stared back at him from Alicia's photograph.

"Holy crap. Is this real?"

"Sure. This is my job, remember? I have a whole deep background created for Marie Hodges, which is why having you here is a serious impediment. Anybody can google Marie Hodges and find a lot of information on her. Where she went to college, a LinkedIn page, everything. It's an alias that will hold up under serious scrutiny."

"That's really cool," he told her. "So now what? We're just waiting?"

"I told you not to come," she reminded him.

She was right. He could have stayed in Moscow,

practiced his repertoire for the Third Round—
but he could practice it just as well in Belgrade.
Without his accompanist and without the Moscow
Orchestra, true, but closer to his violin.

He was really glad to be gone.

In Belgrade, he spent the next day busking—
treating the good folk, residents, and tourists alike,
to his Third Round repertoire: the Mozart and the
Tchaikovsky, repeating both pieces over and over
in different parts of the city. A few people dropped
coins in his open violin case.

Between pieces, he wandered around the city
streets—some charmingly cobblestoned, others
with uniquely disturbing murals, still others that
looked like they'd been dropped from a communist
labor camp.

He switched up the Third Round repertoire for
Adele and Taylor Swift, and the money was much
better. When he played "Let It Be" and "Viva La
Vida," a small crowd gathered, ten or fifteen people,
swaying to the music. He smiled at them, and they
smiled back.

The day passed, and then the next. Much of
Belgrade must have heard the Third Round music
by then. He was trying to decide when he should
return to Moscow when the music dealer in touch
with the thieves confirmed with Alicia that his contacts would be willing to part with the violin for
1.33 million euro. The transfer would go down two

days from now, in a suburb about an hour's drive from the city center. Alicia, as Marie Hodges, would carry a briefcase filled with papers that weighed about as much as 1.33 million euro. Serbian police would be undercover.

"Two days?" Ray said. "I have to leave tomorrow."

"I'll let you know as soon as I hear something."

"Ask them if you can get it tomorrow. Tell them you have to leave Belgrade. You have to play the Third Round in the Tchaikovsky Competition."

She stared at him. "Seriously?"

"Well, just ask if you can get it a day earlier. Say there's another five hundred thousand dollars if you can have it tomorrow."

"You know, that's actually not a bad idea, to show that I'm a very serious buyer."

So she asked the dealer, who relayed it to the thieves. Eventually word came back that the thieves had agreed. The price now was 1.85 million euro.

On the evening of the transfer, Alicia, as Marie Hodges, disappeared early. Ray, in the meantime, hired a town car to take him to the village where the sting would go down. He passed miles of crumbling buildings interspersed with brightly lit new restaurants and shops; eventually the buildings spread out and the evening grew quieter. Yesterday Alicia had donned sunglasses and a wig and reconnoitered the area; she'd drawn him a map showing where he could wait. He handed the map to the driver, who eventually pulled into a parking lot, cut the engine, and pulled out his phone to play a game. Ray's violin was, possibly, just a few feet away.

He waited. Cars passed.

In the end, this was what Ray saw of an international stolen musical instrument sting: Alicia texted him **come** and he was out of the car in a moment, rounding the corner. There was no need to try to figure out where he was going: the night was lit blue with flashing police lights.

Alicia—clearly still undercover—was pinned against a grimy brick wall by an enormous Serbian cop. Several other men were in handcuffs. Almost undetectably she motioned with her eyes toward one tall cop who seemed to be in charge.

"Hi," Ray said, "I think it's my violin. I'm from America."

The cop looked at him, totally confused. He said something in Serbian.

"Violin?" Ray pantomimed. "Can I see it?"

The cop yelled something.

A moment later a tall, well-built man in full police gear, with what looked like a shotgun strapped to his chest, approached them, carrying something violin-shaped. In the light and the movement, Ray could not see. And then he could.

The violin was beautiful, its varnish intact, its body shining. It glowed with an almost painful beauty.

It was not his.

Chapter 31

Day 46: Third Round

He flew back just in time for the practice session with the Moscow Philharmonic Orchestra, which took place next to Red Square in the Zaryadye Philharmonic Concert Hall. No gilded plaster-work, no glittering crystal chandeliers: instead, undulating cream balustrades separated the various seating sections; recessed lighting bathed the entire space in sleek, spare elegance. Despite its enormity, however, the seats hovering all around the stage made the immense space feel very intimate.

He was shell-shocked, beyond depressed: the last thing he wanted was to play Mozart and Tchaikovsky to a huge audience, with millions watching online, and his violin still missing.

As soon as he'd returned to the hotel, Nicole and Janice surrounded him, solicitous and frustrated on his behalf. Janice of course had been very much against his crazy trip to Serbia; Nicole had at least supported him. He saw her mirrored sorrow in her eyes, and that somehow gave him strength.

He was here. He was a finalist at the competition. He would focus. He would kick Russian ass.

The Third Round, accompanied by the world-class Russian Philharmonic, would consist of two concertos, each more than an hour long: Mozart's Concerto no. 5 in A Major and Tchaikovsky's Concerto, composer's edition. Only two musicians would perform each day, on three consecutive days, with the final announcement on the fourth day.

The worst position—the one that all musicians dreaded—was going first. It set the tone, set the bar, set expectations low or high. Because that contestant would be first to go, the audience and the judges often remembered the performance more clearly; then again, after three nights of solid performances, the audiences and the judges often remembered that first performance less clearly. Janice, Nicole, and Ray endlessly debated the ideal spot in the lineup: it was probably fifth or sixth. Unless it was the memorable first or second, of course.

Because of the first drawing of lots, and the whittling down of the contestants, Ray now would play first, at 6:00 p.m.; Mikhail was fourth on Day Two, also at 6:00 p.m. They still had their practice room but also had half an hour each with the Moscow Philharmonic Orchestra—not to play both pieces all the way through but to focus instead on the trickier passages of each concerto.

Nicole had rearranged Ray's schedule so he would practice last, at the very last possible day, with the orchestra. He still only barely made it from the airport—sweating in the back of the cab as the scheduled 2:30 p.m. time grew ever closer. But he made it, with five minutes to spare.

As he got out of the cab, he shook himself. His violin was still gone, but he was still here— a fucking **finalist** at the Tchaikovsky Competition. He folded his brain around the music—it was all about the music now, nothing else. Nicole and Janice met him outside the Great Hall. He hugged them both, but his mind was elsewhere, deep in the Tchaikovsky Concerto. He was only vaguely conscious of the extraordinary building looming in front of him, the people nodding and gesturing to him, Nicole's hand in his own.

When he strode onstage to meet the conductor, he was focused, fully present. **He was a finalist.** He was a world-class musician. The orchestra had to respect him: respect him not for how far he'd come despite the color of his skin, or despite his lost violin, or despite a hundred other reasons why he shouldn't be there: they had to respect him because of what he could do.

He knew they were scrutinizing his playing, and he scrutinized them right back. If the lead-up to the allegro of the Mozart Concerto wasn't at the tempo Ray wanted, he stopped and insisted that the conductor immediately correct it. He wasn't being arrogant, just demanding. He deserved to be there and everyone on the stage playing with him knew it. He used every second of his allotted thirty-minute slot and, when his time had run out, he shook their hands and staggered off the stage, exhausted.

He could have a couple hours' rest before the performance.

That night, when his cue came for the competition, he bounded out, shook hands with the conductor, bowed to the Moscow Philharmonic Orchestra, and bowed at last to the audience. No pink roses allowed, though—competition rules forbade it. The Zaryadye auditorium undulated around him like something alive, and the crowd's deep bellow and applause buoyed him up.

Here he was. His last performance of the competition.

He would remember this forever, he told himself.

His audience would remember this forever, too.

Ray brought the violin to his jaw, closed his eyes. For an instant—less than a breath, less than a blink—regret washed over him: wishing his own violin were here, wishing his grandmother were here. But he could do nothing more. He had done all that he could. It was just him and the music now, and the future was endless.

Drawing his bow into position, he began.

Mozart. He tuned out the world as he talked to Mozart throughout the Concerto no. 5— "Turkish." He summoned all the teaching, all the practice, and poured himself into every precise, pointed note. The opening arpeggio soared into the vast space, and he hung on the high E, demanding his audience—and Mozart—hear him, demanding they open themselves to him. He imagined his notes were water, or mercury, or silver—sliding into their ears, dissolving and thrumming into their blood. Their heartbeats were his.

When he bowed, the applause seemed to last a very long time.

Finally, Tchaikovsky's Concerto.

There were those who would say that only Russians can play Russian music: that it's not in the blood of non-Russians, that Americans or Germans can never truly understand or appreciate the deep and rich culture from whence came Tchaikovsky's glorious concerto.

Ray, of course, would disagree. He would tell you that music is truly a universal language, and that we, the listeners, will always impose our own fears and biases, our own hopes and hungers, on whatever we hear. He would tell you that the rhythm that spurred on Tchaikovsky is the same rhythm that a kid in a redneck North Carolina town would beat with a stick against a fallen tree. It is a rhythm in all of us. Music is about communication—a way of touching your fellow man beyond and above and below language; it is a language all its own. Leonid Molchalin from Juilliard had drilled him hard. Ray took everything he'd learned, along with the sparkle of the water on the Moskva and the taste of his breakfast **kasha**, and he made it clear that he could play "this kind" of music. No one would ever question him again. His G-string notes cut through the orchestra. He commanded the room. He took a few steps forward, daring the audience and the judges to look away. A few times the orchestra's tempo threatened to exceed his, but he pushed right back at them, held them in line.

For the concerto's final movement, he started uncharacteristically slow—a warning shot, daring them, and then winding up the tension, driving forward into a speed that made it seem as if his bow hand were not even part of his body: a flickering mosquito or a hummingbird, barely visible. The melody vibrated off him—clear, uncolored, rich, itself. He forced that orchestra to earn its places in those chairs.

The final note hung in the air like a cloud, and he realized he was grinning from ear to ear.

The audience was on its feet. His shirt was soaked through. Whether or not he won, his fellow finalists would definitely have to work to keep up with him.

Nicole couldn't bring herself to speak after Ray's performance. She just hugged him. Janice joined in. "Your rival, Mikhail Lezenkov, has some big shoes to fill," she said.

"It was like a gigantic ass fell on the stage," Nicole said. "And you just kicked it right off."

During intermission, before the next and final performer of the night—there were only two performances, separated by an intermission—the Russian media mobbed him. He answered their questions, repeated his plea for crowdfunding support—he was up to $4.1 million—signed programs, and then took his seat with the other finalists to listen to the next musician of the night: a Korean woman who delivered a solid, if unremarkable, performance.

The next day was Mikhail's turn. His interpretations of both the Mozart and the Tchaikovsky were light, dazzling, evocative. They were everything that a musician could hope to accomplish, and the audience was rabid, hysterical as they clapped and stomped. "Seemed a little expected," Nicole muttered to Ray while the crowd continued to applaud. "Didn't really wow me. Amazing and all that but, honestly, I think my guy rocked it a little harder."

Privately, in his soul, Ray agreed. He was way better than all of them. And if he'd been playing on his own violin everyone would have known it.

Two nights later, after the final performance, the crowdfunding was up to $4.6 million. He milled with the expectant crowd for the results ceremony. He was tired of the same questions that came at him, but kept trying to provide a consistent bland answer that would ruffle no feathers. Finally they took their seats.

More speeches. Online results had been tallied. Such a difficult choice with so many very qualified performers. Ray tuned out. Really, there were only two: himself and Mikhail. The Chinese woman was solid, but not great. The French guy had been too nervous. The two Russians were brilliant, but Ray didn't think they quite matched Mikhail's style and power.

People were still talking. There went the Russian president, again, with more thoughtful words of praise and inspiration.

More speeches. Online results had been tallied. Such a difficult choice with so many very qualified performers. Ray tuned it out. And now, ladies and gentlemen, the moment that the entire world was awaiting.

The six finalists made their way to the stage. Sixth went to the French guy, fifth to the Chinese, fourth to one of the Russian violinists, and third place went to the Korean.

Two prizes left. The audience was in a frenzy. Several boos had already begun. Maybe they thought it was unnatural for an American to win. He thought about what so many people had said to him so many times before.

You can't do that.

That's for white people.

People like you aren't supposed to like that kind of music.

You're not good enough.

That violin is the only reason you're here.

He was light-headed. The lights were warm and his collar felt too tight. His fingers were tingling, or trembled, he couldn't tell which. All the work, the time, the money he'd spent on preparing for this competition.

The audience fell silent.

"First prize, Mikhail Lezenkov."

The audience erupted. Ray stood tall. Feeling slightly sick, he shook Mikhail's hand, smiled, and posed. Silver medalist. Twenty thousand dollars. **The first American silver medalist. Ever.** He kept replaying the last weeks: he'd come to Russia, competed against the best in the world.

The truth was he'd won the moment he set foot on Russian soil, and now the world knew it. He may have come in second, but he'd gone further than any other American—Black or white. And he hadn't taken lessons from age three, or attended music festivals at age ten, or been drilled relentlessly by elite private teachers.

And, of course, he'd played with no Stradivarius.

Even against these odds, he'd placed second.

The night went on and on: this was the highest an American violinist had ever placed in the competition—Van Cliburn had won, but that was for piano.

Media interviews. Scheduling appointments. Record deals. Much to keep track of. It was all very glittering and exhausting.

They returned to the hotel at 4:00 a.m. He would meet with the competition administration to plot out the upcoming tour schedule, which would begin later that week after the galas had finally come to an end. He wasn't enraptured about quite literally playing second fiddle to Mikhail, but then again, he supposed there were worse things that could have happened.

PART 7

Breaking In

Chapter 32

Day 47: The Violin Case

He had 153 unanswered texts and forty-eight voice mail messages when he woke up the morning after the competition ended: mostly media people who had his cell phone number or industry contacts he'd made over the past few years, all congratulating him on his silver medal. It was monumental. He wondered how he would have done if he hadn't been so distracted.

He almost skipped over the voice mail from Jacob Fischer, thinking it was just another congratulatory message, but listened: "Hi, Ray, I know you're probably in the middle of the competition, and it's not hugely urgent, but can you give me a call when you get a sec? I'll be up. I know there's a time difference—are you five or six hours ahead?" Jacob sounded casual, unhurried.

He picked up on the first ring. "Ray?"

"Hi," Ray said. "You're up late."

He expected congratulations from Jacob, but instead Jacob said, "Glad you called. I was hoping you would. I left a message for Janice, too."

"I don't think she's up yet," Ray said. "What's going on?"

"I found something. In the case."

"What do you mean?"

Violin cases were well-padded, and the alligator-skin case was no exception: with alligator skin encasing it and a lining of padded velvet, there was a reason the Strad had survived so well for so long. Jacob explained that, as he was photographing the case, he noticed a slit cut into the green fabric. Ray had never noticed it: it blended with the rest of the lining, and Ray had never really examined the case that carefully—he'd always focused on the violin, and he'd replaced the case as soon as possible.

Inside the slit in the padded upper compartment, Jacob discovered a faded clasped envelope. Scrawled in pencil on one side, barely legible, were the words **Leon Marks**.

Ray had had the documents all along.

He sat up on the edge of his bed in this foreign country, in this foreign world, and realization washed over him, wave upon wave, making it hard to even sit upright.

It all made sense. **Of course he had the**

documents. Every time he'd seen her, Grandma Nora had asked him about the case, always telling him to bring it next time, asking him if he'd gotten rid of it. Why hadn't she come out and just told him that that was where she'd put PopPop's papers, keeping all of his legacy together in one place? She could have said something—she'd lived for another two years after she'd given him the violin—why hadn't she?

In the meantime, Jacob scanned and sent the documents. Several moments later, the emails hit Ray's inbox.

Two very faded, very creased photographs of an elderly Black man peered up at him. In one the man was standing in front of a house, looking very uncomfortable. In the other he had his arms around two small children. One of them looked like Ray's grandma.

Next, a death certificate: **Leon Marks, b. 1841?, d. Apr 7 1935. Cause of Death: congestive heart failure.**

Last were four sheets of faded yellow notebook paper. The words, scrawling and uneven, were in a child's handwriting.

Chapter 33

Opening the Envelope

My name is Nora. Today I talkd back to my momma and I disrespekt Miss Barbara who lives down the street and my grandpa said hes goin to teech me a lesson. My grandpa tol me to rite down eveything he says so thats what Im doin.

When I was a little boy, I livd in the cabin with my momma, my 2 brothers and my 2 sisters. Eveyday we had to work. It seemd like the only time we didn't do no work was in Church on Sunday. Master Thomas was nice mostly. Espeshelly to momma. She used to say I look just like him.

The missus did not like that. She was

always makin us scrub the floor even when
we had dun it the nite before. You niggers are
only good for workin and singin she always
said. She was a wicket woman that treetd the
slaves reel bad.

One time I watch her tell Master Thomas
that Zeke spilt a pale of feed. She made us all
watch Big Jim the overseer beet him half to
death with rakes and mallets and then cut off
his hand. They took a hot iron with a hook
on the end and jammd it into his stump were
his hand used to be. She said it was goin to
help him. He woodnt never spill nothin else.

My momma wood sing for the Master on
Sundays. Thats when she wood let me sit
with her and the other slaves that cood play
instrawmints. Charles playd the piano in the
house on Sunday and Russell playd the fiddle.
Momma got Russell to teech me at nite when
we finisht workin. She tol me they gone lern you
to play music so you dont never have to Worry
bout gettin beet or gettin sold. You lern it good.

When the Master wanted music I wood
play with Russell, momma and Charles.
When Russell got sick the Master put him in
the field. He workt him like a dog. When he
coodnt work no more, they took him in the
Woods and tyed him up and beet him. They
made us watch while they put his shirt over

his head and whipt him til his skin fell off.
He screemd and screemd. Then we didnt heer
Russell screemin no more.

Thats when Momma tol me to keep playin
that Fiddle so what happn to Russell woodnt
happn to me. I used to play for the field
workers at nite before they went to bed. I
playd and momma sang.

I lernt to play the songs for the master
when people come over and they had partys.
One time Me and momma went with Master
Thomas and his Wife to another house. They
made us play for the masters ther. I think his
name was master Ezra. Him and his wife likd
how I playd and how momma sang. After the
party Master Ezra took my Momma away
that nite.

When it was time for us to go back the nex
morning, Momma was reel sad. She didnt say
nothin the hole way back. Momma was sad
for a long time. She broke 2 a the missus good
teecups. The missus beet her and tol Big Jim
to take her outside with the horses. They made
her plow the fields until she cant walk no more.

I only saw her at nite. She tol me I had
to keep playin. Leon, she said. As long as
you got Breth in you you keep playin that
fiddle. They wont do to you what they did to
Malachi. He was my brother.

He tried to run away. He didnt get far. When
they catchd him they took him to the middl
of the field and made him dig a great big hole.
Then they made him put wood in it. Then they
lit a fire. Big Jim made the other field slaves
put shakls on his hands and ankls and spred
him apart. Them men beet him with a horse
whip then cut off his foot and throwd it into
that fire. Then they cut off his arm and throwd
it into that fire. I wont never forgit how he
screemd and how his skin burnin smelt. They
kept cuttin up his body and throwd it into the
fire. They lafft at him screemin.

When a slave lookt away, they got beet. We
had to wach Malachi be cut up and burnt as
a lesson. I never saw somebody die like that.
Momma tol me as long as I keep playin that
fiddle that wood never happn to me. But I
remembr what happnd to Russell when he
got old and sick.

I used to teech the yungins how to play at
nite after they finisht working. Momma tol
me to help eveybody I cood and that one day
it wood save us.

I playd for the Master and his Wife for
yeers and yeers. Old Charles had died and it
was just me. I tol the Master that some of the
field workers cood play too. It wood be good
for us to play at his Party in the evening. Evey

nite I wood go to teech the field slaves songs. Momma tried to sing but she coodnt sing no more. Me and William and Betty and Abraham playd for the masters Party. Ther was a lot of people. Master Thomas say we did a fine job and the nex day he let me stop work at noon.

Master Thomas always likt to have me around. He always wanted me to play. He treeted me reel fine. Sometimes he let me take food to my momma. Everday he made me play for him. He said it made Him reel happy. When his Wife went to sleep he made me play for him before he went in to sleep nex to her.

Master stopt cuming out of the house after a while. He was gettin sick. He wood lay in his bed all day long. I always stayed with him and playd while he was takin his Medasin and havin his treetmints. He wood lay in his Bed and cry when I playd. He said to me Leon you let me no what the angels will sound like when I get ther. I tol him you aint goin nowere master Thomas sir but he got sicker and sicker and he smelled rite bad. Not even the missus wood go in to see him but I was ther ever day. I playd his faverit tune what seemed like 100 times a day. Then he started gettin better. He got up and walked around sometimes. He was reel slim. He wood make me take my meals

with him since the Missus woodnt see him
no mor. After 3 months Master Thomas got
so slim that he coodnt walk no mor. I still sat
with him and playd ever day. I wont be here
much longer Leon he say to me so I say
were you goin master Thomas sir I say to him.
He just askt me to play him a tune. He say I
made that fiddle sing like my momma used
to. He tol me how he love to heer my momma
sing. He say I was speshel.

Then came a time when he tol me Leon
you been a good boy. You never try to run
away and you do good work. What you want.
Just tell me. I say master Thomas I want my
momma to come back to the house. He tol me
I cant do that my wife the Missus wont have
that. Well then I guess I want to be a free man.

He say to me but if I free you who will play
for me at nite. I say to him I will play for you
master Thomas sir. I wont leev you. I will
play for you as a free man. He thot about that
and he took out some papr and he rote out
what he tol me was my freedom paprs and he
gav me them with my fiddle. I never let them
paprs out o my site. Them papr and my fiddle
kept me alive.

I beggd him on my hands and nees to let
my momma be free too and she wood stay
here and hep him. He tol me he coodnt do

that. I went to tell momma that I was free. I tol her I was goin to find work after master Thomas past and that I was comin back for her to buy her freedom when I made enuff money from my playing. You no what my momma tol me? She tol me dont Never come back to this place. You go be free and dont you Never look back.

Master Thomas died in his Bed. The Missus made me play that song he loved. I lef a few days later. The nex yeer I did come back to find momma but she was Gone.

You no why I tol you all this and made you rite it down? Because Master Thomas was a teribl man. He did teribl things to my momma and to my brother and to many other slaves. Even tho he did all that I still lookt him in the eye and treetd him with respekt. No mattr how mad I was. No mattr how bad things got. I was always respektfl. Even when I didnt get no respekt.

I dont never want you to forget that girl.

I wont never forget this and I have lernt my lesson.

Nora Marks
Age 9

Chapter 34

Day 48: Promenade

And with that final communication from Grandma Nora, Ray called Kim immediately, shared Jacob's documents with her.

Two days later the attorney wrote that he was withdrawing the claim. Would Ray make the document public? It was very damaging to the Marks family, and of course none of this story could be verified. It might all be made up.

Ray was disinclined to respond to their attorney. The Markses and their lawsuit fell away. He didn't feel triumphant: just vaguely uneasy. These white people wouldn't give up so quickly. They'd gotten it into their heads that the violin was theirs for their imaginary niece to play in her imaginary concerts, and there was no arguing with white people.

So he didn't argue. He tried to forget them, let the

press conjecture whatever it wanted; Ray wanted only to play.

Ray and Nicole walked hand in hand along the Moskva River promenade. The sun was warm and glittered on the water. Nannies pushing prams trundled past, and people snacked on the benches.

Ray grabbed Nicole and kissed her long and hard.

"It's over!" She hugged him. "I'm so happy for you."

"Oh my god, I am, too," Ray said. "I can't believe this monkey is finally off my back." Relief kept pouring off him. He'd take a breath and he'd feel some unknown coil in his chest release and fall away; and then another breath, and another coil loosen and disappear. It was really over. "It's like an angel is watching over me."

"More like your grandmother."

"Yeah, I was thinking that, too. I always thought that she was with me. Always."

"That letter she wrote. Do you think it's all true?"

"Yeah. I can't imagine a kid that age coming up with such graphic details. It's the horrible, ugly truth a lot of people refuse to even acknowledge. I don't know how people did it back then. They were treated worse than animals. I thought I had it bad with the comments people make. Calling me a monkey or turning me into a PR stunt. It's nothing compared to what my family went through."

"Try not to think about it," she said, rubbing his back.

"You know what?" he said. "I'm going to use it as a reminder of everything that my family has endured. When I get discouraged, I'm going to take that letter out and read it. Anything that I'm going through won't even compare to the things that used to happen. I wish I could go back and show this to people who told me I was being paranoid and melodramatic."

"You should take this letter for what it is," Nicole said. "Validation. You're doing the right thing with your life. Your great-great-grandfather wasn't a thief. Your family has gone through some crazy stuff. Your grandmother has always been with you. Oh, and one more thing."

"What?"

"Oh, nothing special. Just that this Ray is much nicer to be around than that super stressed-out one."

Ray let out a belly laugh. "Now comes the easy part. Traveling around the world as the Tchaikovsky Competition silver medalist."

"That'll be a breeze," she said. "But at least you can get on with life without these crazy lawsuits."

"You're right." He closed his eyes for a beat, smiled into the sunshine. "The next few months are going to be crazy," he said after a while. They'd seen the schedule: the "busy and interesting" itinerary included touring China, Russia, France, Germany, and several other countries.

The relief continued to pour off Ray, wave upon wave. He hadn't realized how much the Markses' craziness had depleted his mood.

"You know," he said, "I'm going to have to get a manager." Several music management companies had reached out to him, and several record companies kept bugging him about a record deal, but he hadn't called any of them back yet. He felt it would be traitorous to perform without his own violin. Now that he was getting close to the $5 million ransom, it might be only a couple weeks until he had it back. Only $275,000 more to go.

"You really should," she said. "It's stupid for you to spend your time figuring out hotel bookings and car pickups. Managers charge ten percent, right? I wonder if we should look into sharing a part-time personal assistant. It might be cheaper." She really was getting into this. "And we could see who used him—or her—more," she said. "If I used her more, I could pay more, or reimburse you. And vice versa."

"You're really serious," Ray said, looking at her.

"Yeah, why not? Someone to just help make life run more smoothly. Pick up dry cleaning and pick up groceries, and schedule your trips, and pick you up at the airport instead of taking an Uber. I wonder if they'd do laundry and get my car's oil changed?" She looked out across the river, said dreamily, "It really sounds kind of awesome. The question is, who pays for her time when she's sitting at the mechanic's getting my oil changed and she's booking your latest excursion to the Berlin Philharmonic?"

"You pay," he said. "She's getting your oil changed."

"Yeah, but it's your concert."

"She can schedule my concert after she's done with the oil change."

"I wish we could hire her today," Nicole said. "I need to have my oil changed when I get back."

"Didn't you just get one?"

"Yeah, but I'm almost a thousand miles overdue. I'm going to have her keep track of that, too. When my car needs an oil change." Nicole hated putting miles on her car—she loved public transportation and took it as often as possible.

"A thousand miles? Good grief. Why do you drive so much?"

"Don't act like you don't drive a lot."

"Sure I do, but jeez. Was this the last trip to Cleveland?" She'd performed as a substitute for the Cleveland Orchestra a few weeks ago.

"No, when I went to New York that time."

"When did you drive back from New York?"

"When you were with Leonid at Juilliard," she said. "Remember I drove?"

"Oh yeah," he said. "Right." Something curled in the back of his head, a question mark.

"Anyway," he said after a moment, "I really think

we should think about the personal assistant thing." He searched on his phone. "Looks like they'd charge between fifteen and thirty dollars an hour. How many hours do you think you'd need?"

"Say, ten hours a week," Nicole said. "If we each did ten, that would be three hundred dollars a week, or fifteen thousand a year. I think that's way cheaper than a management company. But is it worth spending fifteen thousand dollars to pick up my dry cleaning? Then again, if it's fifteen dollars an hour, it might be worth it."

He wasn't listening anymore, thinking about her driving back to Erie from New York.

She'd flown, not driven.

And then it all made sense.

Chapter 35

Day 56: Marcus Terry

Ray stood in Nicole's living room, staring blankly at a print over her living-room sofa: three cows in a field, a barn, and a few trees on the horizon.

Where to start the search?

She'd rented a house on Windview Place Road in Fairview, a quiet suburb of Erie a couple miles from the Lake. Being so close to Lake Erie made the properties in the area highly sought after. The family of a wealthy orchestra patron actually owned the house—the only reason that Nicole could afford it was that the patron had died, and the family had offered to rent the house to one of the symphony musicians for a couple years while the patron's will worked its way through probate. The house was big for one person: two levels, three bedrooms, a yard that Nicole would mow, complaining, with a push mower once a week. She wasn't much of a homemaker—Erie was clearly just a stepping-stone to bigger orchestras in bigger cities—but she kept the house clean and neat.

He'd called Alicia the moment the plane had touched down at JFK and the seat belt sign had gone off. "I know where it is," he told her.

It was three days after the conversation at the Moskva. Janice and Nicole had returned together to the United States the day after; Ray was supposed to be in Moscow to begin the Tchaikovsky Competition tour. Instead he'd taken a flight to America a day later—after they'd both left.

He hadn't said anything to either Janice or Nicole; he didn't want to arouse any suspicion, especially if he was wrong. He was desperate to tell Janice, but she was traveling with Nicole. It was too risky.

Now that he was back in the United States, he called Alicia, who was still in Europe, tracking down leads to other violins which, Ray now knew, were not his Strad.

"What do you mean?" Alicia asked him. "How? Where is it? Where are you?"

"Nicole has it. Just landed at JFK."

"What? Where is this coming from?"

"She said she drove."

"What?"

"She drove. She said she drove back to Erie. From

New York. She didn't fly out of Newark like she said. She drove."

"Hold on," Alicia had said. "Let me get my notes." Computer keys tapping. "You know of course that she had the most access of anyone, so we've been looking at her the hardest."

"Still?"

"Yep. Following her credit card bills, phone calls. Nothing. No unusual charges, nothing out of the ordinary. Hold on, here it is. No, she flew. She definitely flew from Newark to Erie. I have confirmation from the airlines. Plus we have surveillance footage of her in the airport. And the X-ray footage of her suitcases going through the scanner."

"That doesn't make sense," he'd said. "She told me that she drove from New York."

"It must have been some other time," Alicia had said.

"There was no other time. She hates to drive her car as it is. She was complaining about needing an oil change. She said that she was putting too many miles on her car after the trip from New York. She has never driven to New York since I've known her. Never. She never drives anywhere if she can help it. She takes public transportation. She's like the queen of public transportation. She knows every bus route from here to New York. You should hear about the complicated way she gets from Manhattan to Newark Airport to save four dollars."

"I can't possibly get a warrant to search her house based on a drive back from New York." It was hard to hear her over the noise of the plane: people talking loudly and the thrum of the engines. Then the engines started powering down.

"There's no other explanation," he'd said. "She has to have it. She drove back with it to Erie, which is why it didn't get flagged in the airport. It must have been in one of her suitcases. She had two— I remember really clearly that she had two. I'm going to confront her. I'll wear a wire, I'll get it on tape—"

"You will do nothing of the kind," Alicia told him. "If she doesn't have it, you won't get anywhere. If she does have it, you'll tip her off."

"How am I going to get it back, then?"

"Don't do anything rash, you hear me? I know you're upset, but—"

"Upset? Are you fucking kidding me?" His voice was getting louder. His seatmate was staring at him. He ducked, whispered into the phone, "My girlfriend stole my violin and you don't want me to be upset?"

"Look, I hear you. I'm still in Belgrade. Let me get back and we can regroup. I'll put the art team and the FBI on it in the meantime, and I'll dig in from here. I can get a flight out tomorrow. It's waited this long, it can wait a little bit longer. Let me think it through."

"Great idea," he said. "Can you get a warrant in the meantime?"

"There's not enough for a warrant," she repeated. "Yet."

Around him the other passengers were standing, grabbing luggage, moving down the aisle. He seized the violin case. "Okay. I'm heading to Erie now. I'll wait for you there."

"Don't you dare," she said. "Just stay where you are and don't do anything to tip her off. If she has it, she's hidden it for this long. Don't blow it. Just go back to Charlotte like you planned."

"Okay," he said "I gotta go," and hung up.

Ten minutes later, in the customs line, he thumbed through his Delta Airlines app. Yes, there was a flight to Erie in two hours. He could make it.

That had been four hours ago. Now he stood in Nicole's living room, staring at her living-room walls. Where to start? Over the past year, he'd spent days here. Weeks. Often alone. Was the violin here, all along, in a closet? In her basement? In the attic? How could he search now without giving himself away? How could he have been so close?

Six p.m. He'd timed his arrival after she'd left for rehearsal at the symphony: the Erie Philharmonic had a major performance in a few weeks, which meant that the earliest she'd be back was ten fifteen, ten thirty. Unless they let out early, which they also might do. He had four hours.

He thought back to those days at Grandma Nora's, hunting for PopPop's fiddle in the attic. He'd started by randomly looking in boxes, opening drawers, but soon enough became systematic: proceeding stack by stack, box by box, no matter how unlikely a hiding place. In the end, his system hadn't worked—who knew where Grandma Nora had hidden it all that time; she'd just beamed at him and never told him—but perhaps this time the system would hold him in good stead.

He'd begin in the attic (if there was an attic? he didn't know—and he sure hoped she wasn't hiding his violin in an attic with widely fluctuating temperatures) and work downward. He'd look for anything—a violin-size box, keys to a storage unit, any kind of reference that might seem like a lead. He'd look for hiding places in the drywall, loose floorboards. He'd seen enough movies to know the drill. He couldn't imagine her giving the violin to her parents, or to a friend, for safekeeping. She'd want as few people to know about it as possible.

The attic was a tiny crawl space off the upstairs bathroom. Nothing in it.

Room by room he searched, pulling out every drawer, checking for false bottoms, for loose moldings on walls. Halfway through the upstairs—thank goodness the house wasn't that big—he texted Alicia again: **Did she rent a safe-deposit box?** He waited.

No response. It was after 2:00 a.m. in Belgrade. She must've been asleep.

Nothing in Nicole's closet, apart from what should be. He shook out each shoe in every shoebox, opened every piece of luggage, checked behind every picture, lifted up the mattress, re-made the bed. He'd finished the upstairs—the master bedroom and the spare room she used as a practice room—when Alicia texted back, clearly not asleep: **No. That was the 1st place we looked. Also no storage unit. I'll see u tomorrow. WAIT FOR ME!**

Ray: **Did you check her mom and sister? How about Tina Reed?**

Nicole was close to her mother and sister, who lived outside Harrisburg, and Tina was her best friend at the orchestra.

Alicia: **We asked for all this information from her right after the theft. We've checked them all. I've already contacted Bill Soames to ask him to run a check on everyone again. More tomorrow!!!**

Down the stairs, checking each stair tread. The house was newish—built during the 1980s steel boom—with cheap hollow-core doors and wall-to-wall Berber carpet. There didn't seem to be any structural hiding places. He often stayed over, so she would of course know that he'd be in the house. Wherever she hid it, it had to be somewhere he wouldn't normally go. The basement? The unheated garage out back?

It was nearly 8:00 p.m. when he made a peanut butter sandwich, ate it standing at the sink, staring down at an unwashed coffee mug. She'd be back in a couple hours. "I missed you, so just flew in to see you," he imagined telling her, trying out the words. Could he sound sincere?

On the main level sprawled the kitchen, dining room, living room, half bath/laundry room, foyer. The living room was immaculate. The gray couch sat quietly, yellow pillows staring back at him. The rubber tree plant was shiny and tall. Not a speck of dust on her dark hardwood floors. On the console in the foyer, a pile of mail was neatly stacked. He thumbed through it, as if expecting a postcard from the violin: **Hi, hope you're well, really enjoying my time here in the front closet, wish you were here!**

This was stupid. What had he been thinking? Nicole loved him. She listened to all his family drama—she was there with him when only Aunt Rochelle would speak to him. "You can do this," she would tell him, grabbing his face with both her hands. "You're better than they let you know." She'd pull him close, their foreheads almost touching. "And everyone you meet is better because of you."

But why had she driven back from New York? The hall closet was packed with winter coats. He went through every pocket.

Besides the basement, all that was left were the half bath/laundry room, the dining room, and the kitchen. He dreaded the kitchen—fishing around in the flour, emptying the open boxes of pasta, pouring out the bag of rice—so figured he'd start with the bathroom.

Nothing in the powdered laundry soap. Nothing in the cabinets. Nothing taped to the back of the toilet, or suspended in the toilet tank, the way he heard drug dealers hid their stash. He sat on the toilet and thumbed through the pile of magazines on the shelf next to him. He'd seen them all before, but he was being thorough, right?

There were those old **Men's Health** magazines, which were still arriving addressed to Marcus Terry, the previous tenant, whose subscription had still not run out.

"Who's Marcus Terry?" he'd once asked Nicole when they'd started dating.

"I think that's the guy who used to live here."

He remembered her telling him that the house had sat empty for several months as the heirs tried to decide what to do with it. The patron's estate was complicated, and probate was going to take years, which is why they finally agreed to rent it to a symphony musician.

That conversation with Nicole had been six months ago, and she'd moved into the house more than a year ago. This **Men's Health** issue was from July of this year. The subscription should have run out by now, shouldn't it?

What was the name of the orchestra patron who'd died? He googled the address.

Elizabeth Sutton, beloved wife of Benjamin and mother of James and William, passed away on . . .

No Marcus Terry. Nicole had been the first tenant in the house, he remembered that very clearly. Perhaps Elizabeth Sutton had had a caregiver, though? No mention of his name in the obituary.

Another Google search. Marcus Terry's new address was 3822 Bremer Street, a fifteen-minute drive away.

He texted Alicia: **Can you track down a Marcus Terry, 3822 Bremer Street**

No response. She must be asleep.

It was 9:00 p.m. He had perhaps another hour before Nicole returned. Marcus Terry intrigued him, but he had only a short while to keep searching the house. He spent the next hour going through the kitchen—he searched the refrigerator and the cabinets over the stove, with only the lower cabinets, dining room, and basement left—and then called it quits for the night, let himself out. He'd finish tomorrow. In the meantime he'd drive over to Bremer Street.

Under the streetlights, Marcus Terry's house was in shadow. An ancient Honda Civic, bumper askew, rusted in front of the garage. A light glowed dim from inside the house.

Finally he drove off to check in at the Holiday Inn off the interstate.

Although he was beyond exhausted—his body was still operating on European time—he couldn't sleep. What was Marcus Terry's connection to Nicole? A Google search of **Marcus Terry** turned up a handsome, worked-out man in his early thirties. His dark brown hair hung to his shoulders, framing a square face with very thick eyebrows and a thin moustache. His nose looked like it had been broken a few times. He looked vaguely familiar.

What if Nicole had already gotten rid of the violin? Morning couldn't come soon enough.

When he awoke, dazed and disoriented, at 3:00 a.m.—9:00 a.m. Moscow time—multiple texts from Alicia awaited him. How had he not heard the phone chime?

Alicia: **Marcus Terry is personal trainer at Gold's Gym, West Erie. 34. $15,542 in credit card debt. Been renting 3822 Bremer since last October. Previous address 184 Windview Place. WHERE ARE YOU???**

Alicia: **I've alerted Bill Soames, who will be contacting you momentarily. Flight BEG-EWR arriving 11 AM. DO NOT DO ANYTHING STUPID!! I will call you when I land**

Marcus Terry's previous address, as Nicole had told him, was 184 Windview Place.

What she hadn't told him was that he'd been living there with her in October, when Ray and Nicole first met.

Marcus Terry had moved out shortly after Ray had met her. Why had nobody ever mentioned him to Ray—not Nicole, or Tina, or any of their other friends?

He didn't answer Alicia's texts.

At the all-night Walmart where he'd often shopped with Nicole, he bought a cheap T-shirt and a package of disposable rubber gloves. Then he drove back to 3822 Bremer.

Summer dawn came early, just after five o'clock, illuminating a beat-up house behind an unkempt lawn. The mailbox hung crookedly from the side of the front door. The other houses nearby were equally rough. Two doors down, a car sat on blocks in the driveway. He parked across the street, several driveways away. What time did personal trainers go to work? Nine o'clock? Didn't a lot of people work out before heading to their jobs in the morning? Gold's Gym opened at five thirty.

At 5:10 a.m., a light flicked on. Good thing Ray had arrived early. A figure passed the living-room window and Ray involuntarily ducked down, then laughed at himself. But he stayed low in the seat, waiting.

At 5:23, Marcus Terry opened the front door

and got into his Honda Civic. Ray barely caught a glimpse.

He put on the rubber gloves, stuffed a bunch more in his pocket, just in case.

As soon as Marcus Terry's car turned the corner, Ray was out in the predawn silver light, walking quickly.

Was going to jail for breaking and entering worth getting his violin back?

Hell yes it was.

A chain-link fence ran around the back of the house. Was there a dog? He didn't hear one. He opened the gate, slipped through, wincing as the metal shrieked. A passing car made him move even more quickly.

The back door was locked, and visible from the houses behind it. A big oak tree partially blocked the view, but not well enough. No lights in any of the neighbors' windows. He found a rock in a weed-filled garden bed next to the house. He pulled out the Walmart T-shirt, wrapped the rock in it to muffle the noise, and, with a single tap, broke the window above the doorknob. No going back now.

He reached in, unlocked the door from inside, closed the door behind him. Silence. Only then did he wonder if Marcus Terry had a roommate or a live-in girlfriend. But there'd been only one car in the driveway—unless another hid in the attached garage?

He waited, unmoving, peering out the window to see if anyone had noticed him. Nothing. He set the shirt and the rock down just inside the door, went quickly through the house. He was alone.

The place was a wreck. Clothes and bags were strewn all over the couch. A full ashtray on the coffee table. A Tony's pizza box full of crusts lay open on the floor. Marcus Terry, a personal trainer, sure did a great job with fueling the temple of his body. A sink full of dishes. On the kitchen table, a half gallon of milk that should have been in the refrigerator sat next to a box of Fruity Pebbles. Marcus Terry had left the milk out—did that mean he'd be back soon?

Ray called Gold's Gym. "Hi, can you tell me when Marcus will be done? Does he have a lot of appointments today?" The receptionist checked. He had four appointments, and was done at nine thirty. Could she schedule him a session? What was Ray's name? Ray would text Marcus later. Thanks.

He had, at the most, four hours. Unless an appointment canceled.

In the front hall closet were several boxes of random papers. He scanned them as quickly as possible—tax returns, copies of old bills. In the bedroom, under the bed, were boxes of winter clothes and boots. As he moved to the bedroom closet his phone buzzed: Alicia. He ignored it.

What time did she leave Belgrade again? Had she already returned to the US?

Six forty-five. Back to the kitchen. On the far-left corner of the fridge, beneath a coupon for protein powder and hanging awry, was a photo of a shirtless Marcus Terry hugging a young woman with auburn hair and a single music note tattooed above her wrist: Nicole.

Somehow, despite all this, Ray somehow hadn't believed it.

Through the kitchen cabinets, emptying cans and boxes of food onto the floor. Then adding mismatched cups and plates. Nothing. Was there an attic? A basement?

In the cabinet next to the back door—inches from where he'd left the shirt-wrapped rock— he found a cardboard box packed with more old mail: flyers from moving companies, old gas and electric bills, and a tan oversize clasp envelope stuffed with invoices from Lowrey Storage. There were three invoices dating from this past May to July. At the bottom of the envelope were two identical small silver keys.

A storage unit, rented on May 12.

On May 16, his violin had been stolen.

His phone rang again. Bill Soames this time. He hit DO NOT DISTURB.

By then it was seven thirty and the neighborhood

was coming to life. He decided to get out: a Black man coming out of Marcus Terry's home would, no doubt, raise eyebrows. Ray wasn't going to take the chance that a neighbor would report him. He'd fill in Alicia and Bill Soames, they'd get a warrant, they'd figure this out.

Among the detritus on the living-room floor he found a ratty Erie SeaWolves baseball cap, tucked it low across his eyebrows. He stuffed the manila envelope under his shirt and, carrying the shirt-wrapped rock, unlocked Marcus Terry's front door, removed the rubber gloves, and casually sauntered over to his car, waiting for a "Hey, you!" from the neighbors. No one seemed to notice him. He unlocked the rental and drove off.

A block away, he wrapped the shirt, rock, cap, and gloves in the plastic Walmart shopping bag, tossed it off the bridge into the Trout Run Stream below.

He called Alicia. Her voice mail picked up. By now she would be on a plane heading back to the United States. "Hi, I went to Marcus Terry's house. She knows him. I think they're working together. I found a bunch of receipts and a key to a storage unit in Erie. Lowrey Storage. I'm heading there now."

He hung up. He should call Bill Soames back. Soames would have to fly in, unless he called in some local field agents, which is surely what he'd do. But would they have to get a warrant? Did they have probable cause? Ray had broken into and entered Marcus Terry's house—would that make getting a warrant more difficult?

Plus when Marcus Terry got home after nine thirty, he'd see that someone had smashed the glass in his back door. How long would it take until he noticed that the envelope was missing? It was already eight forty-five.

Lowrey Storage, open twenty-four hours, was 4.3 miles away. He would reach his destination in seven minutes if traffic was light.

He pulled into the parking lot of a big gated building with rows of unheated storage units out back. There was a code to get in the back gate. He didn't have it. He went through the manila envelope, didn't see a code.

In the office, a short burly man with thinning black hair and glasses looked up when the sliding doors opened and Ray came in. His one earring was an iron cross. He had a tattoo of a koi fish on his hairy forearm. "Hi. Can I help you?"

"Hi, yes, I'm in unit 601 and I don't remember the code to get in."

"Okay, let's see what we can do. Name?"

"Marcus Terry."

"I got you right here, Mr. Terry. I'll just need to see some ID."

"I actually ran out of my house without my wallet."

"Sorry, I can't give you the code without any ID."

"Come on, man. Give me a break, please? It's already turning out to be a shitty day. My address is 3822 Bremer Street. My grass needs cutting, my old lady is all up my ass, I'm almost out of gas, and I need to go grocery shopping. What else do you want to know? My shoe size? Ten and a half. Here are the keys, see? And here's an invoice."

The burly man behind the counter smiled sympathetically. "I hear you, bud. I've had those days. Gimme a sec. Here, I'll write it down for you." Ray watched him scrawl the code on a slip of paper.

"Thanks, man. You've literally saved my life." He shook the man's hand, turned to go.

"Excuse me, Mr. Terry?"

Ray froze. "Yeah?"

"This month's payment is two weeks past due."

"Oh, okay. Let me talk to the old lady and have her give you a credit card." He headed out toward the storage units. "This is probably the last month I'll be using it anyway."

"Hey, where are you going?" the man asked.

Ray froze again.

"I thought you said you were 601?"

Ray didn't move.

"That's in here, remember? That's one of the climate-controlled lockers."

Ray shook his head, laughed. "Yeah. Duh. Sorry. I don't know where my head is today." He turned right, toward the interior of the building, and the door slid shut.

He punched in the code. The security door opened. He followed the signs to 601—about halfway down a long hallway lined with dozens of blue corrugated metal doors. Above him a fan clicked on. A few rows over someone rattled something, and then came the sound of glass clinking on cement.

The locker couldn't be that large—doors about three feet wide marched endlessly, side by side, down the corridor.

There was 601. He fumbled in his pocket for the keys. His fingers shook. His hands were sweating and he had to try three times to get the key in the metal padlock. Finally the key slid in, clicked, and the shackle slipped back. He removed the lock, placed it on the ground, pulled back the bolt, and lifted the corrugated metal door.

The unit was shallow—maybe three or four feet deep, with a cement floor. It was completely empty except for a medium-size cardboard box from Amazon, taped closed. He ripped away the tape.

Inside was a cheap black plastic laminate violin case.

He opened it.

PopPop's fiddle—his own most loved Stradivarius violin—grinned up at him, unharmed.

Perfect.

Chapter 36

Aftermath

In the months leading up to the trial, it all came out—and it was so very simple. The morning of the theft, while Ray was showering, Nicole put on a pair of gloves, took out the violin, and stashed it in her small roller bag, using her clothes to pad it. In its place she left the Chuck Taylor shoe and the ransom note. She'd bought the shoe at a Walmart outside Cleveland.

Ray, oblivious, followed her out the door and down to the lobby, slung her roller bags into her taxi, and kissed her goodbye.

The taxi took her to Penn Station, as the GPS and the driver's own testimony corroborated. She exited the taxi, went down to the bowels of Penn Station, her route confirmed by dozens of video cameras along the way. She'd already bought her ticket on New Jersey Transit to Newark Airport, which she'd charged to her Visa.

She stayed on the train one station past Newark Airport, got off at Elizabeth Station wearing a baseball cap—detectives later found the video footage—went across the street to where she'd parked her car in an overnight parking garage. She took out the violin, slipped it in a cheap plastic case that she'd picked up at a pawnshop, slid the case on the back seat floor, and covered it casually with a towel. Then, after locking the car, she caught the next train back to Newark Airport. She'd missed her stop, she told the conductor, waving her Newark ticket.

She'd flown back to Erie and then, that night, when Ray alerted her to the theft, flew back to New York. When they finally left New York, she picked up her car and drove back to Erie with the violin in her back seat. None of the detectives thought of checking her last route from New York back home: the extra miles meant an earlier oil change. Gosh, she hated driving her car. If only she'd taken public transportation.

Pilar Jiménez, who'd delivered their breakfast that morning, was a particular bit of brilliance. Nicole had learned months ago that many of the Saint Jacques housekeeping staff had immigrated illegally. The day before the theft, Nicole had paid the housekeeper $5,000 to deliver the breakfast cart and return to Honduras: if the woman refused, Nicole would report her to US Immigration and Customs Enforcement. The woman took the money and went back to Honduras—a nice red herring to keep the detectives busy.

Back in Erie, Nicole met up with Marcus Terry, who'd already rented the storage locker, and he took the violin in a cardboard box to the unit.

Marcus Terry: her boyfriend. They'd supposedly had a terrible breakup, Marcus was out of her life, and she used a burner phone to communicate with him. Otherwise they stayed apart in case detectives were watching her. He'd been in on the theft from the beginning.

Ray's whole relationship with Nicole was based on her lies. She'd seen an opportunity when she'd met a lonely violinist with a priceless violin—and she'd taken it.

In prison awaiting trial, Nicole reached out several times to Ray: she called, texted, emailed. He wouldn't respond. He wondered if the only reason she wanted to see him was for him to plead with the prosecutors for leniency. He imagined her telling him that Marcus Terry had dreamed up the whole idea—that she went along with it only because Marcus Terry had some diabolical hold over her. Marcus Terry, criminal mastermind and Fruity Pebbles connoisseur.

And then she'd email. He'd deleted several earlier ones, but this email he opened.

Dear Ray,

Are you getting any of my emails?

I know that saying sorry doesn't ease your pain. I never wanted to hurt you.

I know you wont believe me but its true. My idea was that nobody would get hurt. Everybody wins. If Benson paid out the ransom right away like it was supposed to, you would've gotten your violin back before the competition. If they didn't pay it out, you raised the money anyway. In any case you'd get your violin back and I get a nest egg so I don't have to worry so much about making ends meet. Not everybody has your talent and you know I didn't want to stay in a third-rate orchestra all my life. A little more money would have gone a long way. I could've bought a new viola and taken lessons with Caitlin Landuyt. You know how I always wanted to do that. It would've given me a shot. The same shot you had. You can't blame me for wanting the same opportunity you had. It's not my fault. It's Benson's.

Anyway I wanted to write you because I didn't want you to be mad. I love you very much and I just want you to be happy. I just wanted to be happy too.

Please come see me and we can talk about this in person? I really want to see you and talk face to face.

Love,
Nicole

Ray didn't respond and didn't open any of the other dozen emails she sent him in the following couple weeks before he asked the prosecutors to make sure she couldn't contact him again.

The trial took more than a year, and Ray videoed in his testimony from Sweden, where he'd been playing with the Royal Stockholm Philharmonic Orchestra before heading off to a special month-long recital and retreat in Tokyo.

He couldn't forget her. He'd wanted, so many times, to talk to her, to ask her how she could have done this, how she could have done this to him. He'd thought they were in love; he'd thought they shared intimacy and a real connection. Was any of it real? Was it all, and always, about the violin, and the money?

Dear Ray,

I'm sorry for everything I put you through. I want you to know that. I really care for you and you need to know your violin was never in any danger. I would have gotten it back to you no matter what. It was all Marcus's idea, I just went along because he told me to. Please believe me.
The sentencing is coming up next week and it would mean everything to me if you'd just testify on my behalf. Ask the judge for leniency. Please do it. You mean everything to me. I really screwed up and I'm more sorry than you could ever know. Please????

Love,
Nicole

By the time her sentencing rolled around, Ray was back in the United States, playing at a special sold-out exhibition at Berkley.

As Nicole had asked, he wrote a letter to the judge.

Dear Judge Kastenmeier,

Nicole Sellins spent nine months lying and deceiving me. She pretended to love and support me, all while planning to steal my violin. She almost got away with it. She is heartless and manipulative. She wrote me a couple weeks ago asking for leniency. She planned on cheating me and thousands of other people out of millions of dollars. She stole a violin that meant more to me than all the money in the world. Feel free to give her the maximum sentence.

Sincerely,
Ray McMillian

Both Nicole and Marcus Terry ended up going to jail: eight years and a $1.8 million fine for Nicole, and five years and $950,000 fine for Marcus Terry.

Nicole's orchestral career was over. She would be lucky to play in a community orchestra. Ray sometimes wondered what she would do when she got out of prison but tried not to think about her too much.

In the meantime, Ray was playing all over the world. As the violin silver medalist with the Tchaikovsky Competition, great stuff happened. After the first year of traveling internationally, he rediscovered his love of chamber music and formed his own group—the BESK Quartet. They traveled all over the United States, South America, and in Europe; their performances of Schubert, Mozart, Haydn, Shostakovich, Dvořák, and Brahms garnered them dozens of awards and accolades from every major classical music institution. He recorded for Sony, Naxos, and BMI, and his quartet did the same.

Ray made it a point to highlight music by Black and Latinx composers. After all those years fighting and proving wrong the preconceptions that people who looked like him couldn't play the music of dead European white men, he dove into the phenomenal music written by those people who indeed did look like him. William Grant Still was his favorite, and Ray popularized his **Suite for Violin and Piano**; Josephine Reed's **Yellow** coming a close second, and Florence Price's Second Violin Concerto rounding out the top three. Whenever he performed any of these pieces, someone would invariably come up to him and tell him how amazing that piece of music was, as if Ray didn't know. "I'd never heard of her until I heard you play that," the audience member would say, and Ray's reaction was always the same: "You're welcome." He said it with a smile, and meant it.

He was a celebrity, and he never got used to it. Whenever he returned to New York and played at Birdland, the crowd stretched down the block. He made guest appearances in musicals on Broadway and concertos in Carnegie Hall, soloed with the best orchestras on the planet, and dated a super-model for a while.

Ray was living a life he never thought he would have. Once, years later, on the phone with his mother, he asked her if she was still mad at him for not getting that high school job at Popeyes, for not getting his GED and not going to work at the cafeteria hospital with Ricky. She told him that she didn't know what he was talking about and he should stop this foolishness.

Secretly, Ray was a rotten celebrity. He never got used to it, never learned to take it for granted. The photos and adulation and program signing always made him uncomfortable, and after the theft he never ordered room service again. Every day, no matter where he was, he'd find a busker or someone on the street and leave money or help otherwise when he could. He was making a great deal of money and giving a lot of it away as quickly as he got it. He played charity concerts for several different organizations.

He loved Kelly Hall-Tompkins's Music Kitchen, a charity that organized musicians to serve food and play in soup kitchens, and he often volunteered—both to play and to serve the guests. Another charity bought instruments for students who couldn't afford to buy their own: at the inaugural fundraising gala, he played for free, enlisted several musicians—Wynton Marsalis and Trombone Shorty—and donated a hundred thousand dollars to the cause.

Every day, Ray's routine was the same. As soon as he woke, he'd open the Tonareli case to ensure that his violin—PopPop's violin—was nestled inside. Every day it would shine up at him, safe, and his heart would swell in his chest. Many times he'd flash back to that Christmas, long ago, and the memory of opening an alligator-skin case with a loose handle, and he'd breathe in the aroma of mildew, old wood, and Good Luck Dust.

Every night before he went to bed, he'd stash the violin case within easy reach. As he fell asleep, he'd think about the day's events and remember his grandmother's Thanksgiving words to him, seasoned with love, potato peels, and sliced squash: that he work twice as hard as everyone else, that he stand tall and treat others with respect, and that he stay the same "sweet Ray" that Grandma Nora loved so much. He didn't know if he'd succeeded, but he never stopped trying. He had to believe that she would be proud.

Epilogue

That October seemed especially chilly, but maybe it was just the wind creeping between his pants and his socks. He sat on the park bench and breathed deep, admired the red maple across the street, its leaves lit seemingly from within, burning with the end of summer. It made him realize how beautiful everything around him truly was.

"I have to leave a little early if I'm going to make it to Bryce's recital tonight," he said to Janice. "I think maybe I'll start Remy on the Bach A Minor Concerto. If he gets it down, **L'Inverno** should be no problem for him to pick up."

"You still love that piece, don't you?"

"Yeah. It's always been my favorite. I wish I'd performed it more."

"Why don't you perform it next time?"

"Naw. People want to hear more flashy concertos."

Across the street, the steel and glass of the Community Arts Center in Charlotte was the envy of North Carolina for its state-of-the-art performance theater and its multiple practice spaces. Ray had spearheaded its creation three years ago and still loved looking at it.

"Who cares what they want," she said. "It's what you want, remember?"

"Yeah," he said. "I remember. I play because I love it."

"That's right."

"Funny, it seems like a million years later and you're still telling me what I already know."

"No, just a gentle reminder."

Half a block away, a boy was dragging his mother by the hand. Their voices echoed up to him, ghostly in the afternoon light. "Hurry up," he was telling her. "I need to practice before my lesson."

Ray smiled at them both, but neither noticed him.

"Remind you of anyone?" Janice shifted on the bench.

"No, not at all. I was much taller when I was his age."

"True. And I think he's more dedicated," she said.

"I keep meaning to tell you something and it always slips my mind. I wonder why that happens?"

"Old age," she said. "First the memory goes, then the bladder, and then it's all downhill."

"You made this all possible." Ray reached out to the maple tree, to the afternoon sun slanting down, to the building glowing with promise, to the kid and his mom nearly on top of them. "Your belief in me."

"I just encouraged what was already there," she said. "I could tell from the first time I saw you with that school rental how in love with music you were. Despite nobody being there to help. It was inside you. Now you can give it to others. Courage and hope."

"You did. You gave it to me. What a gift."

"Music's the gift. Caring's the gift. And you give it to others now. There are a lot of ways apart from a concert hall to make a difference in someone's life."

As the kid and his mom approached, the little boy broke away and sat down beside Ray. "Mr. Mac," he said, looking up. "I can play the whole sonata now! I practiced every day. Didn't I, Mom?"

"He did," she said, walking over to them. "DeMarcus never missed a day. I don't know what you told him, but it worked."

"That's fantastic. Why don't we go in a few minutes early so you can show me what you can do?"

"Yes, sir!"

Ray, DeMarcus, and his mom crossed the street together. As Ray held the door for them, he looked back at the sunlight pouring like music over an empty park bench.

"Hey. Thanks, Janice."

Author's Note

Music is for everyone. It's not—or at least shouldn't be—an elitist, aristocratic club that you need a membership card to appreciate: it's a language, it's a means of connecting us that is beyond color, beyond race, beyond the shape of your face or the size of your stock portfolio.

Musicians of color, however, are severely under-represented in the classical music world—and that's one of the reasons I wanted to write this book. Look up the statistics: 1.8 percent of musicians perform-ing in classical symphonies are Black; 12 percent are people of color. But for me, day to day, performance by performance, it wasn't about being a statistic: it was about trying to live my life and play the music that I loved, and often being stymied for reasons that seem, even now, incomprehensible. Many of the events in this novel—the wedding scene, the Baton Rouge shakedown, the auditions—come from my own life experiences. Having someone look at you with hatred just because your skin is a different shade from theirs is a devastating feeling that I'd never wish upon anyone. When I share these stories with friends who don't look like me, I get the same reaction: "Things like that don't happen. It's not really like that." They do. It is.

In order to make sense of this chaotic and often perplexing world, we get caught up in trying to shove people into categories. Who can or who can't. Who should and who shouldn't. I, as well as other people who look like me, have often been placed into the **can't** or **shouldn't** category. Only through sheer will and determination can we defy the standards that others have set for us.

As a Black violinist, I have had to work twice as hard as my non-Black counterparts to receive the same benefits. In college, I always had to prove myself and wasn't always successful. I dealt with very real racism, discrimination, and stereotyping from professors, other musicians, and the audience. In a music history class, my professor told us that Black people played Chopin better than white people because of the embedded jungle rhythms in our blood. I was passed over not because I was incapable but because I was perceived as incapable.

Struggle became a normal part of life. At weddings and receptions, I often couldn't be the face of my string quartet because "Blacks aren't as good at this." I was automatically an oddity, rarely seen, whose talents were almost never recognized: "How are you doing that? I had no idea you would be so good. You really surprised me."

I have been fortunate enough to be a guest conductor with several orchestras, including school orchestras. Once I walked into a room full of white middle school kids. I expected their stares. Until I stepped onto the podium, they thought I was there to move equipment. When I asked one of the players to lend me her violin so I could demonstrate how I wanted a passage played, silence ensued. Then, when I tucked the violin under my jaw and showed them what to do, the room let out a collective "wow"; no one had ever seen someone like me play something like that.

It's not fair that people who look a certain way must constantly prove their worth, but at this juncture in history, we're well beyond what's fair. Even after almost forty years of playing violin, I am still confronted with conscious and unconscious discrimination. If I'm playing Handel's **Messiah**—a piece I've performed probably a hundred times on violin and viola—white directors often place a white person on my part, because they don't think I can handle it and my partner will be able to help me. I smile. Then, when my partner—who is usually much less experienced than I am—plays the piece less proficiently than it might be played, I offer advice. My partner is almost always grateful, and Handel's **Messiah** is the better for it.

When I was younger, in high school and in college, I often wanted to give up—until my "Dr. Janice Stevens" came into my life, offering pure and desperately needed encouragement. That kind of mentorship truly changed the direction of my life, and that kind of mentorship is what I try to offer my students today. Being a Black man is great. I love who I am. But it's also a great responsibility— one that I take very seriously. As a teacher of young kids, I realized early on that, for many of my students, I would be the first Black man they actually meet in person. The impression I leave them with will hopefully stay with them for years to come: my speech, appearance, attitude, and demeanor are always professional because I know, like it or not, that I am representing a huge group of people. This doesn't mean that I alter myself to make anyone comfortable: I speak with my normal deep voice, I still rock my earrings, and, if it's a hot day, my tattoos still peek out from my shirtsleeves.

Who you are goes far beyond what you look like. My hope is that Ray's story will inspire all of you—white or Black, Asian or Native American, straight or gay, transgender or cisgender, blond or dark haired, tall or short, big feet or small—to do what you love. Inspire those around you to do what they love, too. It might just pay off.

Alone, we are a solitary violin, a lonely flute, a trumpet singing in the dark.

Together, we are a symphony.

Acknowledgments

First and foremost: To Jeff Kleinman at Folio Literary Management. He's been here every step of the way, going well beyond an agent's usual role—helping shape this book from the first moment I conceived it and always pushing me and demanding my best. Thank you, my friend. This book couldn't have happened without you.

Unimaginable amounts of thank-yous to my mom, Milo Slocumb. I think you did pretty good, Mom. I love you so much—thank you for always being there to support me through everything. To my sister, Dr. Robin Robertson: We've had nothing but fun ever since seventh-grade orchestra—you on cello and me on bass. Whether you're in New York or Denver, I'm grateful that we've always managed to stay close and keep family first. To my older brother, Howard Slocumb, whose ever-present support and love have gotten me through some difficult times: I love you for it. Robin and Howard, now we can play badminton in the backyard again.

Kevin Slocumb: Thank you for everything. If I could be only half as talented as you, I'd be on an entirely different level. I've admired your abilities and gifts for as long as I can remember—you've always been a source of pride and envy for me. One day, I hope, I'll achieve your level of excellence. When we were kids, I had no idea that you wanted to be like me. Now I wish I could turn back the clock and take a few lessons from you—and be a better big brother. We'll always have the memories of making up a dance routine to that Nintendo game **Contra**, and the marching-band comparisons we had to endure, and the mutual love of comics. I love you, dude.

An enormous thanks to the team at Folio Literary Management: Katherine Odom-Tomchin for her day-to-day assistance; Melissa Sarver White, director of international rights, and her colleagues Chiara Panzeri and Madeline Froyd, for their work selling this novel all over the world; Jamie Chambliss, Serin Lee, Samuel Nicol, Carissa McQueen, and Justin Ross, who read multiple iterations of the novel.

A huge shout-out to the delightful Sylvie

Rabineau at William Morris Endeavor and her colleague Nicole Weinroth for believing so intensely in this book and in me as a writer.

Nancy Pearce: Thank you for pushing me to expand what I could do. You didn't let me take the easy way out, always insisting that I do more and try harder. I've tried to make you proud. I hope I succeeded.

Thank you, Robbie Dobson, for believing in and nurturing me. Without your dedication to the skinny kid who didn't even know what fifth position was, I never would have gone to college—let alone majored in music education.

Twenty-five years of the absolute best students on the face of the earth deserve all my heartfelt thanks and love. You guys have been instrumental in shaping me to be the best teacher I could be—from "rap sessions" to kickball games between concerts to **Power Stone 2** tournaments. Some of the best, most impactful moments of my life have been because of you guys, and I deeply appreciate every minute I've spent with you. David, Schotzee is in the house!

Colossal amounts of love and thanks go to Glenn Fry, who has supported me through every step of this process. The encouraging words, the push to explore aspects of this story I never even considered. Thank you with all my heart. I love you.

An immense thank-you to Dr. Dean Maynard for your kindness and kinship. You did so much for me when I needed it most. I love you, bro.

I can say with all confidence that Dr. Rachel Vetter Huang is the reason for so many good things in my life. I literally can't say thank you enough. Thank you for teaching me how to play the violin. Thank you for teaching me how to teach. Thank you for believing in me and instilling a confidence that I had no idea existed. Thank you for allowing me to make mistakes and for steering me back on track. Thank you for making it easy to write Dr. Janice Stevens, one of the most important characters in this book. Thank you thank you thank you thank you thank you.

A tremendous thank-you to Dr. Hao Huang: You always pushed me to be better and to do more. You showed me that something worth doing is worth doing to the best of my abilities.

Tom Schleef, you are gone too soon. Because of you, I'm still here. You meant so much to so many. Your dedication, love, and friendship got me through the worst of times. I am forever grateful. Rest in peace, my friend.

Sachi Rosenbaum, you could teach a course on how to be a great friend. You stood by me with some of the most heartfelt, kindest, most timely words I've ever read. I'll never be able to thank you enough for your selfless acts of giving in the name of friendship.

Ralph Brooker and Jeannie Perron, true friends: Thank you for supporting me in so many different ways. From hospital buddies to quartet partners to hummus tasters. I love you both.

So many people selflessly gave me their time and insights as I researched and learned about violins and the dark world of stolen antiques and antiquities. First and foremost, thanks to Bobby Reed of Hiscox Insurance for insights into how insurance companies deal with incredibly expensive violins. Thanks to Chris Marinelli, Douglas Bort, Mark Kohanski, and, above all, Robert Wittman for sharing their wisdom, experience, insights, and stories. Talking to all of you made it very clear that I'd never make it as an art thief—you were always three steps ahead of me.

A special thanks to Kelly Hall-Tompkins for sharing stories of not only her triumph and success but also her ever-present struggles. Your perspectives helped shape the more difficult subjects I tackled in this novel.

A shout-out to my band, Geppetto's Wüd, and my gaming alliance, DB4E. I love you guys!

Ian Scott William Hargis Bouvier: I love you, buddy. Look at me!

Aim: I love you, dude. You know DC just hasn't been the same without you.

Finally, massive thanks to the Anchor Books team: to my editor, Editorial Director Edward

Kastenmeier, whose keen and thoughtful editing made this novel vastly stronger than it had been; to Publisher Suzanne Herz and Associate Publisher Beth Lamb, whose faith in me is both humbling and astonishing; to Editor Caitlin Landuyt, whose insights into Ray's relationship with his violin really transformed the narrative. Production Editor Kayla Overbey and copy editor Lisa Davis: Your eagle eyes caught thousands of errors, and your graciousness allows me to seem vastly smarter than I am. Thank you, thank you, to Publicity Director James Meader, Director of Marketing Jessica Deitcher, and Social Media Manager Alexa Thompson for your creativity and tirelessness, and to Mark Abrams for designing such a dazzling cover. To all of you at Anchor: I am so proud to be one of your authors.

ABOUT THE AUTHOR

Brendan Nicholaus Slocumb was raised in Fayetteville, North Carolina, and holds a degree in music education (concentrations on violin and viola) from the University of North Carolina at Greensboro. For more than twenty years he has been a public and private school music educator for kindergarten through twelfth grade, teaching general music, band, orchestra, and guitar ensembles. As a violinist, Brendan has performed with orchestras throughout Northern Virginia, Maryland, and Washington, DC. He has also been a frequent adjudicator and guest conductor for district and regional orchestras.

Brendan's a fitness buff who collects comic books and action figures and, in his spare time, performs with his rock band, Geppetto's Wüd.

He is currently working on his second novel.